what did you eat yesterday? 10

fumi yoshinaga

VERTICAL.

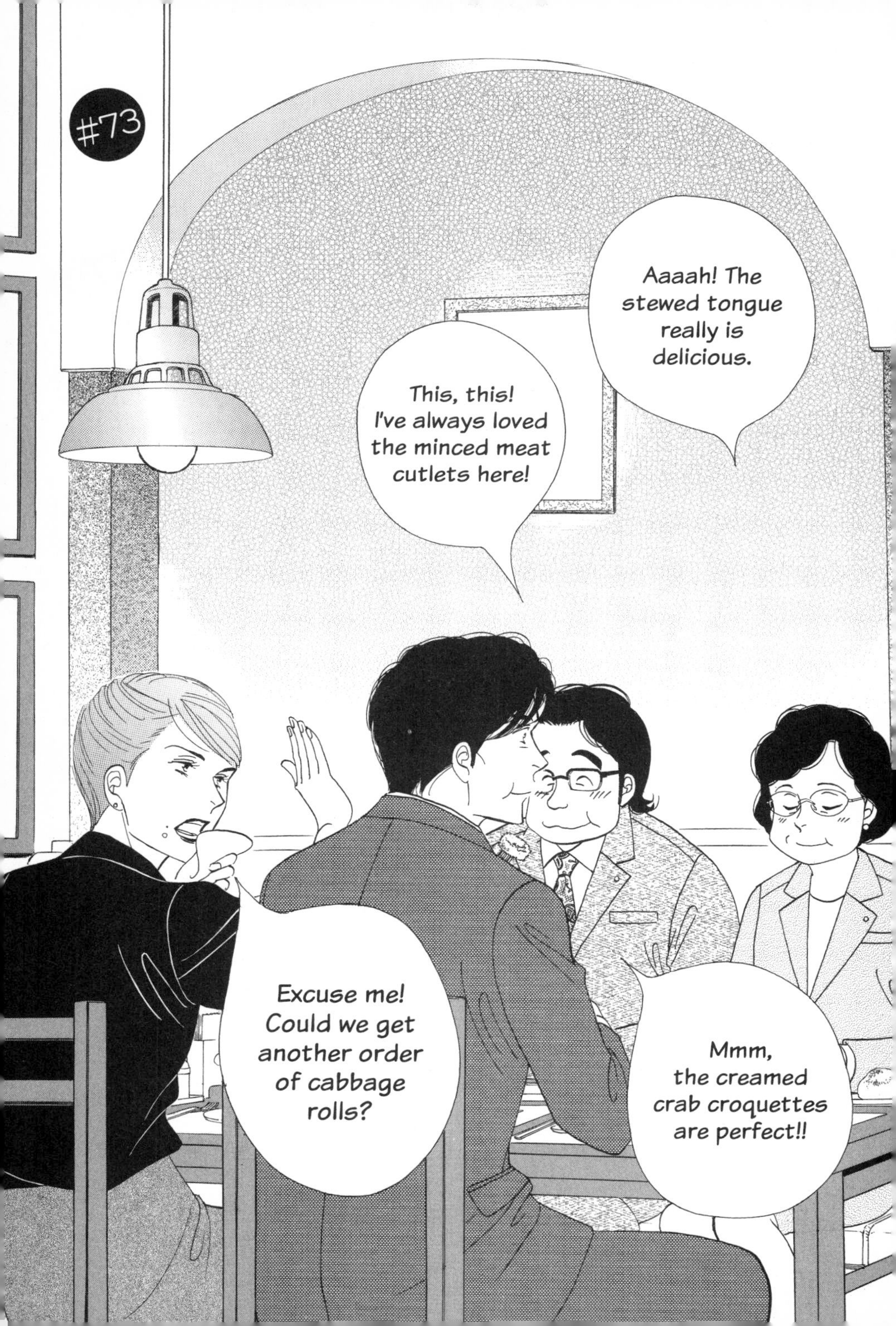
#73
Aaaah! The stewed tongue really is delicious.
This, this! I've always loved the minced meat cutlets here!
Mmm, the creamed crab croquettes are perfect!!
Excuse me! Could we get another order of cabbage rolls?

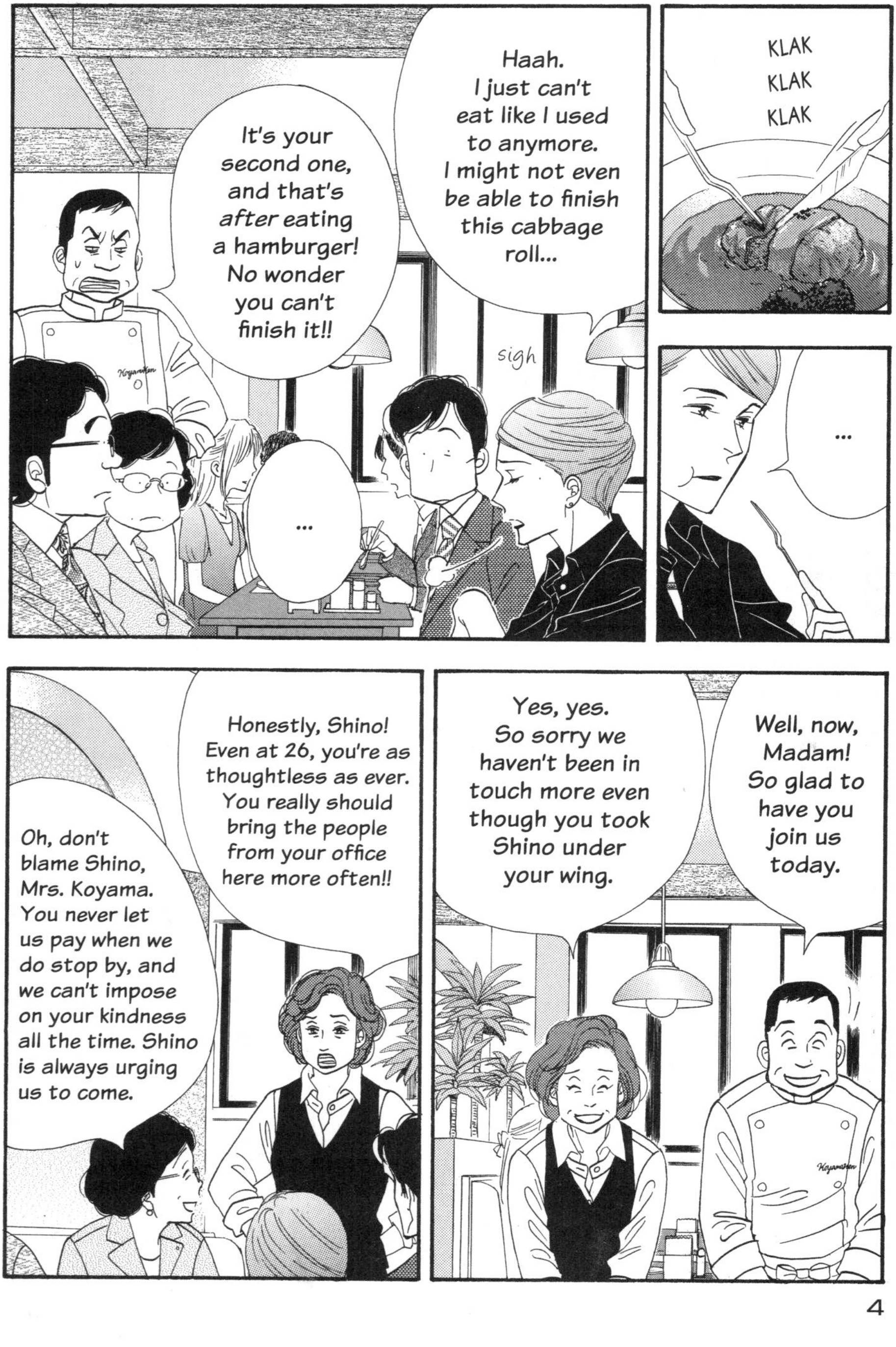
KLAK KLAK KLAK
...
Haah. I just can't eat like I used to anymore. I might not even be able to finish this cabbage roll...
It's your second one, and that's *after* eating a hamburger! No wonder you can't finish it!!
sigh
...
Well, now, Madam! So glad to have you join us today.
Yes, yes. So sorry we haven't been in touch more even though you took Shino under your wing.
Honestly, Shino! Even at 26, you're as thoughtless as ever. You really should bring the people from your office here more often!!
Oh, don't blame Shino, Mrs. Koyama. You never let us pay when we do stop by, and we can't impose on your kindness all the time. Shino is always urging us to come.

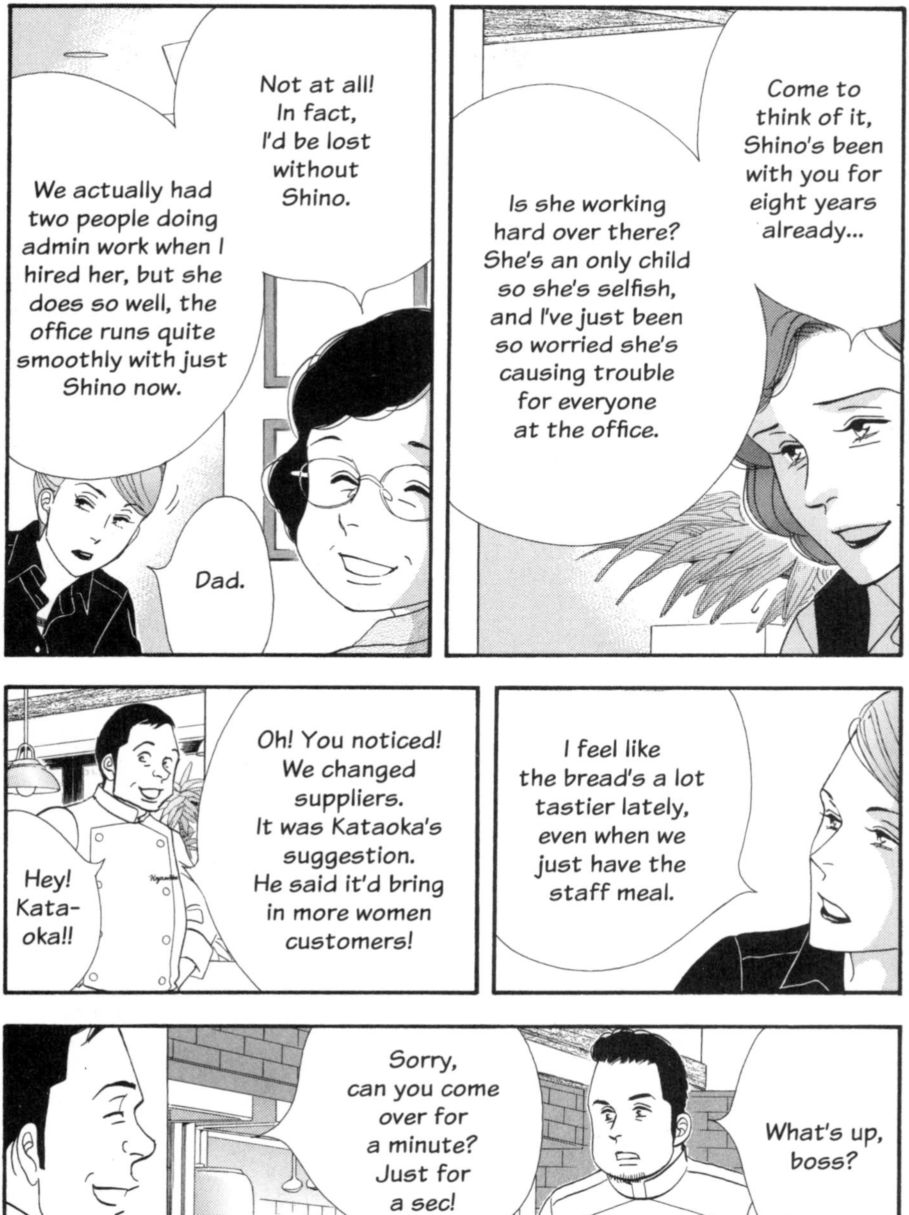
Come to think of it, Shino's been with you for eight years already...
Is she working hard over there? She's an only child so she's selfish, and I've just been so worried she's causing trouble for everyone at the office.
Not at all! In fact, I'd be lost without Shino.
We actually had two people doing admin work when I hired her, but she does so well, the office runs quite smoothly with just Shino now.
Dad.
I feel like the bread's a lot tastier lately, even when we just have the staff meal.
Oh! You noticed! We changed suppliers. It was Kataoka's suggestion. He said it'd bring in more women customers!
Hey! Kata-oka!!
What's up, boss?
Sorry, can you come over for a minute? Just for a sec!

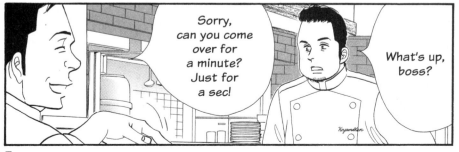

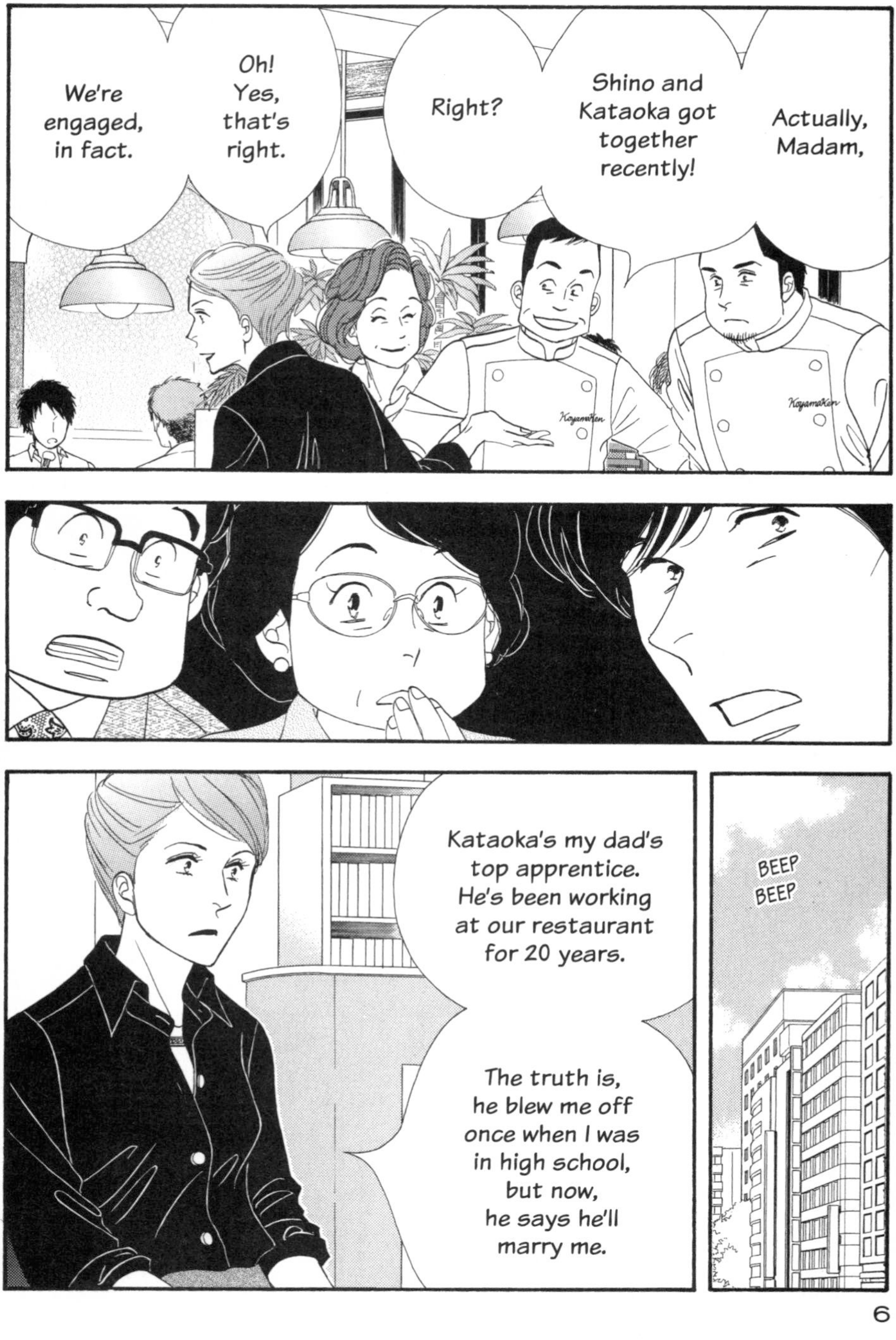
Actually, Madam,
Shino and Kataoka got together recently!
Right?
Oh! Yes, that's right.
We're engaged, in fact.
BEEP BEEP
Kataoka's my dad's top apprentice. He's been working at our restaurant for 20 years.
The truth is, he blew me off once when I was in high school, but now, he says he'll marry me.

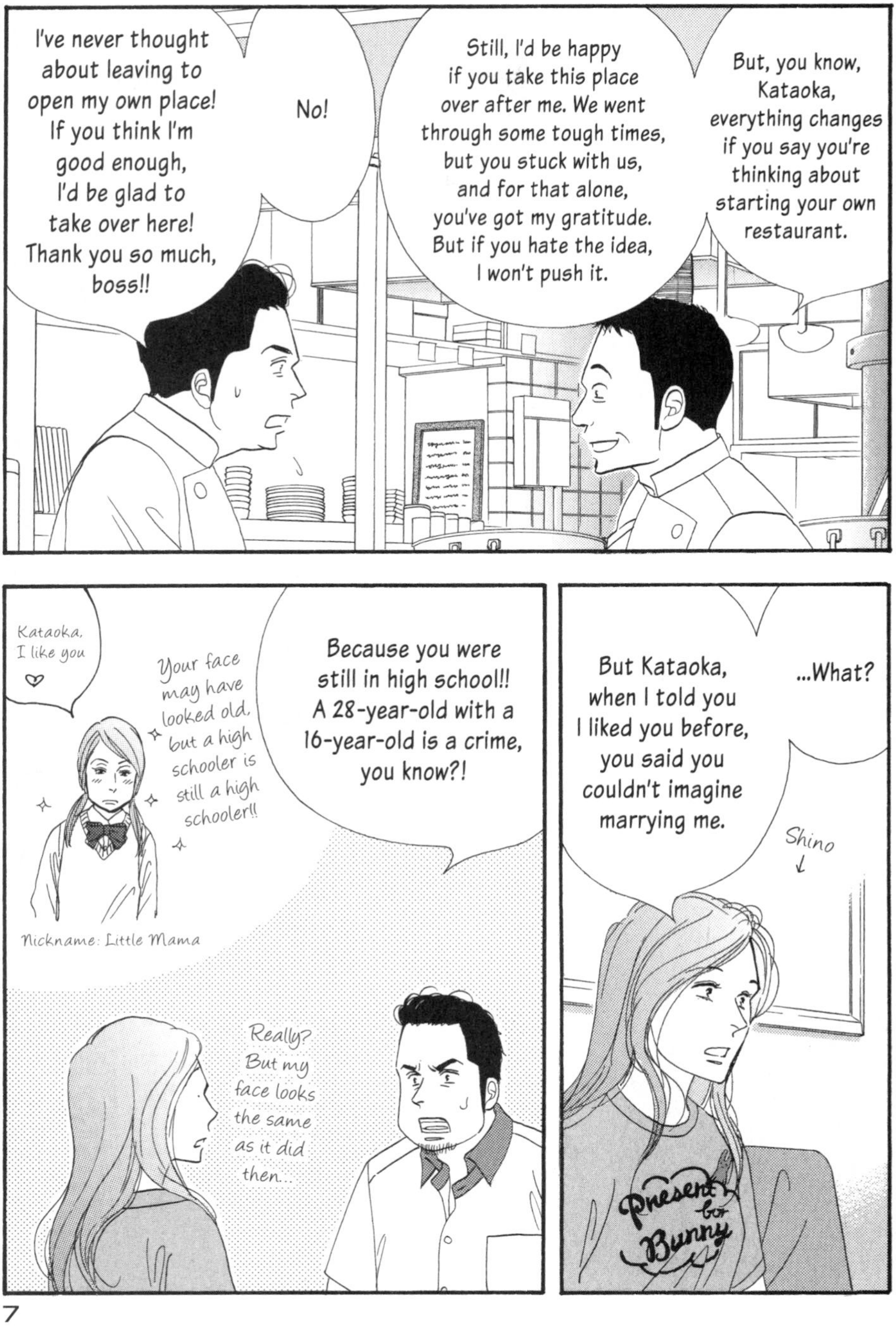

But, you know, Kataoka, everything changes if you say you're thinking about starting your own restaurant.
Still, I'd be happy if you take this place over after me. We went through some tough times, but you stuck with us, and for that alone, you've got my gratitude. But if you hate the idea, I won't push it.
No!
I've never thought about leaving to open my own place! If you think I'm good enough, I'd be glad to take over here! Thank you so much, boss!!
...What?
But Kataoka, when I told you I liked you before, you said you couldn't imagine marrying me.
Shino
Because you were still in high school!! A 28-year-old with a 16-year-old is a crime, you know?!
Kataoka, I like you
Your face may have looked old, but a high schooler is still a high schooler!!
Nickname: Little Mama
Really? But my face looks the same as it did then...
Present for Bunny

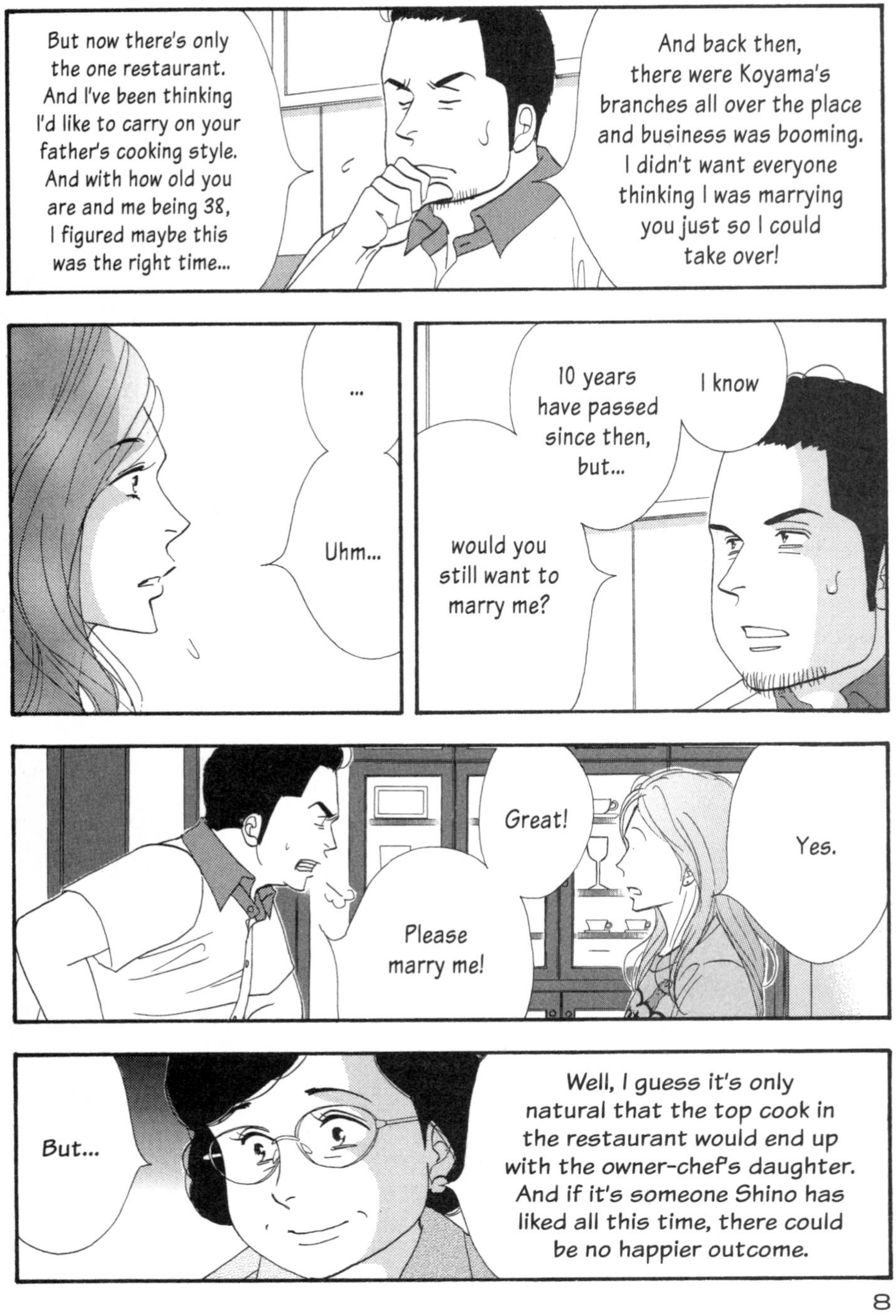
And back then, there were Koyama's branches all over the place and business was booming. I didn't want everyone thinking I was marrying you just so I could take over!
But now there's only the one restaurant. And I've been thinking I'd like to carry on your father's cooking style. And with how old you are and me being 38, I figured maybe this was the right time...
I know
10 years have passed since then, but...
would you still want to marry me?
...
Uhm...
Yes.
Great!
Please marry me!
Well, I guess it's only natural that the top cook in the restaurant would end up with the owner-chef's daughter. And if it's someone Shino has liked all this time, there could be no happier outcome.
But...

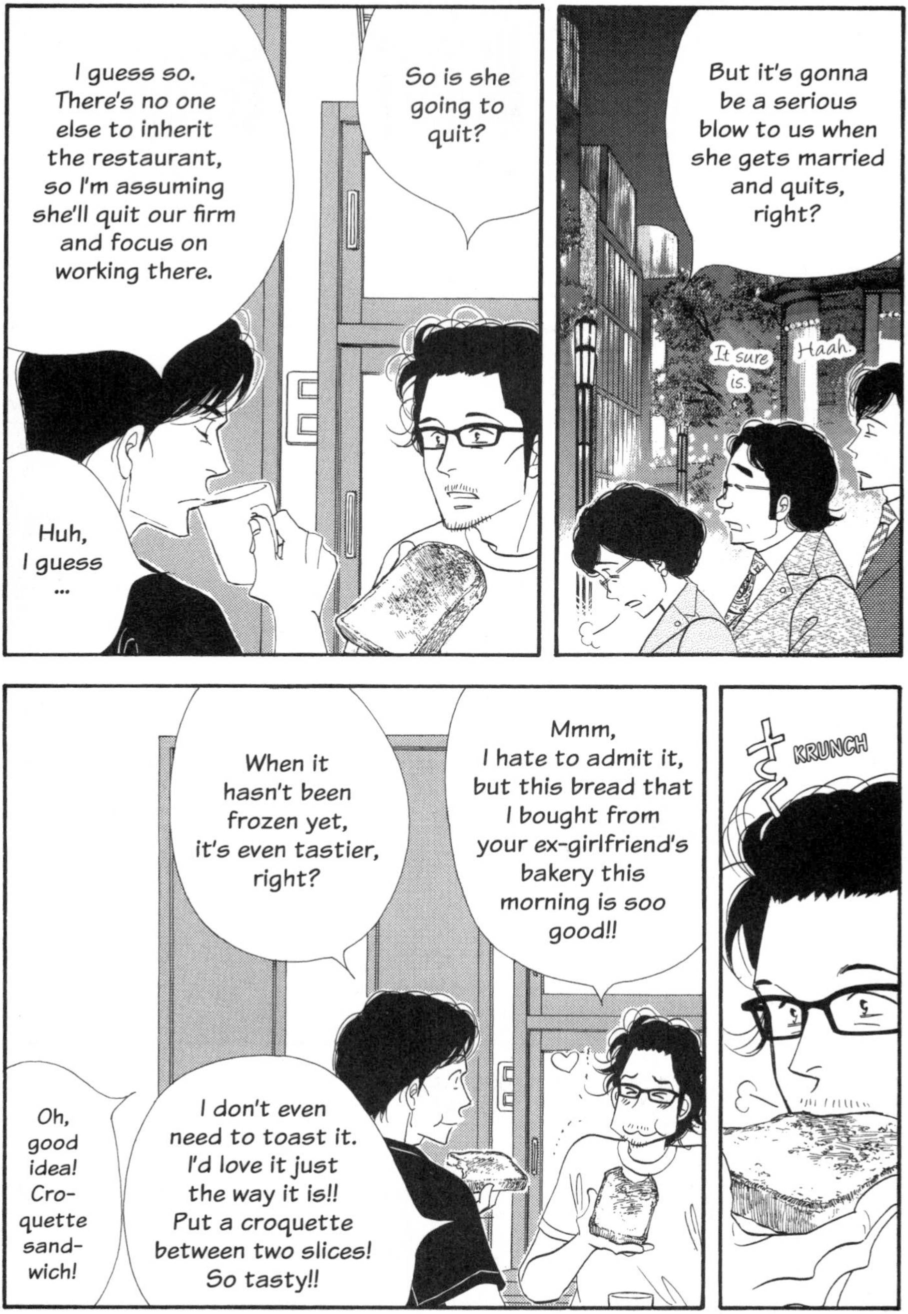
But it's gonna be a serious blow to us when she gets married and quits, right?
Haah.
It sure is.
So is she going to quit?
I guess so. There's no one else to inherit the restaurant, so I'm assuming she'll quit our firm and focus on working there.
Huh, I guess ...
さく
KRUNCH
Mmm, I hate to admit it, but this bread that I bought from your ex-girlfriend's bakery this morning is soo good!!
When it hasn't been frozen yet, it's even tastier, right?
I don't even need to toast it. I'd love it just the way it is!! Put a croquette between two slices! So tasty!!
Oh, good idea! Cro-quette sand-wich!

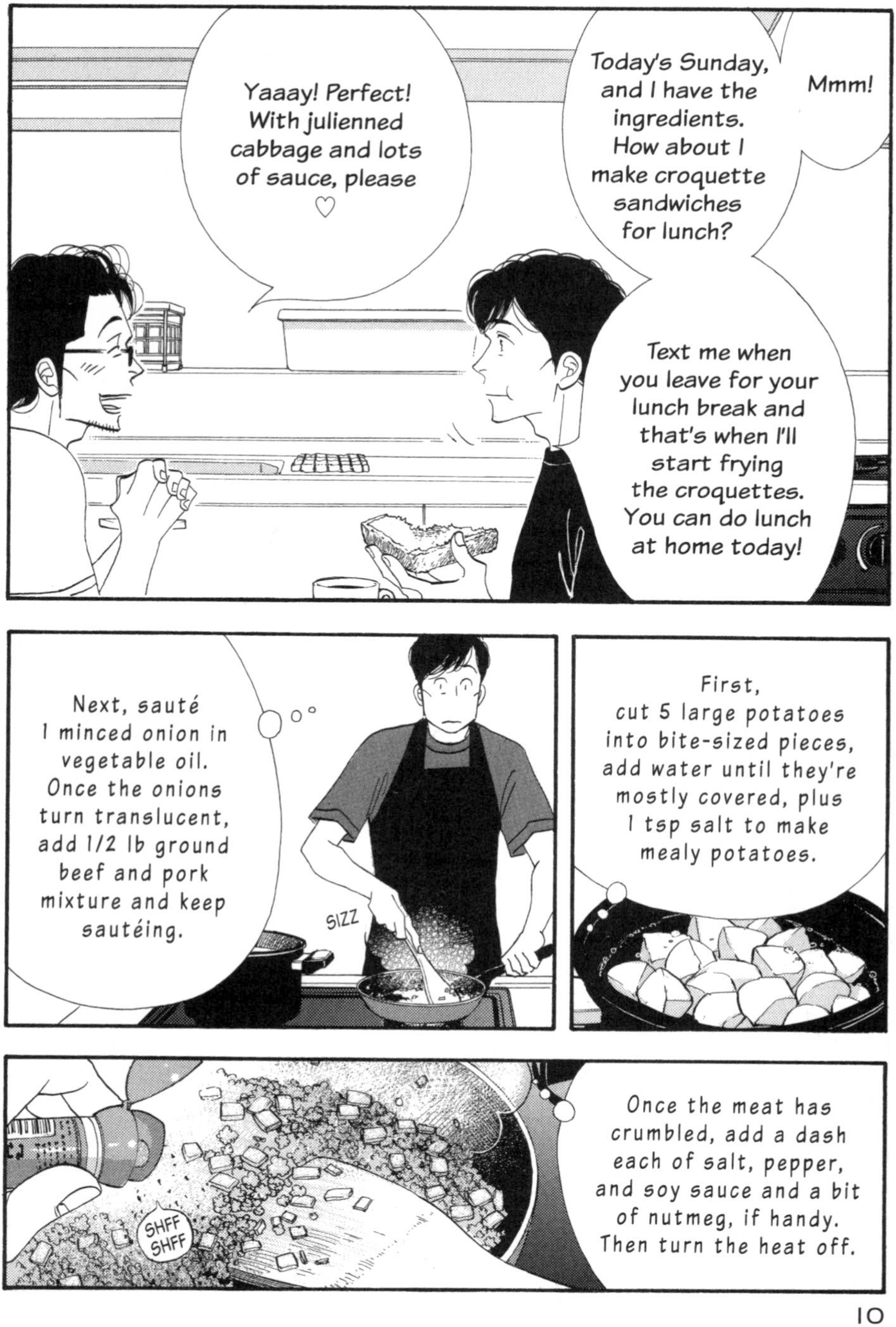
Today's Sunday, and I have the ingredients. How about I make croquette sandwiches for lunch?
Yaaay! Perfect! With julienned cabbage and lots of sauce, please ♡
Mmm!
Text me when you leave for your lunch break and that's when I'll start frying the croquettes. You can do lunch at home today!
First, cut 5 large potatoes into bite-sized pieces, add water until they're mostly covered, plus 1 tsp salt to make mealy potatoes.
Next, sauté 1 minced onion in vegetable oil. Once the onions turn translucent, add 1/2 lb ground beef and pork mixture and keep sautéing.
SIZZ
Once the meat has crumbled, add a dash each of salt, pepper, and soy sauce and a bit of nutmeg, if handy. Then turn the heat off.
SHFF SHFF

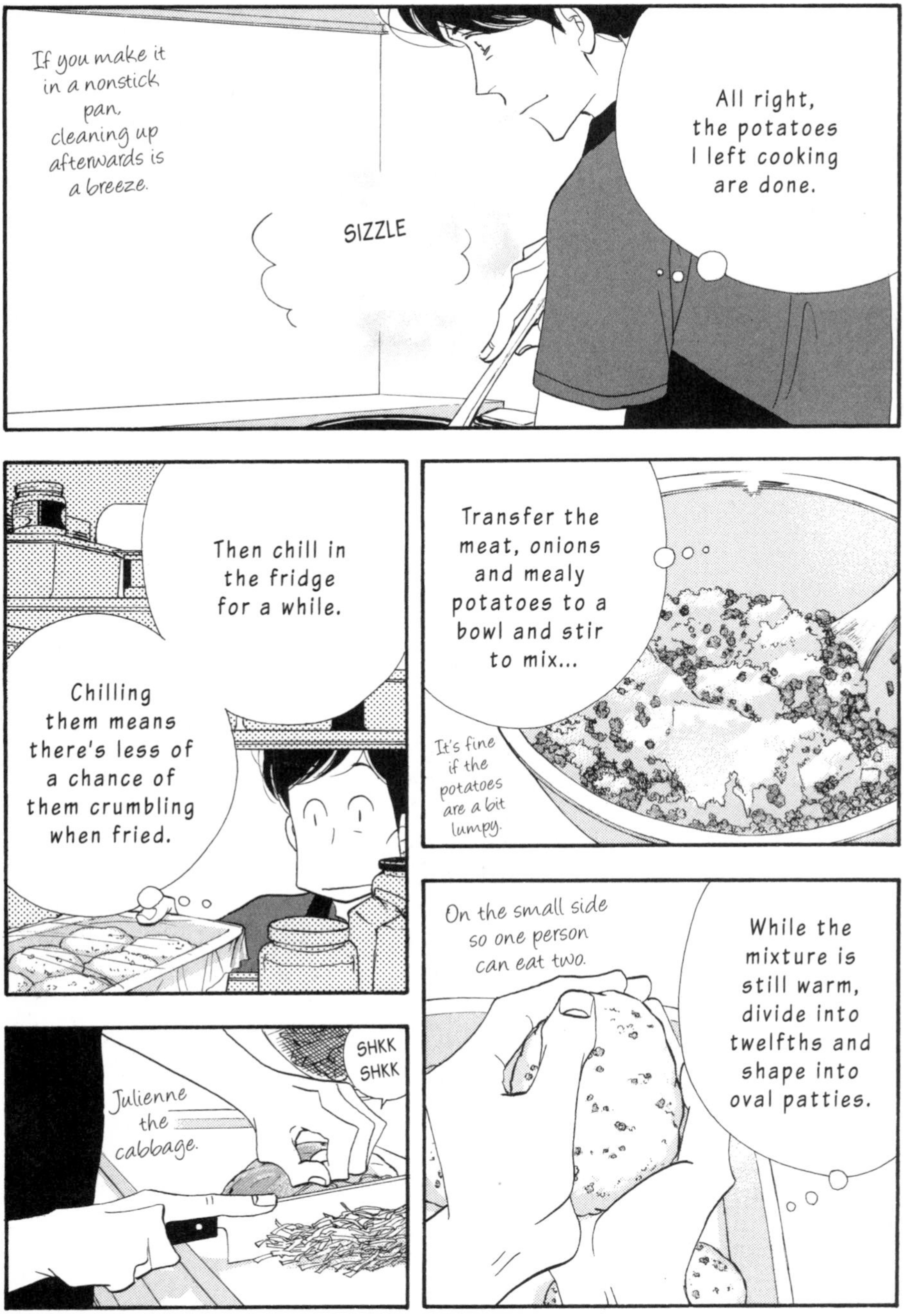
All right, the potatoes I left cooking are done.
If you make it in a nonstick pan, cleaning up afterwards is a breeze.
SIZZLE
Transfer the meat, onions and mealy potatoes to a bowl and stir to mix...
It's fine if the potatoes are a bit lumpy.
While the mixture is still warm, divide into twelfths and shape into oval patties.
On the small side so one person can eat two.
Then chill in the fridge for a while.
Chilling them means there's less of a chance of them crumbling when fried.
SHKK SHKK
Julienne the cabbage.

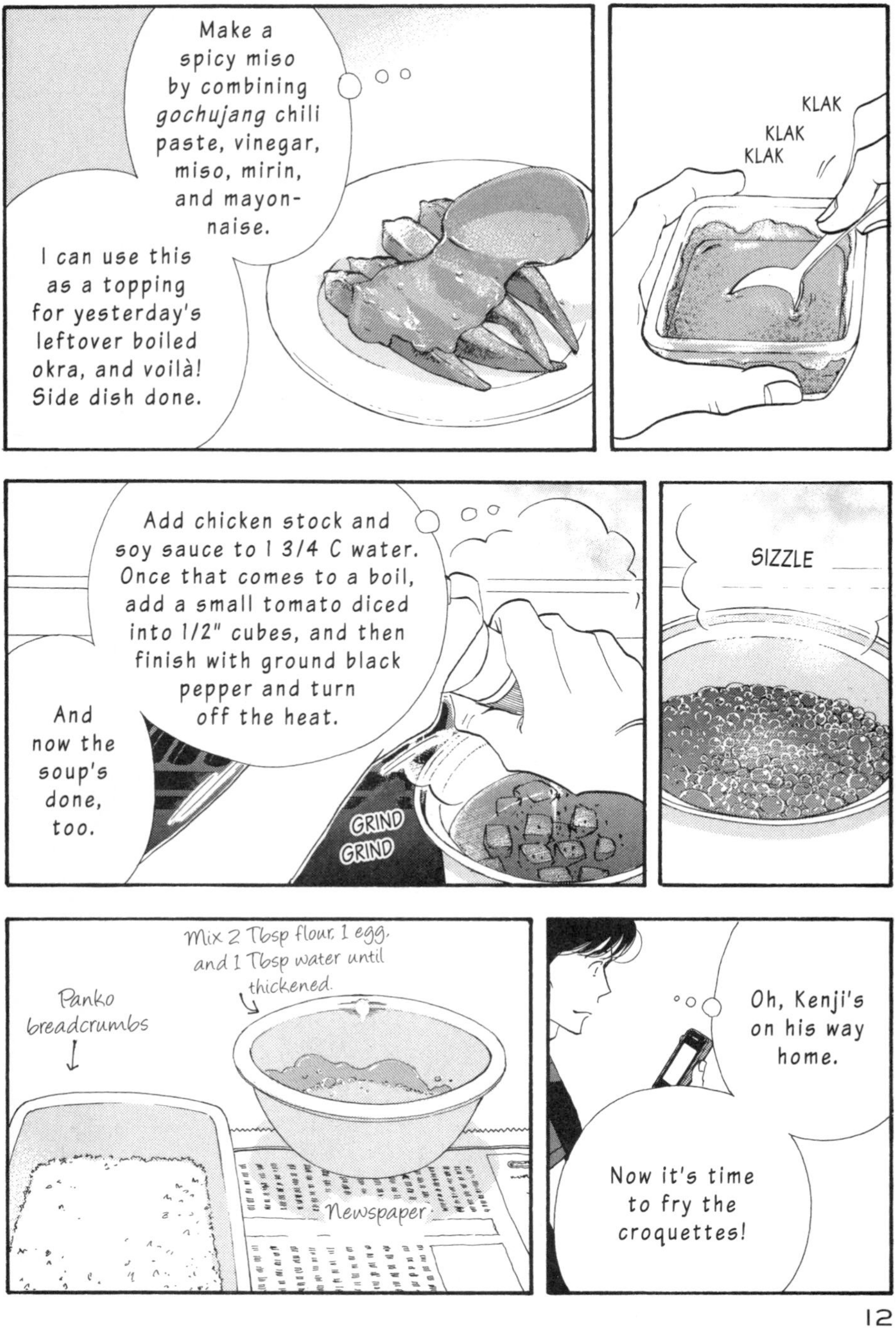
KLAK
KLAK
KLAK
Make a spicy miso by combining *gochujang* chili paste, vinegar, miso, mirin, and mayon-naise.
I can use this as a topping for yesterday's leftover boiled okra, and voilà! Side dish done.
SIZZLE
Add chicken stock and soy sauce to 1 3/4 C water. Once that comes to a boil, add a small tomato diced into 1/2" cubes, and then finish with ground black pepper and turn off the heat.
GRIND GRIND
And now the soup's done, too.
Oh, Kenji's on his way home.
Now it's time to fry the croquettes!
Mix 2 Tbsp flour, 1 egg, and 1 Tbsp water until thickened.
Panko breadcrumbs
Newspaper

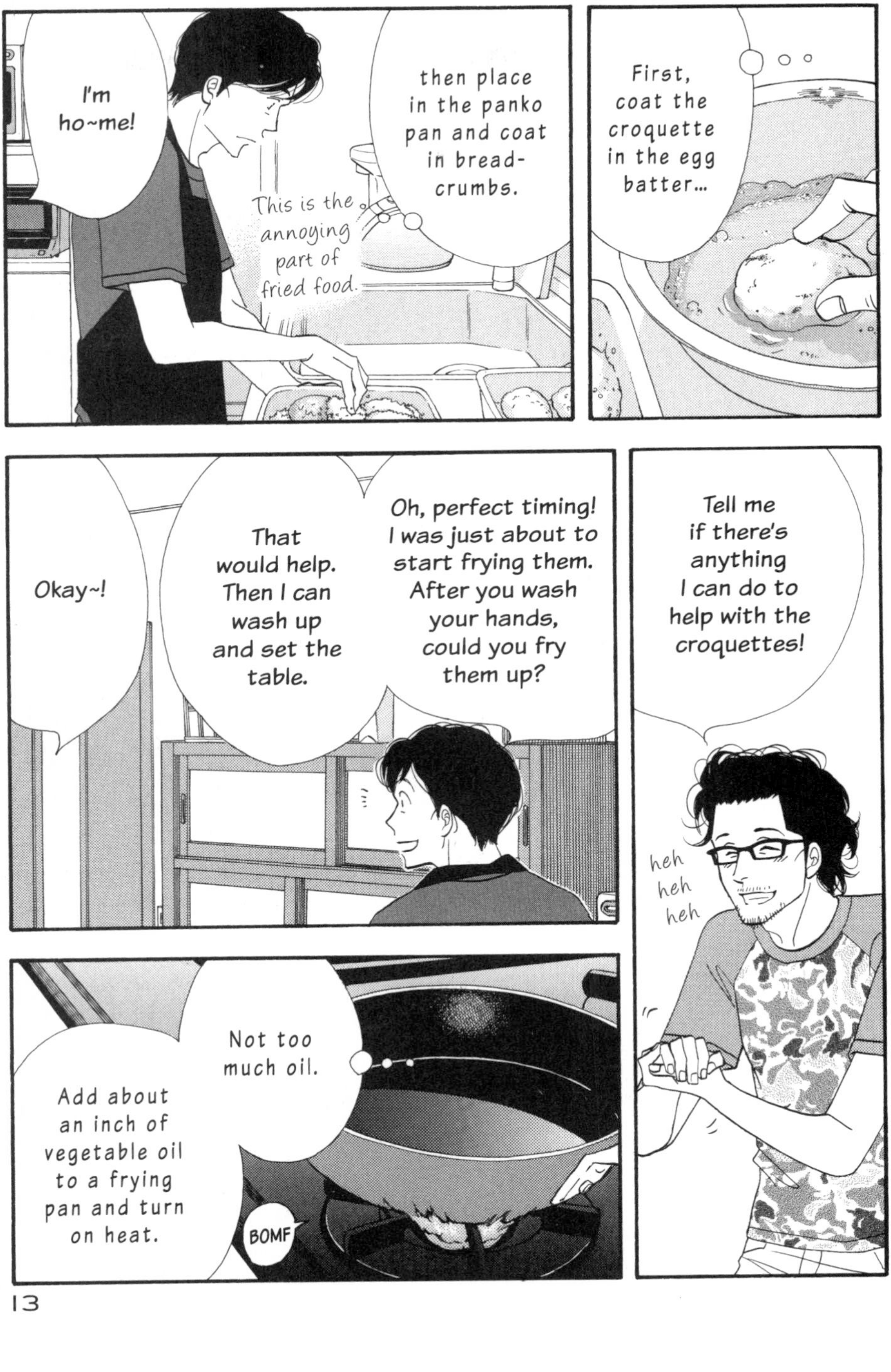
First, coat the croquette in the egg batter...
then place in the panko pan and coat in bread-crumbs.
This is the annoying part of fried food.
I'm ho~me!
Tell me if there's anything I can do to help with the croquettes!
heh heh heh
Oh, perfect timing! I was just about to start frying them. After you wash your hands, could you fry them up?
That would help. Then I can wash up and set the table.
Okay~!
Not too much oil.
Add about an inch of vegetable oil to a frying pan and turn on heat.
BOMF

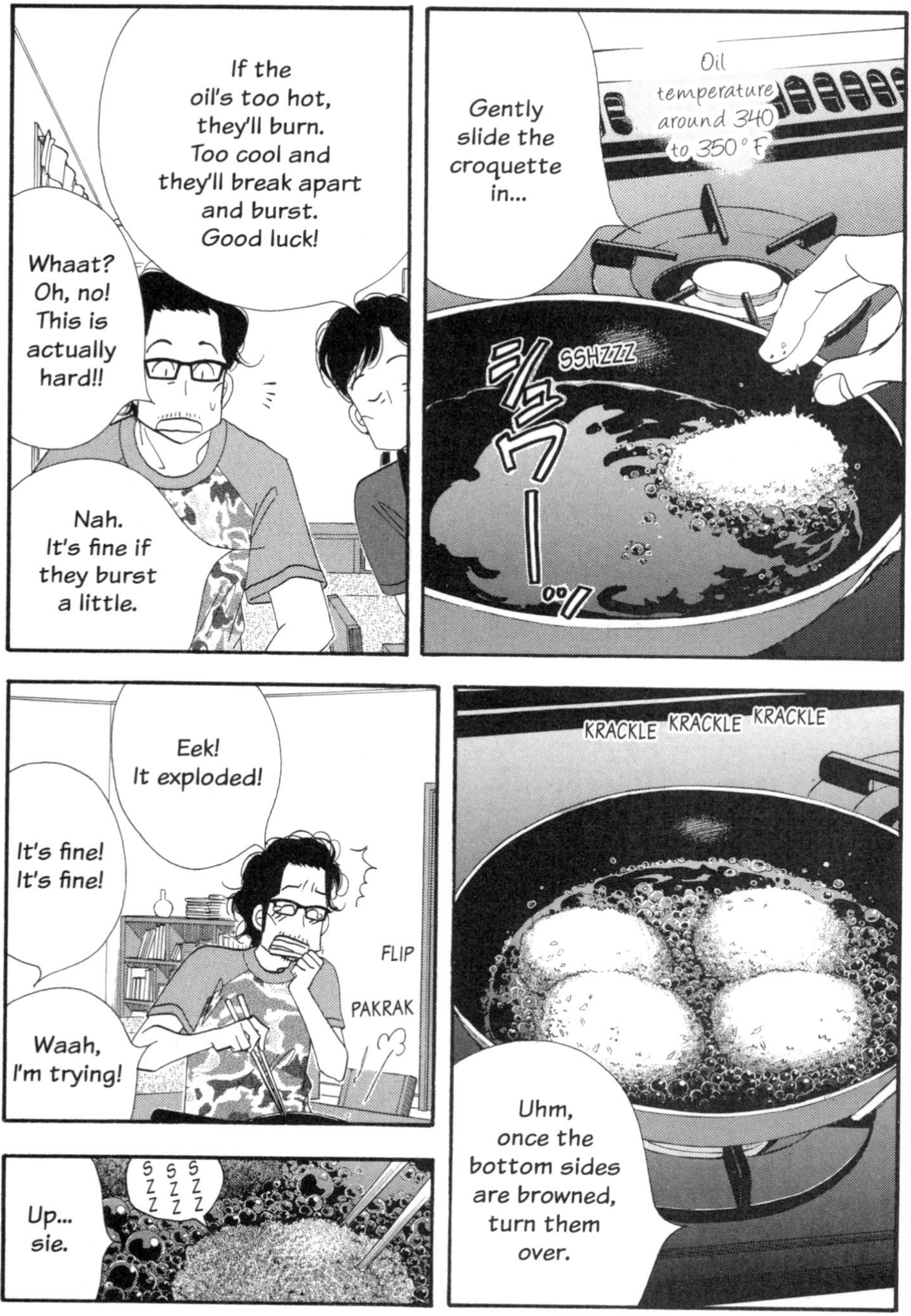
Oil temperature around 340 to 350°F
Gently slide the croquette in...
SSHZZZ
If the oil's too hot, they'll burn. Too cool and they'll break apart and burst. Good luck!
Whaat? Oh, no! This is actually hard!!
Nah. It's fine if they burst a little.
KRACKLE KRACKLE KRACKLE
Uhm, once the bottom sides are browned, turn them over.
Eek! It exploded!
It's fine! It's fine!
FLIP
PAKRAK
Waah, I'm trying!
SSS
ZZZ
ZZZ
Up... sie.

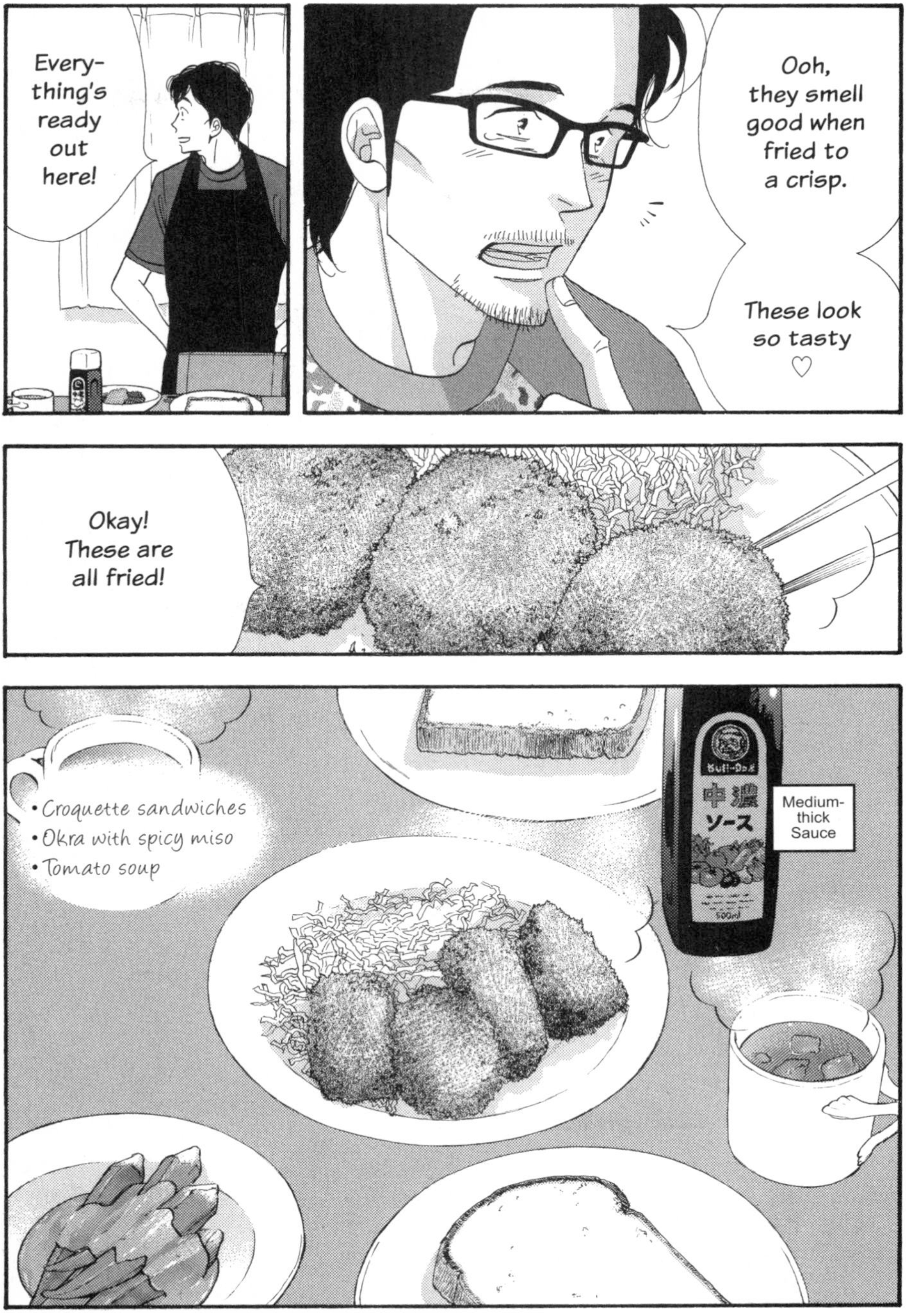
Ooh, they smell good when fried to a crisp.
These look so tasty ♡
Every-thing's ready out here!
Okay! These are all fried!
• Croquette sandwiches
• Okra with spicy miso
• Tomato soup
中濃
ソース
Medium-thick Sauce

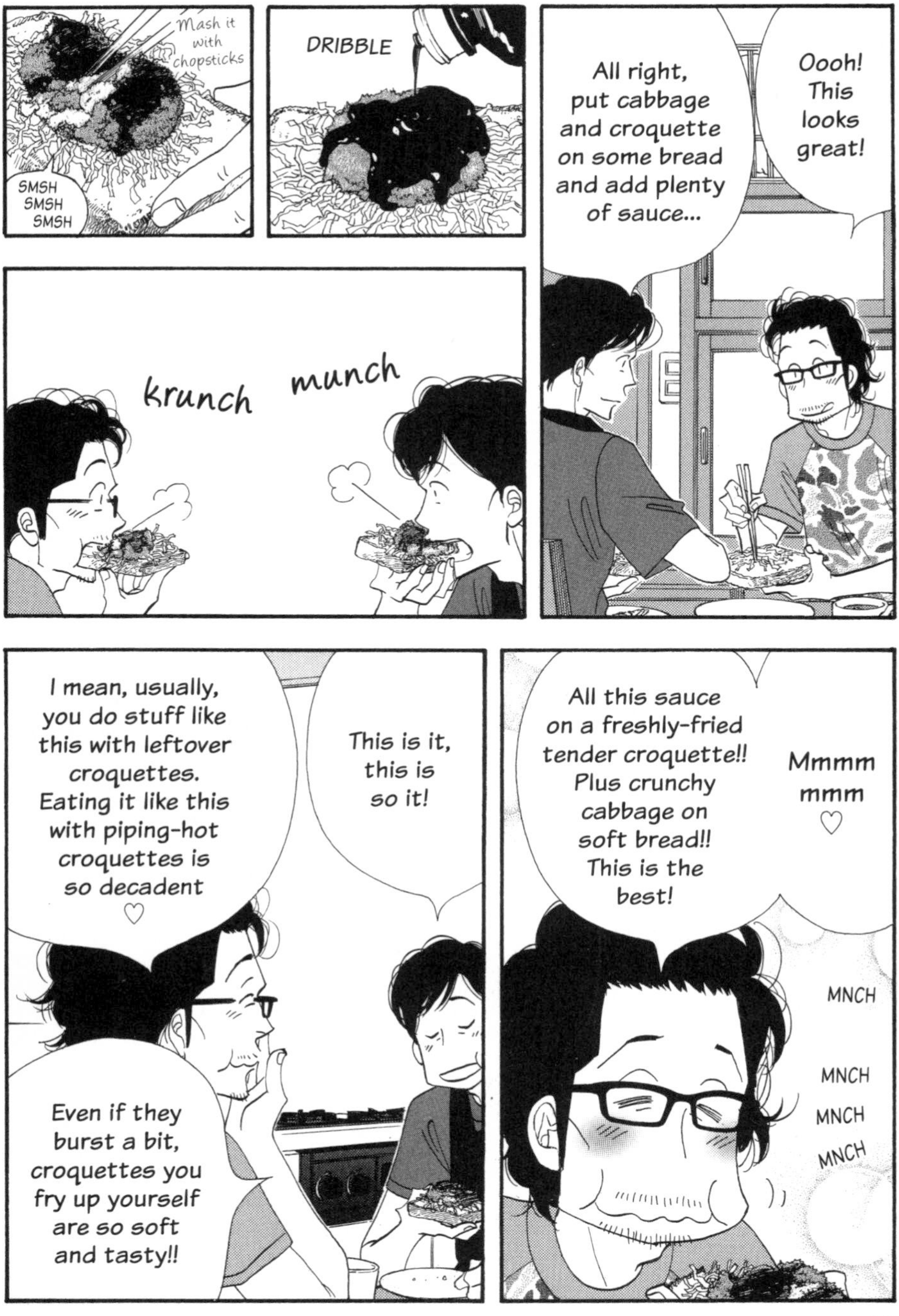
Oooh! This looks great!
All right, put cabbage and croquette on some bread and add plenty of sauce...
DRIBBLE
Mash it with chopsticks
SMSH SMSH SMSH
munch
krunch
Mmmm mmm ♡
All this sauce on a freshly-fried tender croquette!! Plus crunchy cabbage on soft bread!! This is the best!
MNCH
MNCH
MNCH
MNCH
This is it, this is so it!
I mean, usually, you do stuff like this with leftover croquettes. Eating it like this with piping-hot croquettes is so decadent ♡
Even if they burst a bit, croquettes you fry up yourself are so soft and tasty!!

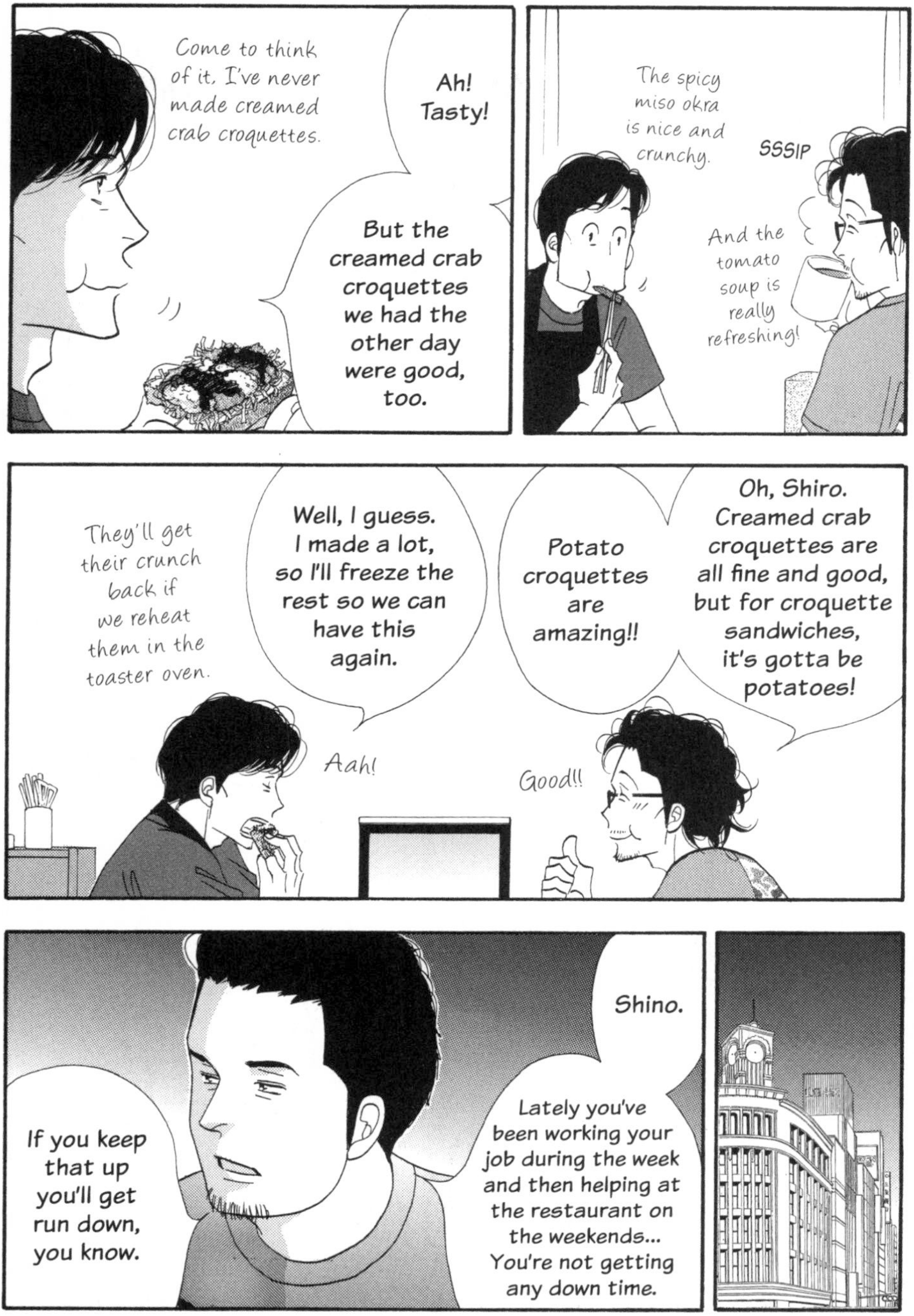
The spicy miso okra is nice and crunchy.
SSSIP
And the tomato soup is really refreshing!
Ah! Tasty!
But the creamed crab croquettes we had the other day were good, too.
Come to think of it, I've never made creamed crab croquettes.
Oh, Shiro. Creamed crab croquettes are all fine and good, but for croquette sandwiches, it's gotta be potatoes!
Potato croquettes are amazing!!
Good!!
Well, I guess. I made a lot, so I'll freeze the rest so we can have this again.
They'll get their crunch back if we reheat them in the toaster oven.
Aah!
Shino.
Lately you've been working your job during the week and then helping at the restaurant on the weekends... You're not getting any down time.
If you keep that up you'll get run down, you know.

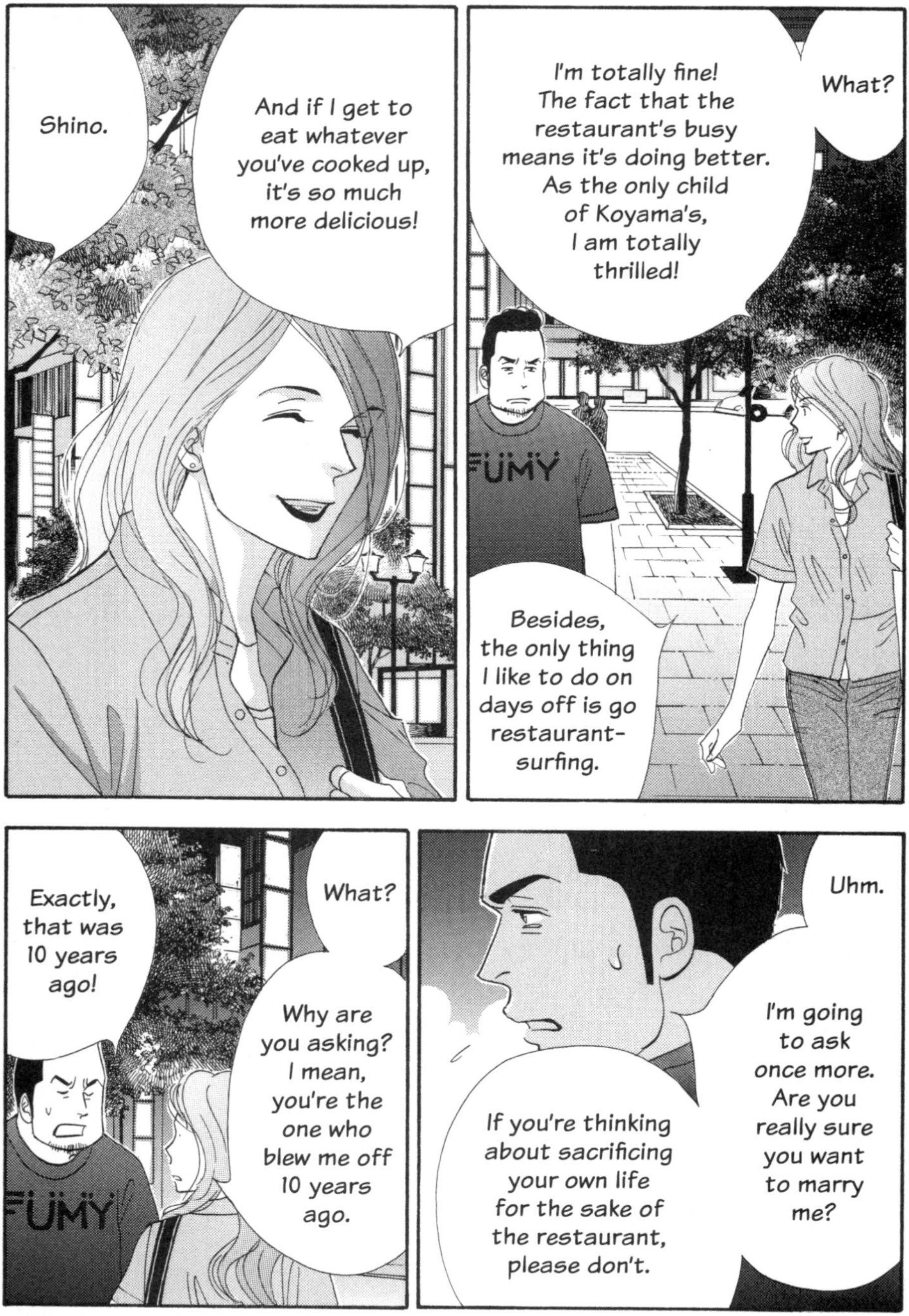
What?
I'm totally fine! The fact that the restaurant's busy means it's doing better. As the only child of Koyama's, I am totally thrilled!
Besides, the only thing I like to do on days off is go restaurant-surfing.
And if I get to eat whatever you've cooked up, it's so much more delicious!
Shino.
Uhm.
I'm going to ask once more. Are you really sure you want to marry me?
If you're thinking about sacrificing your own life for the sake of the restaurant, please don't.
What?
Why are you asking? I mean, you're the one who blew me off 10 years ago.
Exactly, that was 10 years ago!

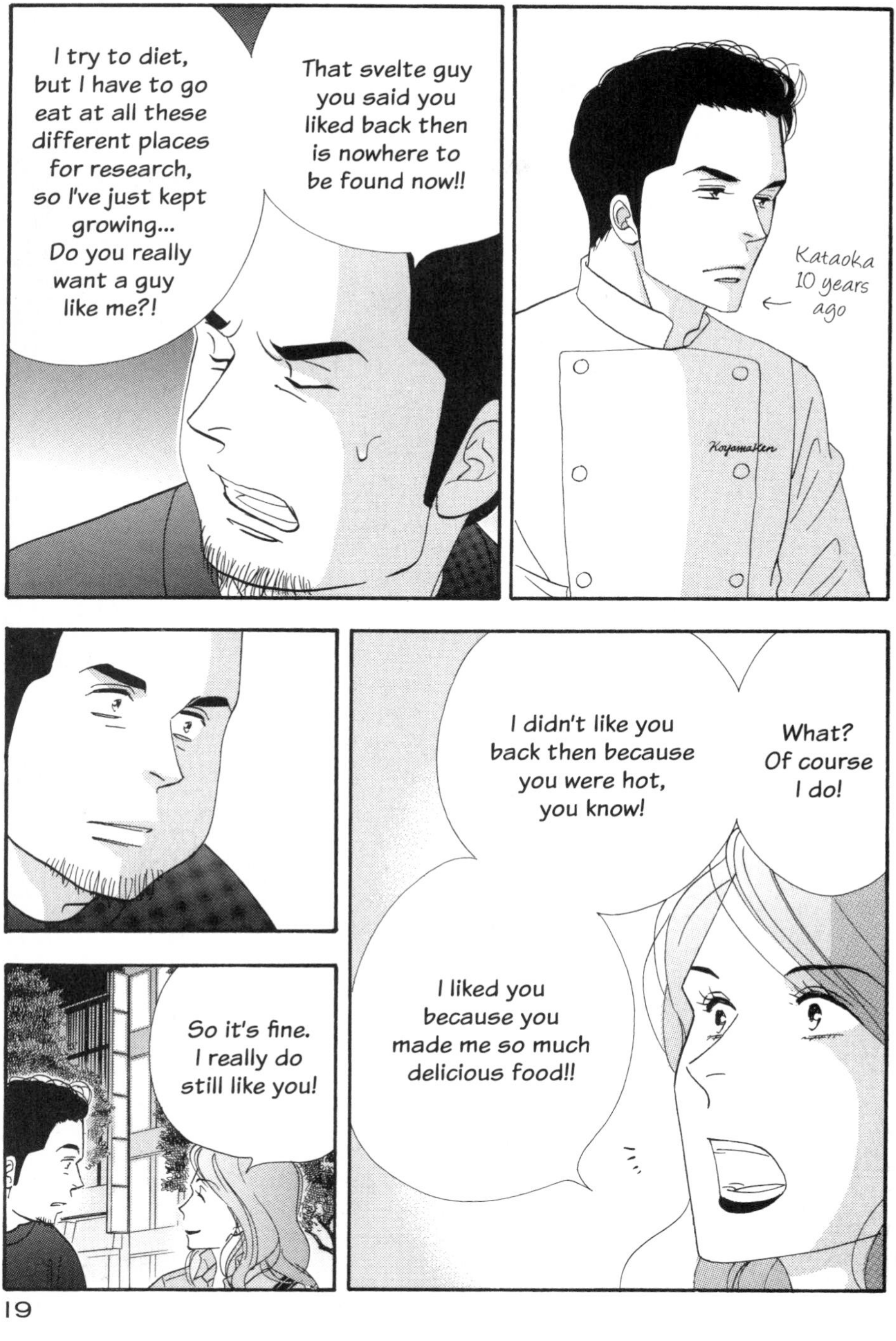
Kataoka 10 years ago
That svelte guy you said you liked back then is nowhere to be found now!!
I try to diet, but I have to go eat at all these different places for research, so I've just kept growing... Do you really want a guy like me?!
What? Of course I do!
I didn't like you back then because you were hot, you know!
I liked you because you made me so much delicious food!!
So it's fine. I really do still like you!

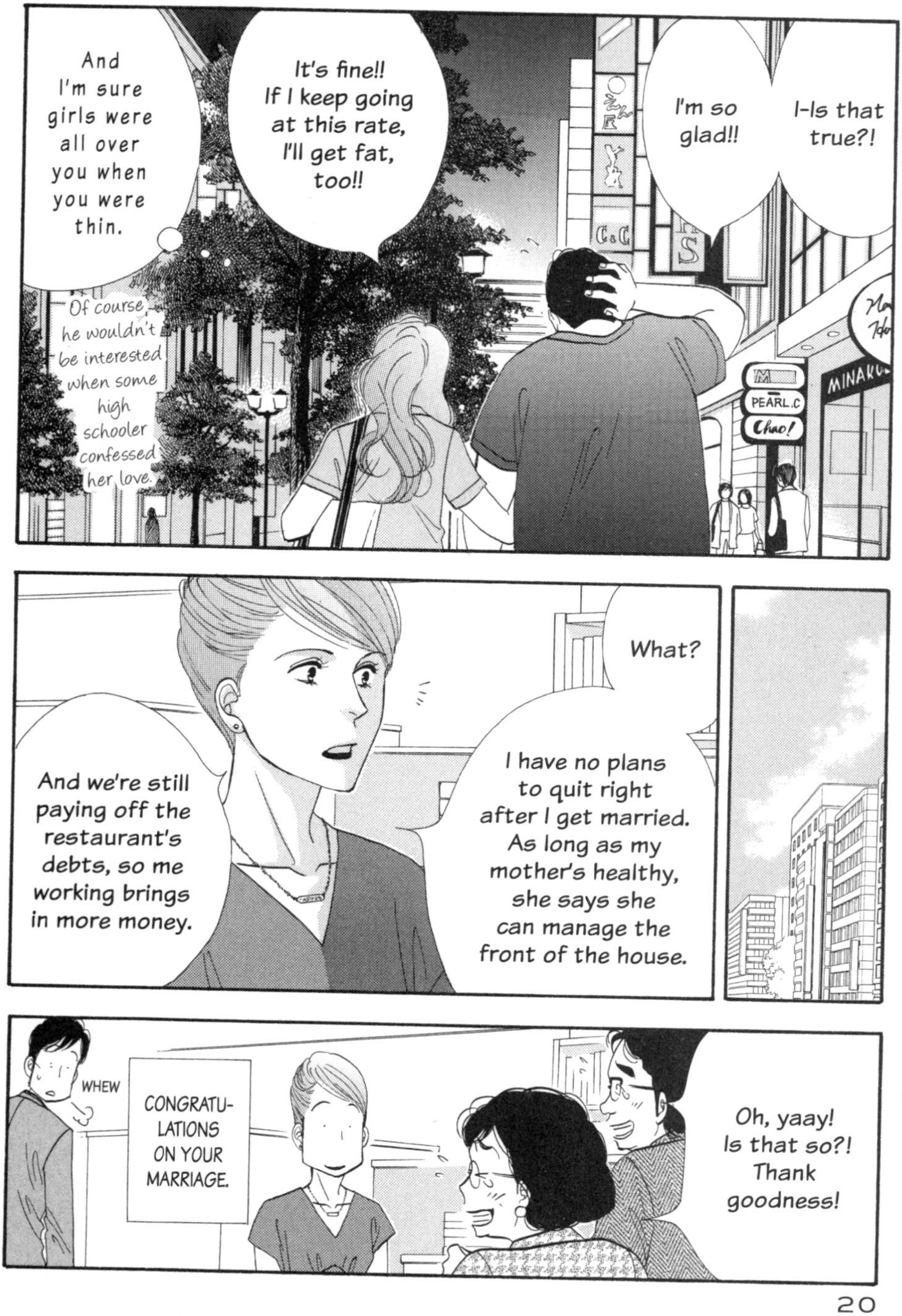
I-Is that true?!
I'm so glad!!
It's fine!! If I keep going at this rate, I'll get fat, too!!
And I'm sure girls were all over you when you were thin.
Of course, he wouldn't be interested when some high schooler confessed her love.
PEARL.C
Chao!
What?
I have no plans to quit right after I get married. As long as my mother's healthy, she says she can manage the front of the house.
And we're still paying off the restaurant's debts, so me working brings in more money.
Oh, yaay! Is that so?! Thank goodness!
CONGRATULATIONS ON YOUR MARRIAGE.
WHEW

Since everything inside
the **croquette** is cooked,
you can freeze them before coating
in panko and frying them.
This meal takes a bit of effort,
so it's best to make plenty,
enough for two or three days,
and then freeze everything except
the portion you'll serve that day.

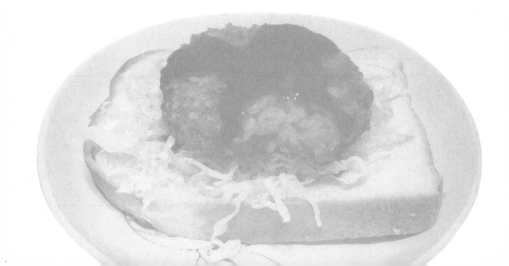

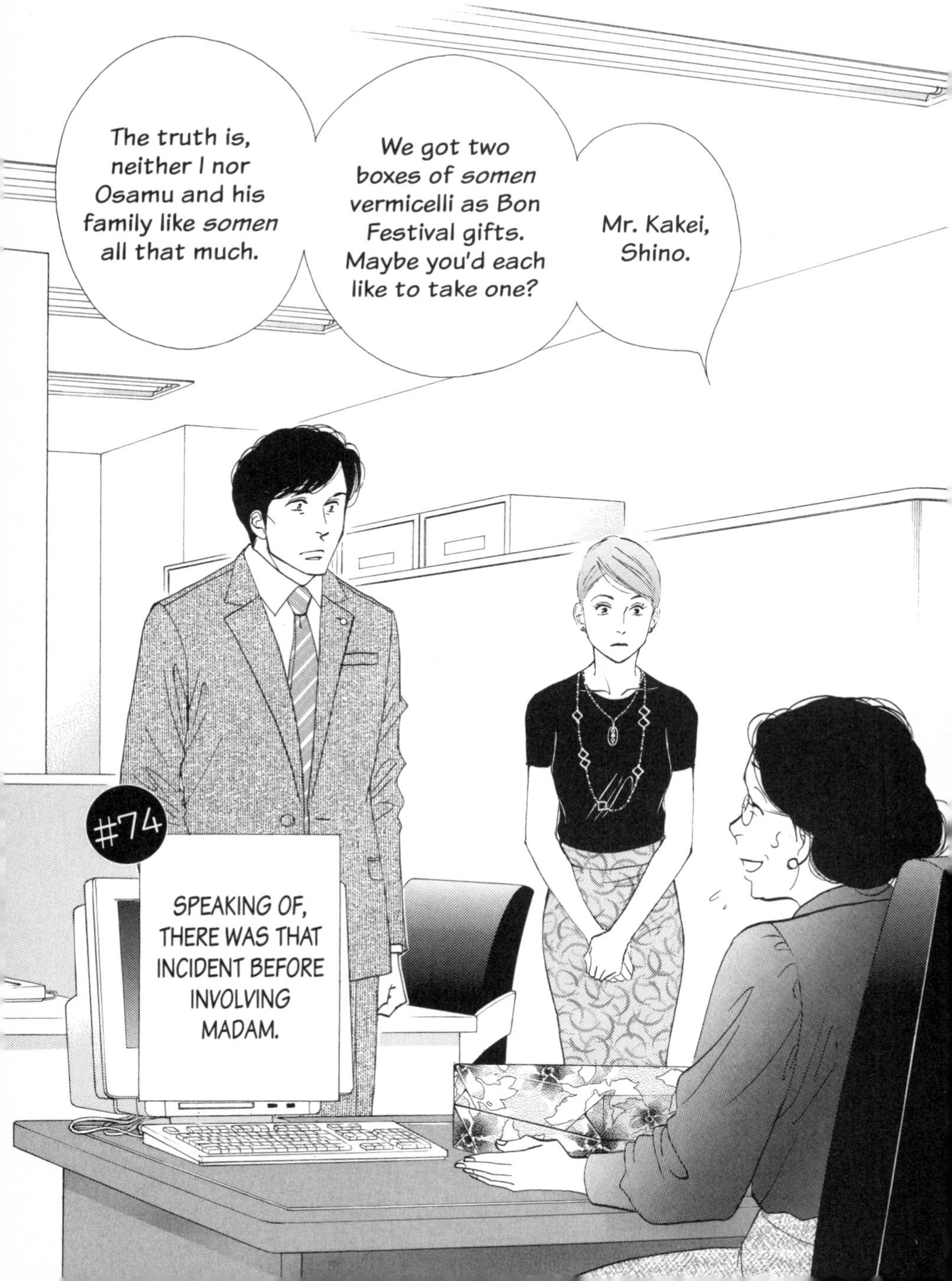
Mr. Kakei, Shino.
We got two boxes of *somen* vermicelli as Bon Festival gifts. Maybe you'd each like to take one?
The truth is, neither I nor Osamu and his family like *somen* all that much.
#74
SPEAKING OF, THERE WAS THAT INCIDENT BEFORE INVOLVING MADAM.

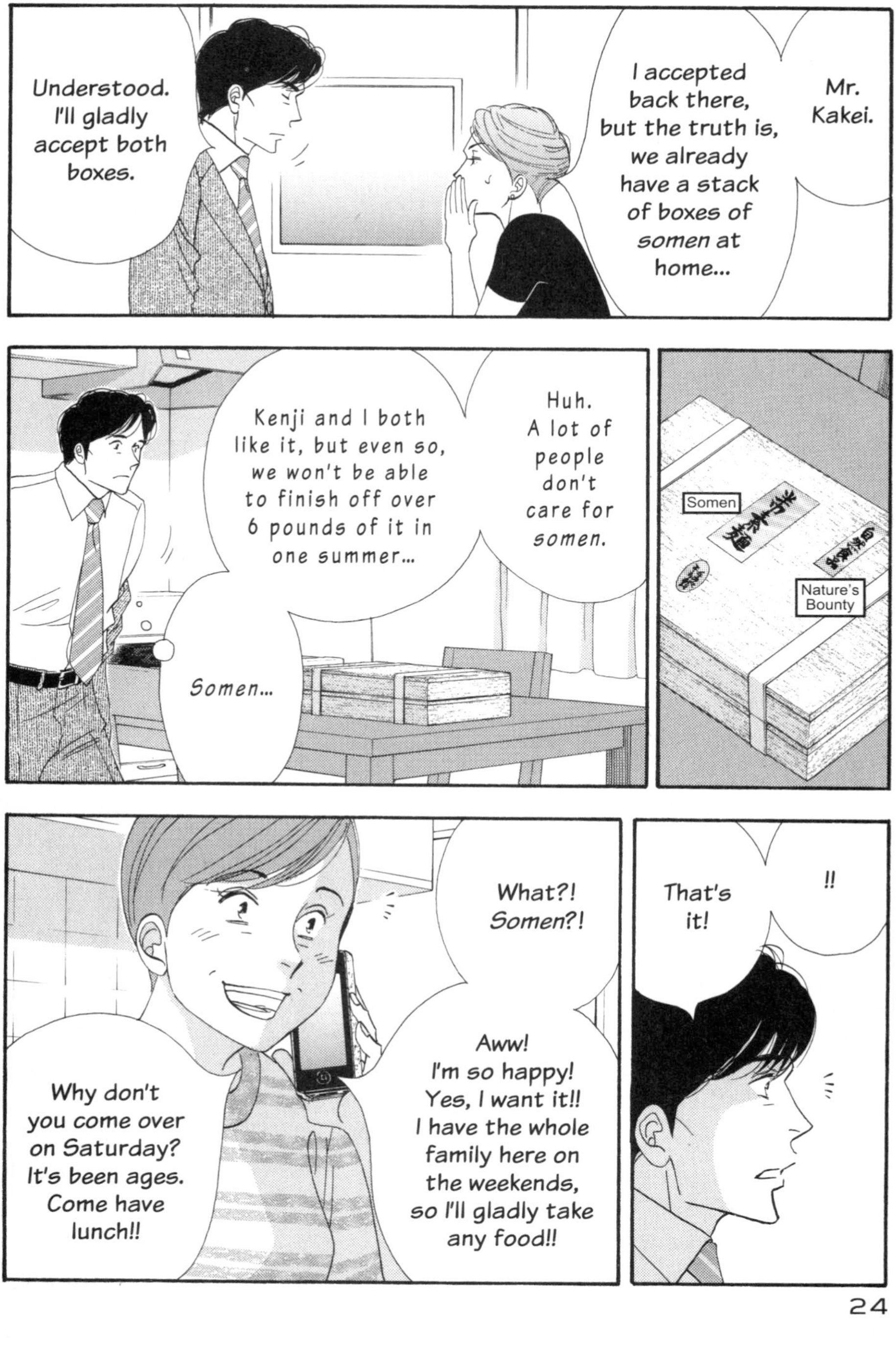
Mr. Kakei.
I accepted back there, but the truth is, we already have a stack of boxes of *somen* at home...
Understood. I'll gladly accept both boxes.
Somen
Nature's Bounty
Huh. A lot of people don't care for *somen*.
Kenji and I both like it, but even so, we won't be able to finish off over 6 pounds of it in one summer...
Somen...
!!
That's it!
What?! *Somen*?!
Aww! I'm so happy! Yes, I want it!! I have the whole family here on the weekends, so I'll gladly take any food!!
Why don't you come over on Saturday? It's been ages. Come have lunch!!

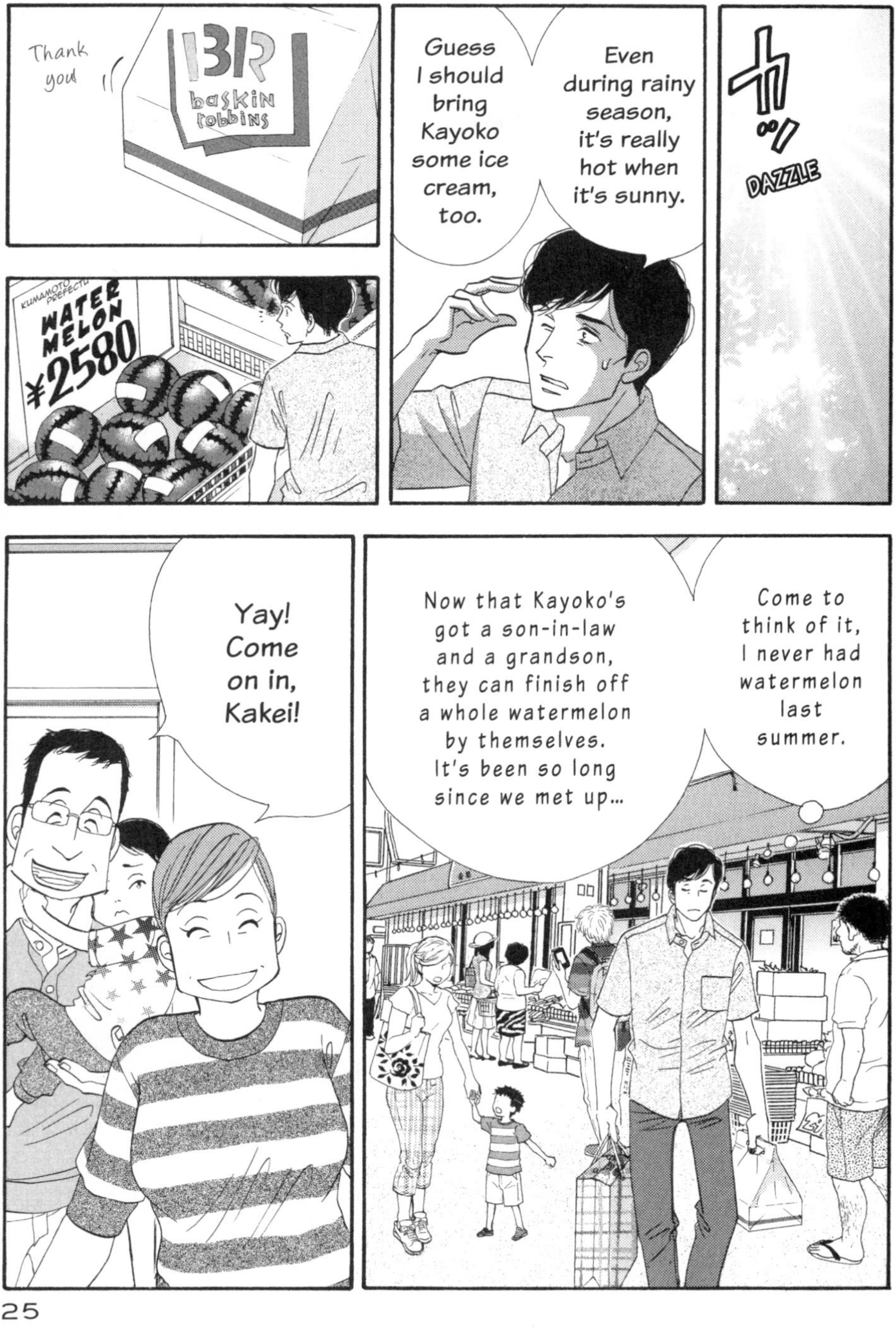
DAZZLE
Even during rainy season, it's really hot when it's sunny.
Guess I should bring Kayoko some ice cream, too.
Thank you
baskin robbins
KUMAMOTO PREFECTU
WATER MELON ¥2580
Come to think of it, I never had watermelon last summer.
Now that Kayoko's got a son-in-law and a grandson, they can finish off a whole watermelon by themselves. It's been so long since we met up...
Yay! Come on in, Kakei!

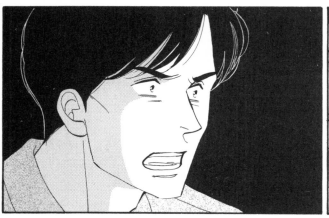

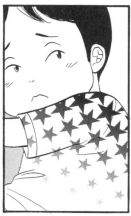

Ah! Hello, Mr. Kakei!
Hi. I'm Watanabe. It's been a while.
A-Amazing. Your son turned into a human being in the brief time I haven't seen him?!
Goro! Come play with Grandpa!
Ha ha ha! He's still just a little bug!
He's a year and eight months now, but he's pretty shy. Sorry about that.
Here we go.
Sit tight for just a bit. I'm gonna make lunch right now!

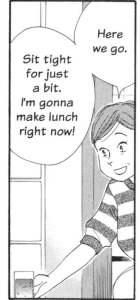

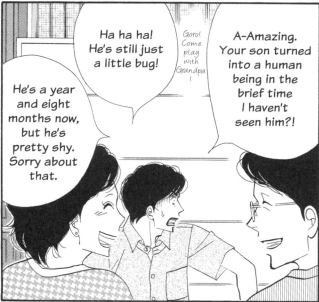

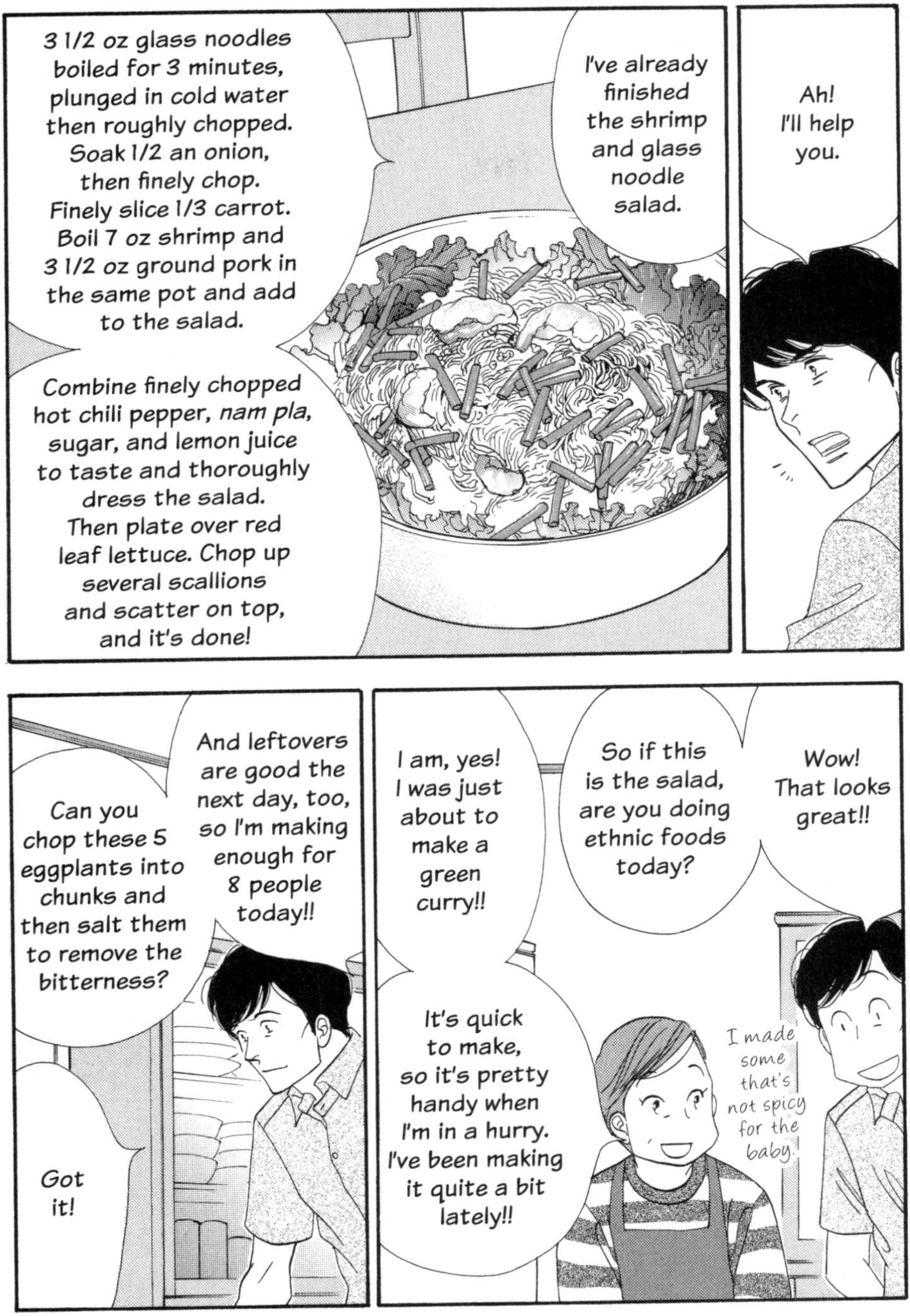
Ah! I'll help you.
I've already finished the shrimp and glass noodle salad.
3 1/2 oz glass noodles boiled for 3 minutes, plunged in cold water then roughly chopped. Soak 1/2 an onion, then finely chop. Finely slice 1/3 carrot. Boil 7 oz shrimp and 3 1/2 oz ground pork in the same pot and add to the salad.
Combine finely chopped hot chili pepper, *nam pla*, sugar, and lemon juice to taste and thoroughly dress the salad. Then plate over red leaf lettuce. Chop up several scallions and scatter on top, and it's done!
Wow! That looks great!!
So if this is the salad, are you doing ethnic foods today?
I am, yes! I was just about to make a green curry!!
It's quick to make, so it's pretty handy when I'm in a hurry. I've been making it quite a bit lately!!
I made some that's not spicy for the baby.
And leftovers are good the next day, too, so I'm making enough for 8 people today!!
Can you chop these 5 eggplants into chunks and then salt them to remove the bitterness?
Got it!

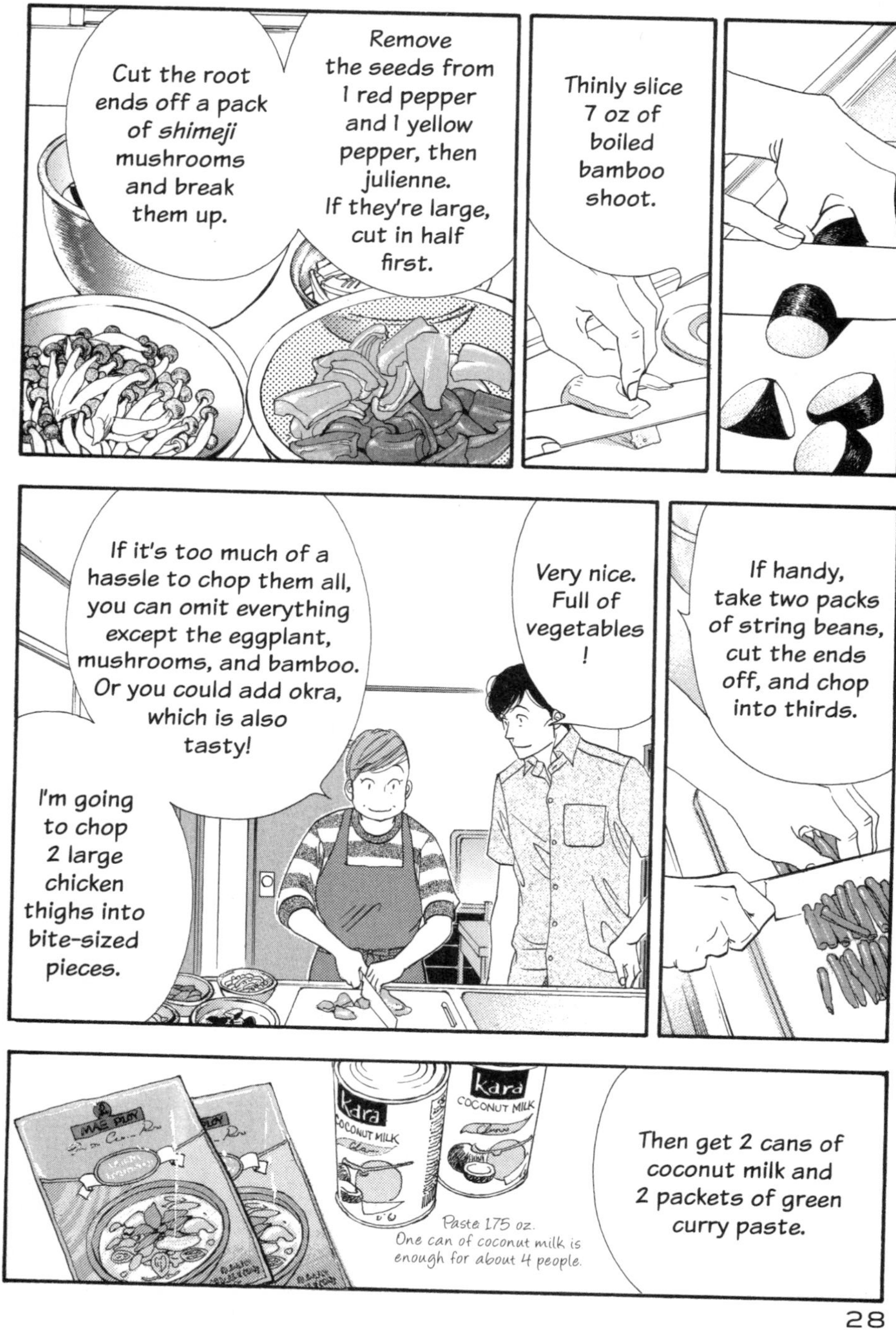
Thinly slice 7 oz of boiled bamboo shoot.
Remove the seeds from 1 red pepper and 1 yellow pepper, then julienne. If they're large, cut in half first.
Cut the root ends off a pack of *shimeji* mushrooms and break them up.
If handy, take two packs of string beans, cut the ends off, and chop into thirds.
Very nice. Full of vegetables!
If it's too much of a hassle to chop them all, you can omit everything except the eggplant, mushrooms, and bamboo. Or you could add okra, which is also tasty!
I'm going to chop 2 large chicken thighs into bite-sized pieces.
Then get 2 cans of coconut milk and 2 packets of green curry paste.
Paste 175 oz.
One can of coconut milk is enough for about 4 people.

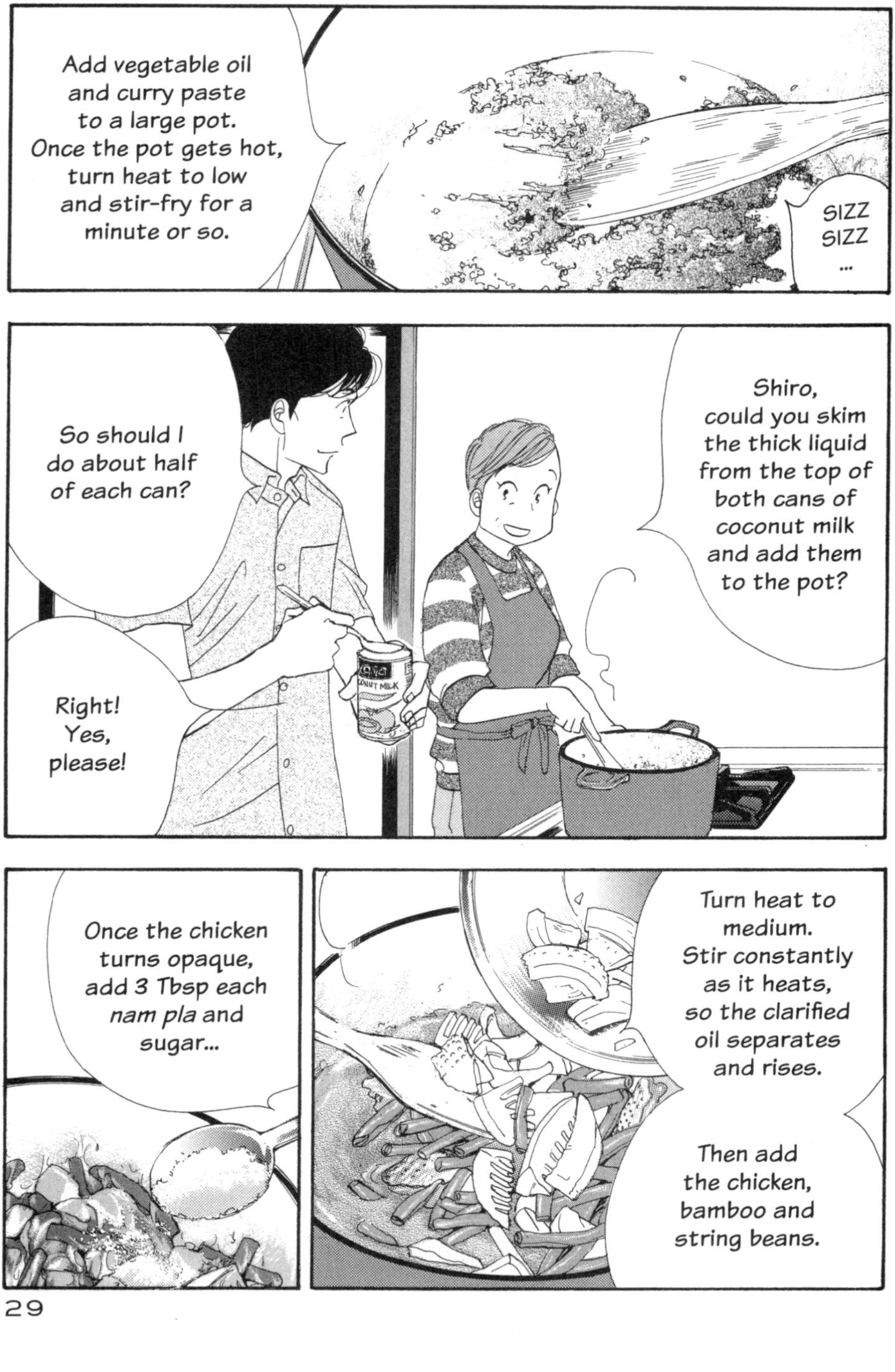
Add vegetable oil and curry paste to a large pot. Once the pot gets hot, turn heat to low and stir-fry for a minute or so.
SIZZ SIZZ ...
Shiro, could you skim the thick liquid from the top of both cans of coconut milk and add them to the pot?
So should I do about half of each can?
Right! Yes, please!
Turn heat to medium. Stir constantly as it heats, so the clarified oil separates and rises.
Then add the chicken, bamboo and string beans.
Once the chicken turns opaque, add 3 Tbsp each *nam pla* and sugar...

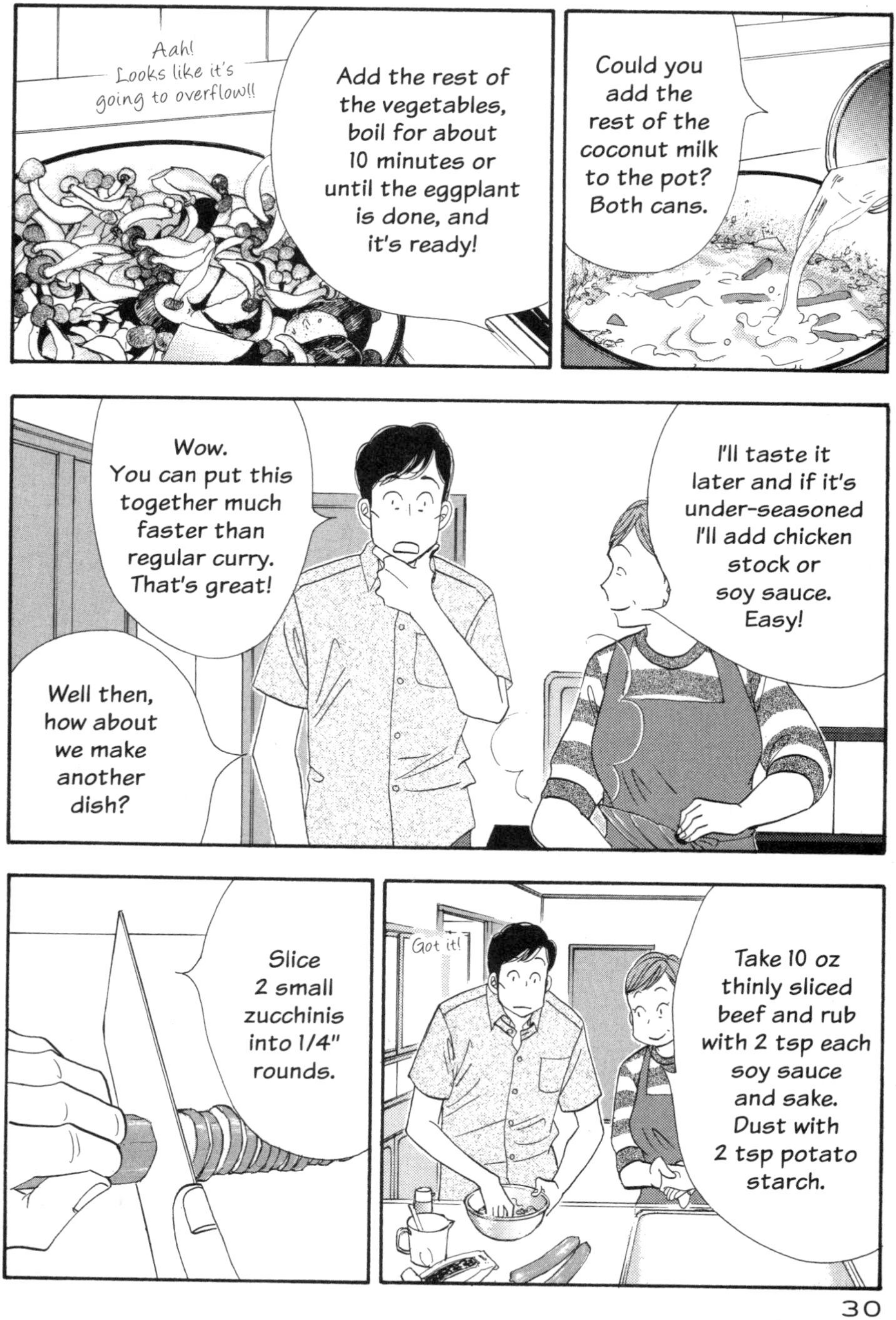
Could you add the rest of the coconut milk to the pot? Both cans.
Add the rest of the vegetables, boil for about 10 minutes or until the eggplant is done, and it's ready!
Aah! Looks like it's going to overflow!!
I'll taste it later and if it's under-seasoned I'll add chicken stock or soy sauce. Easy!
Wow. You can put this together much faster than regular curry. That's great!
Well then, how about we make another dish?
Take 10 oz thinly sliced beef and rub with 2 tsp each soy sauce and sake. Dust with 2 tsp potato starch.
Got it!
Slice 2 small zucchinis into 1/4" rounds.

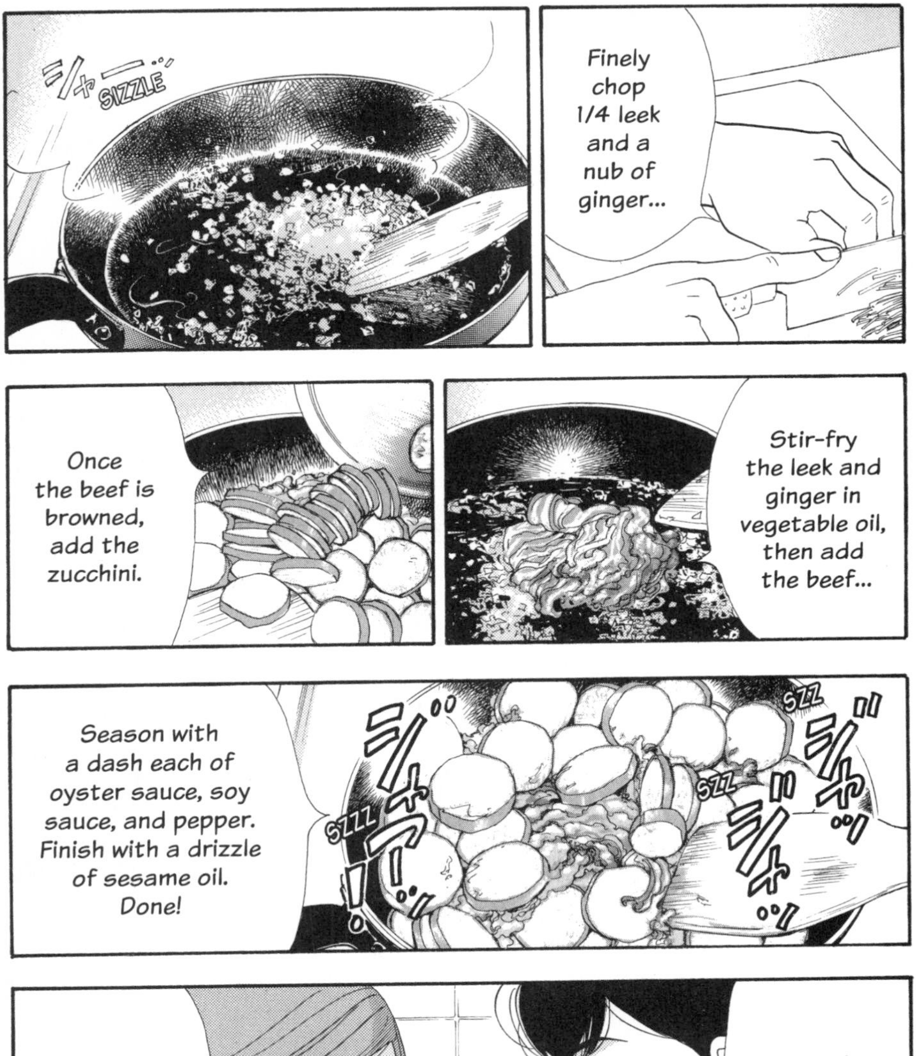
Finely chop 1/4 leek and a nub of ginger...
SIZZLE
Stir-fry the leek and ginger in vegetable oil, then add the beef...
Once the beef is browned, add the zucchini.
SZZ
SZZ
Season with a dash each of oyster sauce, soy sauce, and pepper. Finish with a drizzle of sesame oil. Done!
SZZZ
Wow! Chinese-style zucchini!
Lunch is ready, everyone!

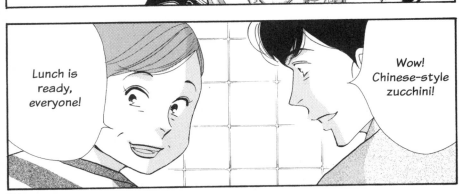

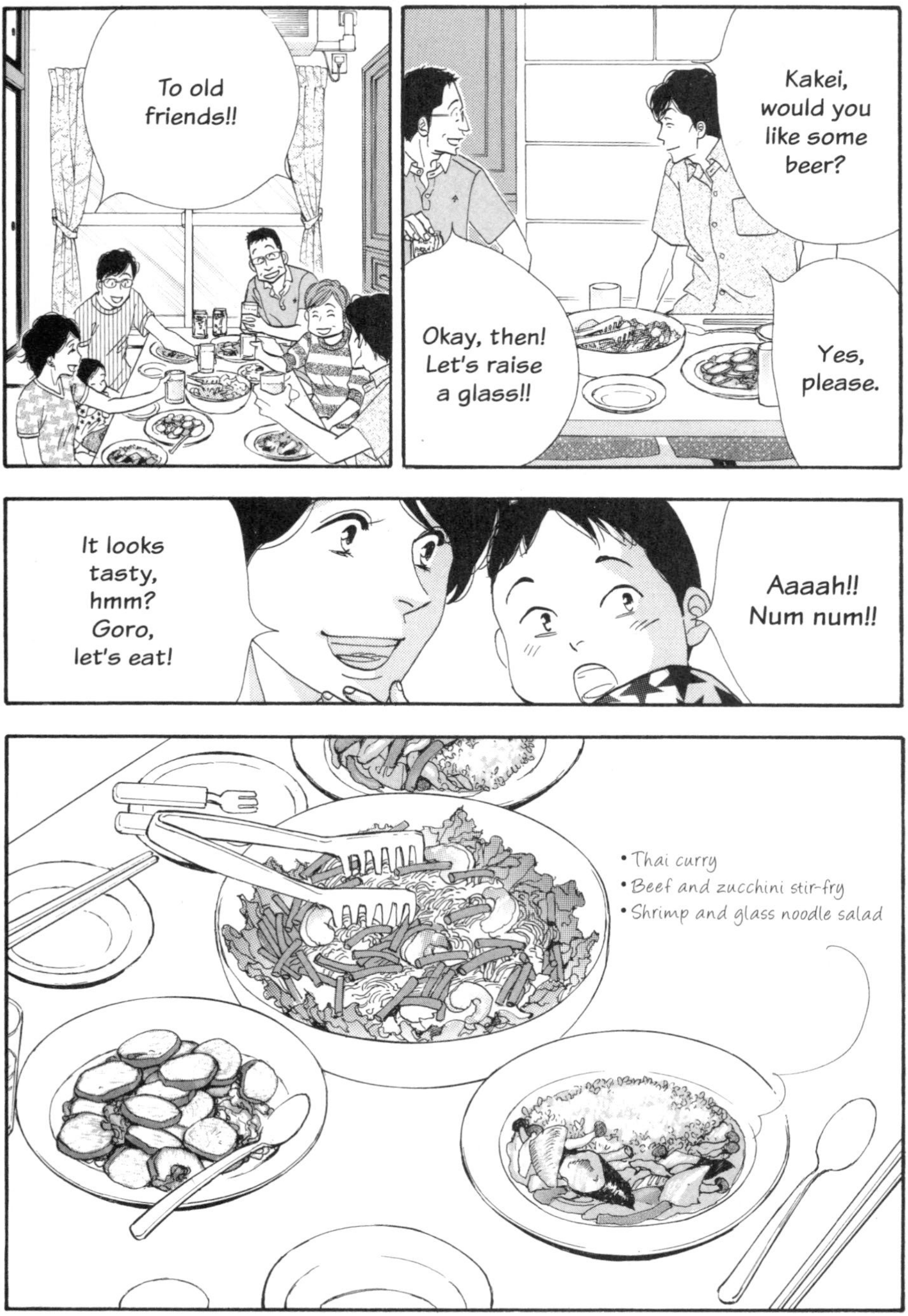
Kakei, would you like some beer?
Yes, please.
Okay, then! Let's raise a glass!!
To old friends!!
Aaaah!! Num num!!
It looks tasty, hmm? Goro, let's eat!
• Thai curry
• Beef and zucchini stir-fry
• Shrimp and glass noodle salad

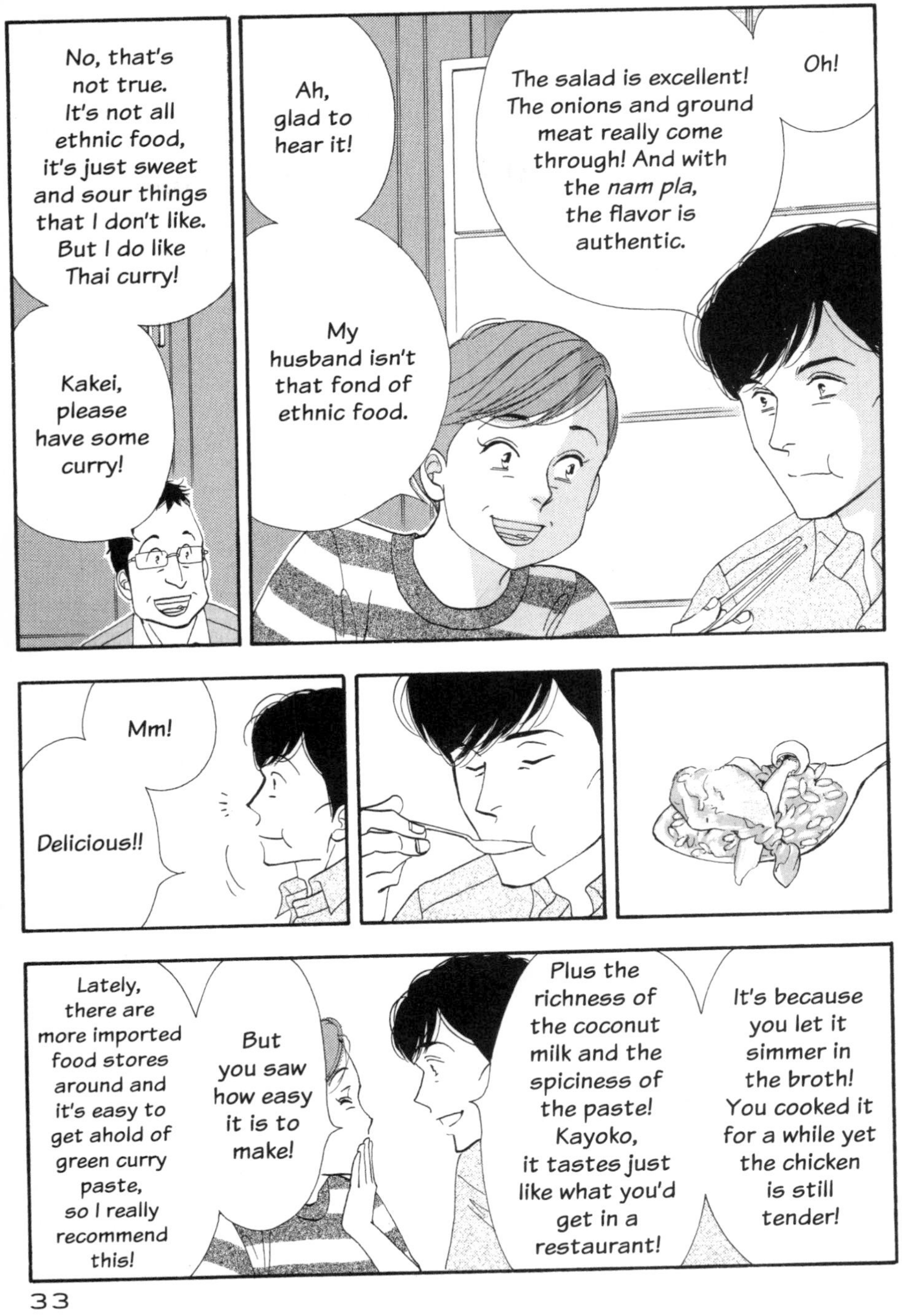
Oh!
The salad is excellent! The onions and ground meat really come through! And with the *nam pla*, the flavor is authentic.
Ah, glad to hear it!
My husband isn't that fond of ethnic food.
No, that's not true. It's not all ethnic food, it's just sweet and sour things that I don't like. But I do like Thai curry!
Kakei, please have some curry!
Mm!
Delicious!!
It's because you let it simmer in the broth! You cooked it for a while yet the chicken is still tender!
Plus the richness of the coconut milk and the spiciness of the paste! Kayoko, it tastes just like what you'd get in a restaurant!
But you saw how easy it is to make!
Lately, there are more imported food stores around and it's easy to get ahold of green curry paste, so I really recommend this!

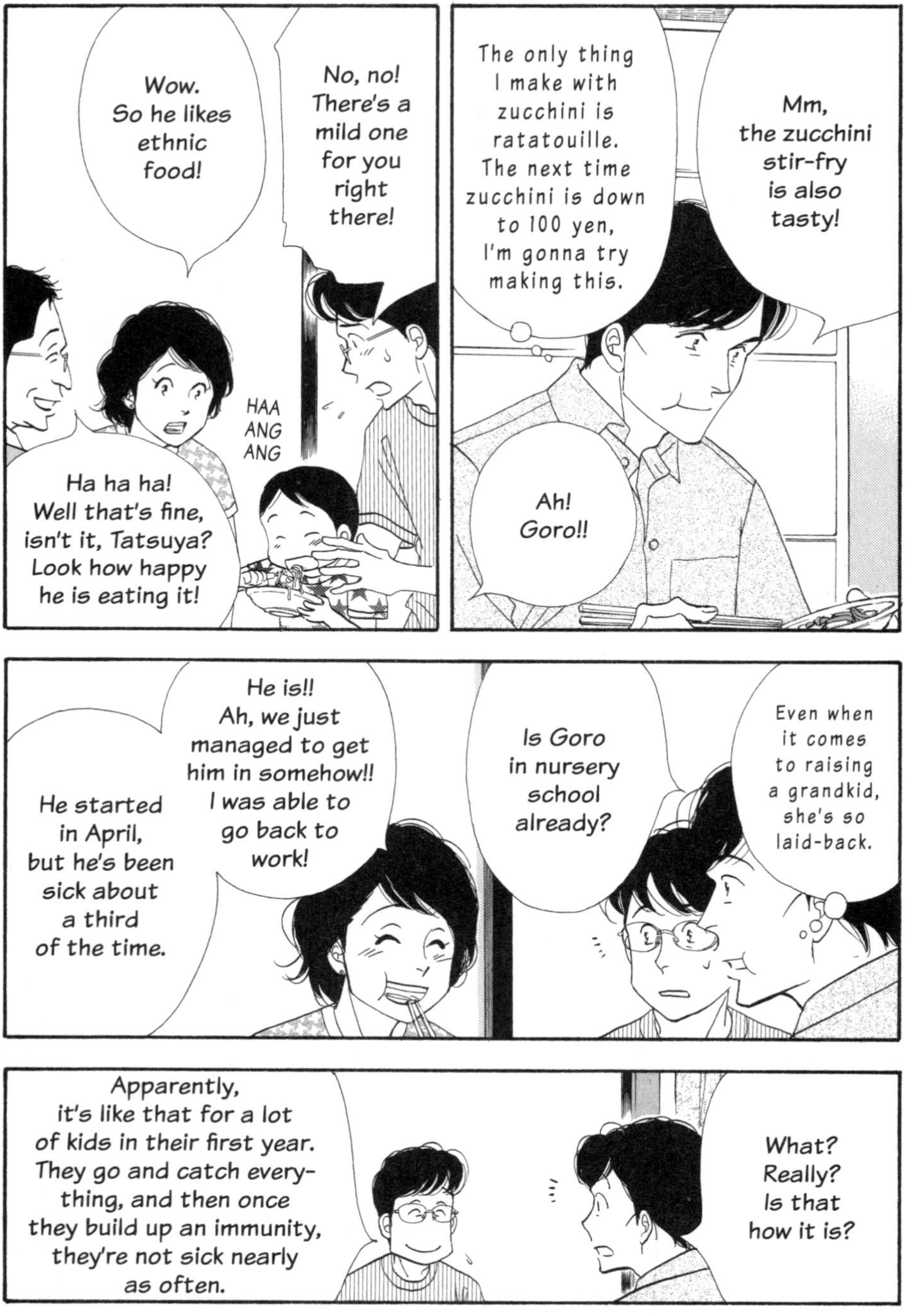
Mm, the zucchini stir-fry is also tasty!
The only thing I make with zucchini is ratatouille. The next time zucchini is down to 100 yen, I'm gonna try making this.
Ah! Goro!!
No, no! There's a mild one for you right there!
Wow. So he likes ethnic food!
HAA ANG ANG
Ha ha ha! Well that's fine, isn't it, Tatsuya? Look how happy he is eating it!
Even when it comes to raising a grandkid, she's so laid-back.
Is Goro in nursery school already?
He is!! Ah, we just managed to get him in somehow!! I was able to go back to work!
He started in April, but he's been sick about a third of the time.
What? Really? Is that how it is?
Apparently, it's like that for a lot of kids in their first year. They go and catch every-thing, and then once they build up an immunity, they're not sick nearly as often.

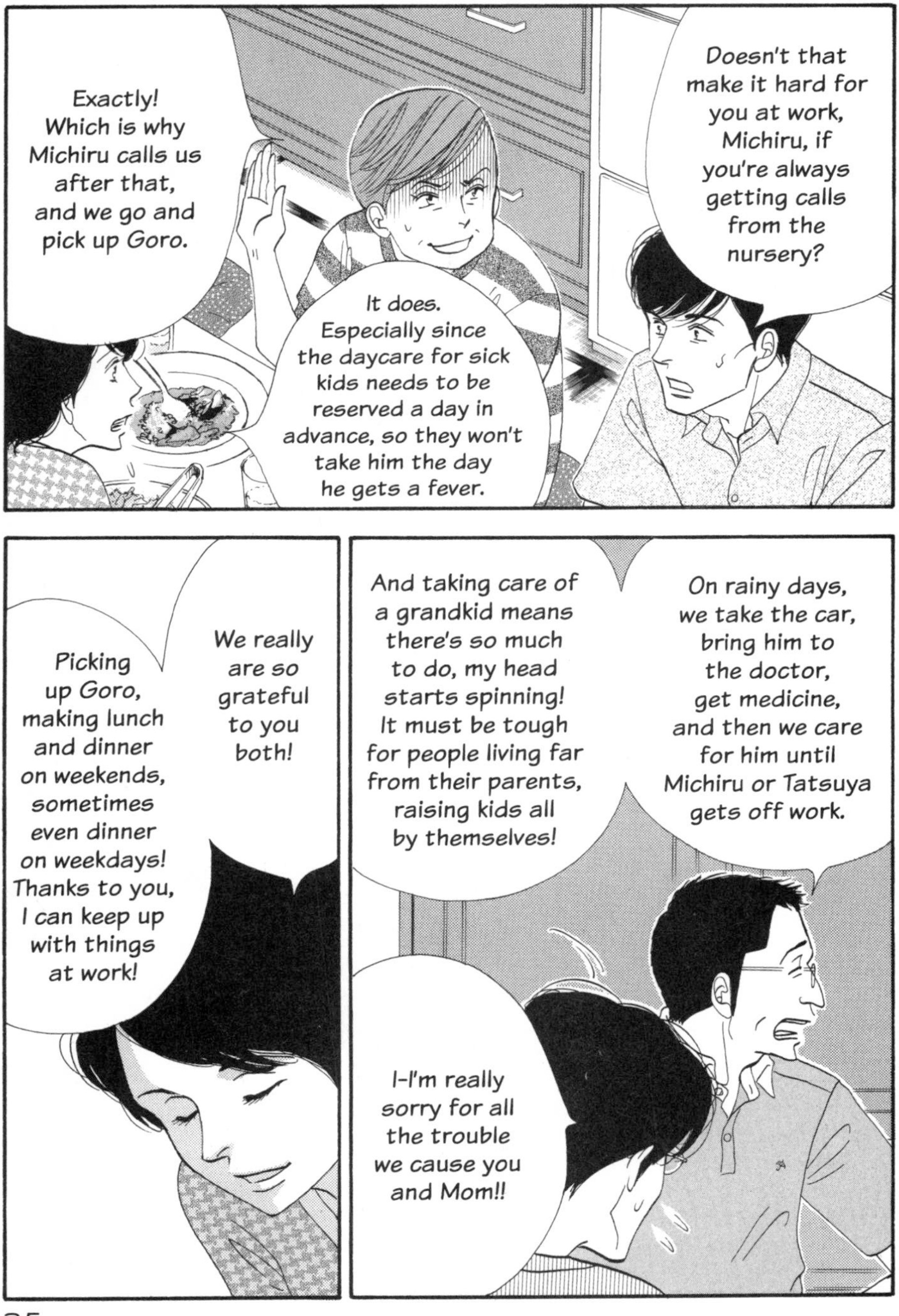
Doesn't that make it hard for you at work, Michiru, if you're always getting calls from the nursery?
Exactly! Which is why Michiru calls us after that, and we go and pick up Goro.
It does. Especially since the daycare for sick kids needs to be reserved a day in advance, so they won't take him the day he gets a fever.
On rainy days, we take the car, bring him to the doctor, get medicine, and then we care for him until Michiru or Tatsuya gets off work.
And taking care of a grandkid means there's so much to do, my head starts spinning! It must be tough for people living far from their parents, raising kids all by themselves!
I-I'm really sorry for all the trouble we cause you and Mom!!
We really are so grateful to you both!
Picking up Goro, making lunch and dinner on weekends, sometimes even dinner on weekdays! Thanks to you, I can keep up with things at work!

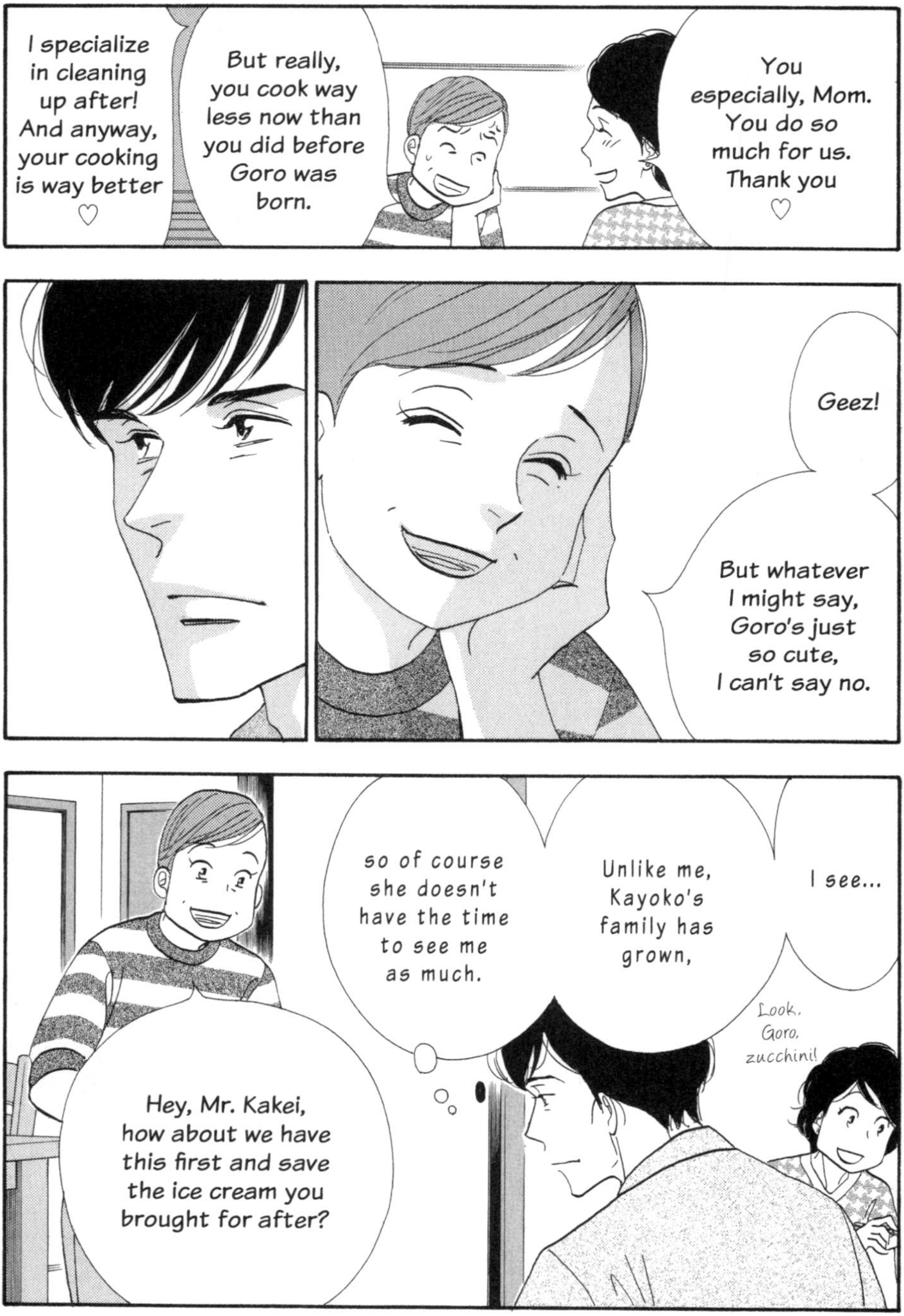
You especially, Mom. You do so much for us. Thank you ♡
But really, you cook way less now than you did before Goro was born.
I specialize in cleaning up after! And anyway, your cooking is way better ♡
Geez!
But whatever I might say, Goro's just so cute, I can't say no.
I see...
Unlike me, Kayoko's family has grown,
so of course she doesn't have the time to see me as much.
Look, Goro, zucchini!
Hey, Mr. Kakei, how about we have this first and save the ice cream you brought for after?

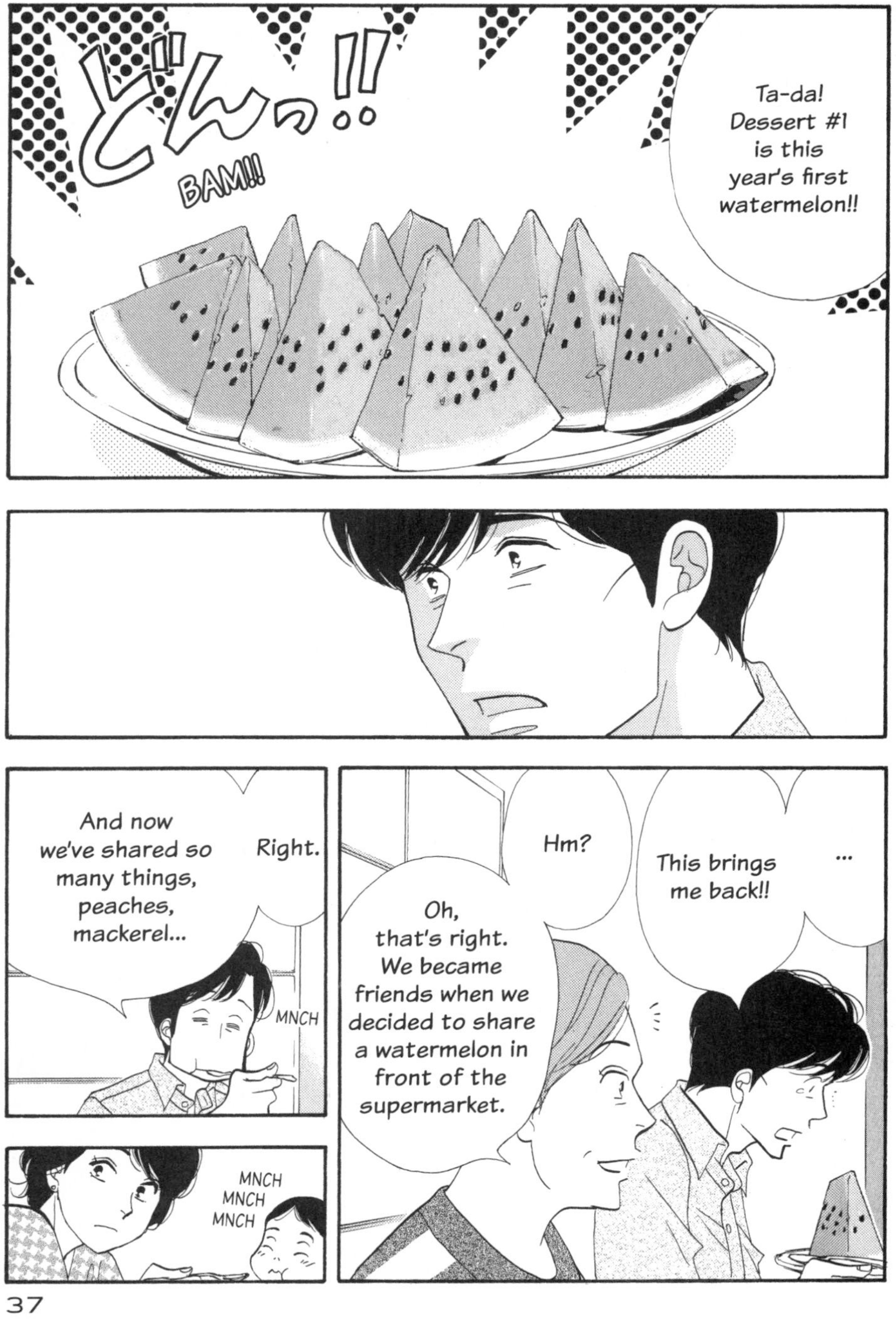
Ta-da! Dessert #1 is this year's first watermelon!!
どんっ!!
BAM!!
...
This brings me back!!
Hm?
Oh, that's right. We became friends when we decided to share a watermelon in front of the supermarket.
Right.
And now we've shared so many things, peaches, mackerel...
MNCH
MNCH MNCH MNCH

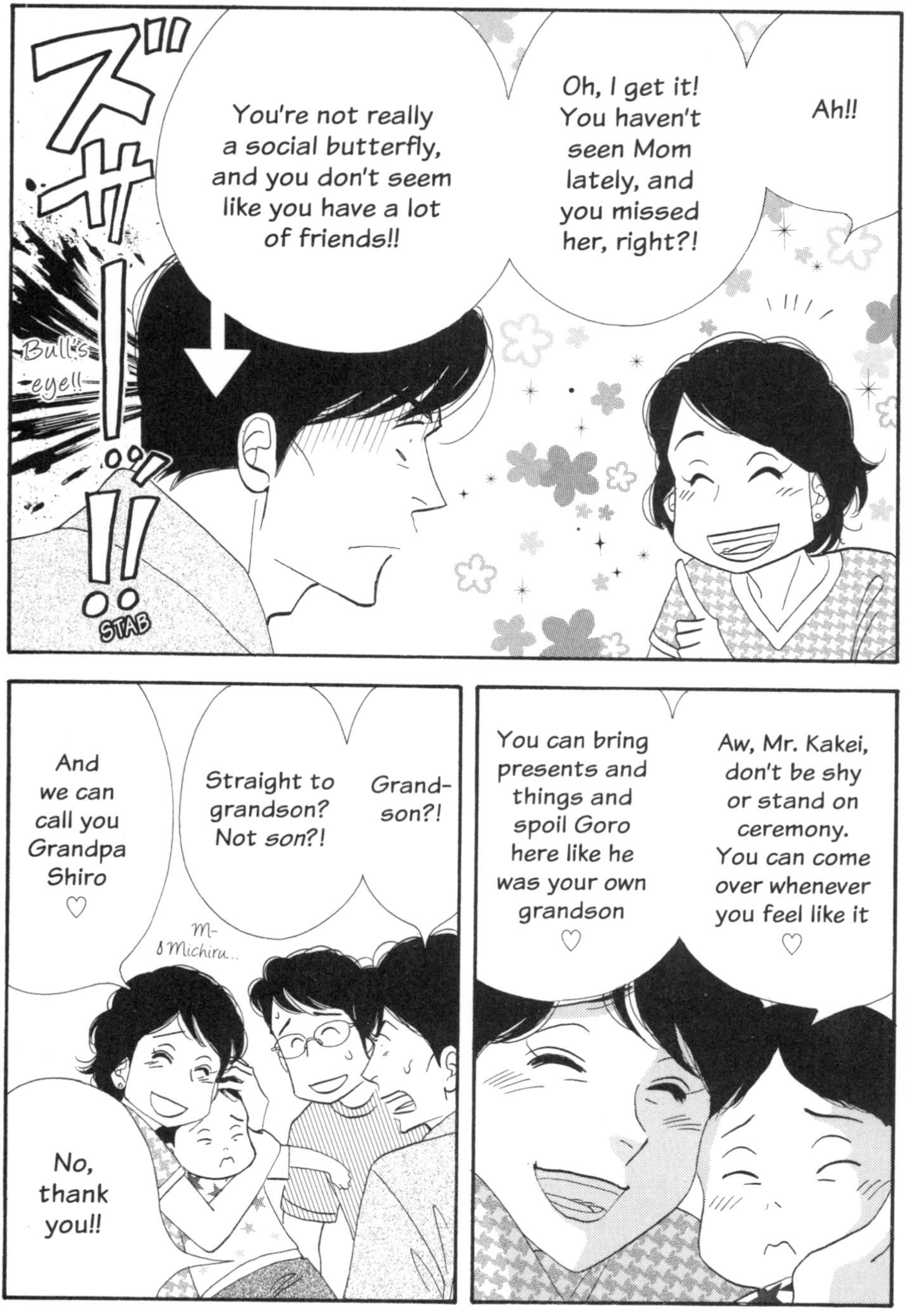
Ah!!
Oh, I get it! You haven't seen Mom lately, and you missed her, right?!
You're not really a social butterfly, and you don't seem like you have a lot of friends!!
Bull's eye!!
STAB
Aw, Mr. Kakei, don't be shy or stand on ceremony. You can come over whenever you feel like it ♡
You can bring presents and things and spoil Goro here like he was your own grandson ♡
Grand-son?!
Straight to grandson? Not son?!
And we can call you Grandpa Shiro ♡
M-Michiru..
No, thank you!!

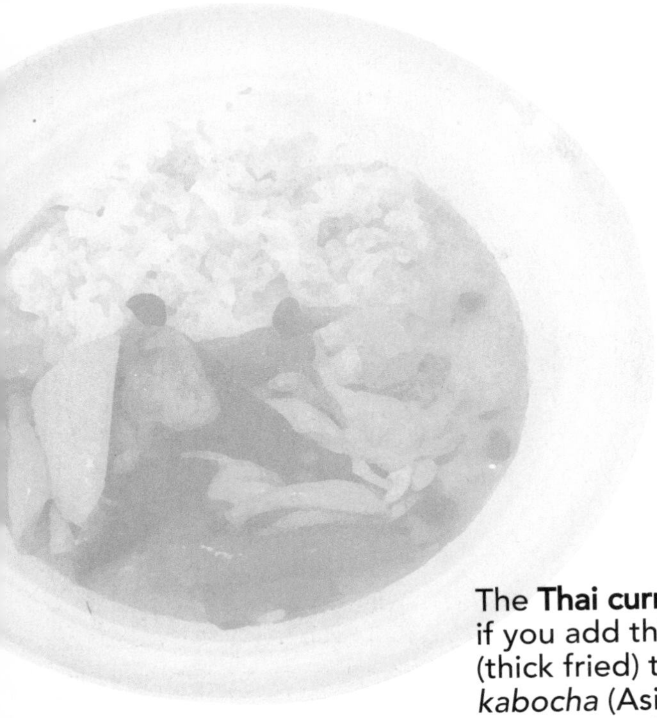

The **Thai curry** is also tasty if you add things like *atsuage* (thick fried) tofu, shrimp or *kabocha* (Asian pumpkin). But if you add too many ingredients, the pan will overflow. I think one packet of curry paste and one can of coconut milk is enough for six servings.

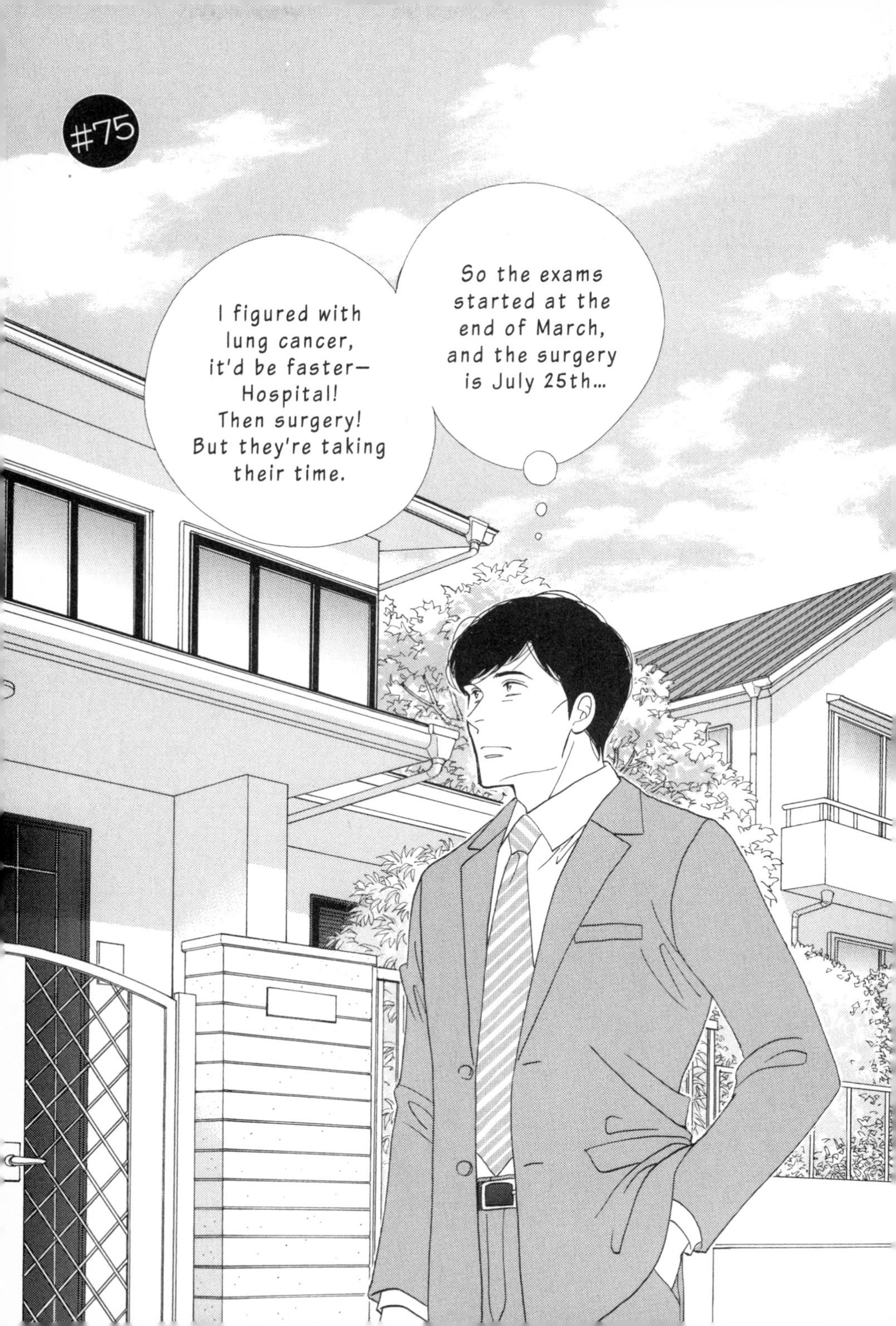
#75
So the exams started at the end of March, and the surgery is July 25th…
I figured with lung cancer, it'd be faster— Hospital! Then surgery! But they're taking their time.

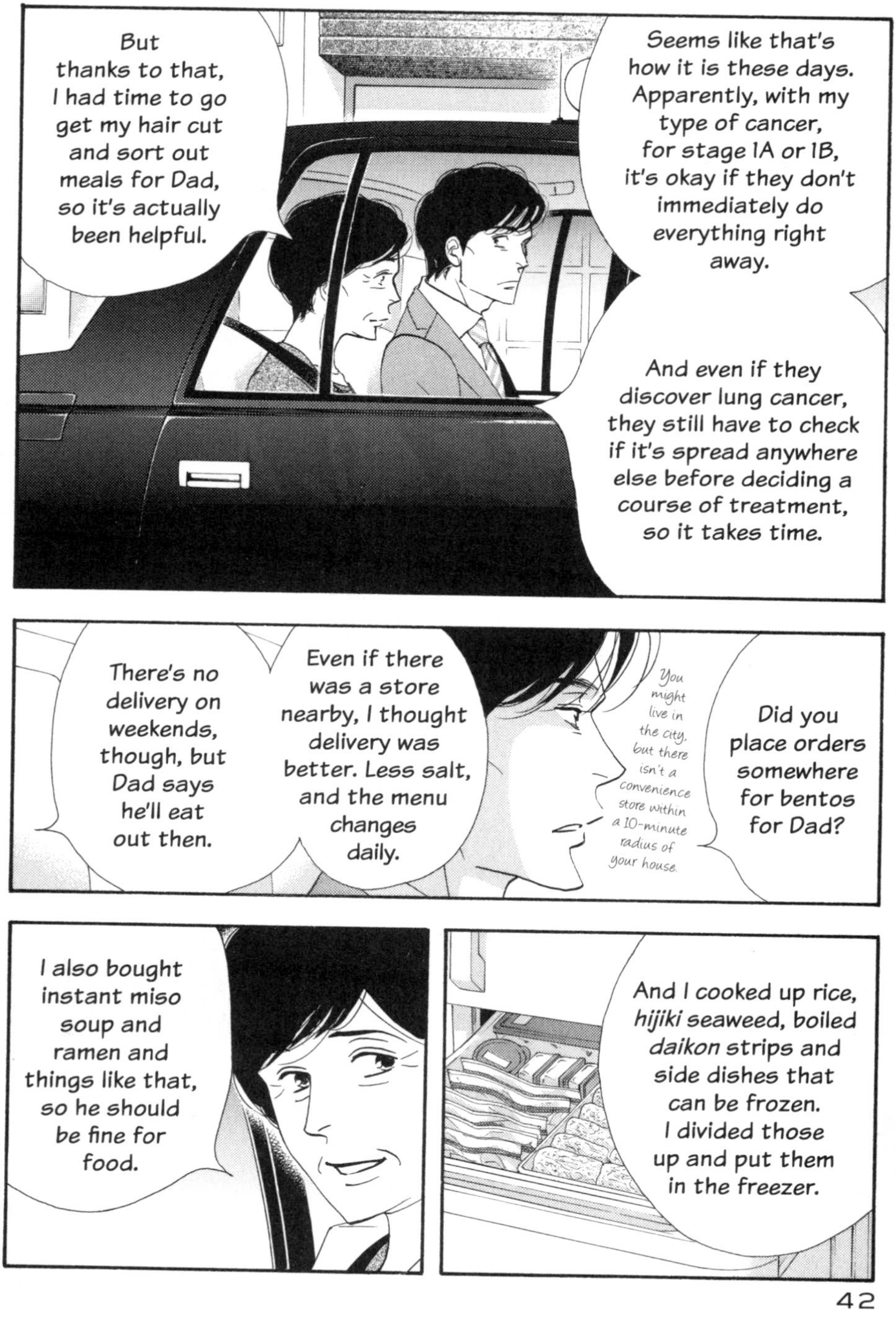
Seems like that's how it is these days. Apparently, with my type of cancer, for stage 1A or 1B, it's okay if they don't immediately do everything right away.
And even if they discover lung cancer, they still have to check if it's spread anywhere else before deciding a course of treatment, so it takes time.
But thanks to that, I had time to go get my hair cut and sort out meals for Dad, so it's actually been helpful.
Did you place orders somewhere for bentos for Dad?
You might live in the city, but there isn't a convenience store within a 10-minute radius of your house.
Even if there was a store nearby, I thought delivery was better. Less salt, and the menu changes daily.
There's no delivery on weekends, though, but Dad says he'll eat out then.
And I cooked up rice, hijiki seaweed, boiled daikon strips and side dishes that can be frozen. I divided those up and put them in the freezer.
I also bought instant miso soup and ramen and things like that, so he should be fine for food.

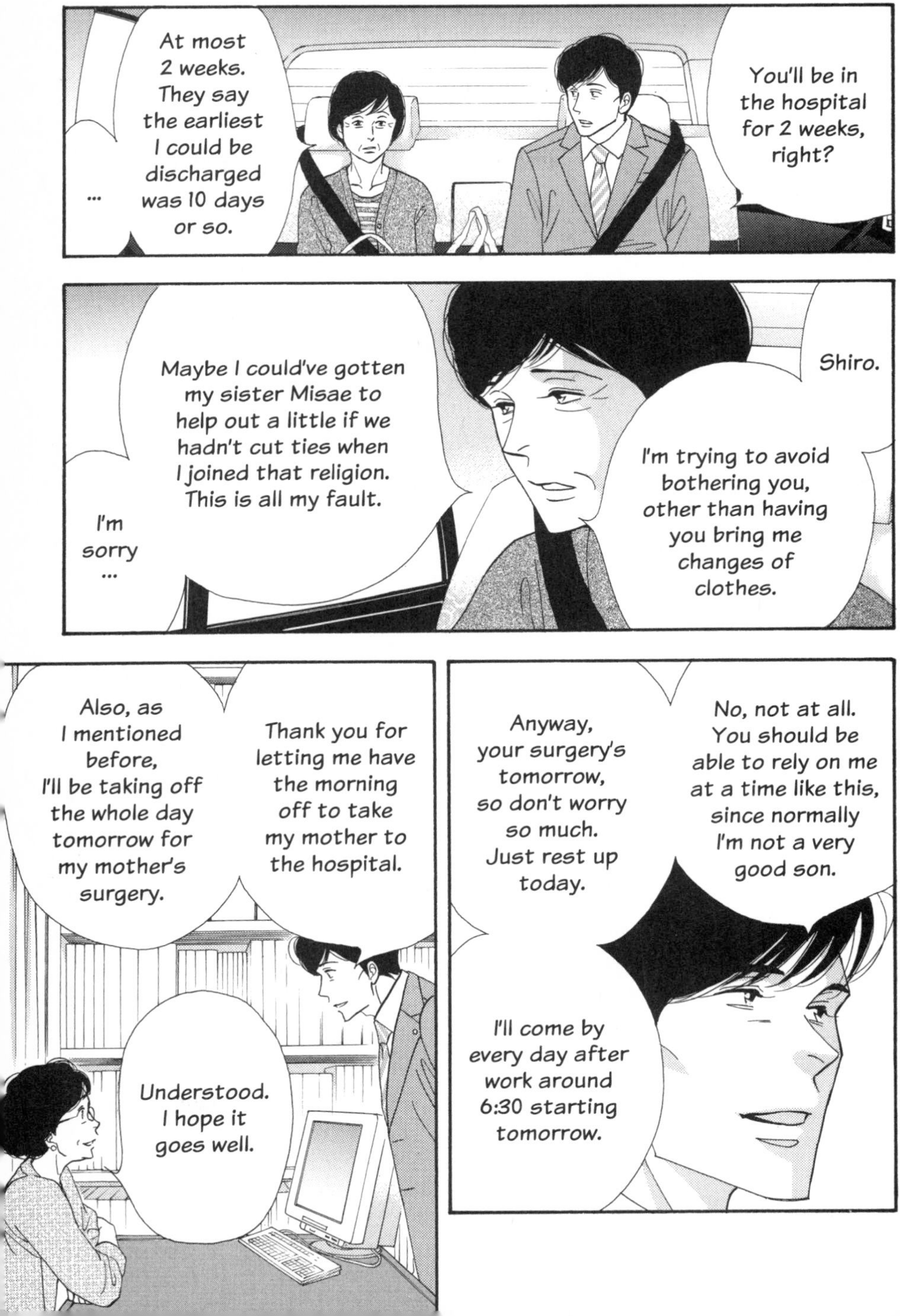
You'll be in the hospital for 2 weeks, right?
At most 2 weeks. They say the earliest I could be discharged was 10 days or so.
...
Shiro.
I'm trying to avoid bothering you, other than having you bring me changes of clothes.
Maybe I could've gotten my sister Misae to help out a little if we hadn't cut ties when I joined that religion. This is all my fault.
I'm sorry ...
No, not at all. You should be able to rely on me at a time like this, since normally I'm not a very good son.
Anyway, your surgery's tomorrow, so don't worry so much. Just rest up today.
I'll come by every day after work around 6:30 starting tomorrow.
Thank you for letting me have the morning off to take my mother to the hospital.
Also, as I mentioned before, I'll be taking off the whole day tomorrow for my mother's surgery.
Understood. I hope it goes well.

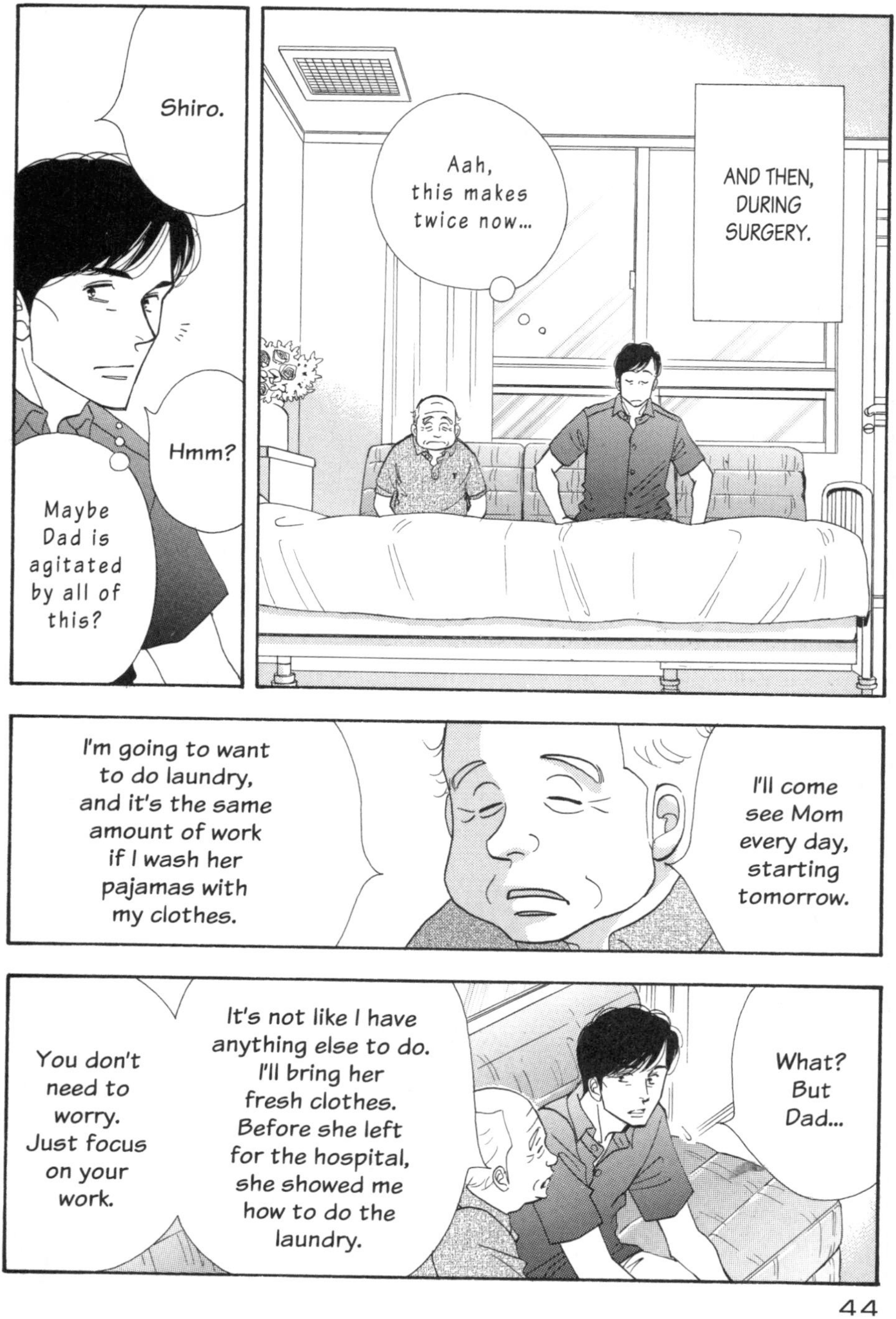
AND THEN, DURING SURGERY.
Aah, this makes twice now...
Shiro.
Hmm?
Maybe Dad is agitated by all of this?
I'll come see Mom every day, starting tomorrow.
I'm going to want to do laundry, and it's the same amount of work if I wash her pajamas with my clothes.
What? But Dad...
It's not like I have anything else to do. I'll bring her fresh clothes. Before she left for the hospital, she showed me how to do the laundry.
You don't need to worry. Just focus on your work.

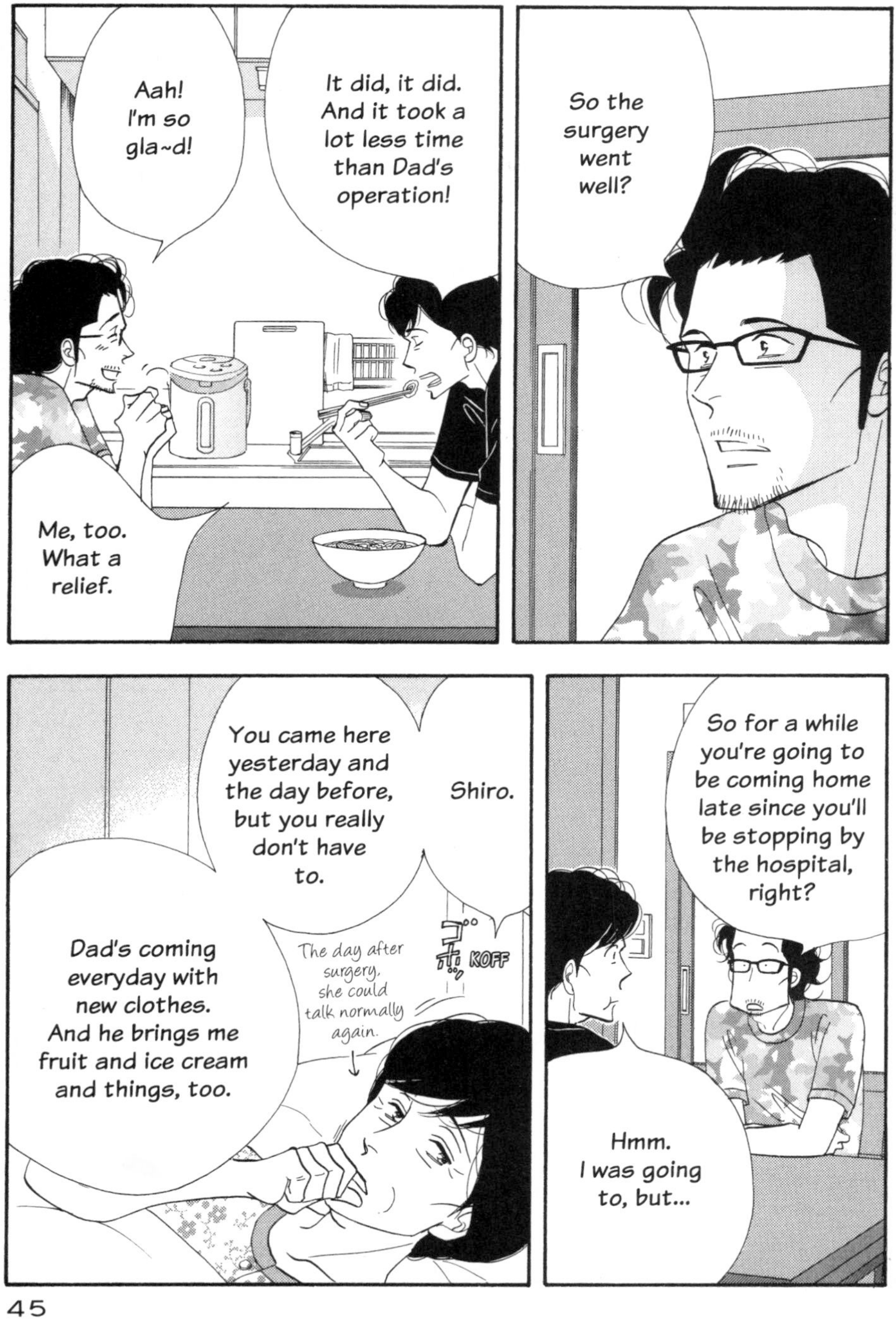
So the surgery went well?
It did, it did. And it took a lot less time than Dad's operation!
Aah! I'm so gla~d!
Me, too. What a relief.
So for a while you're going to be coming home late since you'll be stopping by the hospital, right?
Hmm. I was going to, but...
Shiro.
You came here yesterday and the day before, but you really don't have to.
KOFF
The day after surgery, she could talk normally again.
Dad's coming everyday with new clothes. And he brings me fruit and ice cream and things, too.

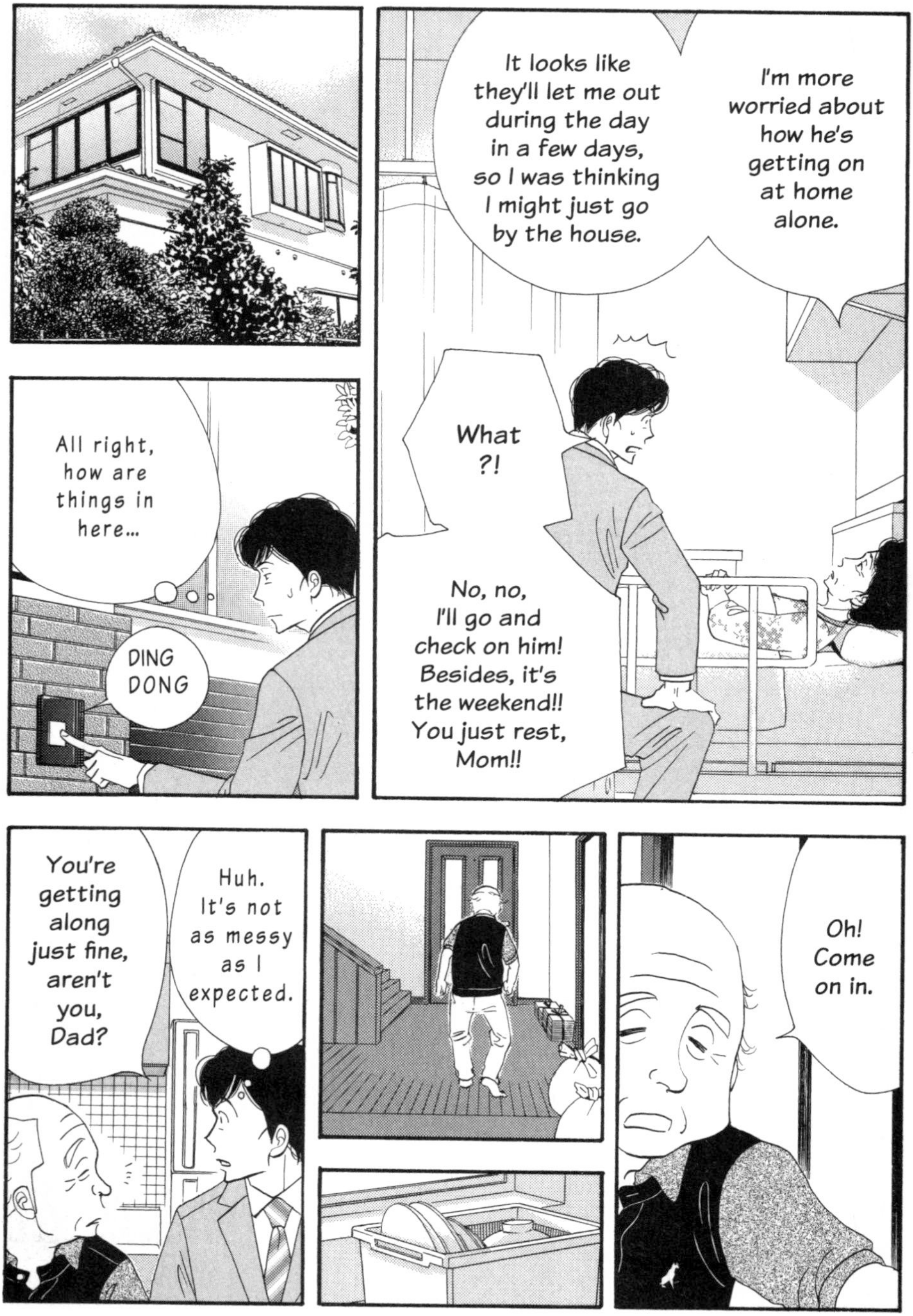
I'm more worried about how he's getting on at home alone.
It looks like they'll let me out during the day in a few days, so I was thinking I might just go by the house.
What?!
No, no, I'll go and check on him! Besides, it's the weekend!! You just rest, Mom!!
All right, how are things in here...
DING DONG
Oh! Come on in.
Huh. It's not as messy as I expected.
You're getting along just fine, aren't you, Dad?

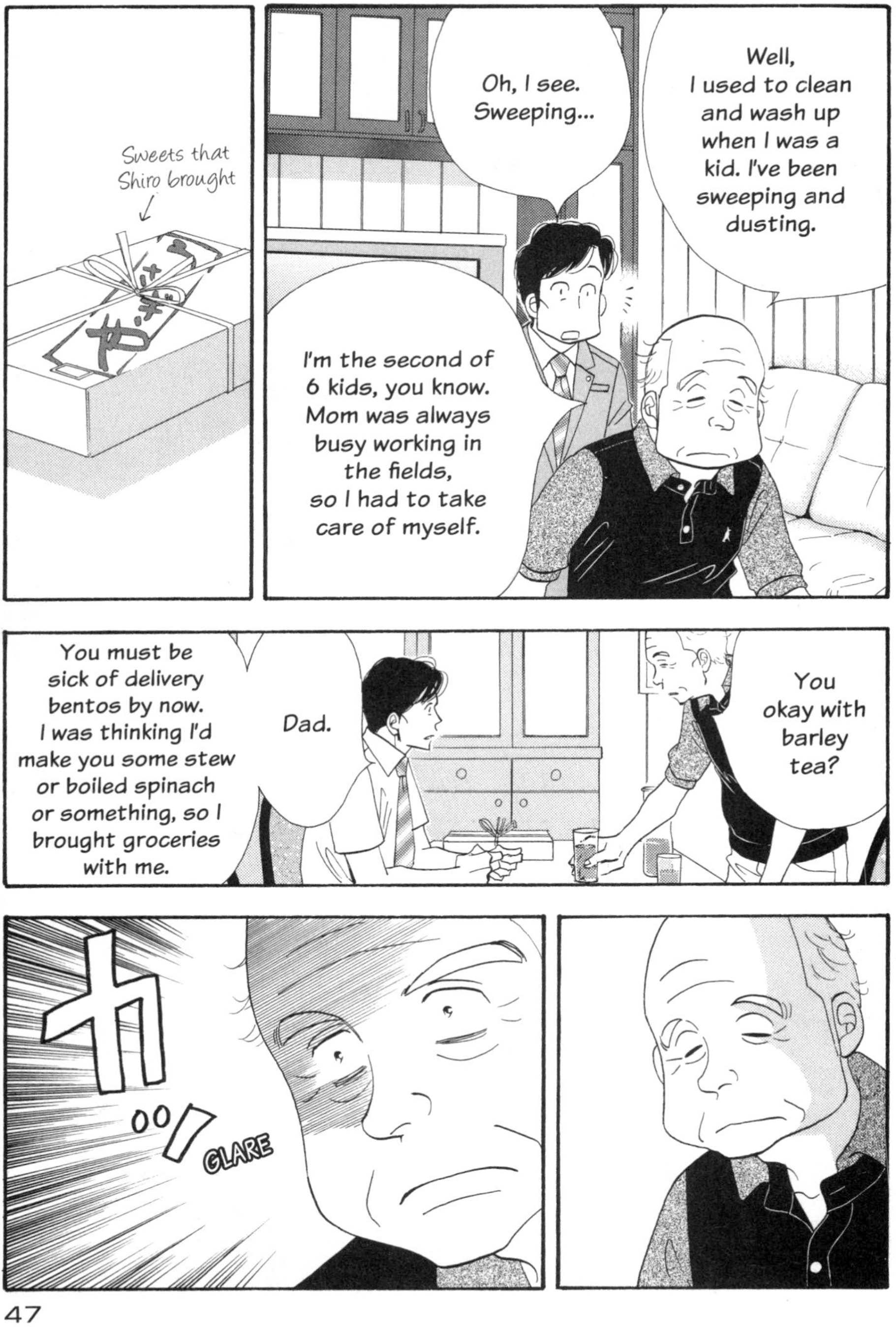

Well, I used to clean and wash up when I was a kid. I've been sweeping and dusting.
Oh, I see. Sweeping...
I'm the second of 6 kids, you know. Mom was always busy working in the fields, so I had to take care of myself.
Sweets that Shiro brought
You okay with barley tea?
Dad.
You must be sick of delivery bentos by now. I was thinking I'd make you some stew or boiled spinach or something, so I brought groceries with me.
GLARE

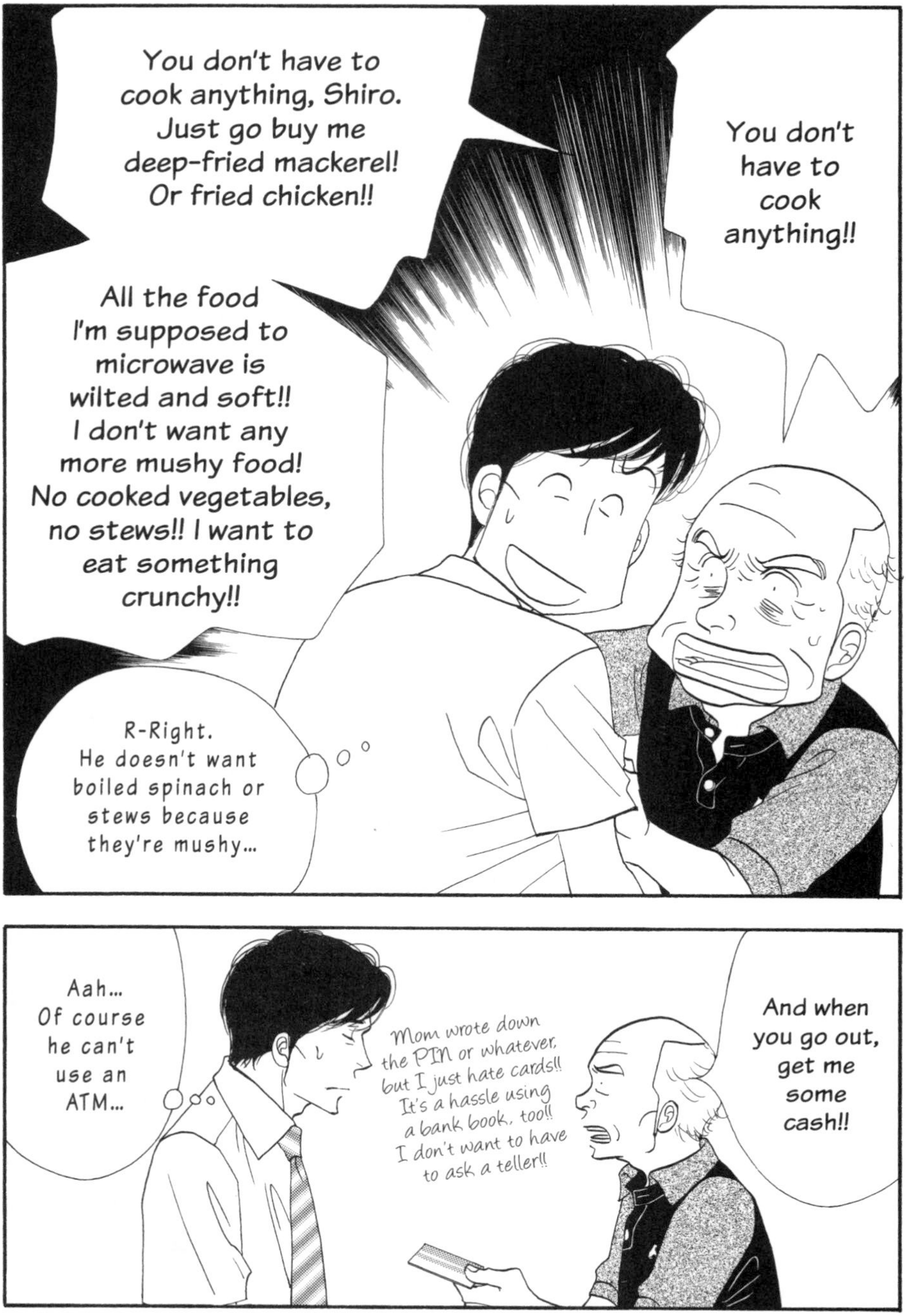

You don't have to cook anything!!
You don't have to cook anything, Shiro. Just go buy me deep-fried mackerel! Or fried chicken!!
All the food I'm supposed to microwave is wilted and soft!! I don't want any more mushy food! No cooked vegetables, no stews!! I want to eat something crunchy!!
R-Right. He doesn't want boiled spinach or stews because they're mushy...
And when you go out, get me some cash!!
Mom wrote down the PIN or whatever, but I just hate cards!! It's a hassle using a bank book, too!! I don't want to have to ask a teller!!
Aah... Of course he can't use an ATM...

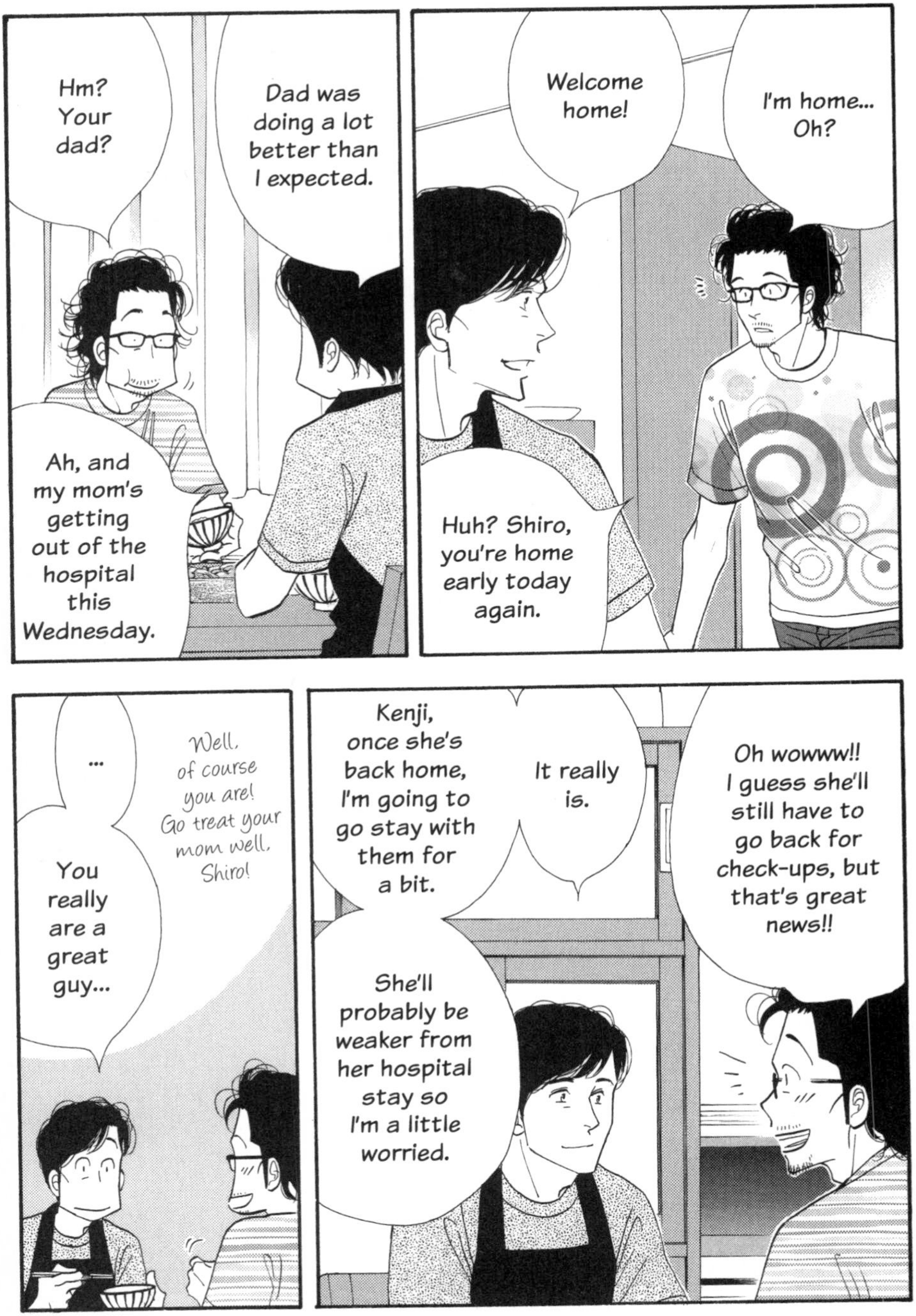
I'm home... Oh?
Welcome home!
Huh? Shiro, you're home early today again.
Dad was doing a lot better than I expected.
Hm? Your dad?
Ah, and my mom's getting out of the hospital this Wednesday.
Oh wowww!! I guess she'll still have to go back for check-ups, but that's great news!!
It really is.
Kenji, once she's back home, I'm going to go stay with them for a bit.
She'll probably be weaker from her hospital stay so I'm a little worried.
...
You really are a great guy...
Well, of course you are! Go treat your mom well, Shiro!

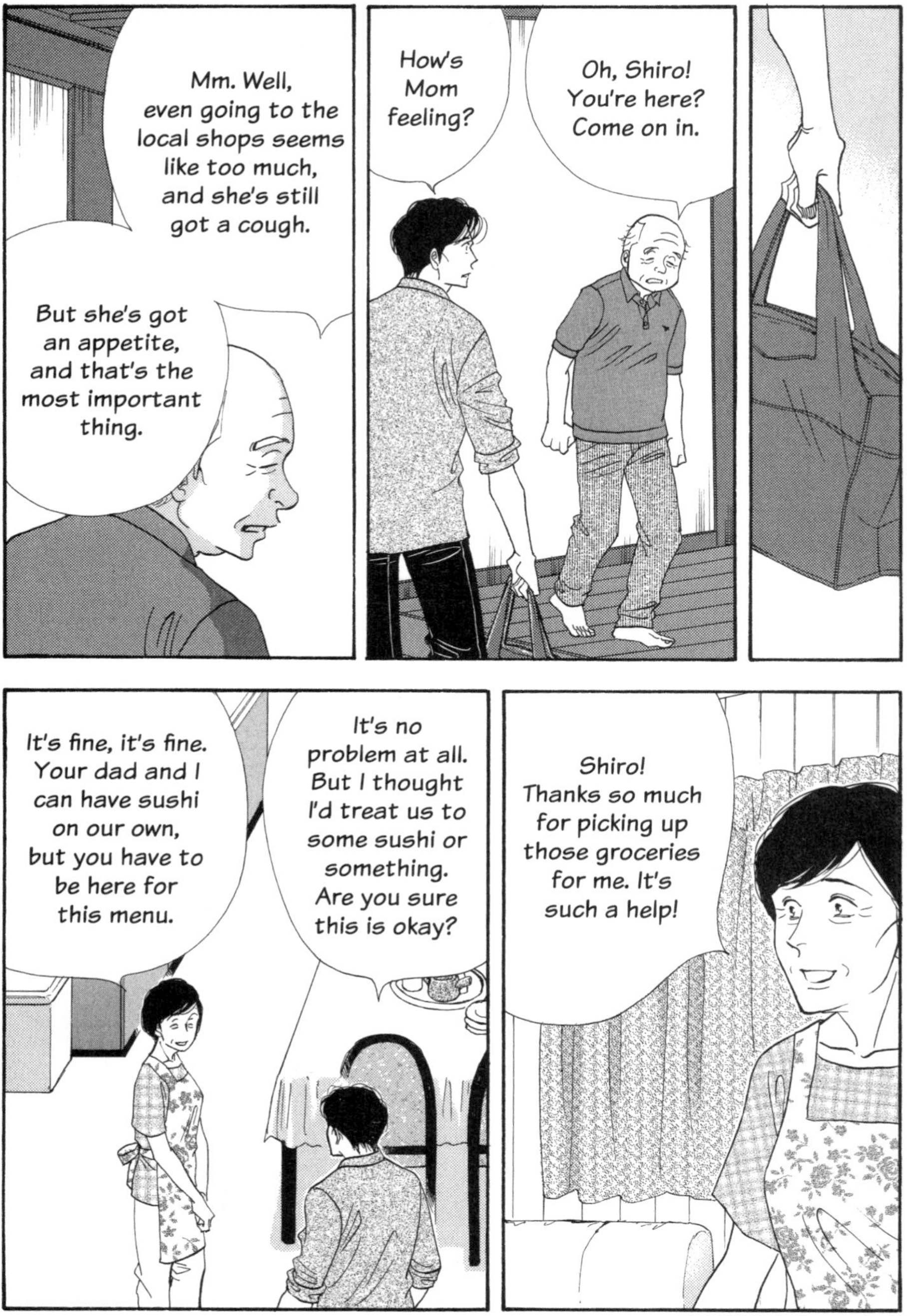
Oh, Shiro! You're here? Come on in.
How's Mom feeling?
Mm. Well, even going to the local shops seems like too much, and she's still got a cough.
But she's got an appetite, and that's the most important thing.
Shiro! Thanks so much for picking up those groceries for me. It's such a help!
It's no problem at all. But I thought I'd treat us to some sushi or something. Are you sure this is okay?
It's fine, it's fine. Your dad and I can have sushi on our own, but you have to be here for this menu.

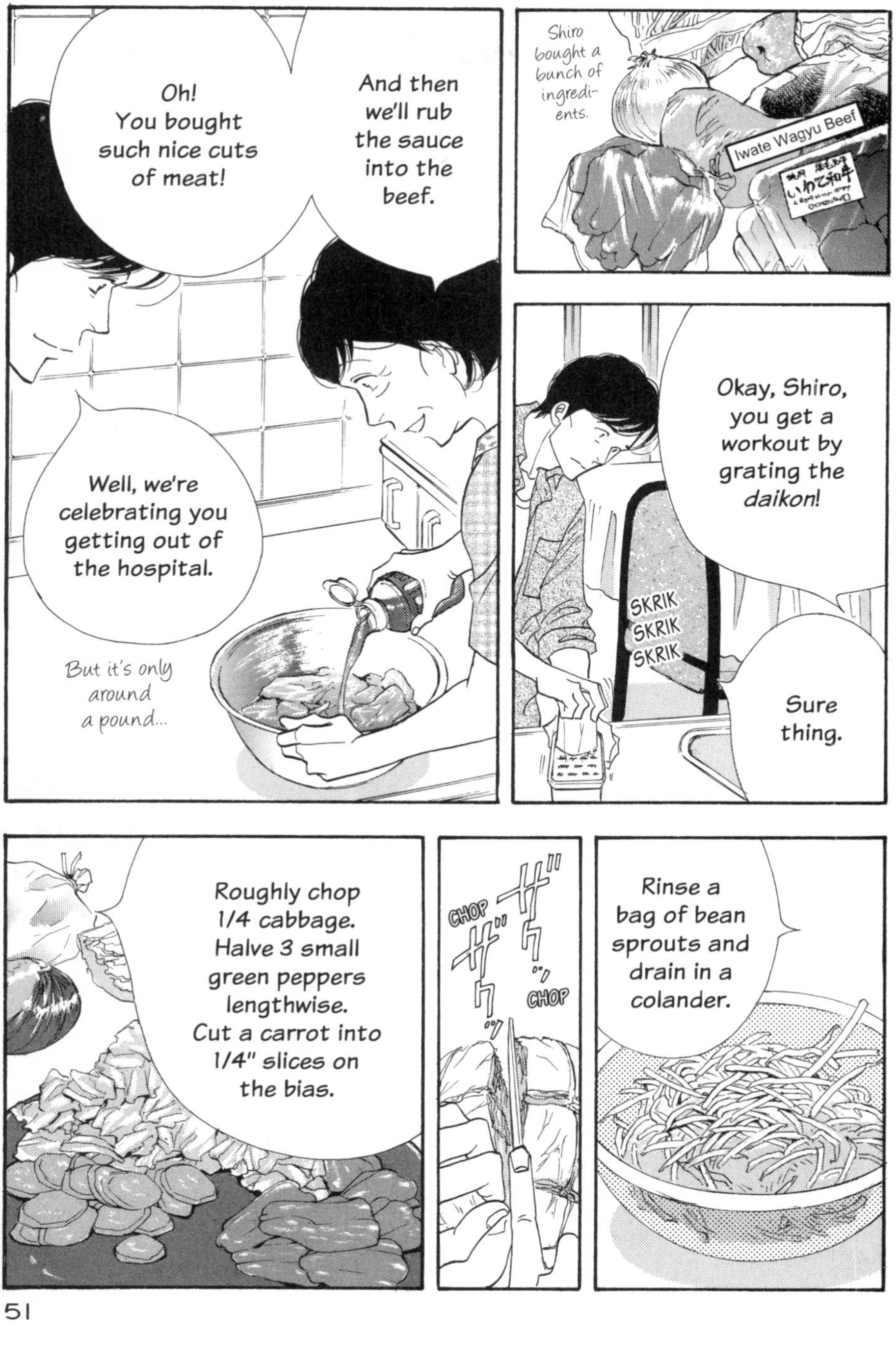
Shiro bought a bunch of ingredi-ents.
Iwate Wagyu Beef
いわて和牛
Okay, Shiro, you get a workout by grating the *daikon*!
SKRIK SKRIK SKRIK
Sure thing.
And then we'll rub the sauce into the beef.
Oh! You bought such nice cuts of meat!
Well, we're celebrating you getting out of the hospital.
But it's only around a pound...
Rinse a bag of bean sprouts and drain in a colander.
CHOP
CHOP
Roughly chop 1/4 cabbage. Halve 3 small green peppers lengthwise. Cut a carrot into 1/4" slices on the bias.

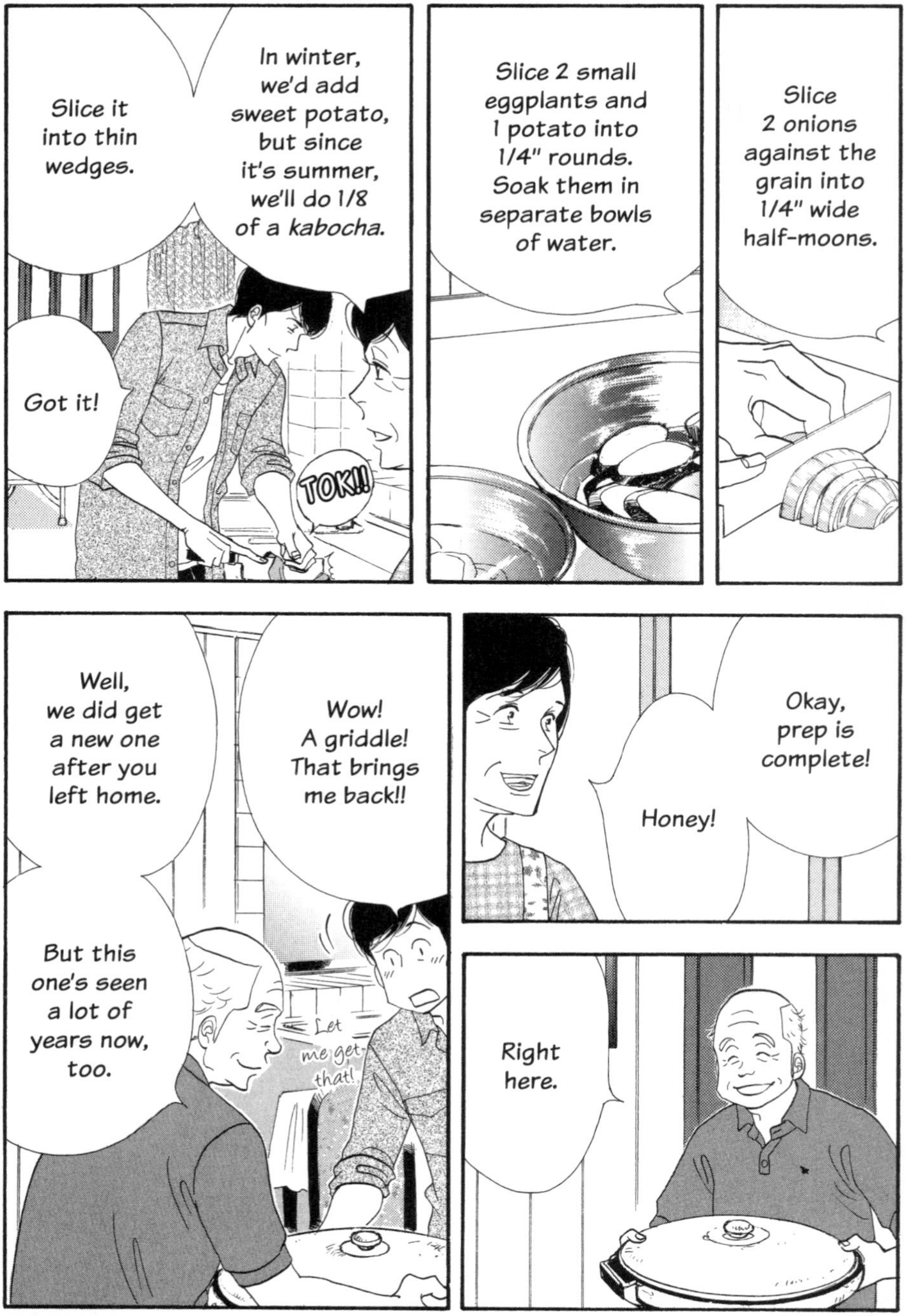
Slice 2 onions against the grain into 1/4" wide half-moons.
Slice 2 small eggplants and 1 potato into 1/4" rounds. Soak them in separate bowls of water.
In winter, we'd add sweet potato, but since it's summer, we'll do 1/8 of a *kabocha*.
Slice it into thin wedges.
Got it!
TOK!!
Okay, prep is complete!
Honey!
Right here.
Wow! A griddle! That brings me back!!
Well, we did get a new one after you left home.
Let me get that!
But this one's seen a lot of years now, too.

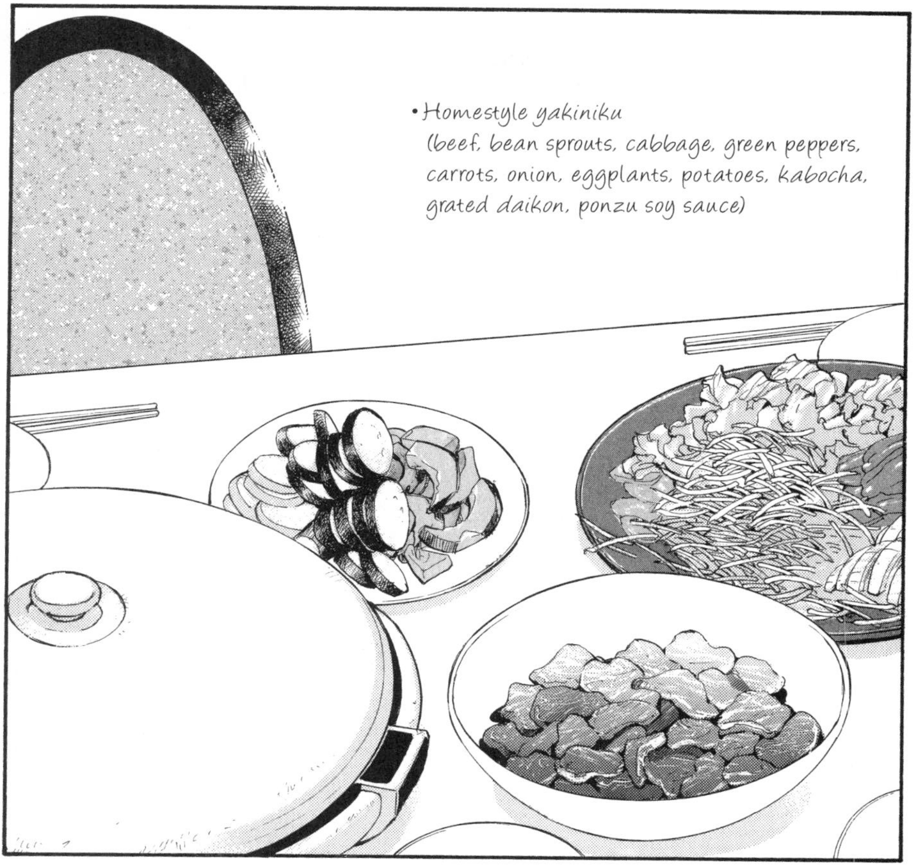
•Homestyle yakiniku
(beef, bean sprouts, cabbage, green peppers, carrots, onion, eggplants, potatoes, kabocha, grated daikon, ponzu soy sauce)

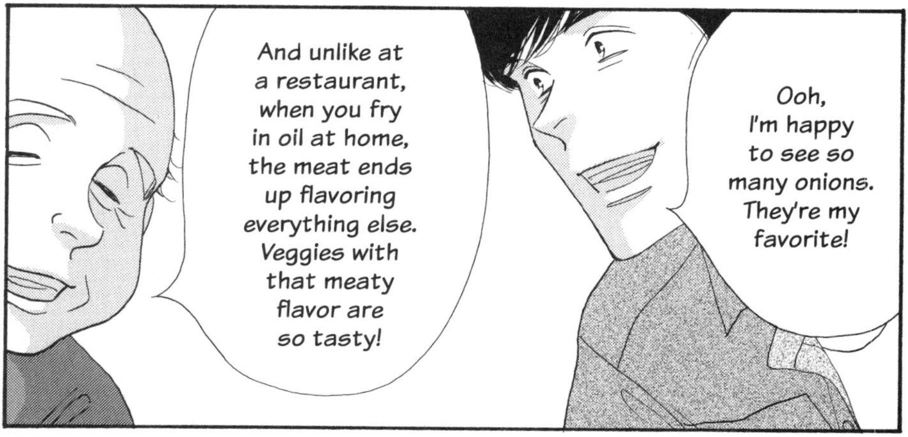
Ooh, I'm happy to see so many onions. They're my favorite!
And unlike at a restaurant, when you fry in oil at home, the meat ends up flavoring everything else. Veggies with that meaty flavor are so tasty!

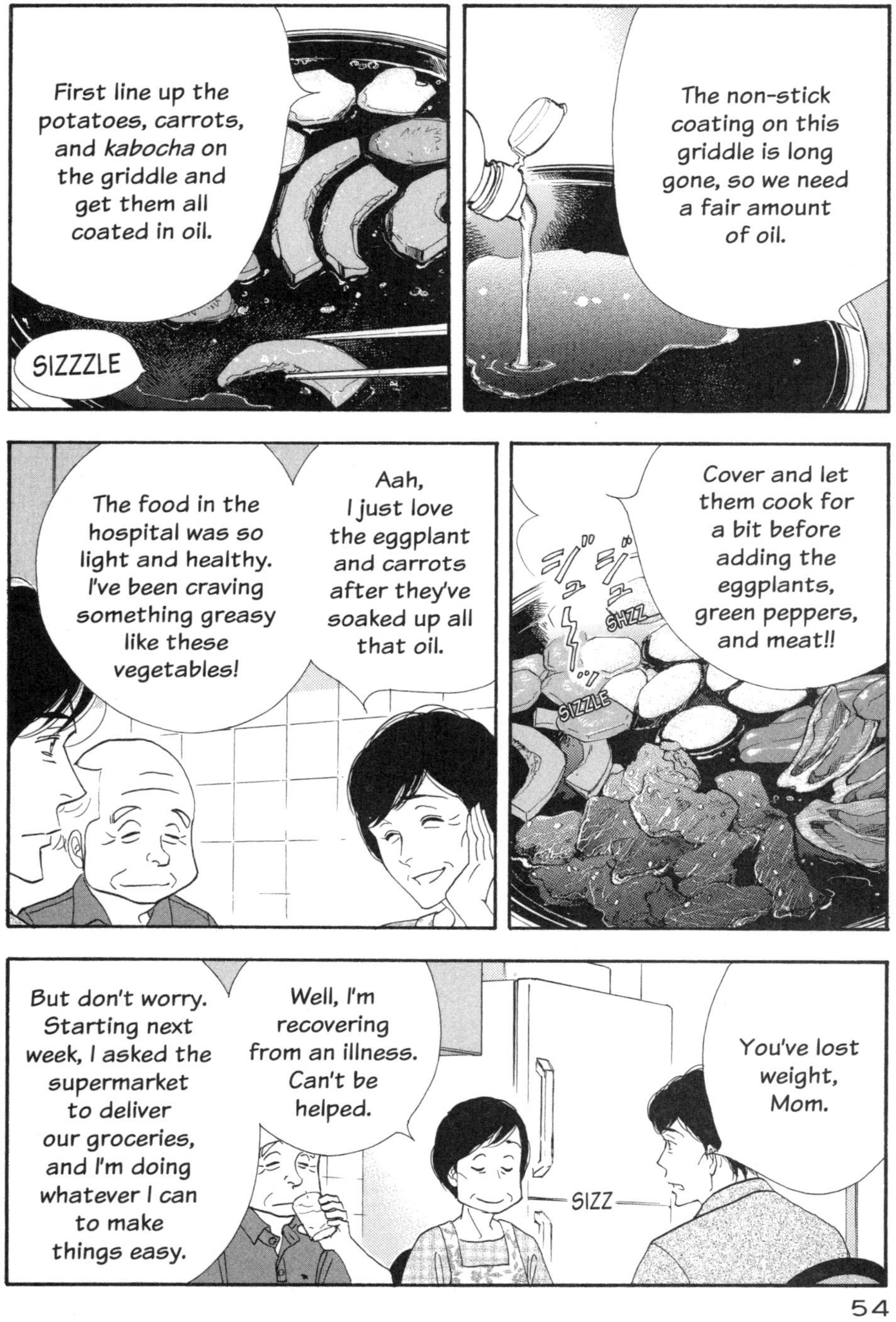
The non-stick coating on this griddle is long gone, so we need a fair amount of oil.
First line up the potatoes, carrots, and *kabocha* on the griddle and get them all coated in oil.
SIZZZLE
Cover and let them cook for a bit before adding the eggplants, green peppers, and meat!!
SHZZ
SIZZLE
Aah, I just love the eggplant and carrots after they've soaked up all that oil.
The food in the hospital was so light and healthy. I've been craving something greasy like these vegetables!
You've lost weight, Mom.
Well, I'm recovering from an illness. Can't be helped.
SIZZ
But don't worry. Starting next week, I asked the supermarket to deliver our groceries, and I'm doing whatever I can to make things easy.

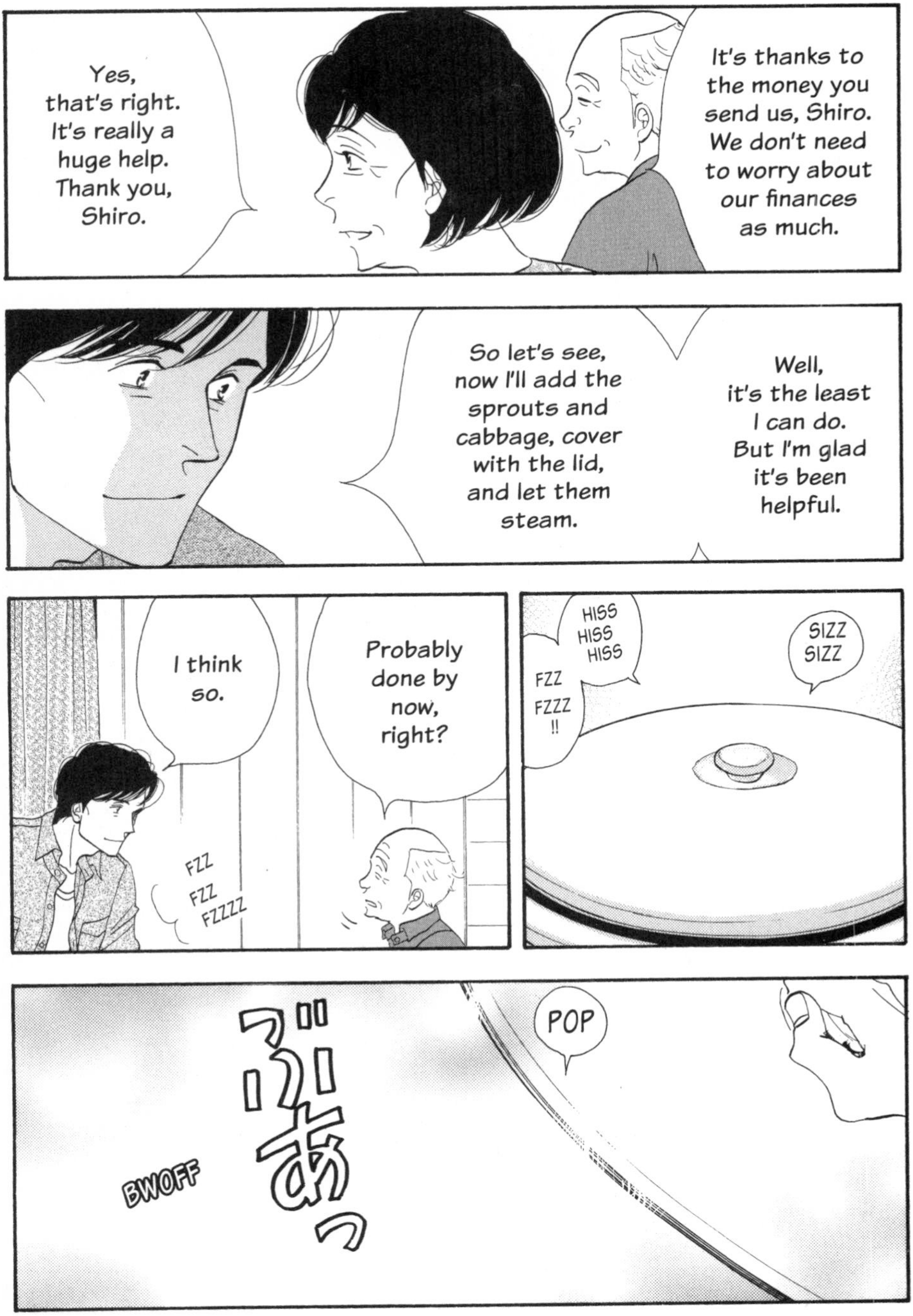
It's thanks to the money you send us, Shiro. We don't need to worry about our finances as much.
Yes, that's right. It's really a huge help. Thank you, Shiro.
Well, it's the least I can do. But I'm glad it's been helpful.
So let's see, now I'll add the sprouts and cabbage, cover with the lid, and let them steam.
SIZZ SIZZ
HISS HISS HISS
FZZ FZZZ !!
Probably done by now, right?
I think so.
FZZ FZZ FZZZZ
POP
ぶあっ
BWOFF

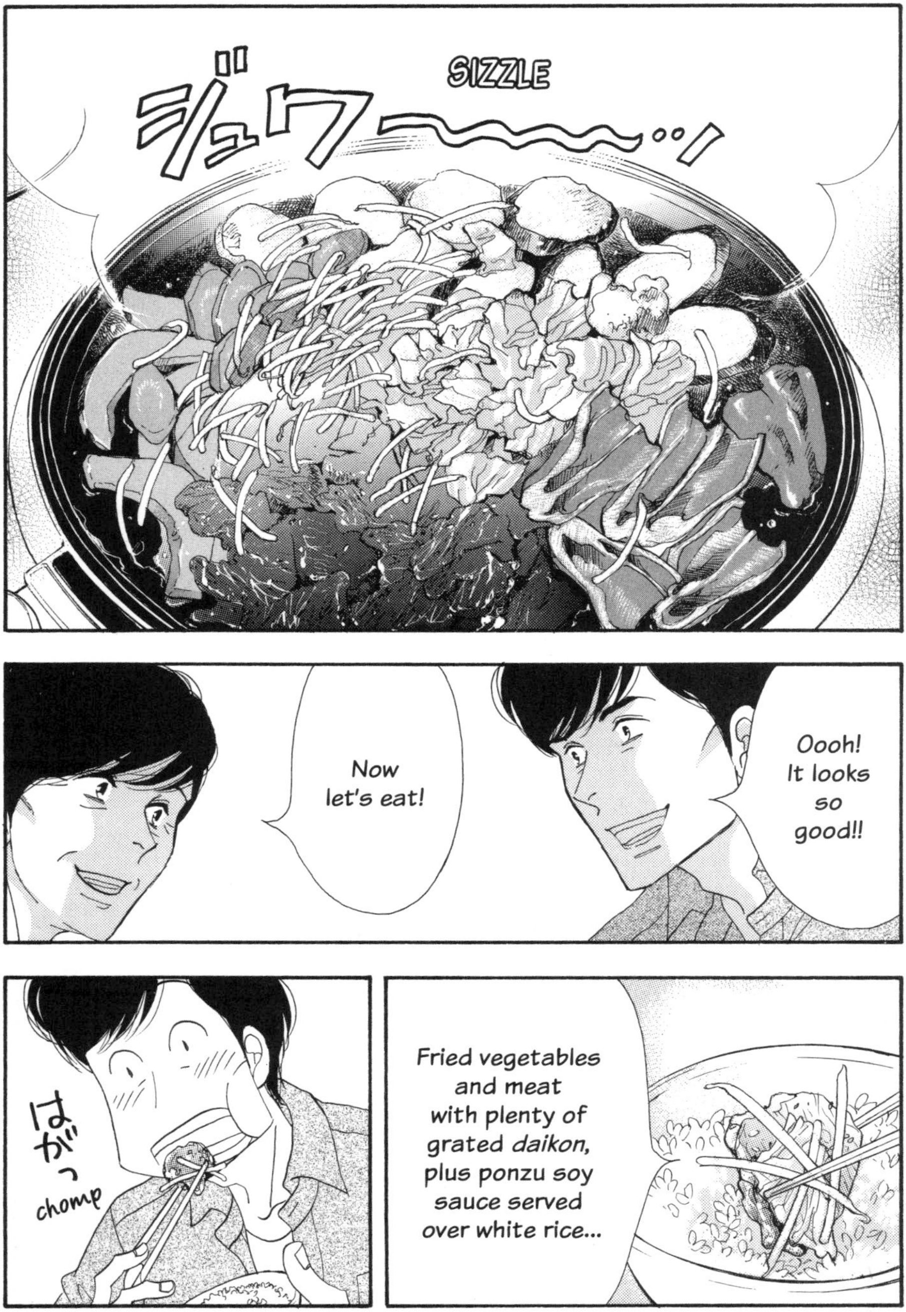
ジュワ〜〜〜ッ!
SIZZLE
Oooh! It looks so good!!
Now let's eat!
Fried vegetables and meat with plenty of grated *daikon*, plus ponzu soy sauce served over white rice...
はがっ
chomp

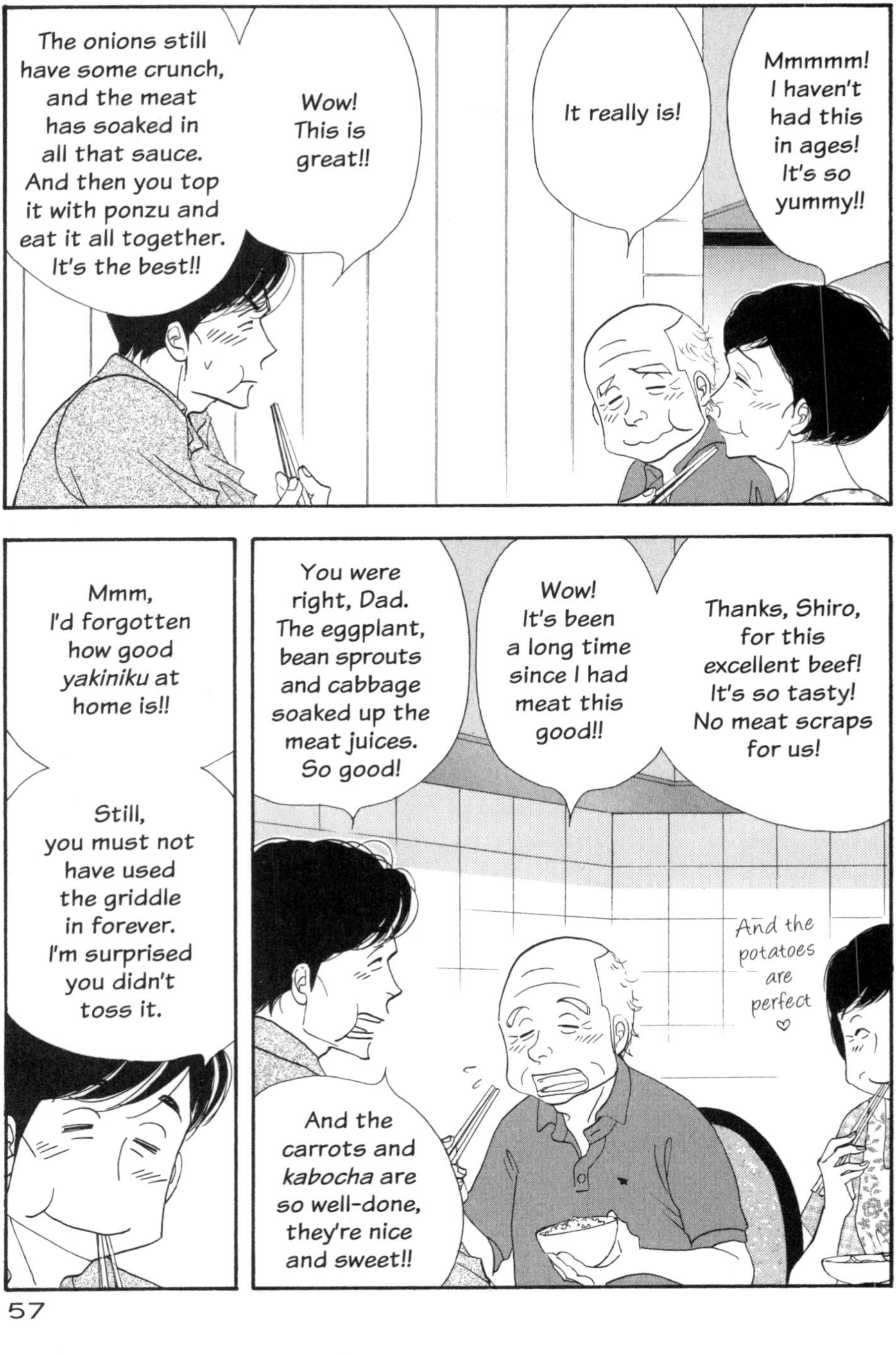
Mmmmm! I haven't had this in ages! It's so yummy!!
It really is!
Wow! This is great!!
The onions still have some crunch, and the meat has soaked in all that sauce. And then you top it with ponzu and eat it all together. It's the best!!
Thanks, Shiro, for this excellent beef! It's so tasty! No meat scraps for us!
Wow! It's been a long time since I had meat this good!!
You were right, Dad. The eggplant, bean sprouts and cabbage soaked up the meat juices. So good!
And the potatoes are perfect ♡
And the carrots and *kabocha* are so well-done, they're nice and sweet!!
Mmm, I'd forgotten how good *yakiniku* at home is!!
Still, you must not have used the griddle in forever. I'm surprised you didn't toss it.

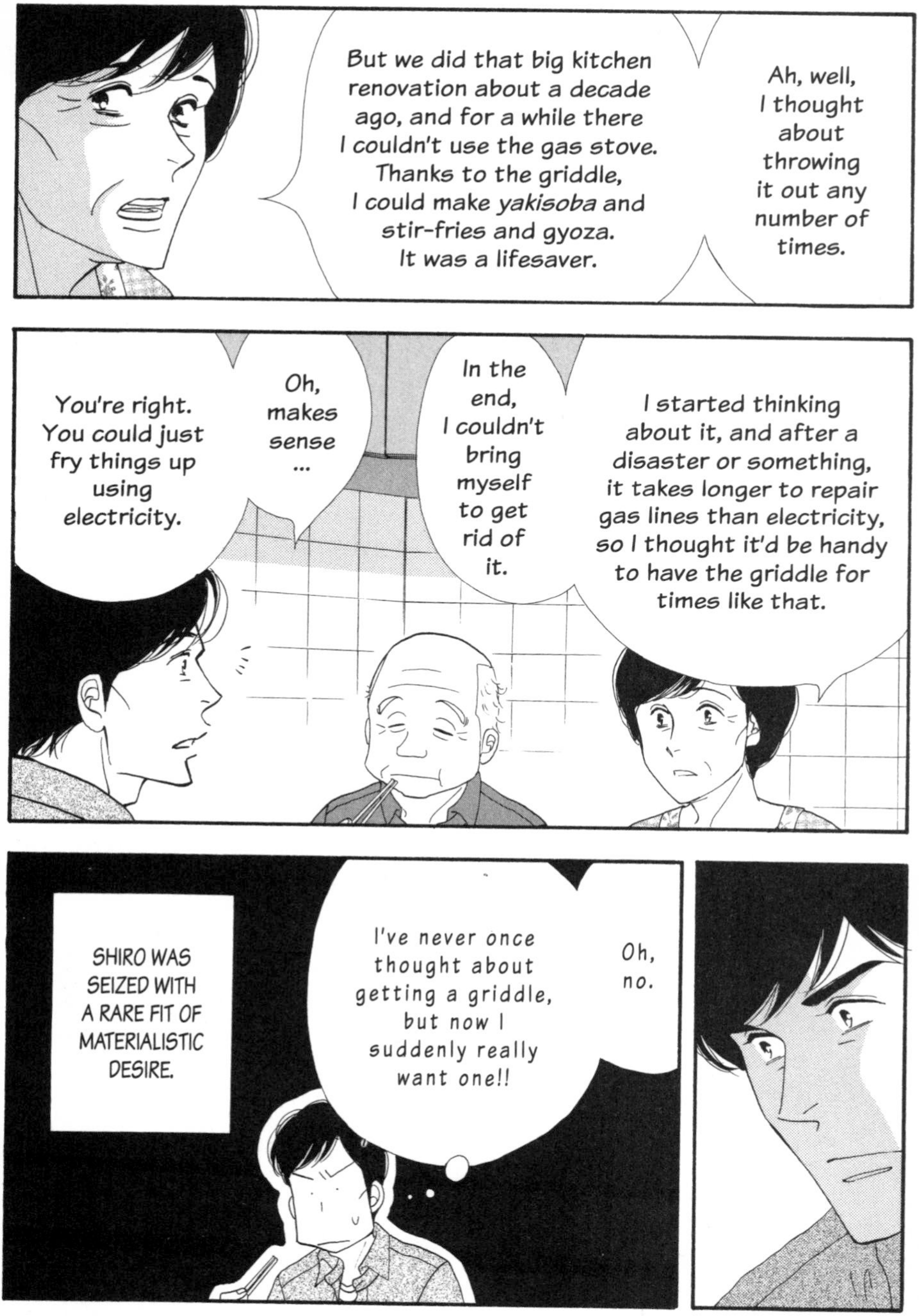
Ah, well, I thought about throwing it out any number of times.
But we did that big kitchen renovation about a decade ago, and for a while there I couldn't use the gas stove. Thanks to the griddle, I could make *yakisoba* and stir-fries and gyoza. It was a lifesaver.
I started thinking about it, and after a disaster or something, it takes longer to repair gas lines than electricity, so I thought it'd be handy to have the griddle for times like that.
In the end, I couldn't bring myself to get rid of it.
Oh, makes sense ...
You're right. You could just fry things up using electricity.
Oh, no.
I've never once thought about getting a griddle, but now I suddenly really want one!!
SHIRO WAS SEIZED WITH A RARE FIT OF MATERIALISTIC DESIRE.

Homestyle *yakiniku* is also delicious with sweet potatoes instead of regular potatoes. *Kabocha*, potatoes, and sweet potatoes are all vegetables that take a while to cook through, so try lightly microwaving them before frying. *Shiitake* mushrooms and *shishito* frying peppers are also tasty in this dish.

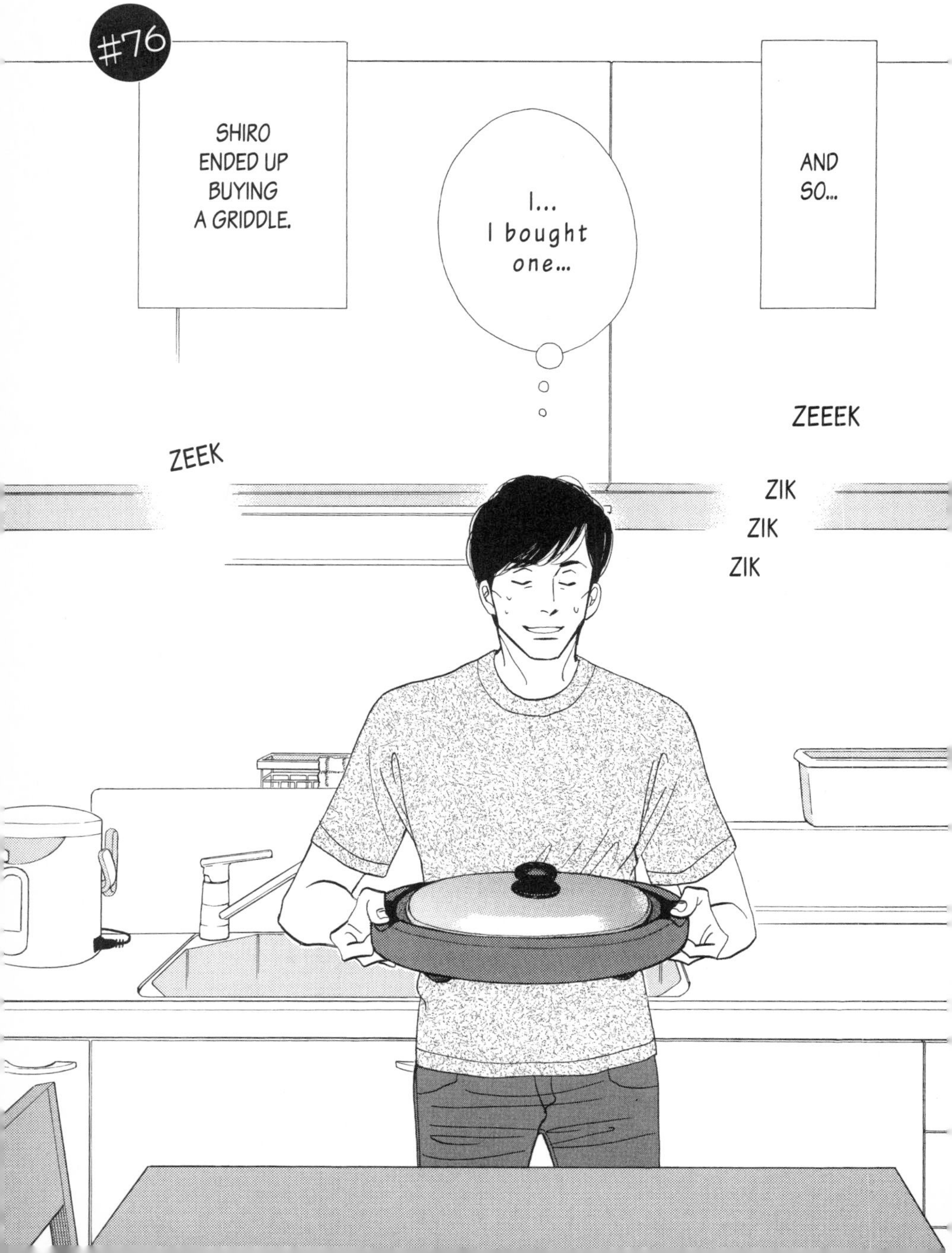
#76
AND SO...
I... I bought one...
SHIRO ENDED UP BUYING A GRIDDLE.
ZEEEK
ZIK ZIK ZIK
ZEEK

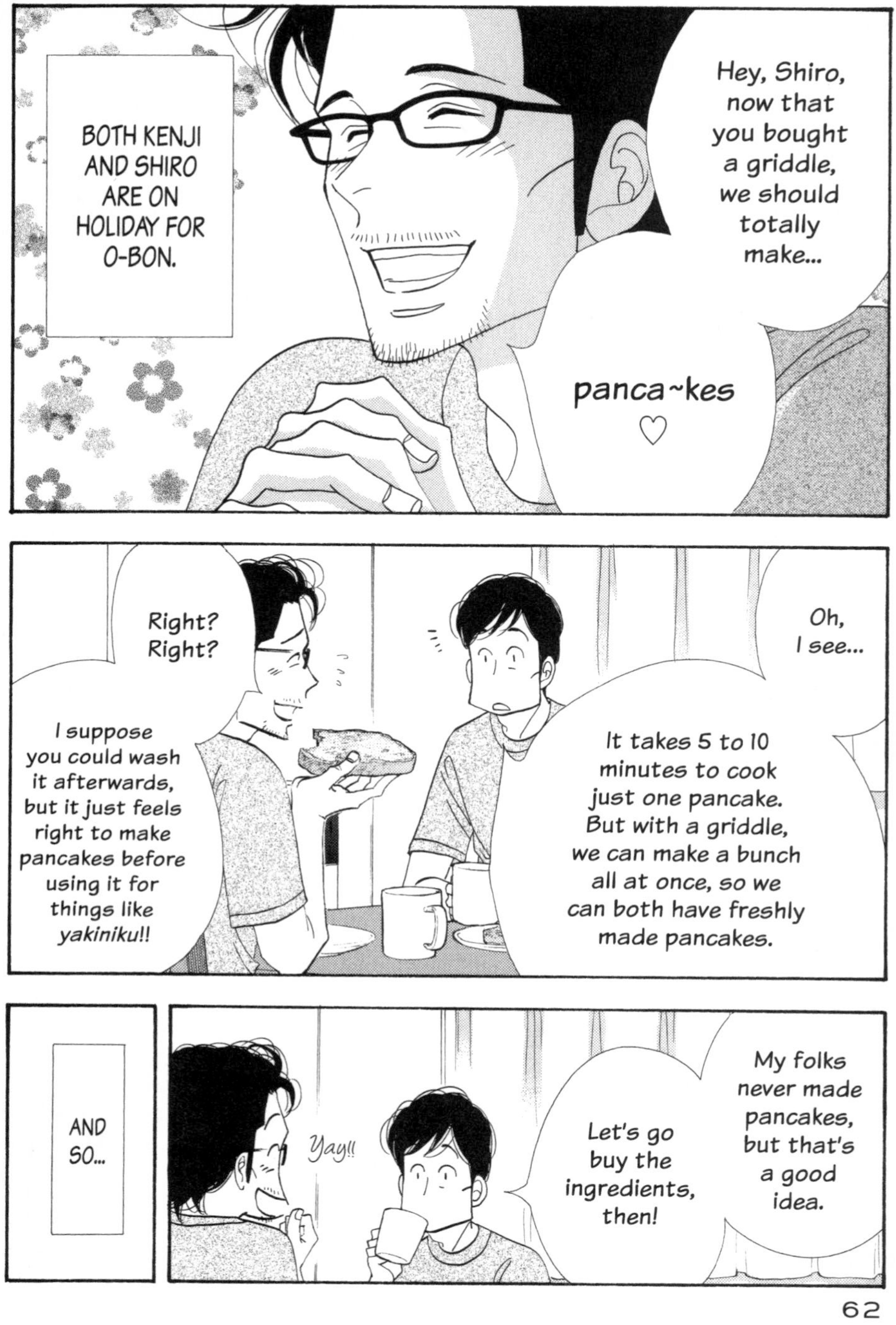
Hey, Shiro, now that you bought a griddle, we should totally make...
panca~kes ♡
BOTH KENJI AND SHIRO ARE ON HOLIDAY FOR O-BON.
Oh, I see...
It takes 5 to 10 minutes to cook just one pancake. But with a griddle, we can make a bunch all at once, so we can both have freshly made pancakes.
Right? Right?
I suppose you could wash it afterwards, but it just feels right to make pancakes before using it for things like *yakiniku*!!
My folks never made pancakes, but that's a good idea.
Let's go buy the ingredients, then!
Yay!!
AND SO...

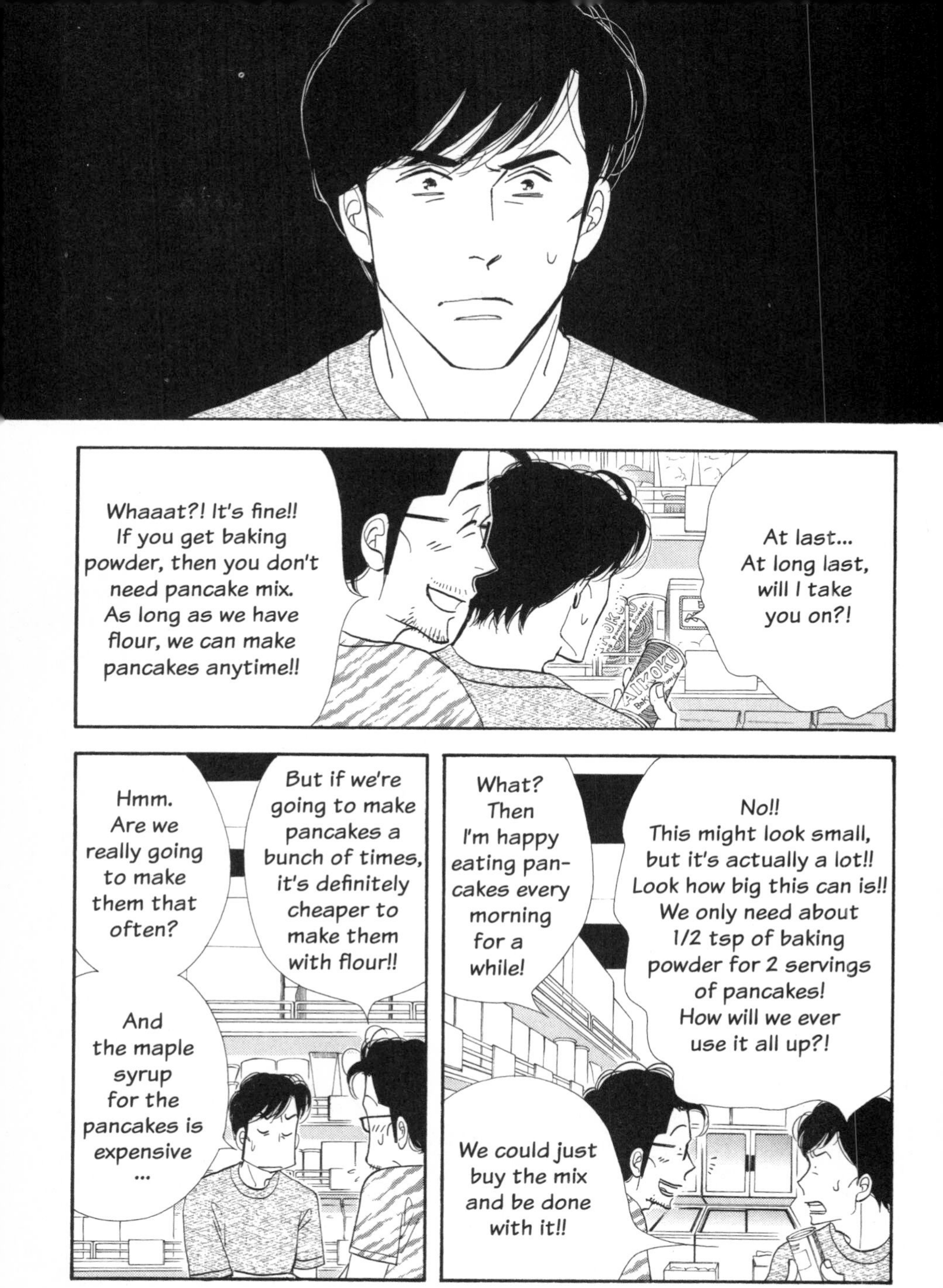
At last... At long last, will I take you on?!
Whaaat?! It's fine!! If you get baking powder, then you don't need pancake mix. As long as we have flour, we can make pancakes anytime!!
No!! This might look small, but it's actually a lot!! Look how big this can is!! We only need about 1/2 tsp of baking powder for 2 servings of pancakes! How will we ever use it all up?!
What? Then I'm happy eating pancakes every morning for a while!
We could just buy the mix and be done with it!!
But if we're going to make pancakes a bunch of times, it's definitely cheaper to make them with flour!!
Hmm. Are we really going to make them that often?
And the maple syrup for the pancakes is expensive ...

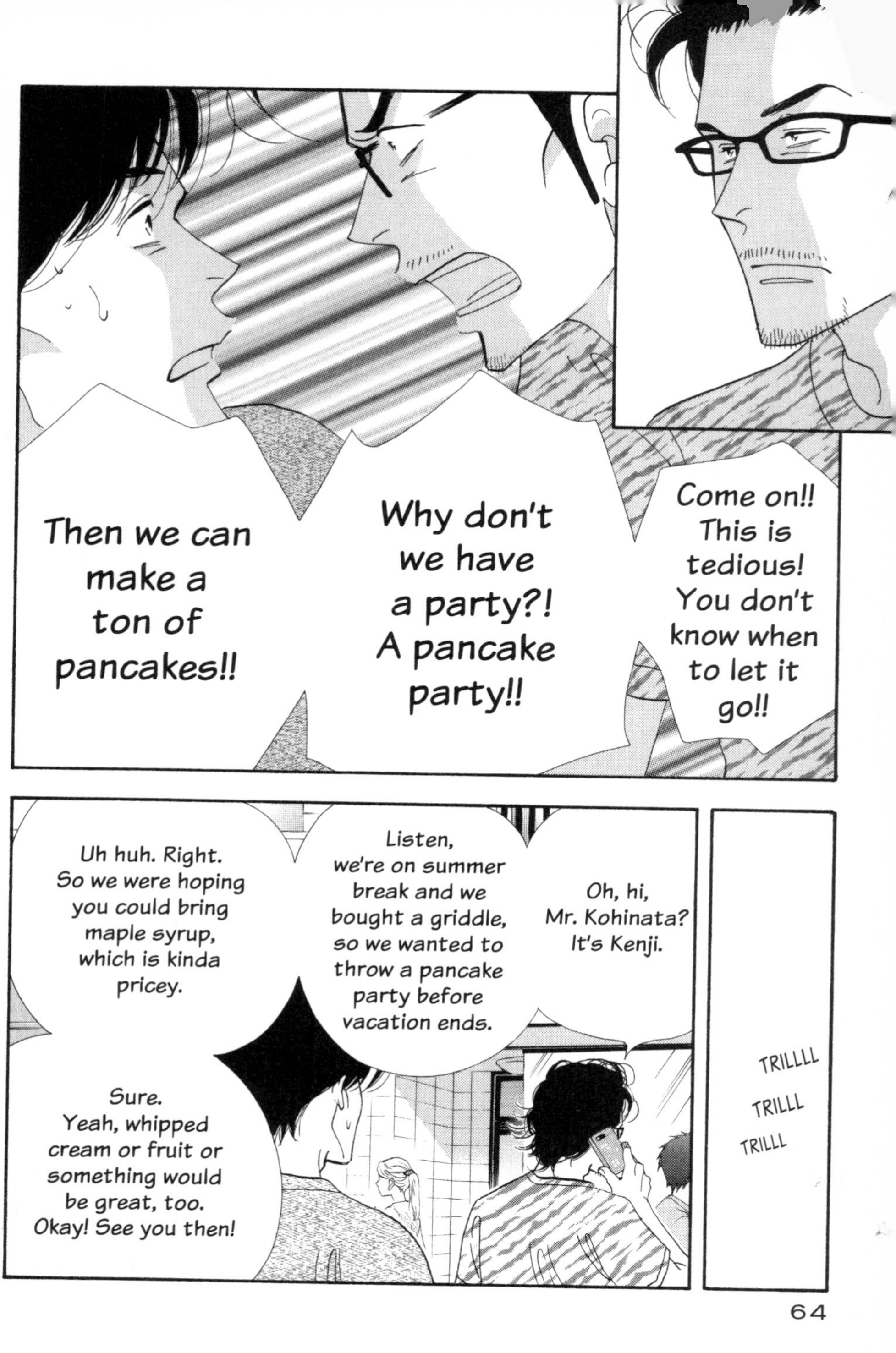
Come on!! This is tedious! You don't know when to let it go!!
Why don't we have a party?! A pancake party!!
Then we can make a ton of pancakes!!
TRILLLL
TRILLL
TRILLL
Oh, hi, Mr. Kohinata? It's Kenji.
Listen, we're on summer break and we bought a griddle, so we wanted to throw a pancake party before vacation ends.
Uh huh. Right. So we were hoping you could bring maple syrup, which is kinda pricey.
Sure. Yeah, whipped cream or fruit or something would be great, too. Okay! See you then!

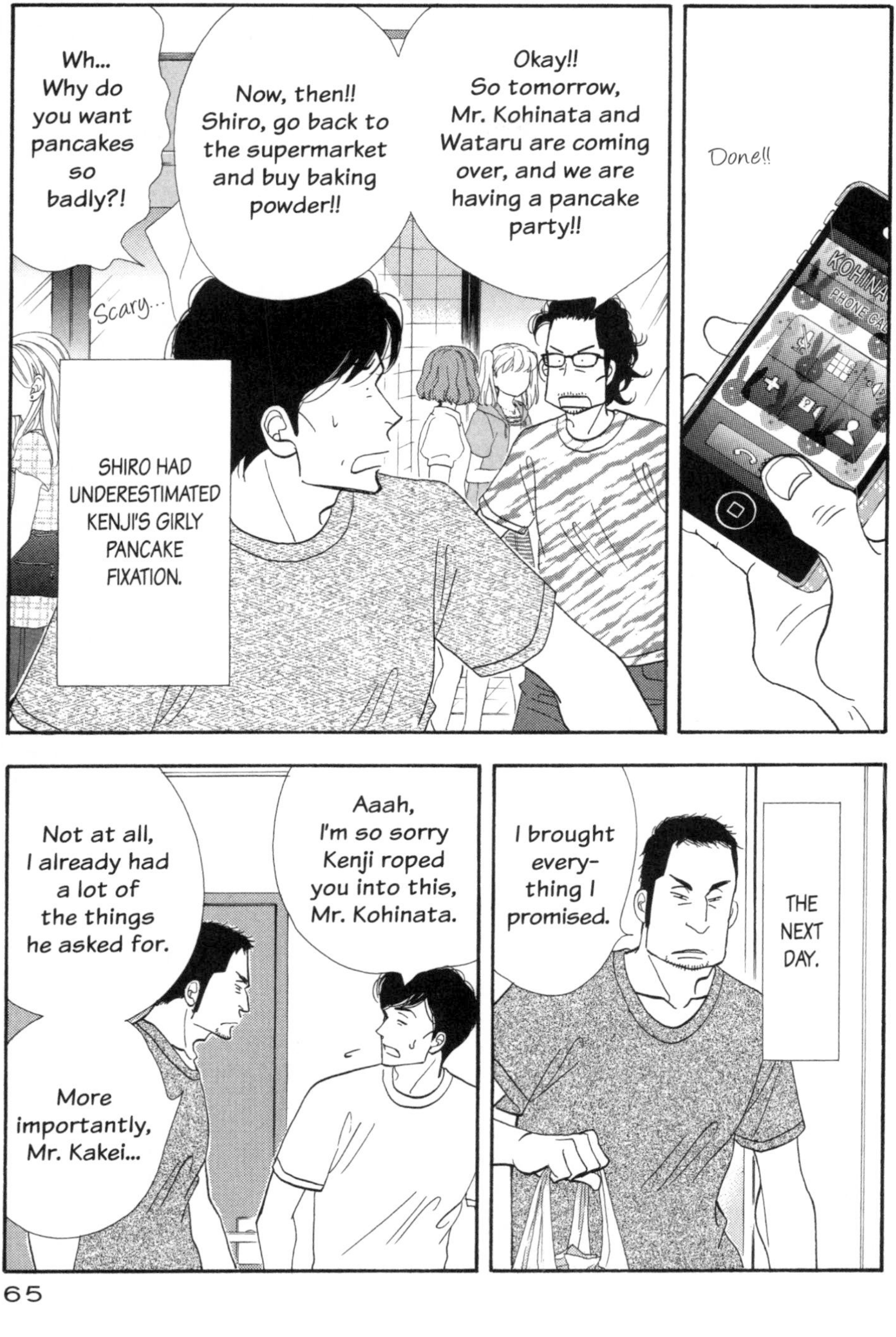
Done!!
Okay!! So tomorrow, Mr. Kohinata and Wataru are coming over, and we are having a pancake party!!
Now, then!! Shiro, go back to the supermarket and buy baking powder!!
Wh... Why do you want pancakes so badly?!
Scary...
SHIRO HAD UNDERESTIMATED KENJI'S GIRLY PANCAKE FIXATION.
THE NEXT DAY.
I brought every-thing I promised.
Aaah, I'm so sorry Kenji roped you into this, Mr. Kohinata.
Not at all, I already had a lot of the things he asked for.
More importantly, Mr. Kakei...

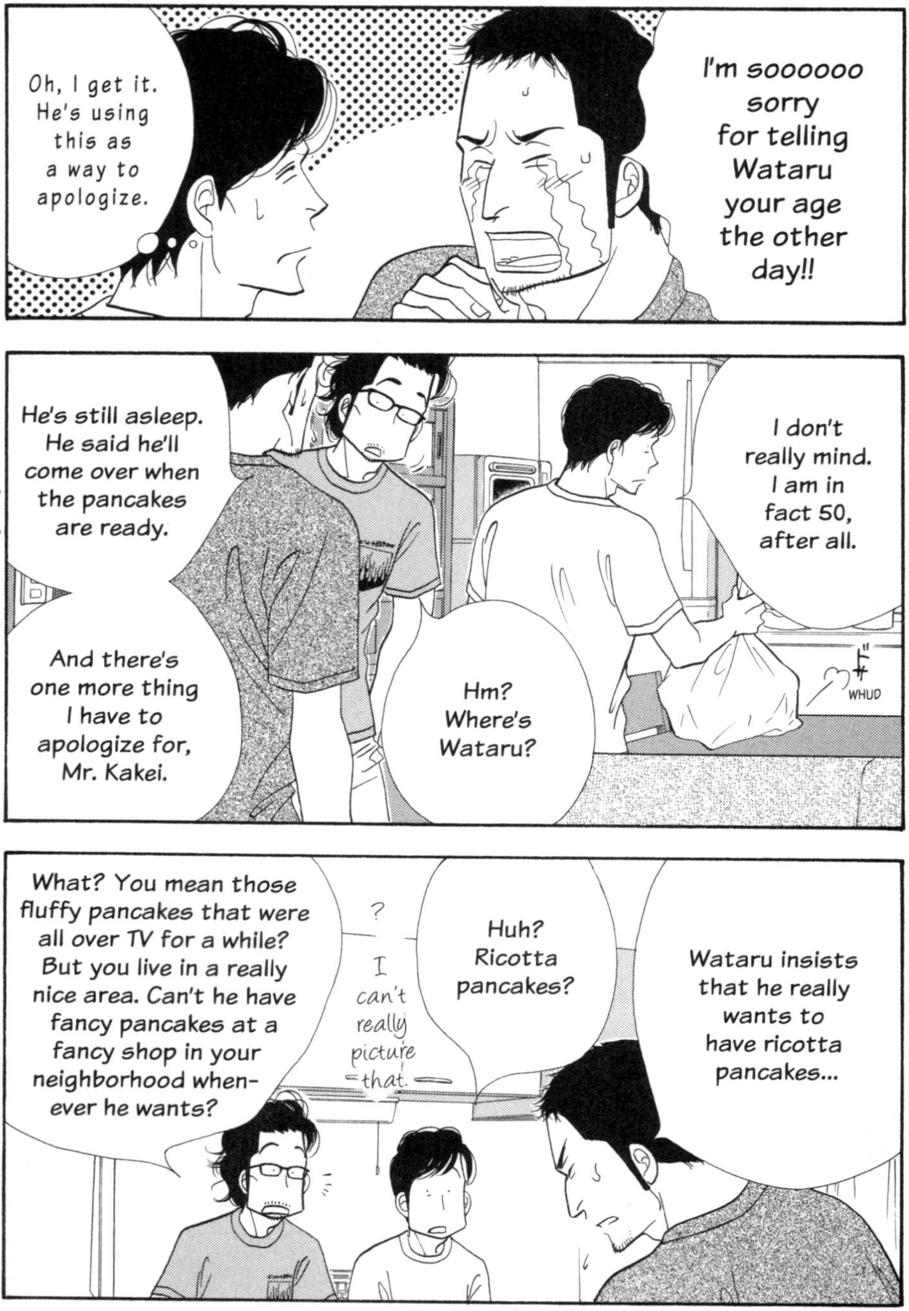
I'm sooooo sorry for telling Wataru your age the other day!!
Oh, I get it. He's using this as a way to apologize.
I don't really mind. I am in fact 50, after all.
WHUD
Hm? Where's Wataru?
He's still asleep. He said he'll come over when the pancakes are ready.
And there's one more thing I have to apologize for, Mr. Kakei.
Wataru insists that he really wants to have ricotta pancakes...
Huh? Ricotta pancakes?
?
I can't really picture that.
What? You mean those fluffy pancakes that were all over TV for a while? But you live in a really nice area. Can't he have fancy pancakes at a fancy shop in your neighborhood whenever he wants?

He's just gonna eat them...

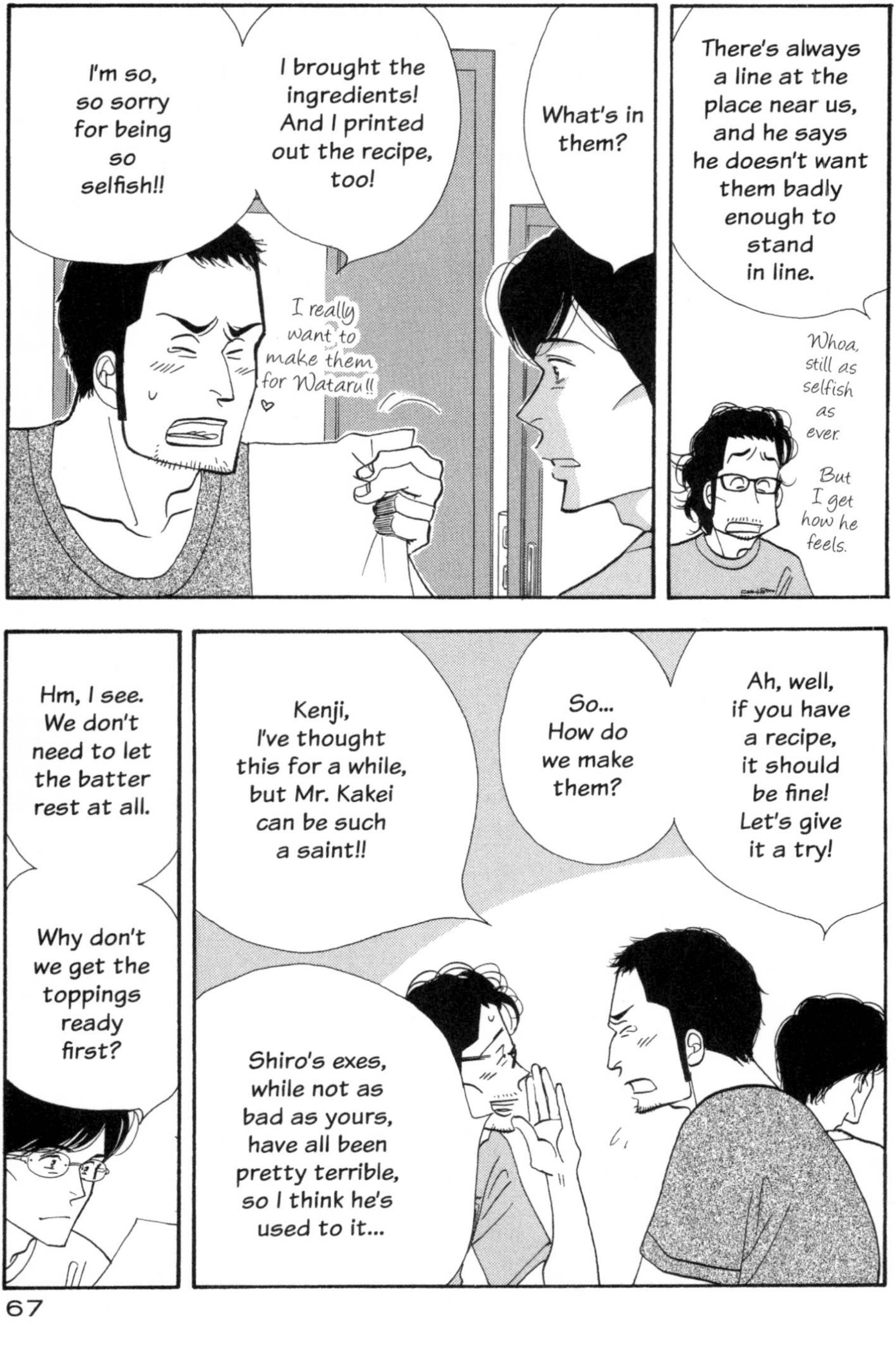
There's always a line at the place near us, and he says he doesn't want them badly enough to stand in line.
Whoa, still as selfish as ever.
But I get how he feels.
What's in them?
I brought the ingredients! And I printed out the recipe, too!
I'm so, so sorry for being so selfish!!
I really want to make them for Wataru!!
Ah, well, if you have a recipe, it should be fine! Let's give it a try!
So... How do we make them?
Kenji, I've thought this for a while, but Mr. Kakei can be such a saint!!
Shiro's exes, while not as bad as yours, have all been pretty terrible, so I think he's used to it...
Hm, I see. We don't need to let the batter rest at all.
Why don't we get the toppings ready first?

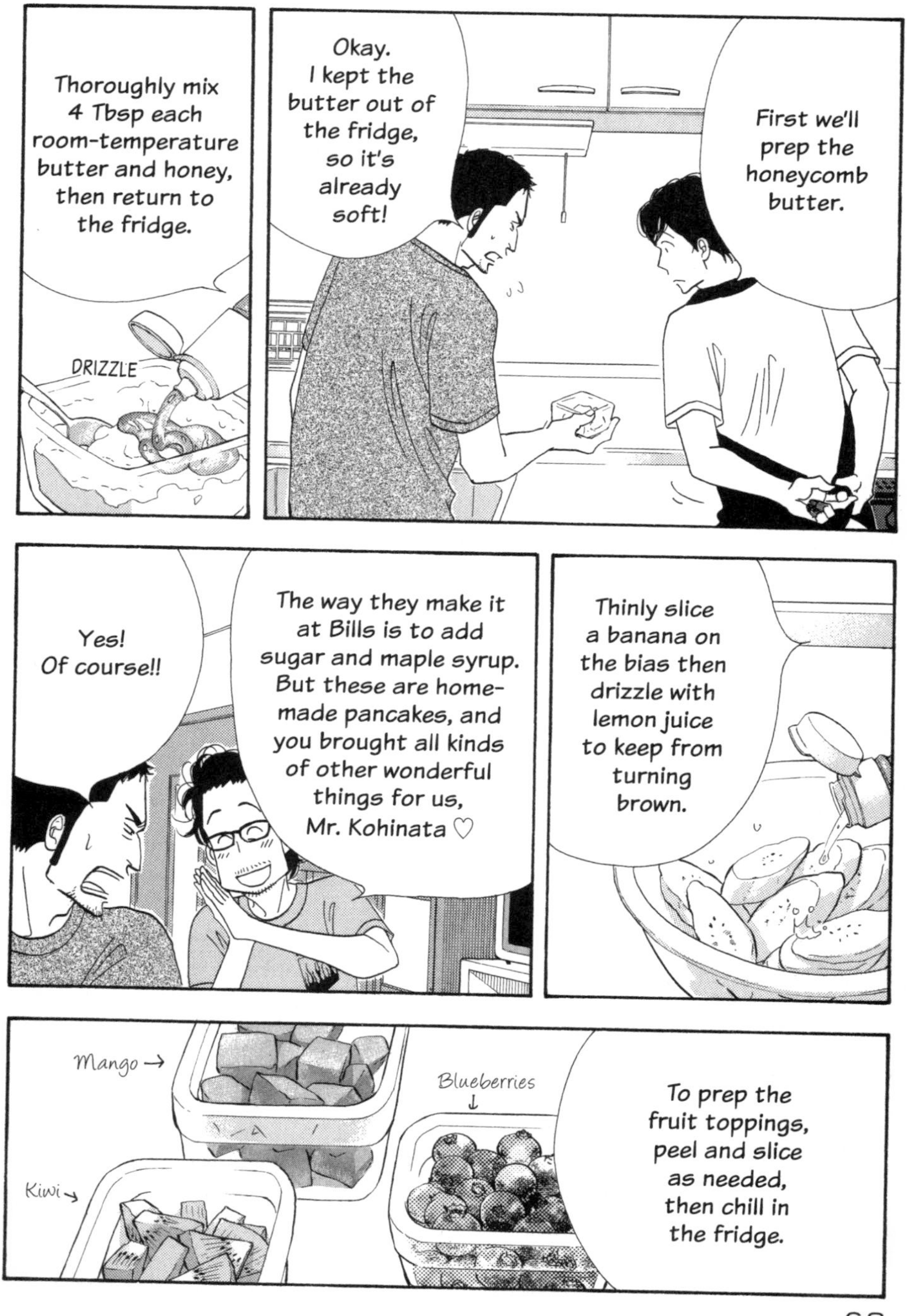
First we'll prep the honeycomb butter.
Okay. I kept the butter out of the fridge, so it's already soft!
Thoroughly mix 4 Tbsp each room-temperature butter and honey, then return to the fridge.
DRIZZLE
Thinly slice a banana on the bias then drizzle with lemon juice to keep from turning brown.
The way they make it at Bills is to add sugar and maple syrup. But these are home-made pancakes, and you brought all kinds of other wonderful things for us, Mr. Kohinata ♡
Yes! Of course!!
To prep the fruit toppings, peel and slice as needed, then chill in the fridge.
Blueberries
Mango
Kiwi

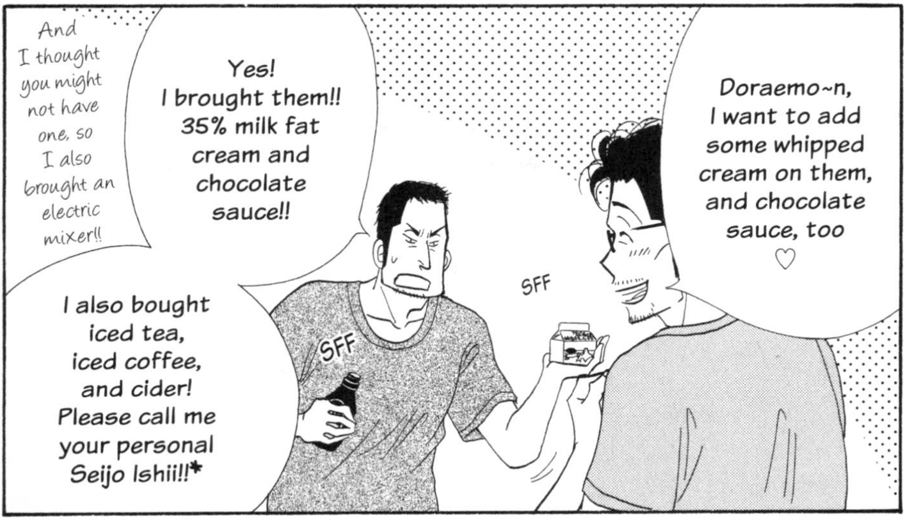
Doraemo~n, I want to add some whipped cream on them, and chocolate sauce, too ♡
Yes! I brought them!! 35% milk fat cream and chocolate sauce!!
And I thought you might not have one, so I also brought an electric mixer!!
SFF
SFF
I also bought iced tea, iced coffee, and cider! Please call me your personal Seijo Ishii!!*

* High-end grocery store

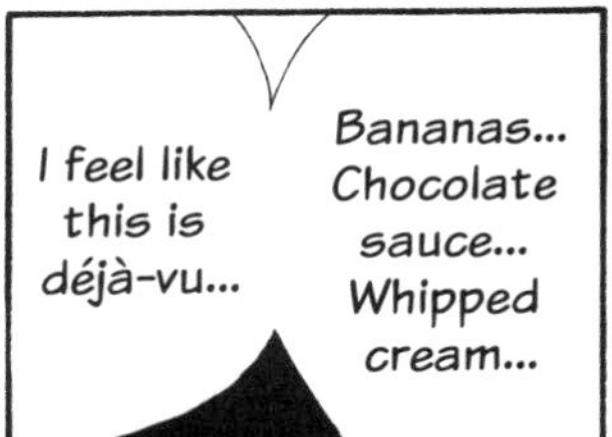
Bananas... Chocolate sauce... Whipped cream...
I feel like this is déjà-vu...

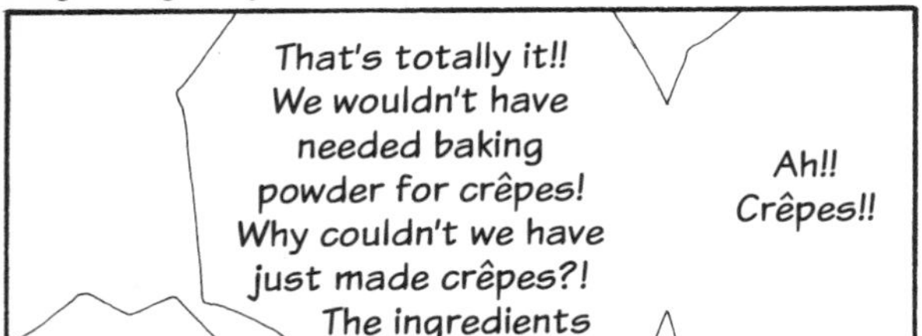
Ah!! Crêpes!!
That's totally it!! We wouldn't have needed baking powder for crêpes! Why couldn't we have just made crêpes?! The ingredients are basically the same!!
What?! What are you saying, Shiro?! They're totally different!! And there's no point in making crêpes on a griddle!!

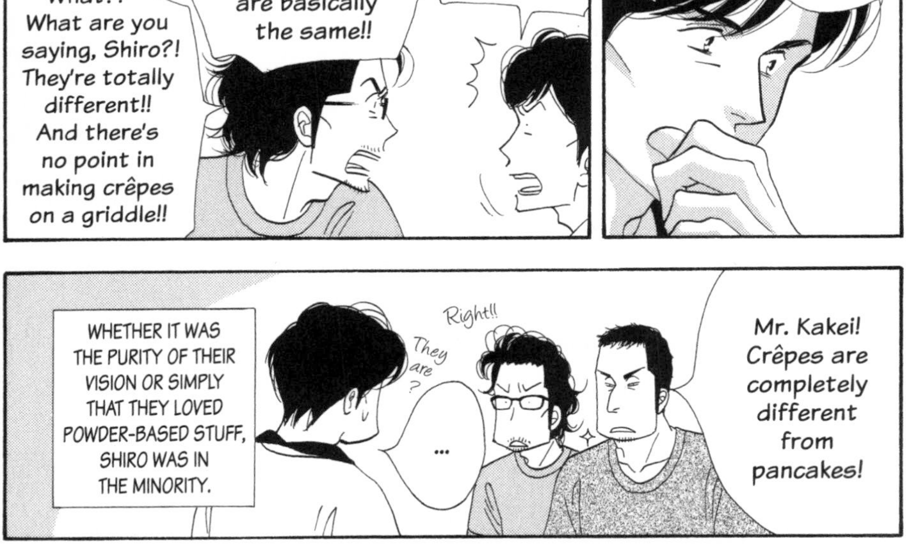
Mr. Kakei! Crêpes are completely different from pancakes!
Right!!
They are?
...
WHETHER IT WAS THE PURITY OF THEIR VISION OR SIMPLY THAT THEY LOVED POWDER-BASED STUFF, SHIRO WAS IN THE MINORITY.

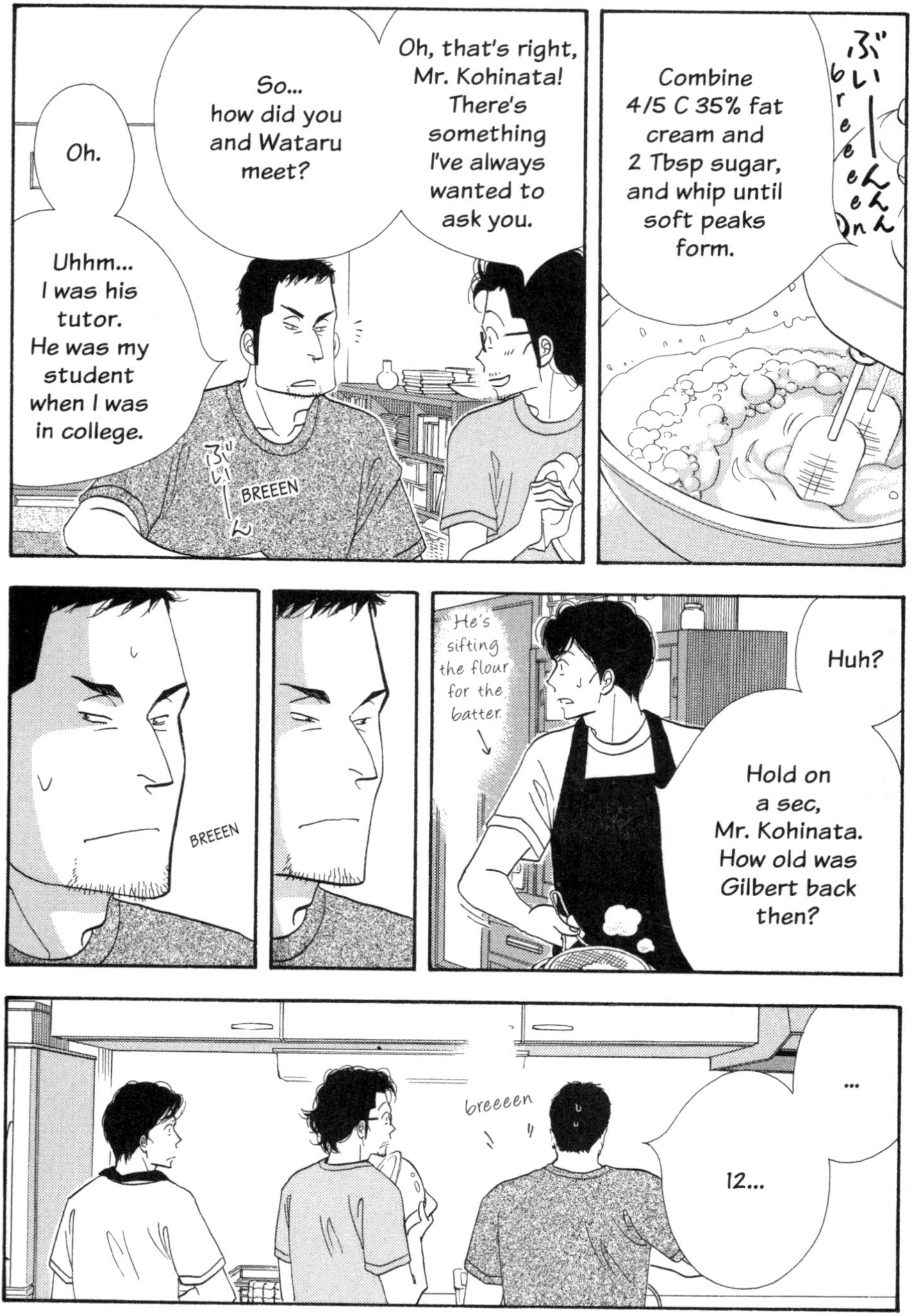

ぶいーんん
breeeen
Combine 4/5 C 35% fat cream and 2 Tbsp sugar, and whip until soft peaks form.
Oh, that's right, Mr. Kohinata! There's something I've always wanted to ask you.
So... how did you and Wataru meet?
Oh.
Uhhm... I was his tutor. He was my student when I was in college.
ぶいーん
BREEEN
Huh?
Hold on a sec, Mr. Kohinata. How old was Gilbert back then?
He's sifting the flour for the batter.
BREEEN
...
12...
breeeen

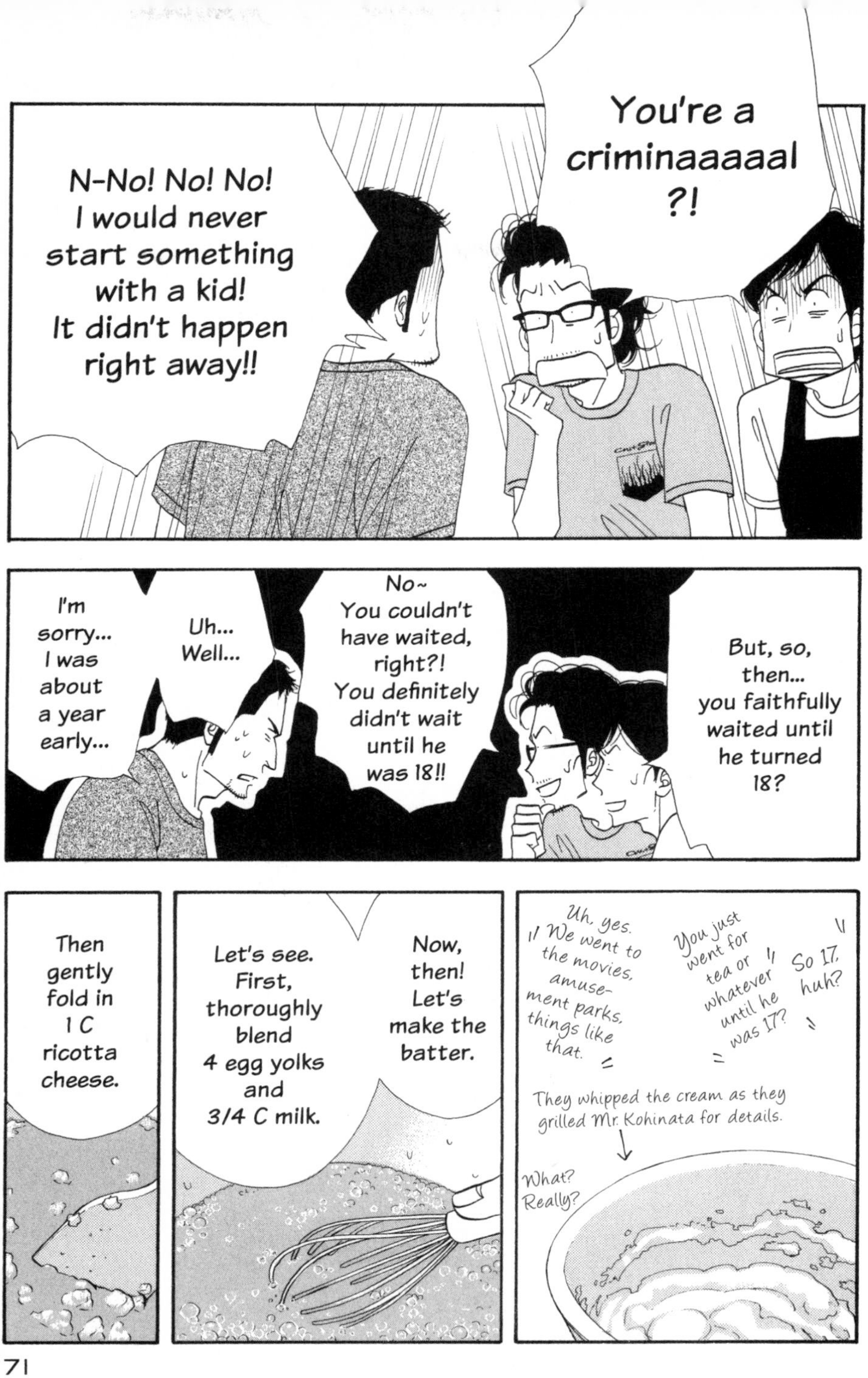
You're a criminaaaaal ?!
N-No! No! No! I would never start something with a kid! It didn't happen right away!!
But, so, then... you faithfully waited until he turned 18?
No~ You couldn't have waited, right?! You definitely didn't wait until he was 18!!
Uh... Well...
I'm sorry... I was about a year early...
So 17, huh?
You just went for tea or whatever until he was 17?
Uh, yes. We went to the movies, amusement parks, things like that.
They whipped the cream as they grilled Mr. Kohinata for details.
What? Really?
Now, then! Let's make the batter.
Let's see. First, thoroughly blend 4 egg yolks and 3/4 C milk.
Then gently fold in 1 C ricotta cheese.

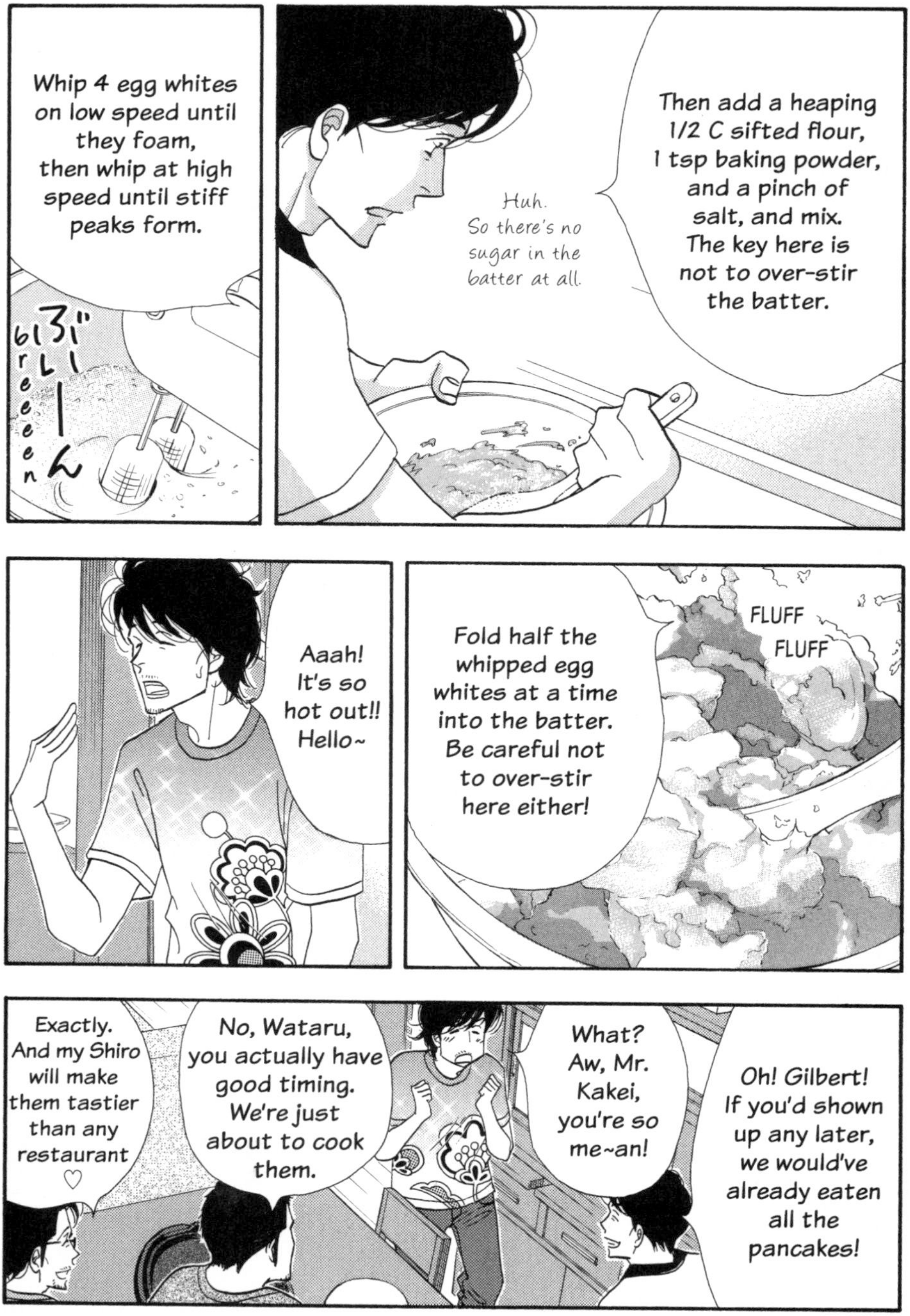

Then add a heaping 1/2 C sifted flour, 1 tsp baking powder, and a pinch of salt, and mix. The key here is not to over-stir the batter.
Huh. So there's no sugar in the batter at all.
Whip 4 egg whites on low speed until they foam, then whip at high speed until stiff peaks form.
ぶぃーん
breeeeen
Fold half the whipped egg whites at a time into the batter. Be careful not to over-stir here either!
FLUFF
FLUFF
Aaah! It's so hot out!! Hello~
Oh! Gilbert! If you'd shown up any later, we would've already eaten all the pancakes!
What? Aw, Mr. Kakei, you're so me~an!
No, Wataru, you actually have good timing. We're just about to cook them.
Exactly. And my Shiro will make them tastier than any restaurant ♡

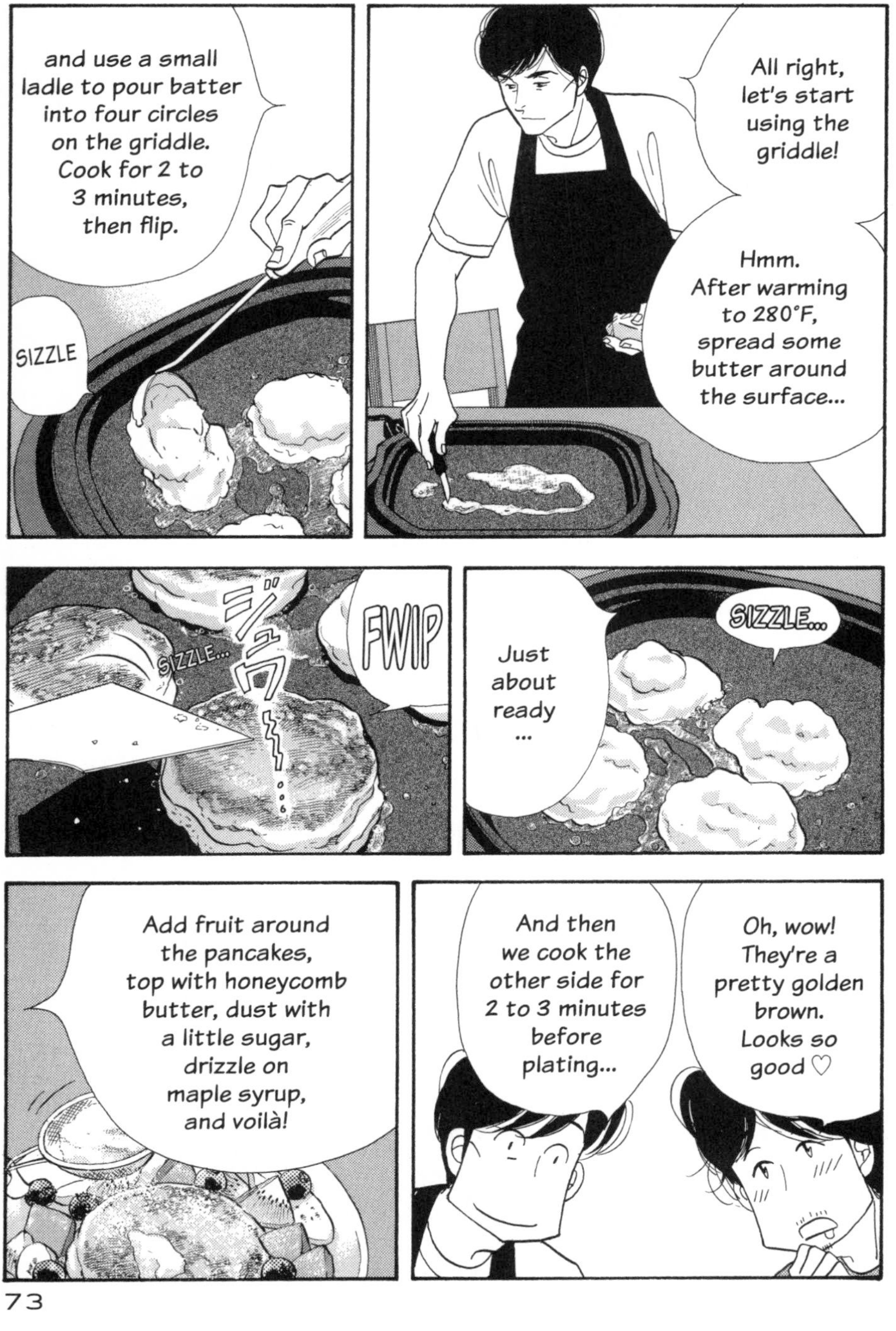
All right, let's start using the griddle!
Hmm. After warming to 280°F, spread some butter around the surface...
and use a small ladle to pour batter into four circles on the griddle. Cook for 2 to 3 minutes, then flip.
SIZZLE
SIZZLE...
Just about ready ...
FWIP
ジュウ
SIZZLE...
Oh, wow! They're a pretty golden brown. Looks so good ♡
And then we cook the other side for 2 to 3 minutes before plating...
Add fruit around the pancakes, top with honeycomb butter, dust with a little sugar, drizzle on maple syrup, and voilà!

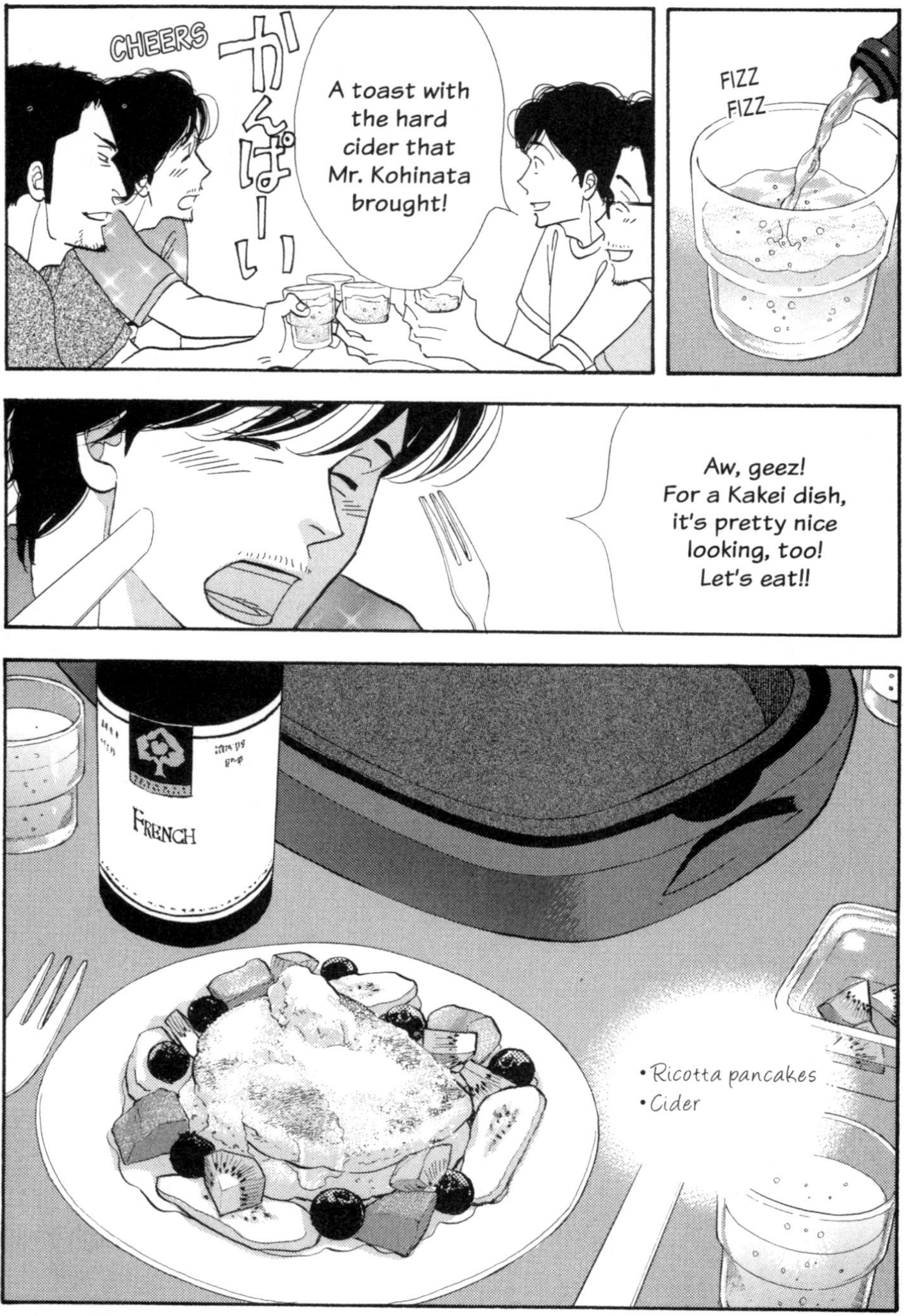
FIZZ FIZZ
かんぱーい
CHEERS
A toast with the hard cider that Mr. Kohinata brought!
Aw, geez! For a Kakei dish, it's pretty nice looking, too! Let's eat!!
FRENCH
•Ricotta pancakes
•Cider

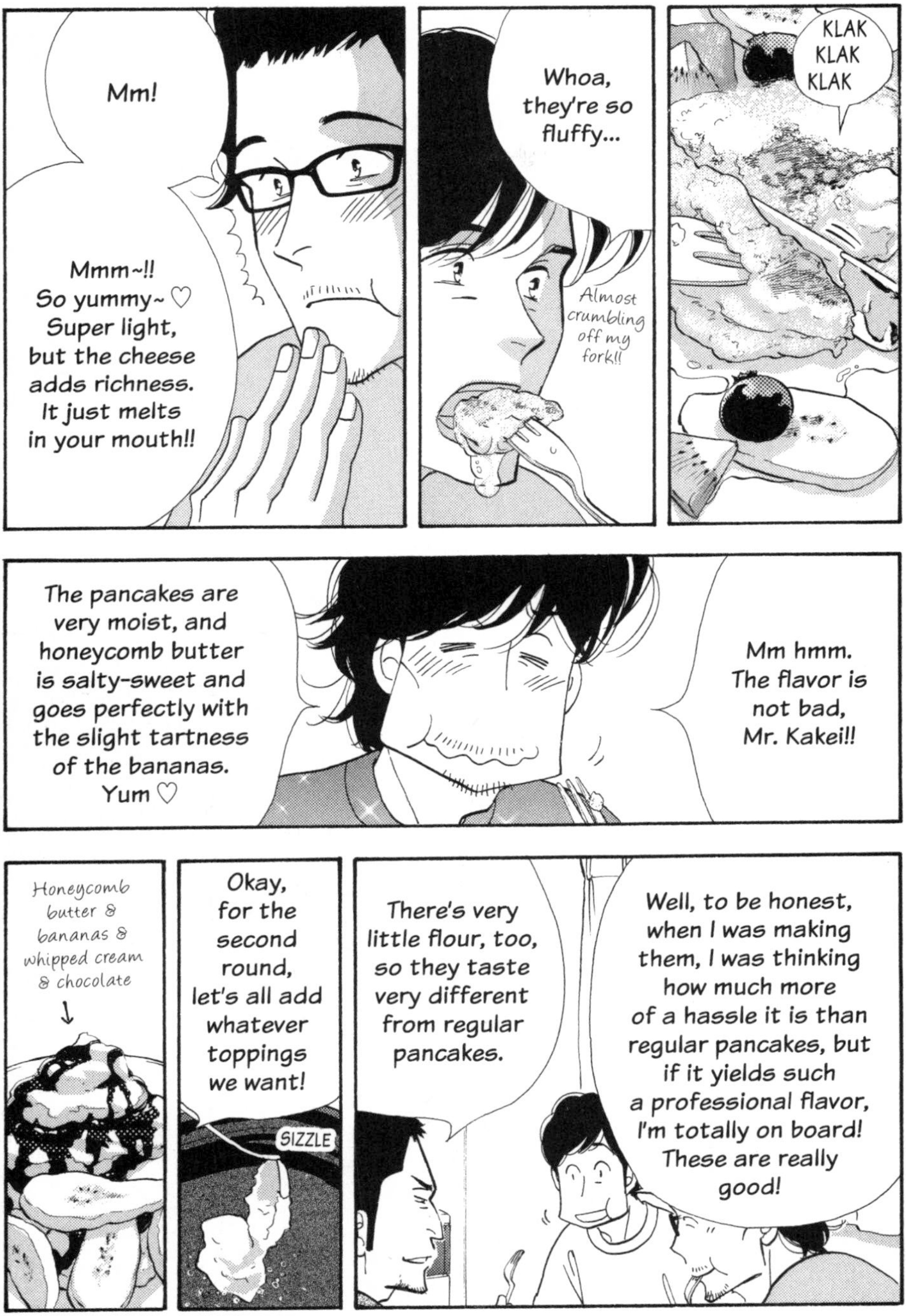
KLAK KLAK KLAK
Whoa, they're so fluffy...
Almost crumbling off my fork!!
Mm!
Mmm~!! So yummy~ ♡ Super light, but the cheese adds richness. It just melts in your mouth!!
Mm hmm. The flavor is not bad, Mr. Kakei!!
The pancakes are very moist, and honeycomb butter is salty-sweet and goes perfectly with the slight tartness of the bananas. Yum ♡
Well, to be honest, when I was making them, I was thinking how much more of a hassle it is than regular pancakes, but if it yields such a professional flavor, I'm totally on board! These are really good!
There's very little flour, too, so they taste very different from regular pancakes.
Okay, for the second round, let's all add whatever toppings we want!
SIZZLE
Honeycomb butter & bananas & whipped cream & chocolate

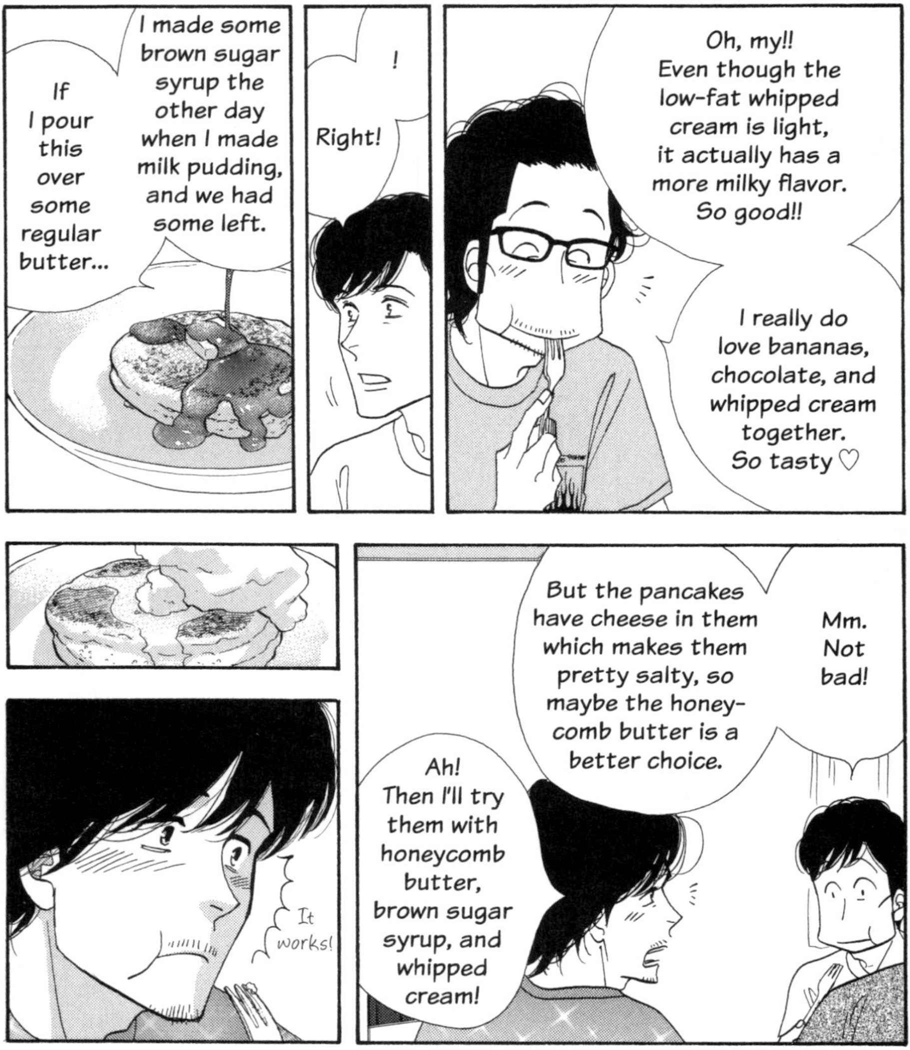
Oh, my!! Even though the low-fat whipped cream is light, it actually has a more milky flavor. So good!!
I really do love bananas, chocolate, and whipped cream together. So tasty ♡
!
Right!
I made some brown sugar syrup the other day when I made milk pudding, and we had some left.
If I pour this over some regular butter...
Mm. Not bad!
But the pancakes have cheese in them which makes them pretty salty, so maybe the honey-comb butter is a better choice.
Ah! Then I'll try them with honeycomb butter, brown sugar syrup, and whipped cream!
It works!
Oh, man! The whipped cream is doing a good job! That particular flavor of brown sugar syrup really works with dairy! Yum ♡
I didn't think I'd get to eat something like this. Make pancakes at home again ♡
Wataru, I'm so glad you're happy!

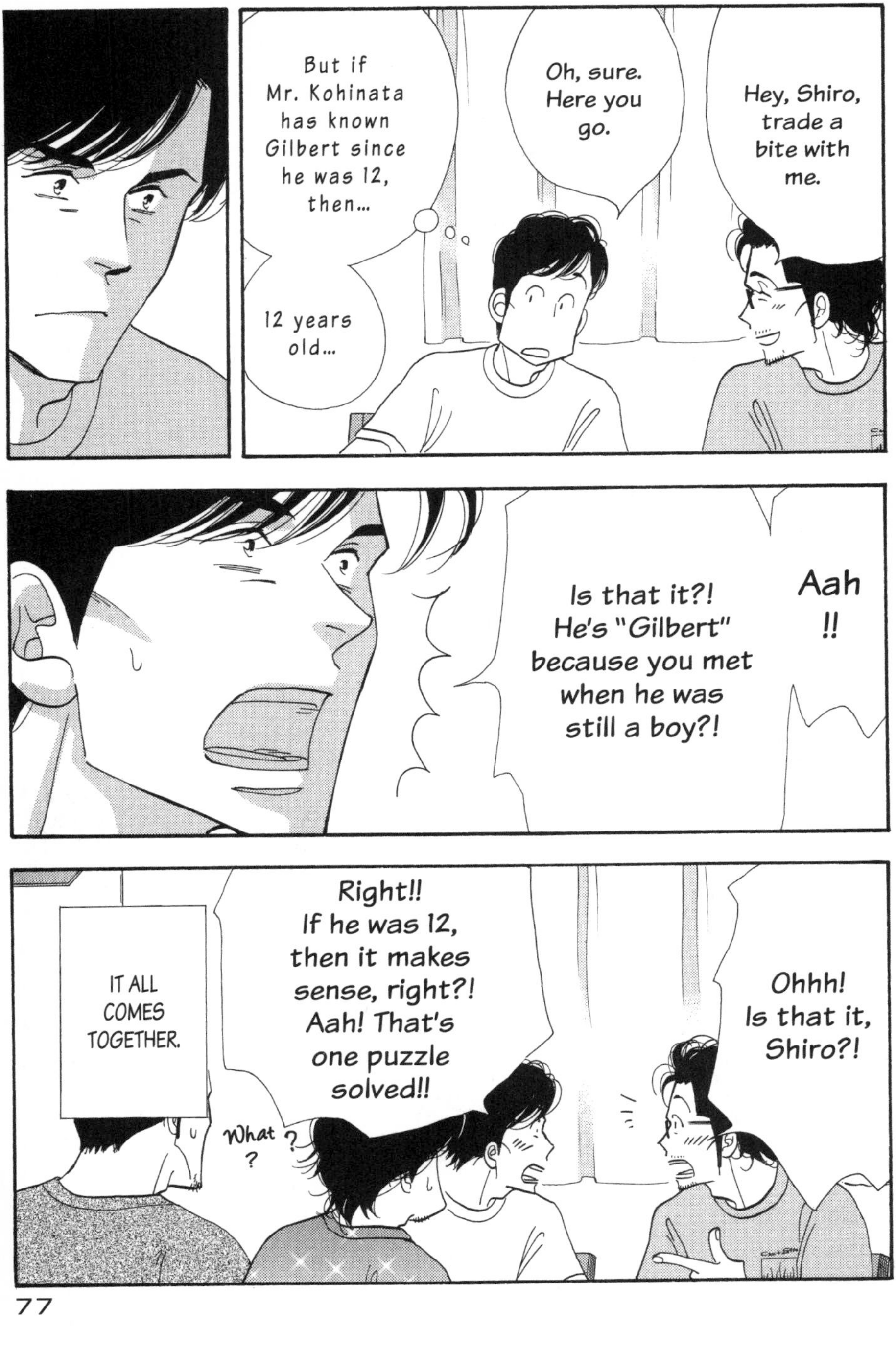
Hey, Shiro, trade a bite with me.
Oh, sure. Here you go.
But if Mr. Kohinata has known Gilbert since he was 12, then...
12 years old...
Aah!!
Is that it?! He's "Gilbert" because you met when he was still a boy?!
Ohhh! Is that it, Shiro?!
Right!! If he was 12, then it makes sense, right?! Aah! That's one puzzle solved!!
What??
IT ALL COMES TOGETHER.

The price of ricotta cheese is usually around 400 or 450 yen for 100 g (3 1/2 oz) (as of June 2015).
There's not a lot of flour, so the pancakes feel like they disappear in a puff in your mouth— much lighter than regular pancakes. The best thing about **homemade pancakes** is that you can have as much of whatever topping you like, so if you try them, please enjoy all the toppings you love that you can't get in a restaurant.

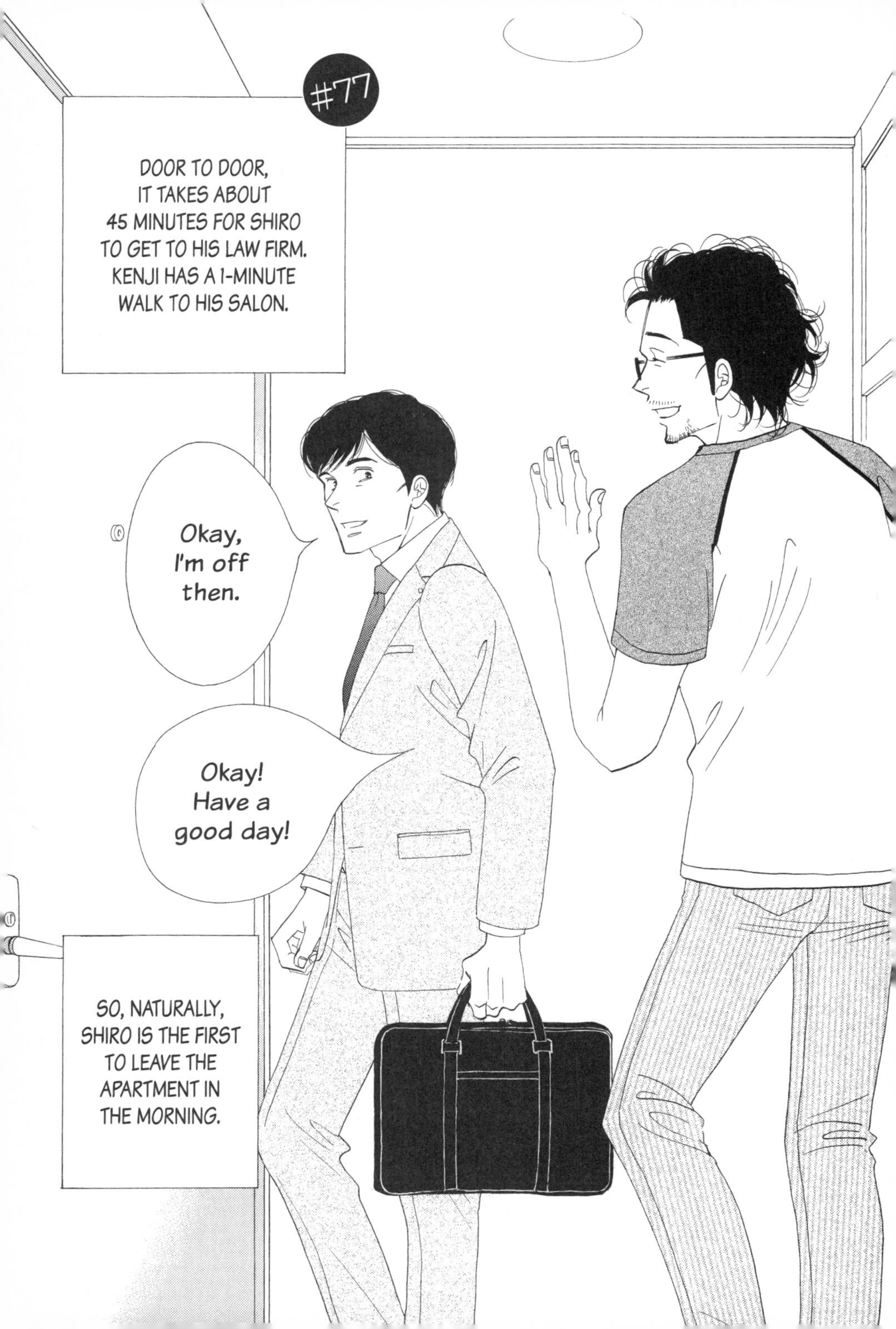
#77
DOOR TO DOOR, IT TAKES ABOUT 45 MINUTES FOR SHIRO TO GET TO HIS LAW FIRM. KENJI HAS A 1-MINUTE WALK TO HIS SALON.
Okay, I'm off then.
Okay! Have a good day!
SO, NATURALLY, SHIRO IS THE FIRST TO LEAVE THE APARTMENT IN THE MORNING.

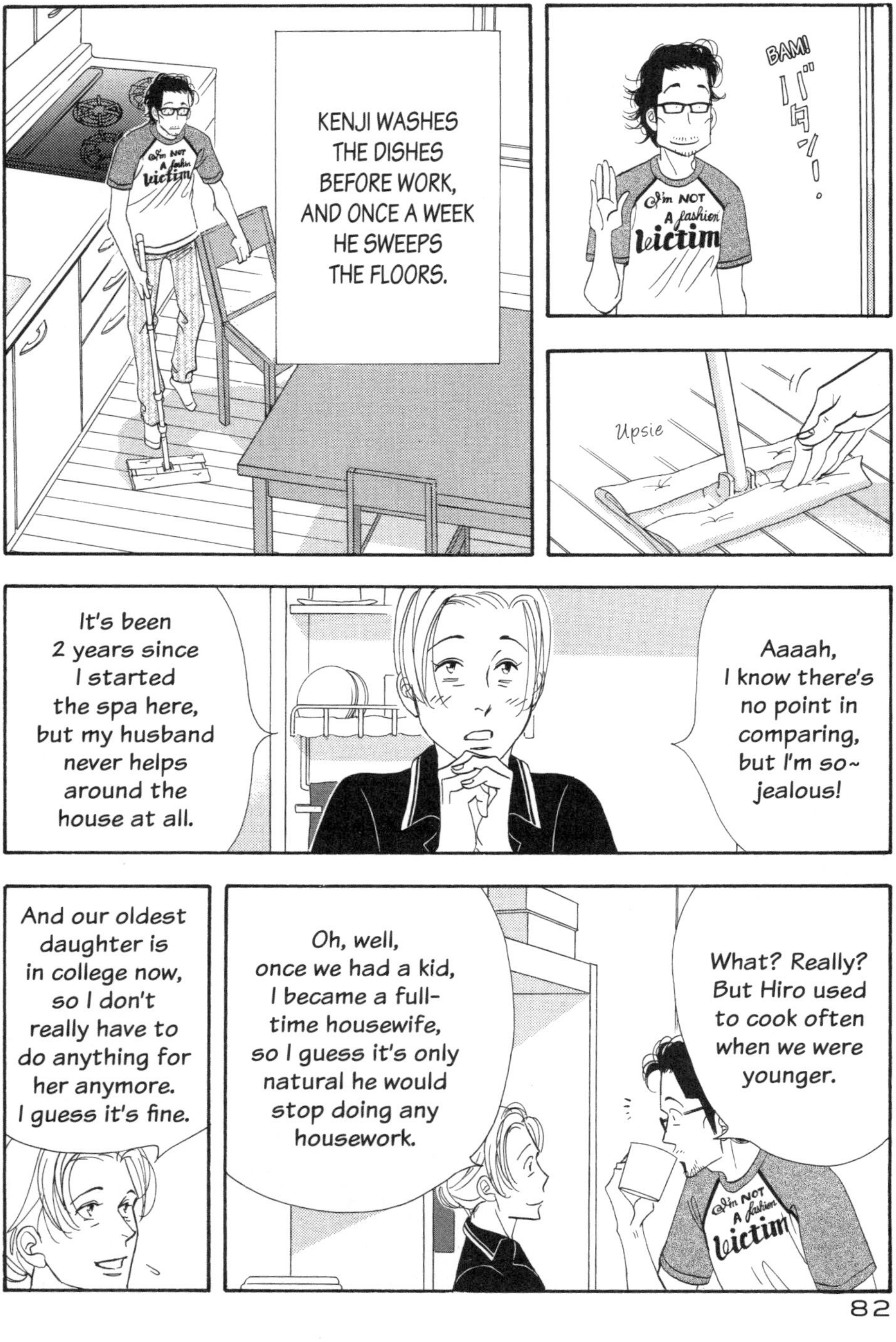
BAM!
バタン！
Upsie
KENJI WASHES THE DISHES BEFORE WORK, AND ONCE A WEEK HE SWEEPS THE FLOORS.
Aaaah, I know there's no point in comparing, but I'm so~ jealous!
It's been 2 years since I started the spa here, but my husband never helps around the house at all.
What? Really? But Hiro used to cook often when we were younger.
Oh, well, once we had a kid, I became a full-time housewife, so I guess it's only natural he would stop doing any housework.
And our oldest daughter is in college now, so I don't really have to do anything for her anymore. I guess it's fine.

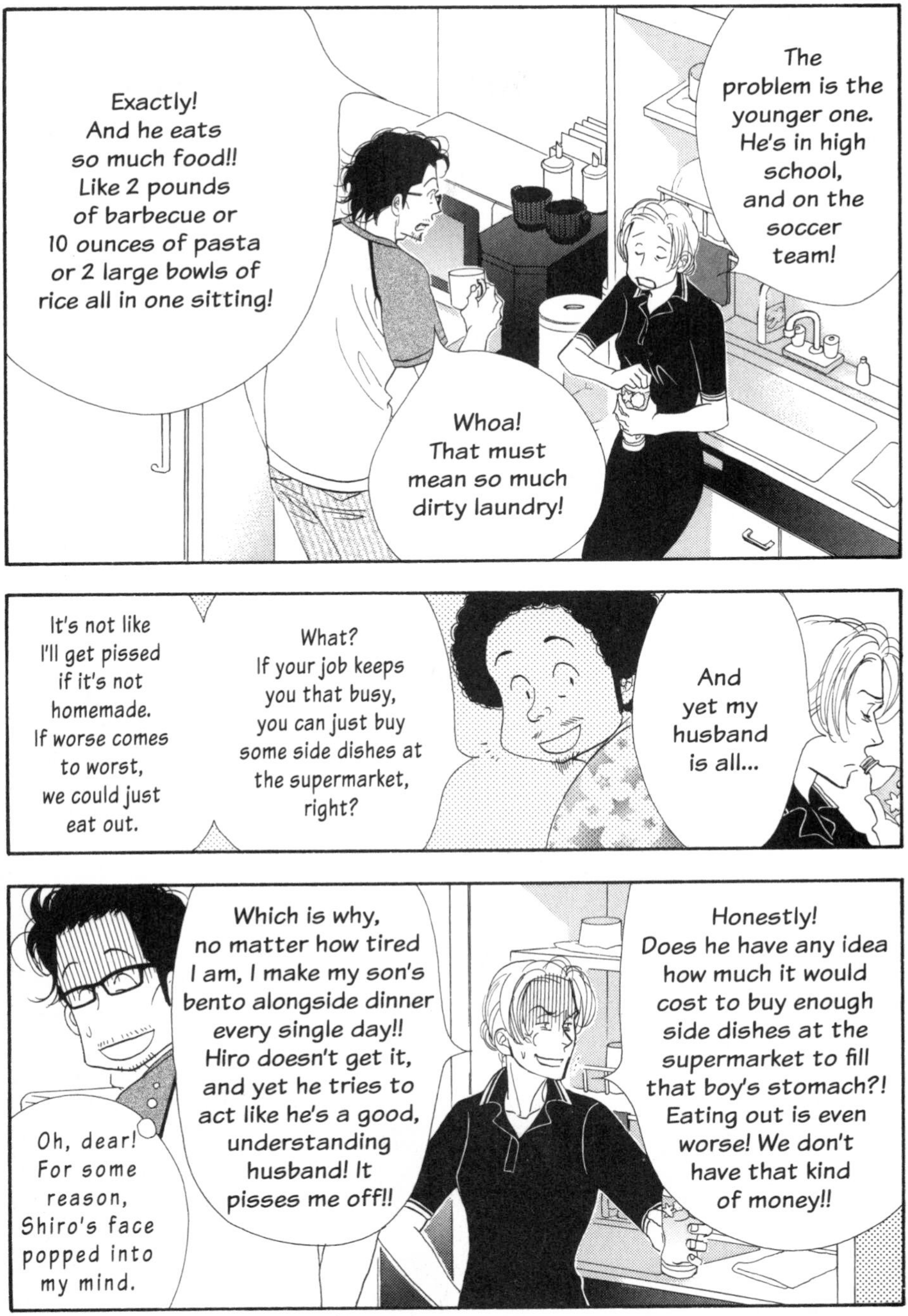
The problem is the younger one. He's in high school, and on the soccer team!
Exactly! And he eats so much food!! Like 2 pounds of barbecue or 10 ounces of pasta or 2 large bowls of rice all in one sitting!
Whoa! That must mean so much dirty laundry!
And yet my husband is all...
What? If your job keeps you that busy, you can just buy some side dishes at the supermarket, right?
It's not like I'll get pissed if it's not homemade. If worse comes to worst, we could just eat out.
Honestly! Does he have any idea how much it would cost to buy enough side dishes at the supermarket to fill that boy's stomach?! Eating out is even worse! We don't have that kind of money!!
Which is why, no matter how tired I am, I make my son's bento alongside dinner every single day!! Hiro doesn't get it, and yet he tries to act like he's a good, understanding husband! It pisses me off!!
Oh, dear! For some reason, Shiro's face popped into my mind.

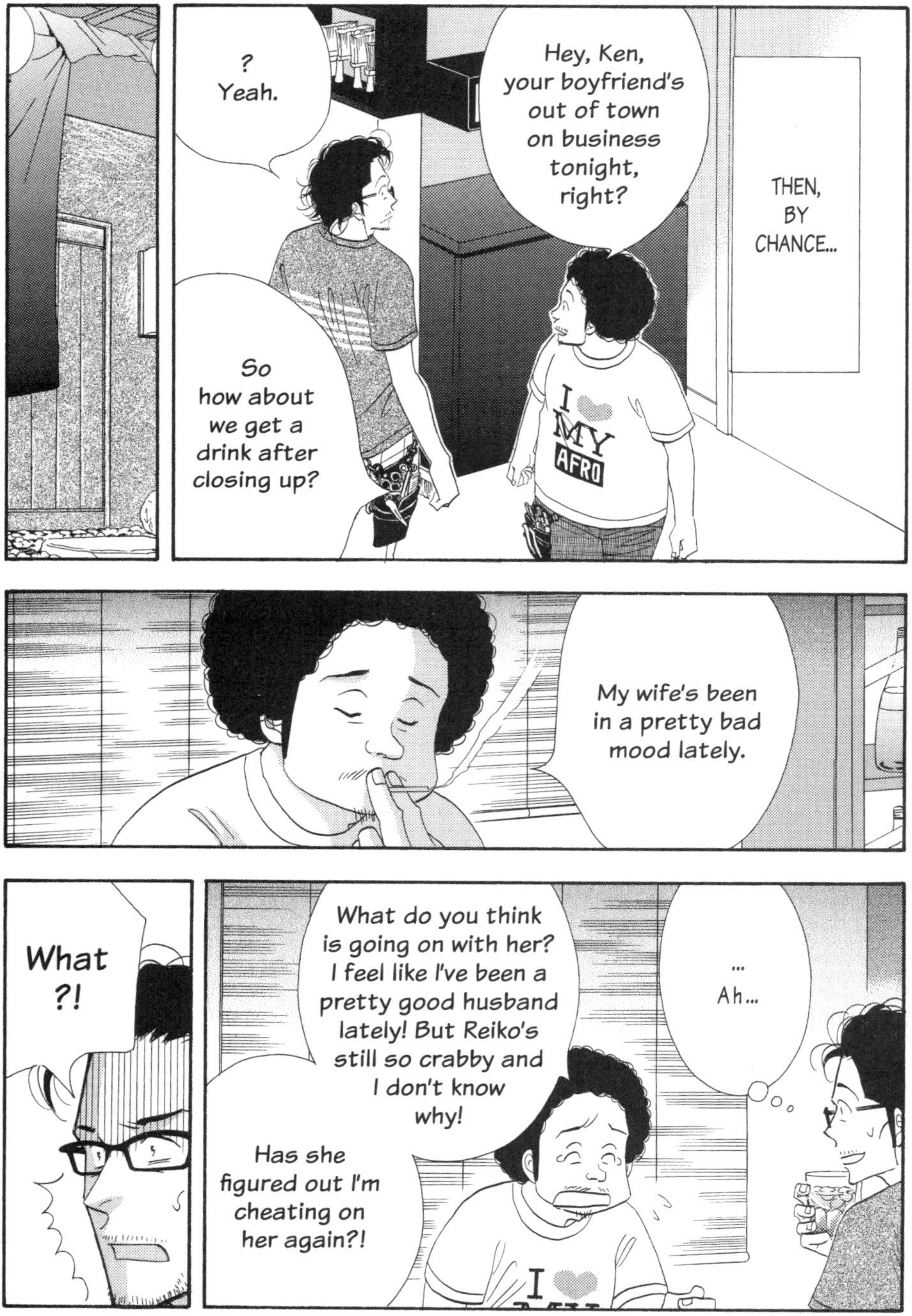
THEN, BY CHANCE...
Hey, Ken, your boyfriend's out of town on business tonight, right?
? Yeah.
So how about we get a drink after closing up?
I ♥ MY AFRO
My wife's been in a pretty bad mood lately.
... Ah...
What do you think is going on with her? I feel like I've been a pretty good husband lately! But Reiko's still so crabby and I don't know why!
Has she figured out I'm cheating on her again?!
What ?!

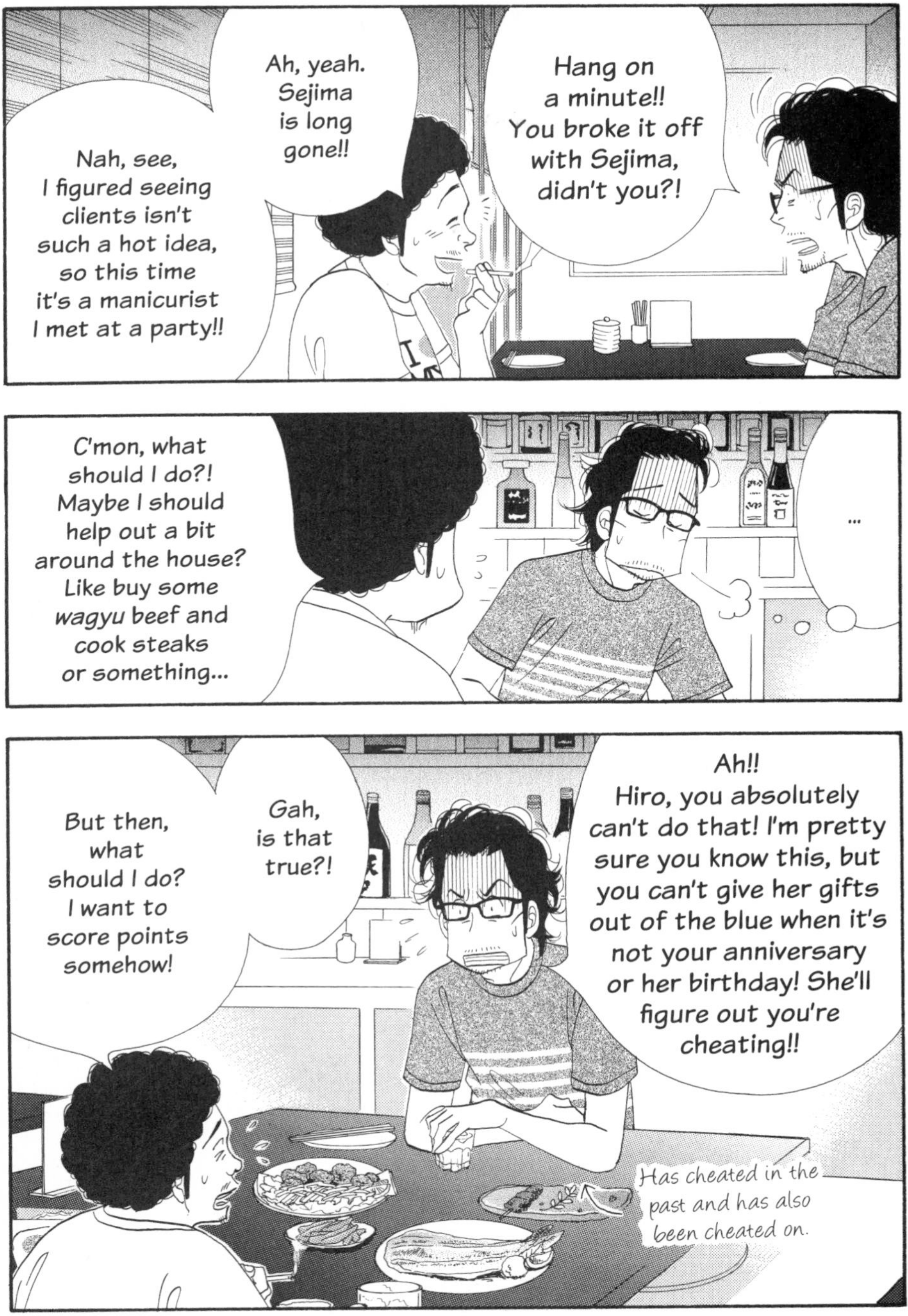
Hang on a minute!! You broke it off with Sejima, didn't you?!
Ah, yeah. Sejima is long gone!!
Nah, see, I figured seeing clients isn't such a hot idea, so this time it's a manicurist I met at a party!!
...
C'mon, what should I do?! Maybe I should help out a bit around the house? Like buy some *wagyu* beef and cook steaks or something...
Ah!! Hiro, you absolutely can't do that! I'm pretty sure you know this, but you can't give her gifts out of the blue when it's not your anniversary or her birthday! She'll figure out you're cheating!!
Gah, is that true?!
But then, what should I do? I want to score points somehow!
Has cheated in the past and has also been cheated on.

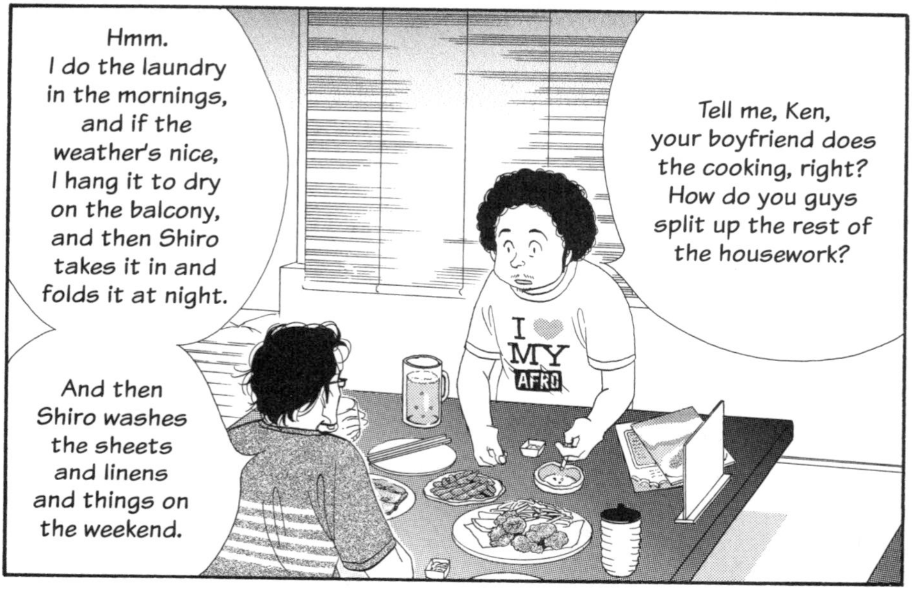
Tell me, Ken, your boyfriend does the cooking, right? How do you guys split up the rest of the housework?
I ♥ MY AFRO
Hmm. I do the laundry in the mornings, and if the weather's nice, I hang it to dry on the balcony, and then Shiro takes it in and folds it at night.
And then Shiro washes the sheets and linens and things on the weekend.

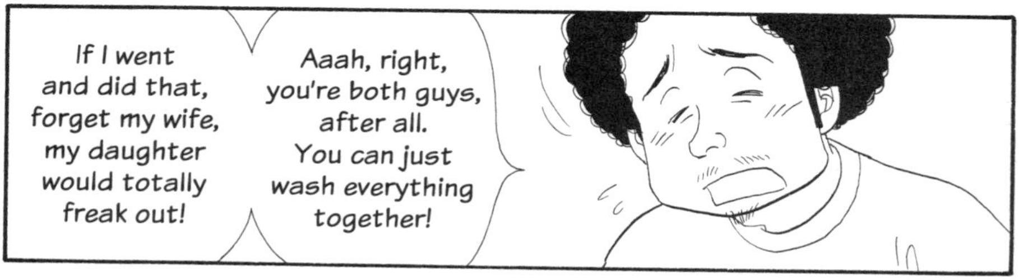
Aaah, right, you're both guys, after all. You can just wash everything together!
If I went and did that, forget my wife, my daughter would totally freak out!

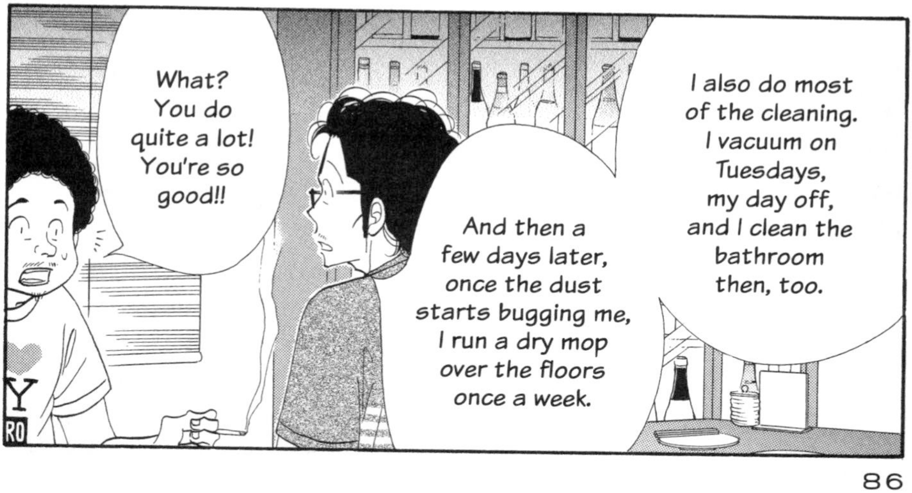
I also do most of the cleaning. I vacuum on Tuesdays, my day off, and I clean the bathroom then, too.
And then a few days later, once the dust starts bugging me, I run a dry mop over the floors once a week.
What? You do quite a lot! You're so good!!

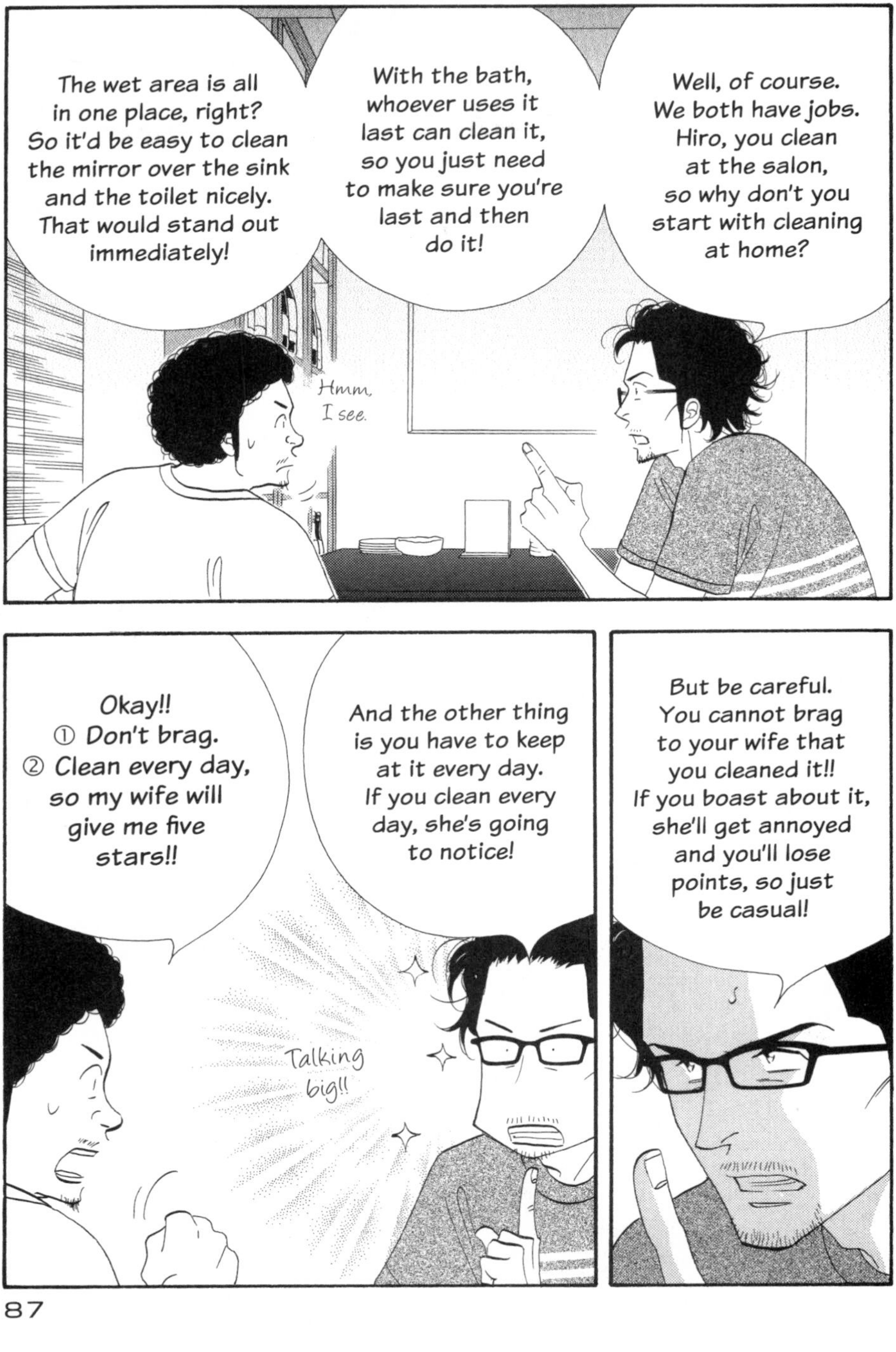
Well, of course. We both have jobs. Hiro, you clean at the salon, so why don't you start with cleaning at home?
With the bath, whoever uses it last can clean it, so you just need to make sure you're last and then do it!
The wet area is all in one place, right? So it'd be easy to clean the mirror over the sink and the toilet nicely. That would stand out immediately!
Hmm, I see.
But be careful. You cannot brag to your wife that you cleaned it!! If you boast about it, she'll get annoyed and you'll lose points, so just be casual!
And the other thing is you have to keep at it every day. If you clean every day, she's going to notice!
Okay!! ① Don't brag. ② Clean every day, so my wife will give me five stars!!
Talking big!!

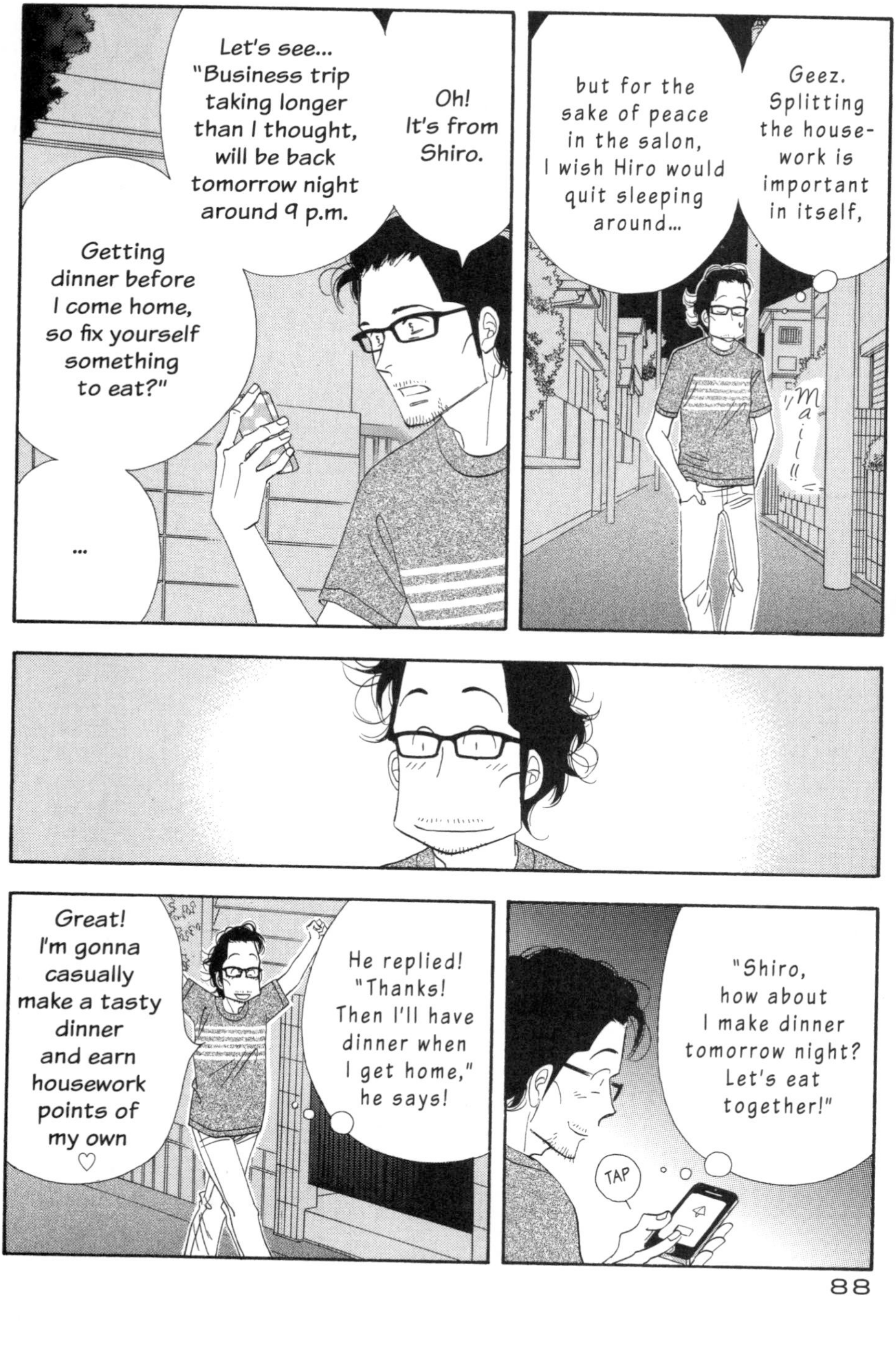
Geez. Splitting the house-work is important in itself,
but for the sake of peace in the salon, I wish Hiro would quit sleeping around...
Mail!!
Oh! It's from Shiro.
Let's see... "Business trip taking longer than I thought, will be back tomorrow night around 9 p.m.
Getting dinner before I come home, so fix yourself something to eat?"
...
"Shiro, how about I make dinner tomorrow night? Let's eat together!"
TAP
He replied! "Thanks! Then I'll have dinner when I get home," he says!
Great! I'm gonna casually make a tasty dinner and earn housework points of my own ♡

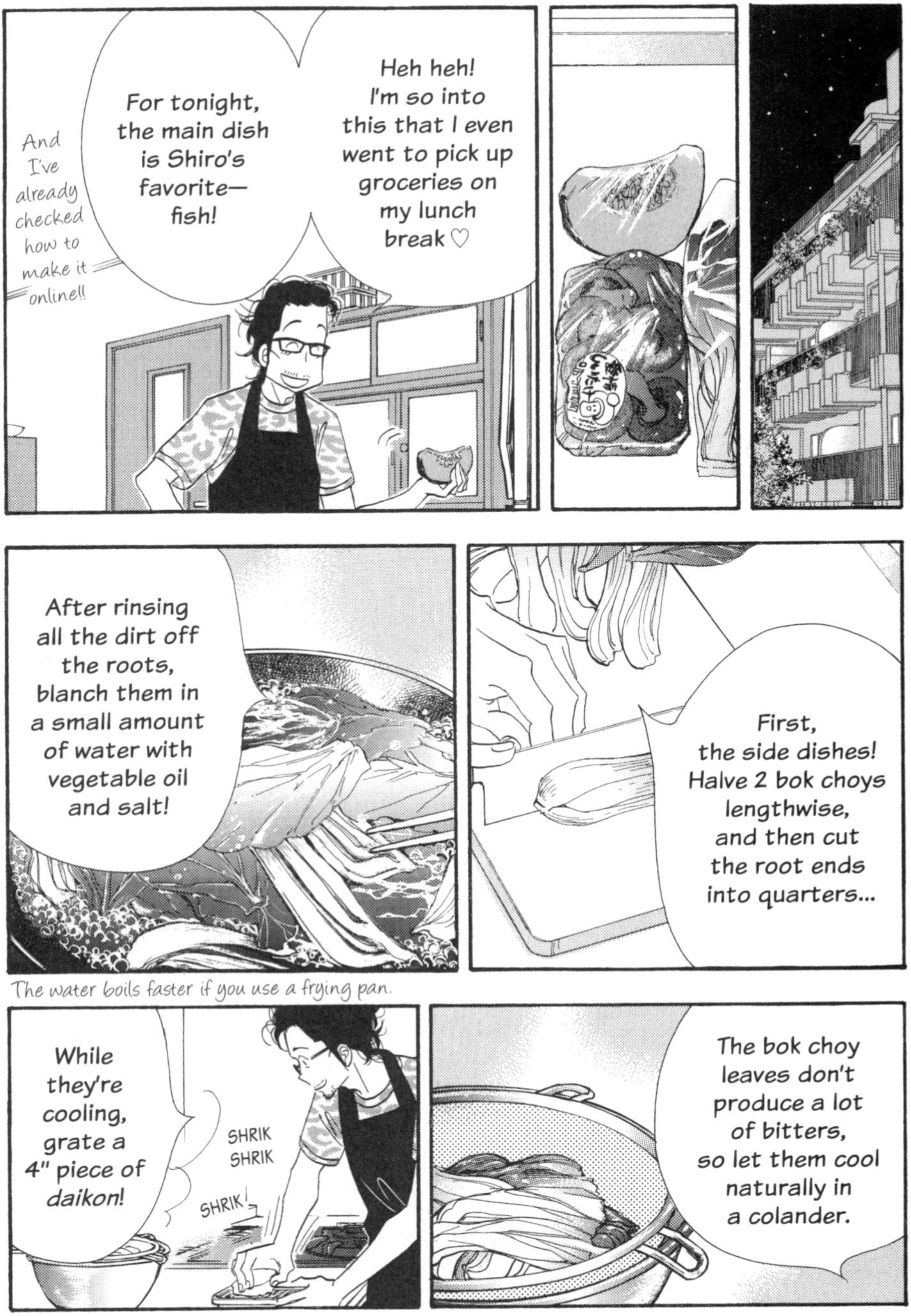
Heh heh! I'm so into this that I even went to pick up groceries on my lunch break ♡
For tonight, the main dish is Shiro's favorite—fish!
And I've already checked how to make it online!!
First, the side dishes! Halve 2 bok choys lengthwise, and then cut the root ends into quarters...
After rinsing all the dirt off the roots, blanch them in a small amount of water with vegetable oil and salt!
The water boils faster if you use a frying pan.
The bok choy leaves don't produce a lot of bitters, so let them cool naturally in a colander.
While they're cooling, grate a 4" piece of daikon!
SHRIK SHRIK
SHRIK

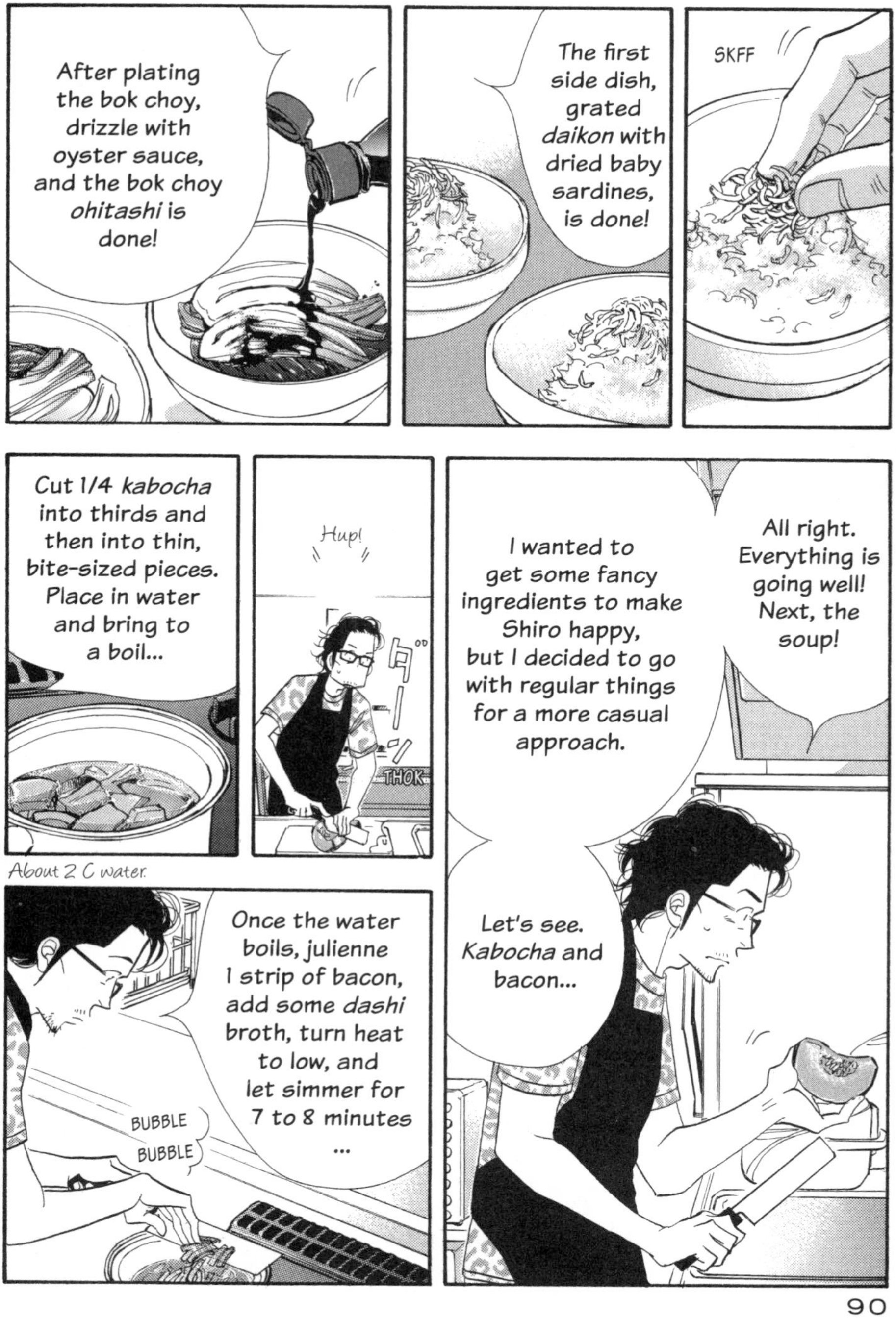
SKFF
The first side dish, grated *daikon* with dried baby sardines, is done!
After plating the bok choy, drizzle with oyster sauce, and the bok choy *ohitashi* is done!
All right. Everything is going well! Next, the soup!
I wanted to get some fancy ingredients to make Shiro happy, but I decided to go with regular things for a more casual approach.
Let's see. *Kabocha* and bacon...
Hup!
THOK
Cut 1/4 *kabocha* into thirds and then into thin, bite-sized pieces. Place in water and bring to a boil...
About 2 C water.
Once the water boils, julienne 1 strip of bacon, add some *dashi* broth, turn heat to low, and let simmer for 7 to 8 minutes ...
BUBBLE
BUBBLE

Over very low heat so the ingredients don't crumble.
BUBBLE
BUBBLE
BUBBLE
Once the *kabocha* is done, turn off heat. The bacon adds salt, so dissolve only a little miso into the broth.
Grind in black pepper, and the *kabocha* and bacon miso soup is done!
GRIND
GRIND
WHEEW
Oh, no!! I just stood there and waited for the *kabocha* to cook!!
Waah!! I still haven't done anything for the main dish!!
Let's see. First, the sauce!
Slowly, slowly.
TOK
TOK
Slice 1/2 onion into wedges, 1/4 carrot into thin sticks, and thinly slice 2 *shiitake* mushrooms.
Dissolve 1 Tbsp potato starch in 2 Tbsp water to make the thickener...
KLAK
KLAK
KLAK

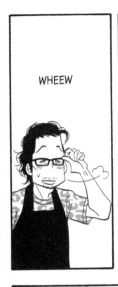

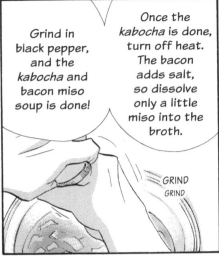

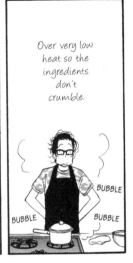

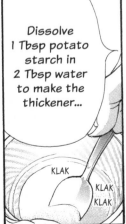

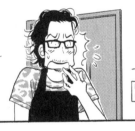

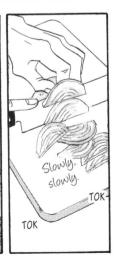

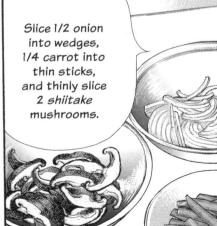

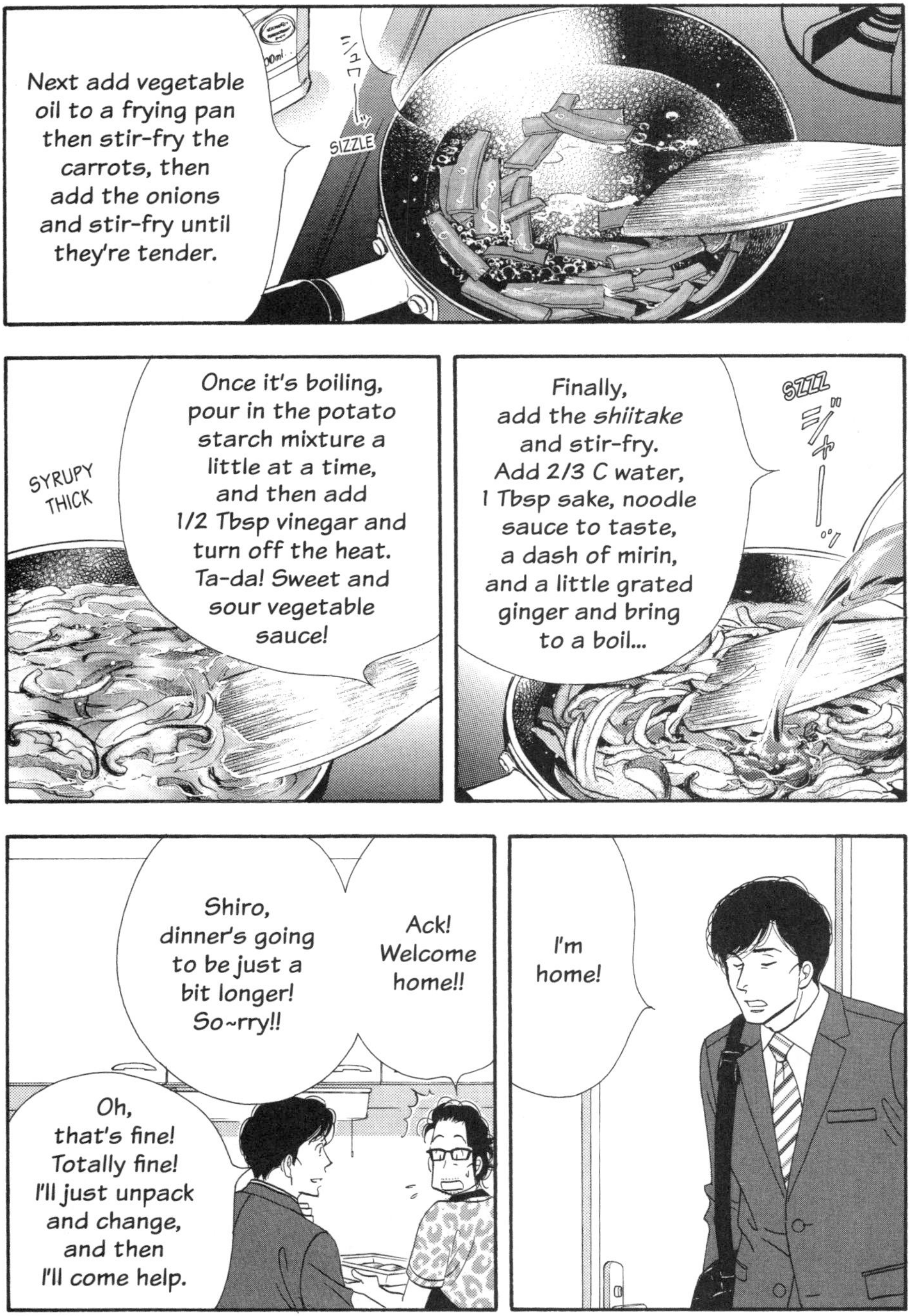
Next add vegetable oil to a frying pan then stir-fry the carrots, then add the onions and stir-fry until they're tender.
SIZZLE
SZZZ
Finally, add the *shiitake* and stir-fry. Add 2/3 C water, 1 Tbsp sake, noodle sauce to taste, a dash of mirin, and a little grated ginger and bring to a boil...
Once it's boiling, pour in the potato starch mixture a little at a time, and then add 1/2 Tbsp vinegar and turn off the heat. Ta-da! Sweet and sour vegetable sauce!
SYRUPY THICK
I'm home!
Ack! Welcome home!!
Shiro, dinner's going to be just a bit longer! So~rry!!
Oh, that's fine! Totally fine! I'll just unpack and change, and then I'll come help.

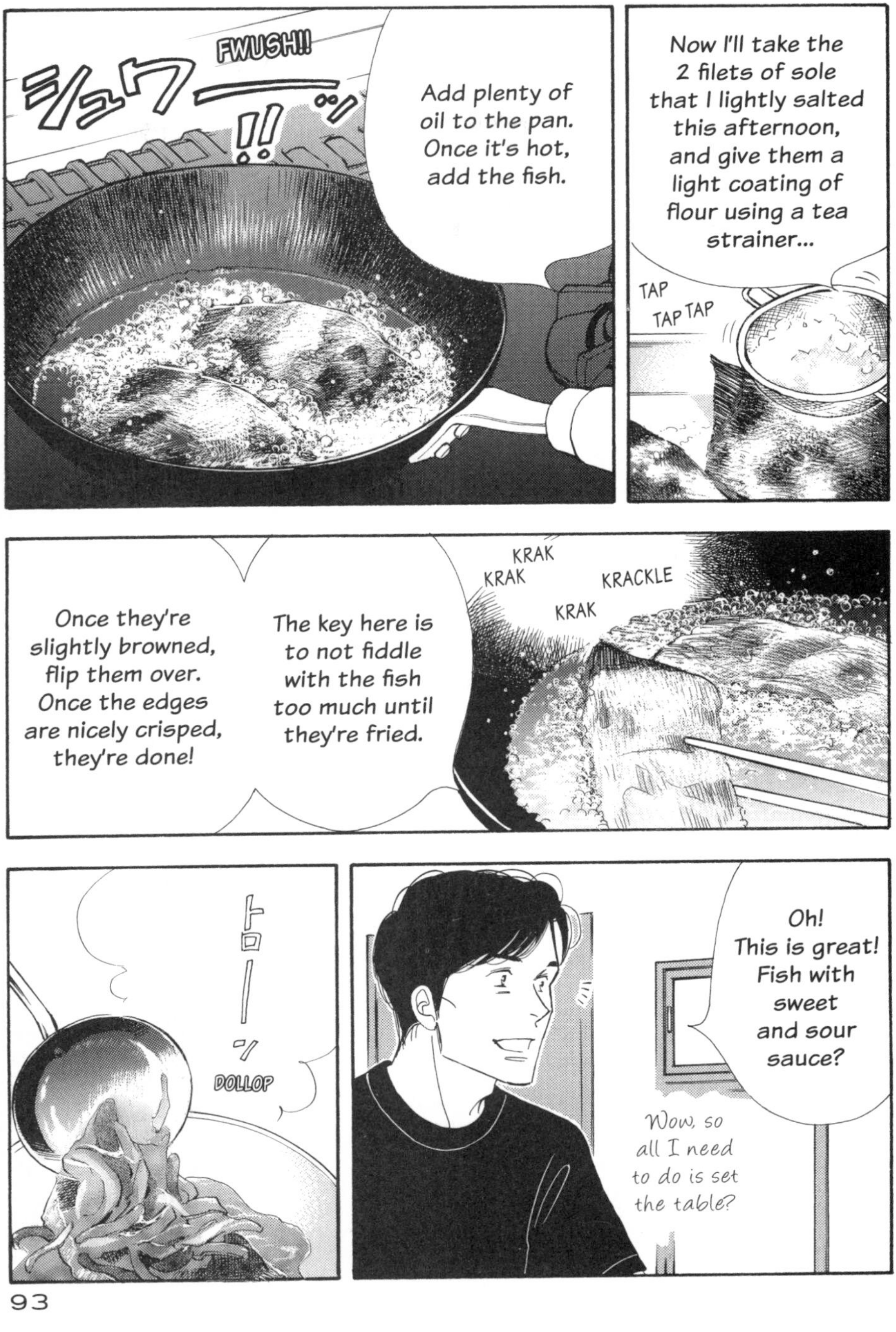
Now I'll take the 2 filets of sole that I lightly salted this afternoon, and give them a light coating of flour using a tea strainer...
TAP
TAP TAP
シュワーーッ!!
FWUSH!!
Add plenty of oil to the pan. Once it's hot, add the fish.
KRAK
KRAK
KRACKLE
KRAK
The key here is to not fiddle with the fish too much until they're fried.
Once they're slightly browned, flip them over. Once the edges are nicely crisped, they're done!
Oh! This is great! Fish with sweet and sour sauce?
Wow, so all I need to do is set the table?
トローッ
DOLLOP

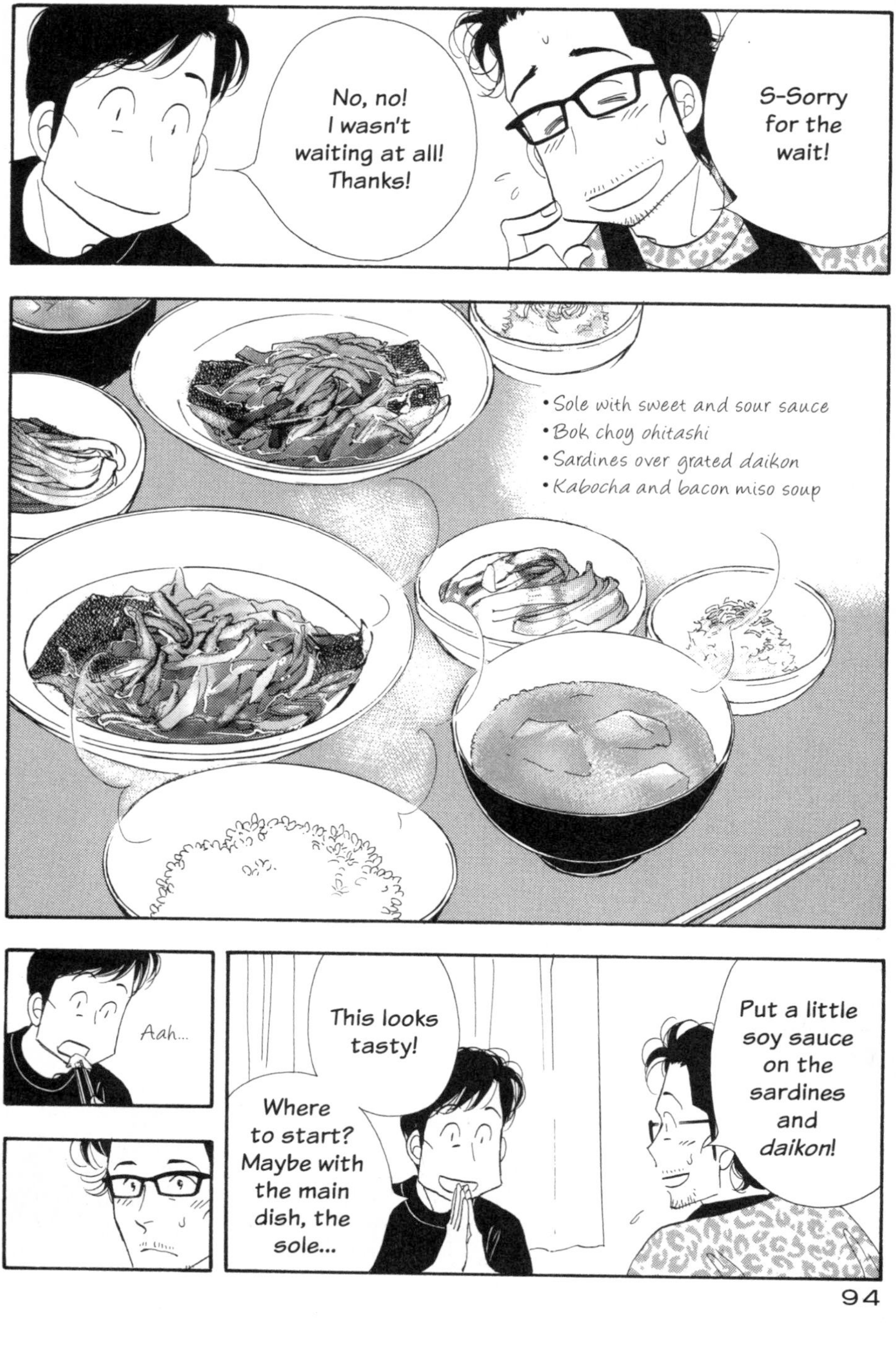
S-Sorry for the wait!
No, no! I wasn't waiting at all! Thanks!
•Sole with sweet and sour sauce
•Bok choy ohitashi
•Sardines over grated daikon
•Kabocha and bacon miso soup
Put a little soy sauce on the sardines and daikon!
This looks tasty!
Where to start? Maybe with the main dish, the sole...
Aah...

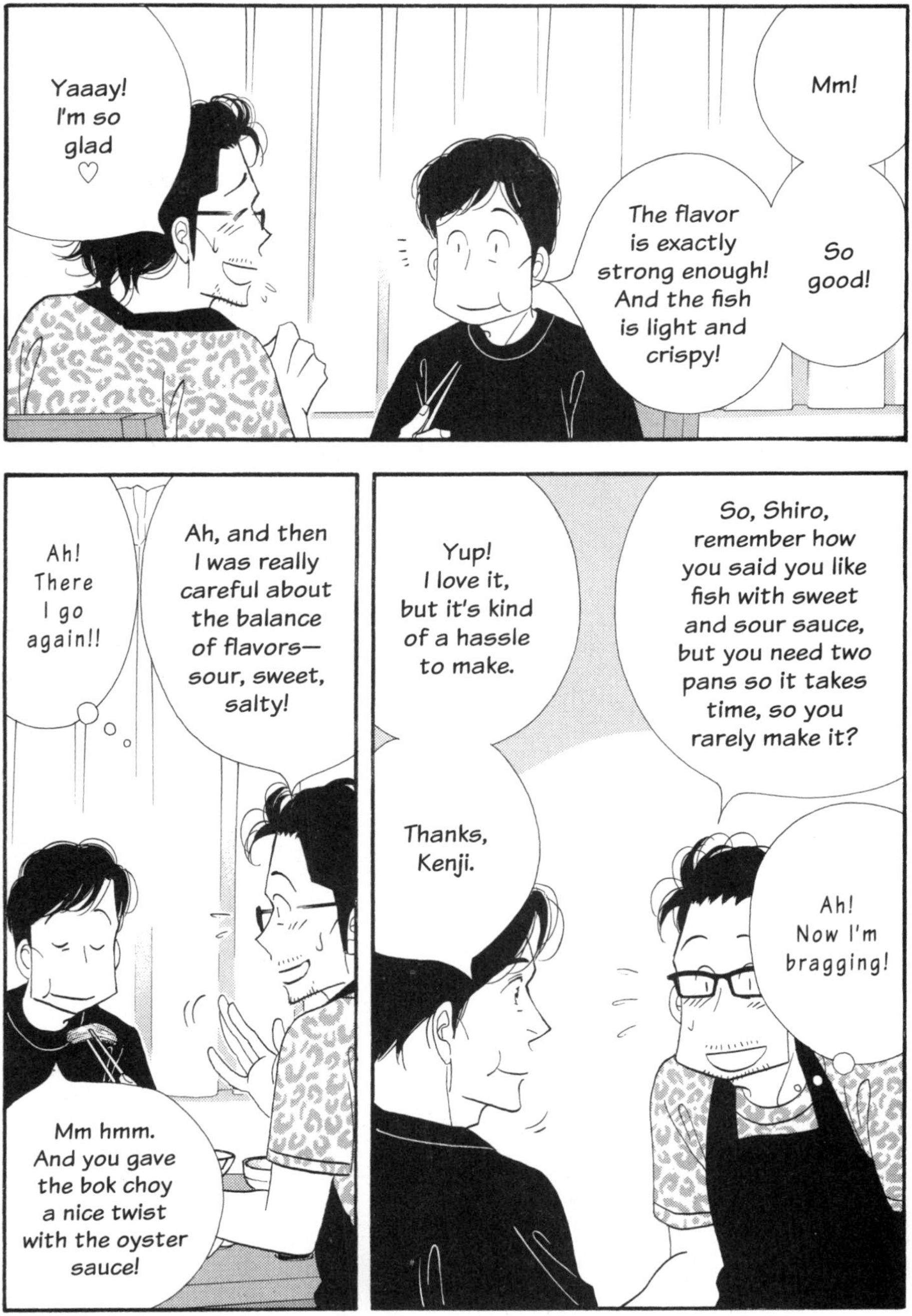
Mm!
So good!
The flavor is exactly strong enough! And the fish is light and crispy!
Yaaay! I'm so glad ♡
So, Shiro, remember how you said you like fish with sweet and sour sauce, but you need two pans so it takes time, so you rarely make it?
Yup! I love it, but it's kind of a hassle to make.
Thanks, Kenji.
Ah! Now I'm bragging!
Ah, and then I was really careful about the balance of flavors—sour, sweet, salty!
Ah! There I go again!!
Mm hmm. And you gave the bok choy a nice twist with the oyster sauce!

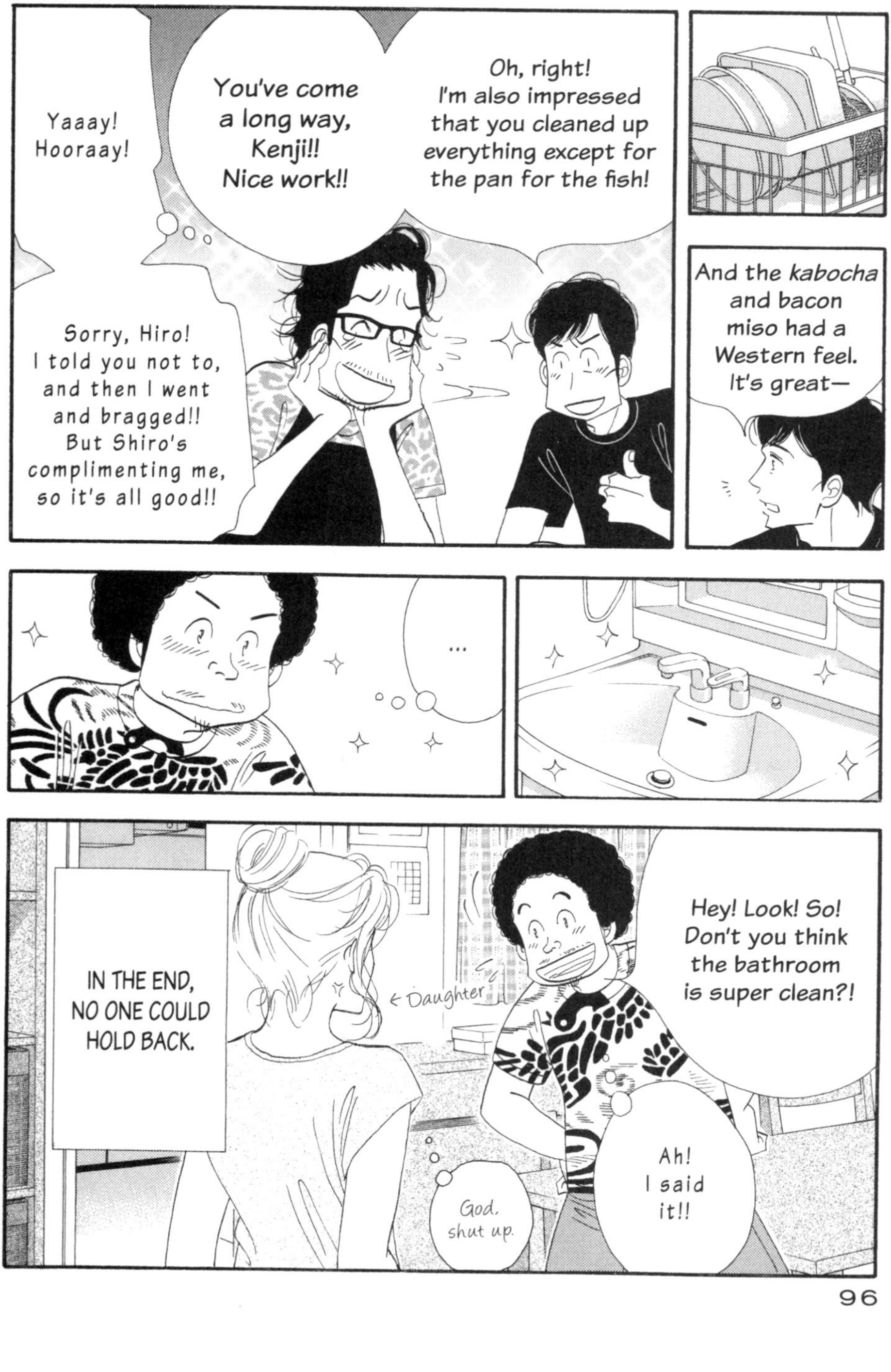
And the *kabocha* and bacon miso had a Western feel. It's great—
Oh, right! I'm also impressed that you cleaned up everything except for the pan for the fish!
You've come a long way, Kenji!! Nice work!!
Yaaay! Hooraay!
Sorry, Hiro! I told you not to, and then I went and bragged!! But Shiro's complimenting me, so it's all good!!
...
Hey! Look! So! Don't you think the bathroom is super clean?!
← Daughter
Ah! I said it!!
God, shut up.
IN THE END, NO ONE COULD HOLD BACK.

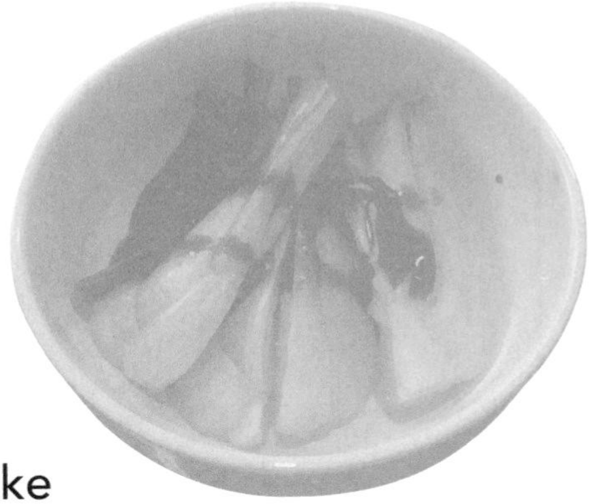

Besides sole,
other light, white fish like
Spanish mackerel,
sea bream, and perch are
all delicious with this
sweet and sour sauce.
Another vegetable besides
bok choy that pairs well with
oyster sauce is boiled
green beans.

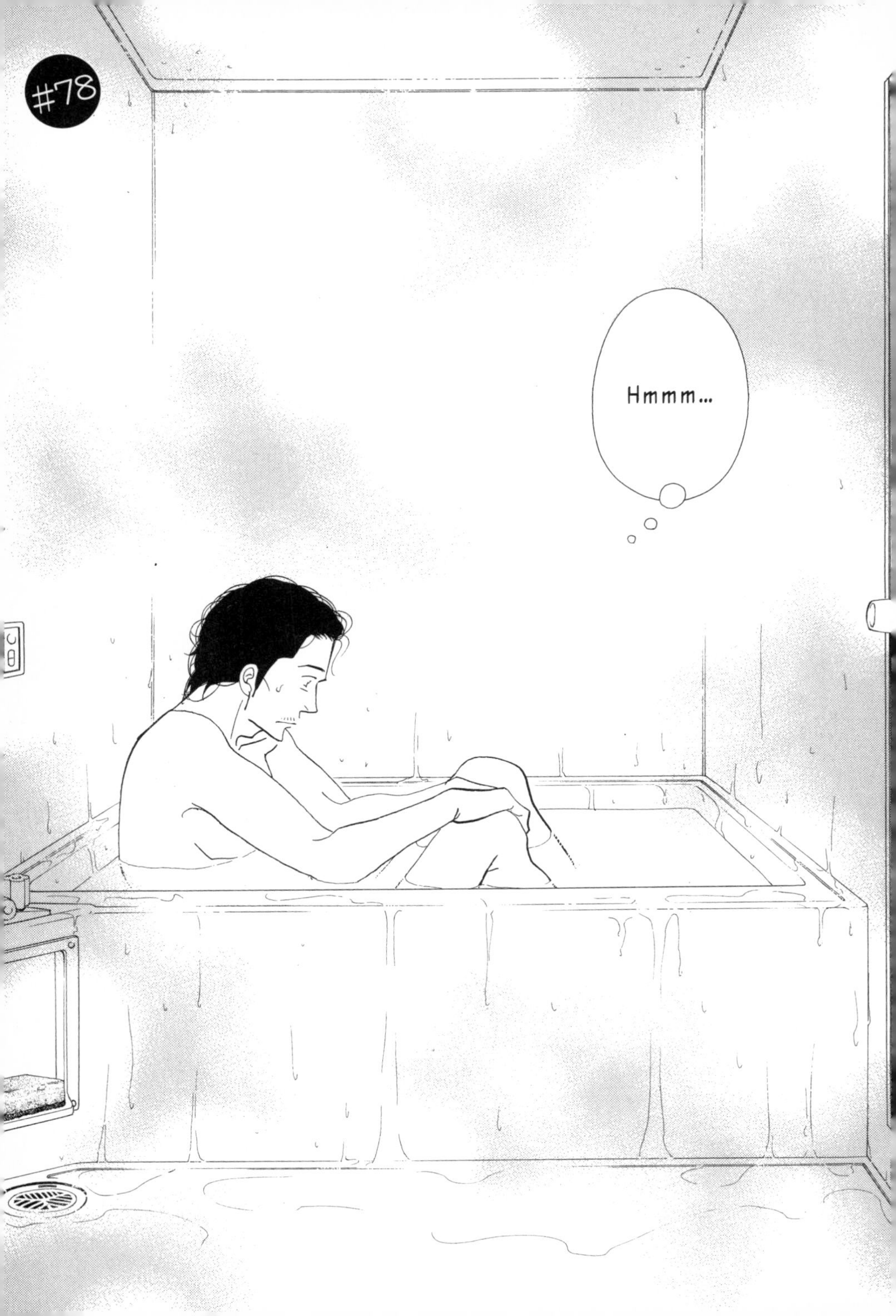
#78
Hmmm...

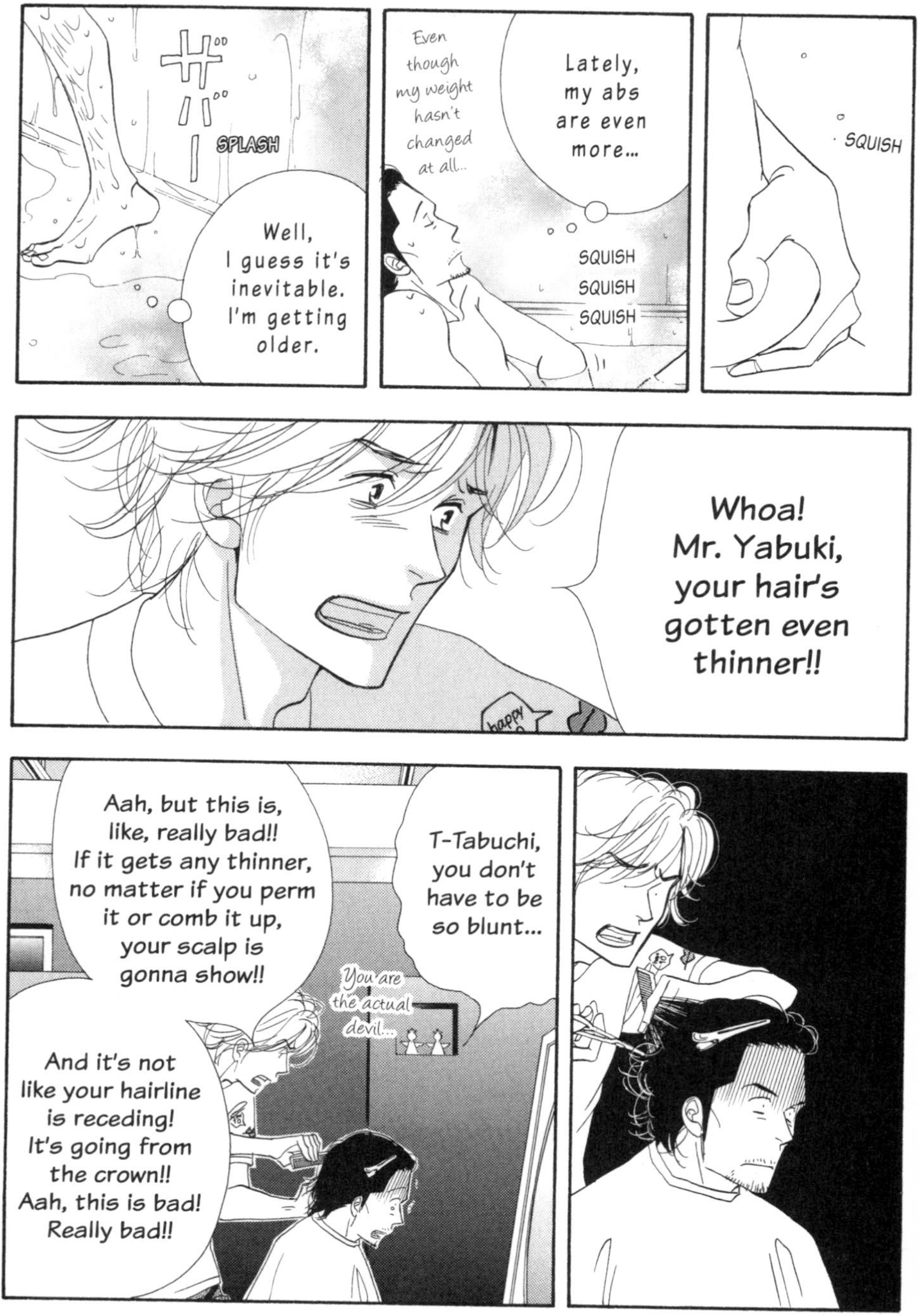
SQUISH
Lately, my abs are even more...
Even though my weight hasn't changed at all...
SQUISH
SQUISH
SQUISH
SPLASH
Well, I guess it's inevitable. I'm getting older.
Whoa! Mr. Yabuki, your hair's gotten even thinner!!
Aah, but this is, like, really bad!! If it gets any thinner, no matter if you perm it or comb it up, your scalp is gonna show!!
T-Tabuchi, you don't have to be so blunt...
You are the actual devil...
And it's not like your hairline is receding! It's going from the crown!! Aah, this is bad! Really bad!!

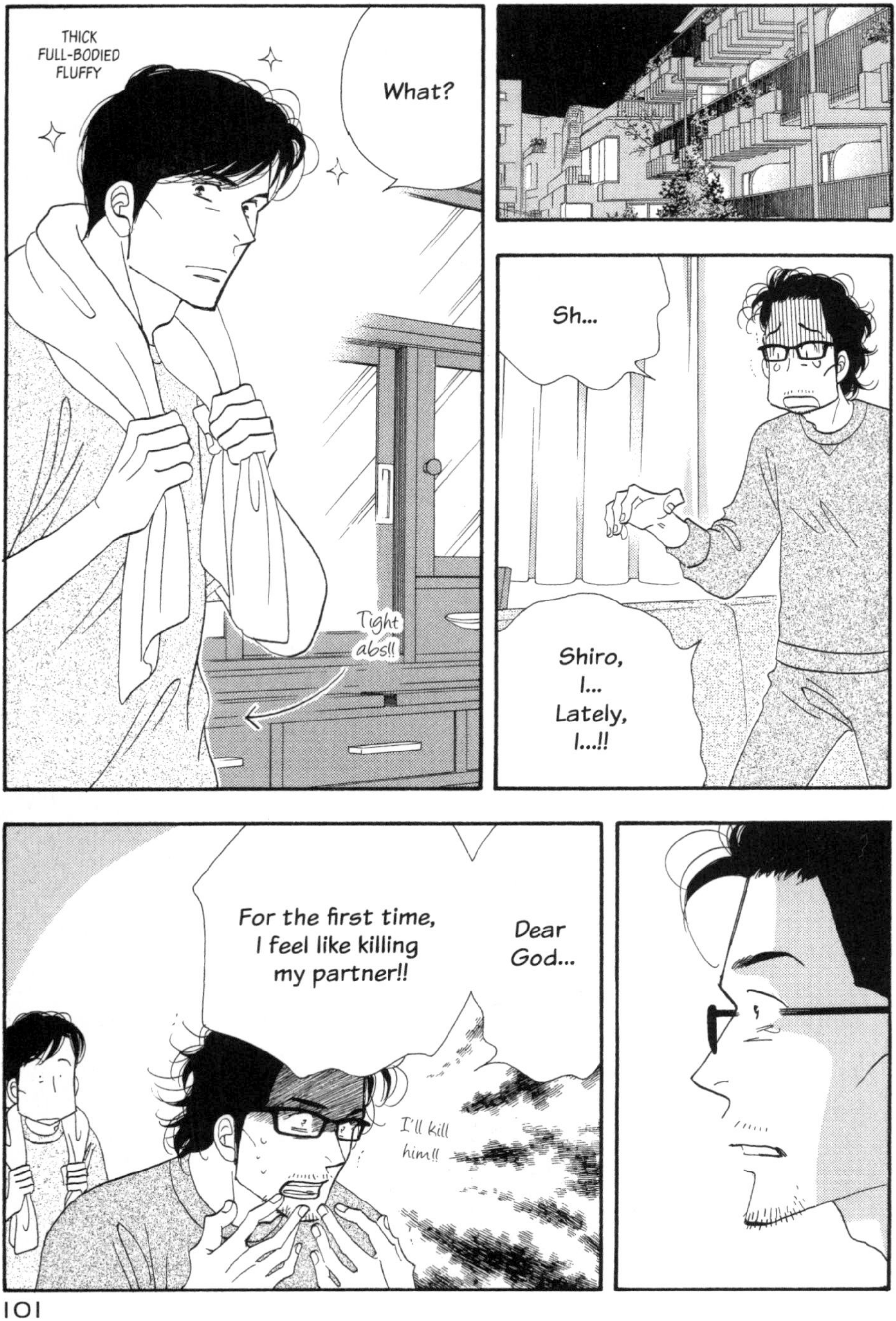
Sh...
Shiro, I... Lately, I...!!
THICK FULL-BODIED FLUFFY
What?
Tight abs!!
Dear God...
For the first time, I feel like killing my partner!!
I'll kill him!!

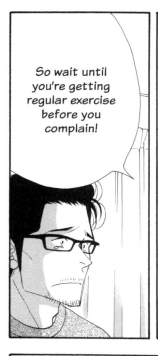

Look, Kenji.
The hair is one thing, but for the body, I've been going to the gym for nearly 20 years now. I make sure to swim at least half a mile once or twice a week to keep in shape!
So wait until you're getting regular exercise before you complain!
Waaah! You're too right! I can't even make a grumbling noise!
But I know all that!! I know perfectly well that it's only because I have a slim build to start with, plus the fact that you make me such healthy dinners, that I've managed to make it this far without exercising!!
If you know that, then thank your lucky stars and hurry up and join my gym. They're doing a promotion right now, so it's free to join.
But I can't swim, so I can't just pop into the pool and come home like you do!

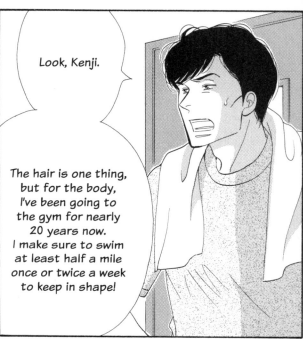

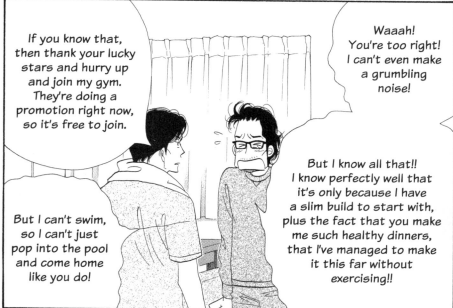

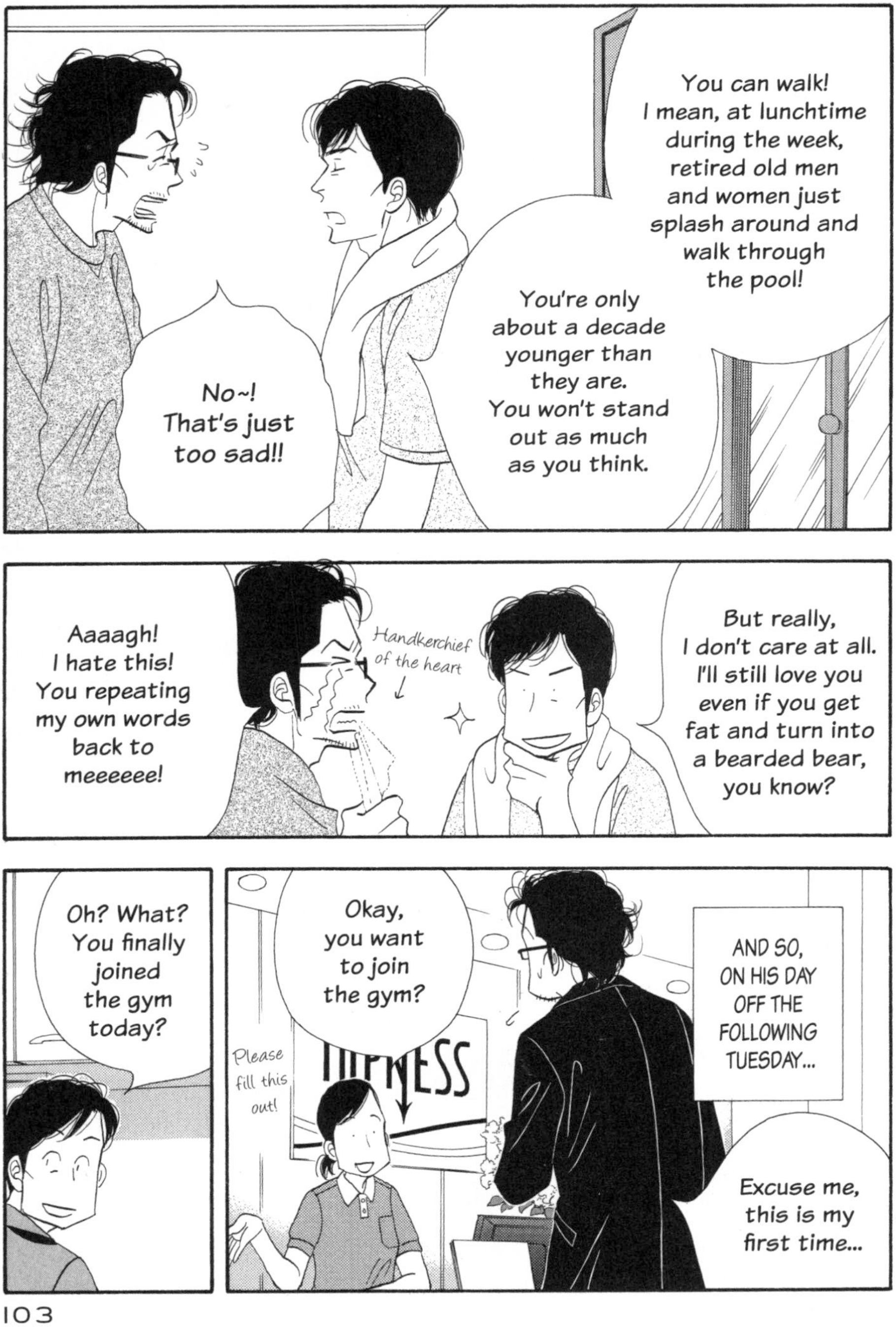
You can walk! I mean, at lunchtime during the week, retired old men and women just splash around and walk through the pool!
You're only about a decade younger than they are. You won't stand out as much as you think.
No~! That's just too sad!!
But really, I don't care at all. I'll still love you even if you get fat and turn into a bearded bear, you know?
Handkerchief of the heart
Aaaagh! I hate this! You repeating my own words back to meeeeee!
AND SO, ON HIS DAY OFF THE FOLLOWING TUESDAY...
Excuse me, this is my first time...
Okay, you want to join the gym?
Please fill this out!
Oh? What? You finally joined the gym today?

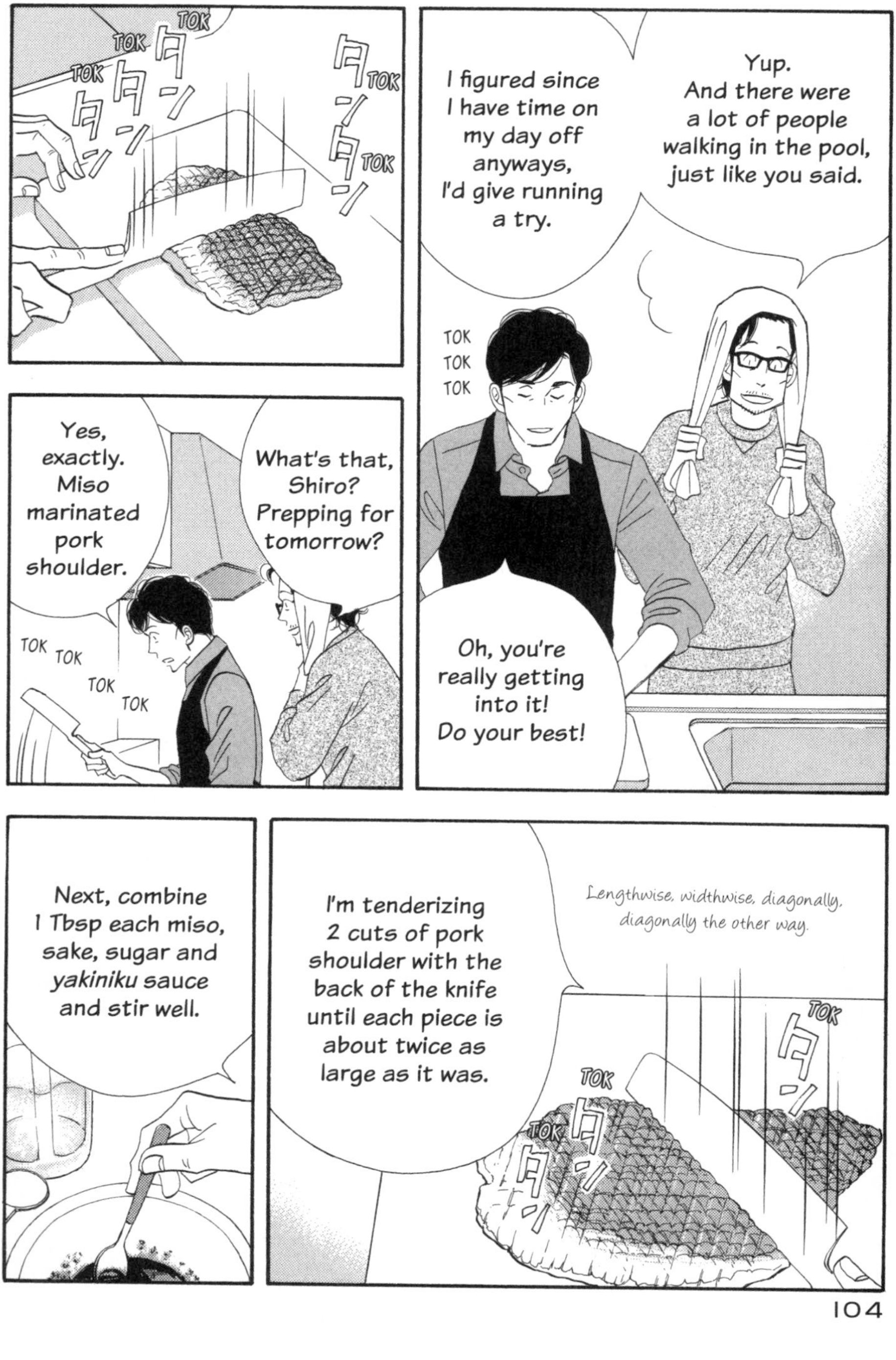
Yup.
And there were a lot of people walking in the pool, just like you said.
I figured since I have time on my day off anyways, I'd give running a try.
TOK TOK TOK
Oh, you're really getting into it! Do your best!
TOK TOK TOK TOK TOK TOK
What's that, Shiro? Prepping for tomorrow?
Yes, exactly. Miso marinated pork shoulder.
TOK TOK TOK TOK
I'm tenderizing 2 cuts of pork shoulder with the back of the knife until each piece is about twice as large as it was.
Lengthwise, widthwise, diagonally, diagonally the other way.
TOK TOK TOK
Next, combine 1 Tbsp each miso, sake, sugar and *yakiniku* sauce and stir well.

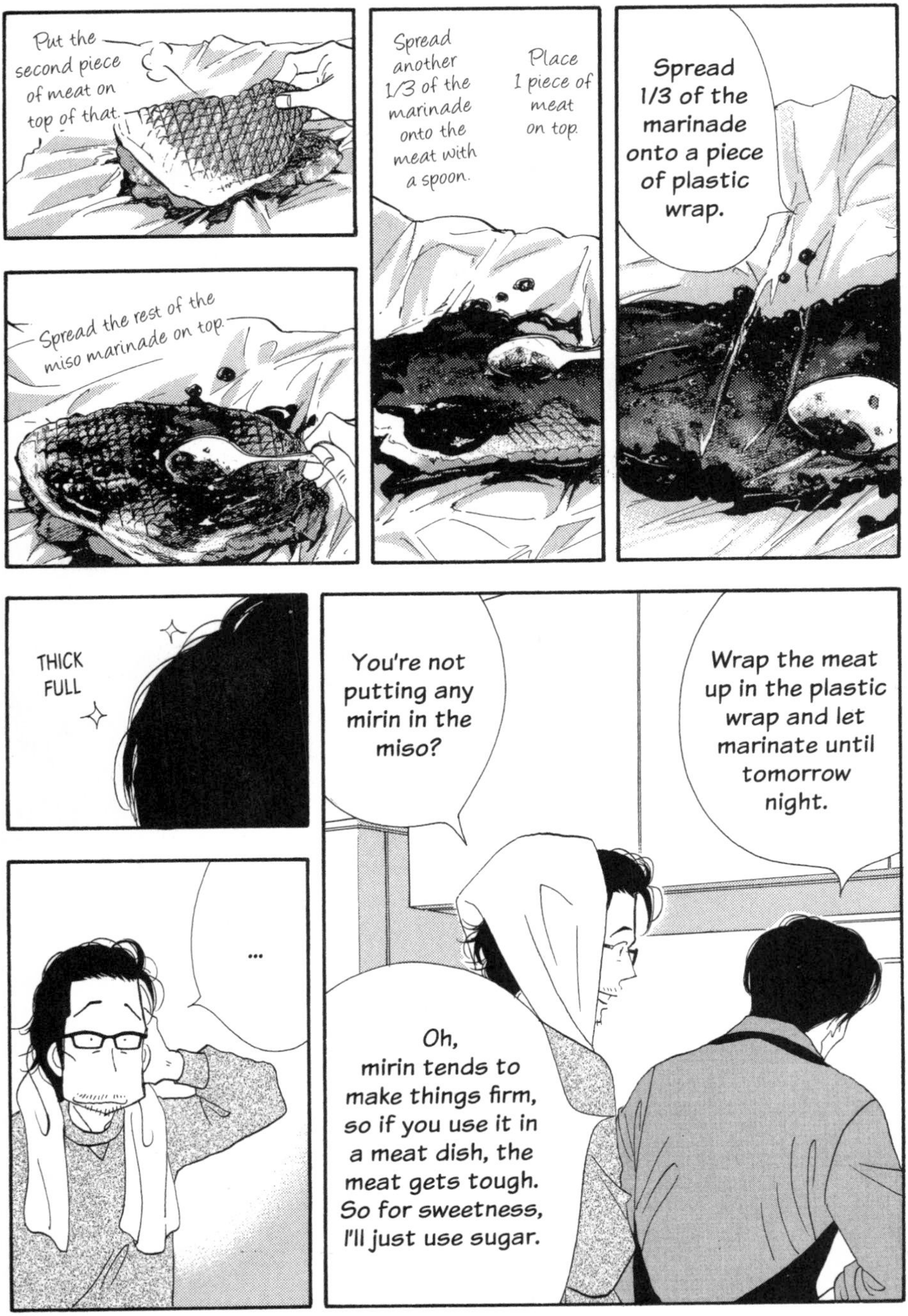
Spread 1/3 of the marinade onto a piece of plastic wrap.
Place 1 piece of meat on top.
Spread another 1/3 of the marinade onto the meat with a spoon.
Put the second piece of meat on top of that.
Spread the rest of the miso marinade on top.
Wrap the meat up in the plastic wrap and let marinate until tomorrow night.
You're not putting any mirin in the miso?
Oh, mirin tends to make things firm, so if you use it in a meat dish, the meat gets tough. So for sweetness, I'll just use sugar.
THICK
FULL
...

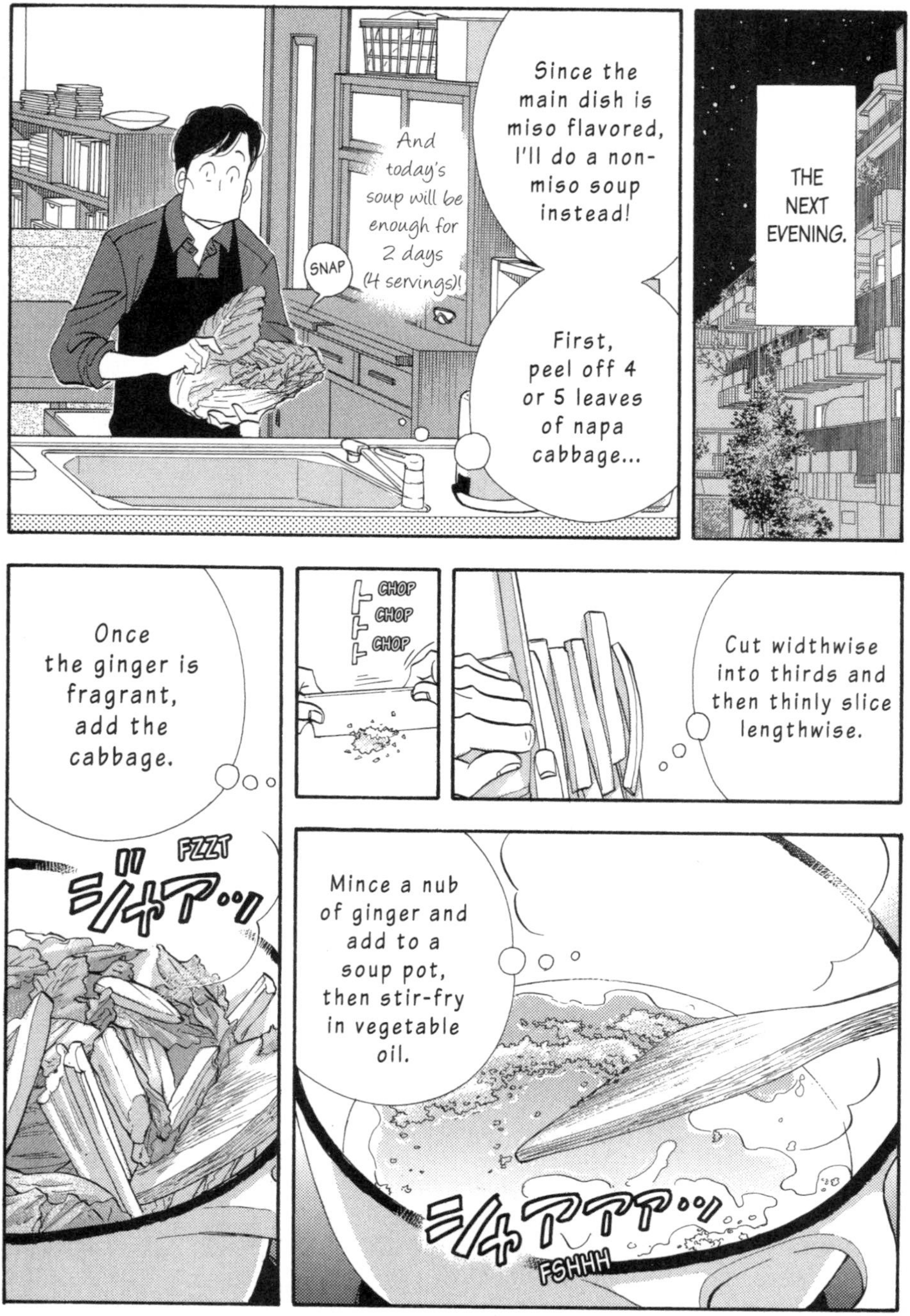
THE NEXT EVENING.
Since the main dish is miso flavored, I'll do a non-miso soup instead!
First, peel off 4 or 5 leaves of napa cabbage...
And today's soup will be enough for 2 days (4 servings)!
SNAP
Cut widthwise into thirds and then thinly slice lengthwise.
CHOP
CHOP
CHOP
Mince a nub of ginger and add to a soup pot, then stir-fry in vegetable oil.
FSHHH
Once the ginger is fragrant, add the cabbage.
FZZT

POP
Add 1 can of water-packed scallops, 1 light C water, and a dash of chicken bouillon, and simmer.
Okay, while that's cooking, I'll drain the tofu.
Wrap 1/4 block of tofu in a paper towel and microwave for 1 minute...
BEEP BEEP BEEP
Once it's heated up, wrap tofu in a fresh paper towel.
Careful not to burn yourself!!
Place a weight on top and let sit for a while.
The cabbage should be cooked through by now. Add 1 C milk.
BUBBLE
BUBBLE
BUBBLE

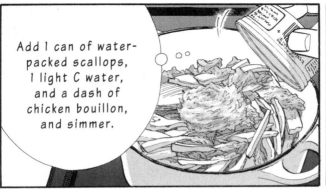

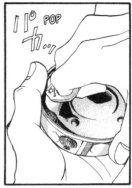

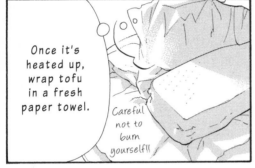

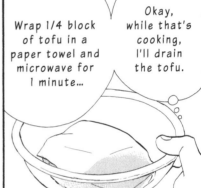

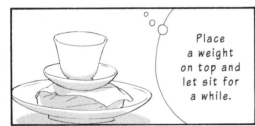

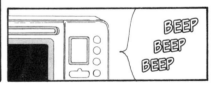

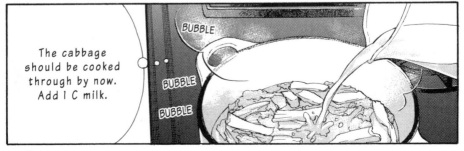

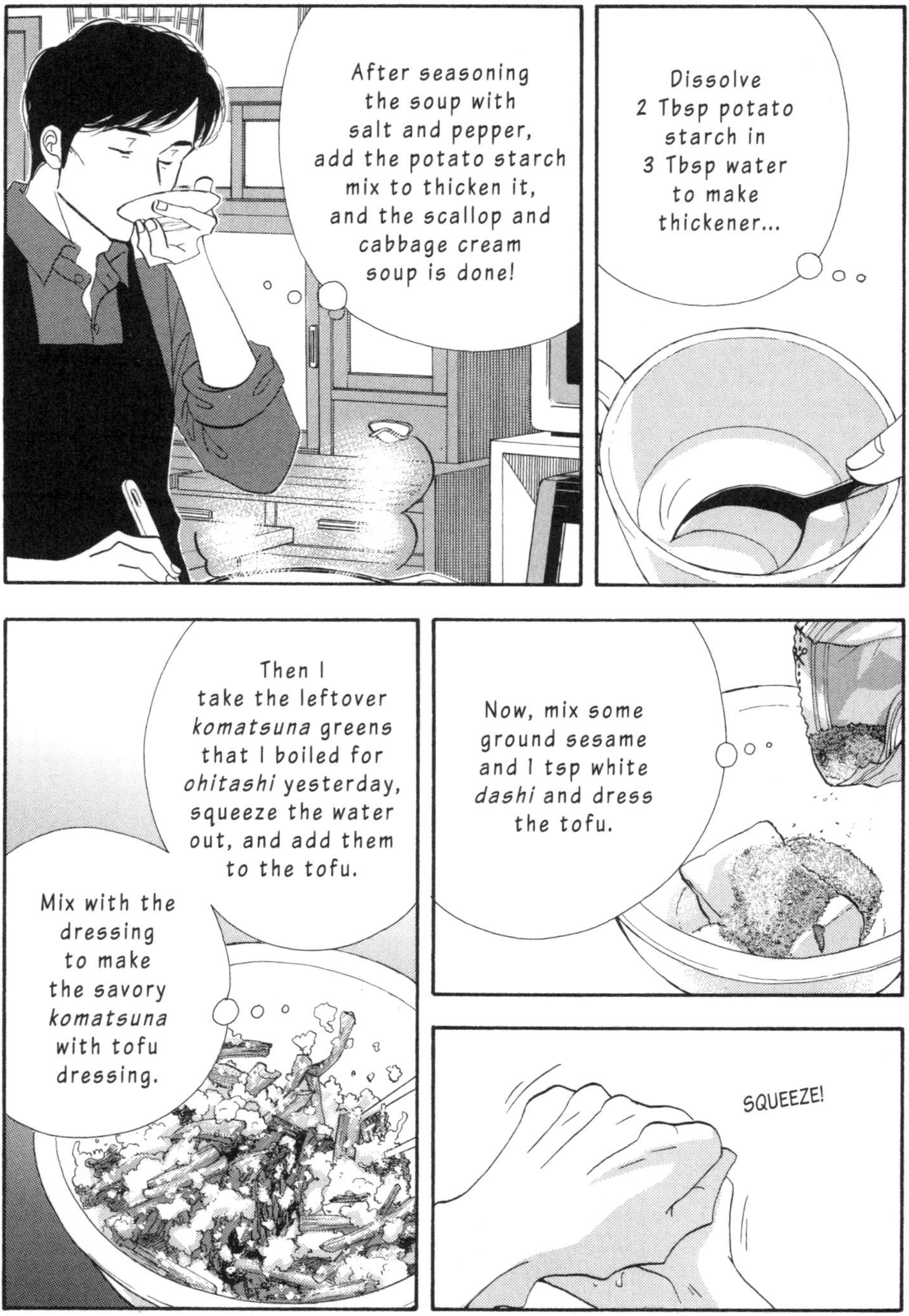
Dissolve 2 Tbsp potato starch in 3 Tbsp water to make thickener...
After seasoning the soup with salt and pepper, add the potato starch mix to thicken it, and the scallop and cabbage cream soup is done!
Now, mix some ground sesame and 1 tsp white dashi and dress the tofu.
SQUEEZE!
Then I take the leftover komatsuna greens that I boiled for ohitashi yesterday, squeeze the water out, and add them to the tofu.
Mix with the dressing to make the savory komatsuna with tofu dressing.

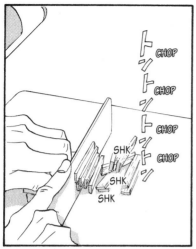

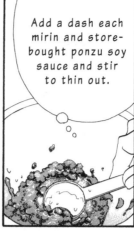

Remove the pit from an *umeboshi* plum and then mash.
Add a dash each mirin and store-bought ponzu soy sauce and stir to thin out.
トントントントン
CHOP
CHOP
CHOP
CHOP
SHK
SHK
SHK
Take a 4" piece of yam, halve lengthwise, and slice into thin rectangles before roughly mixing in the plum dressing.
Add a little wasabi and a packet of shredded nori seaweed, and the plum-dressed yam is done.
Of course, you can use crushed nori instead of shredded.
Now all that's left is to wait for Kenji to come home, and then I'll cook up the miso marinated pork!
I'm home!

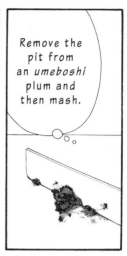

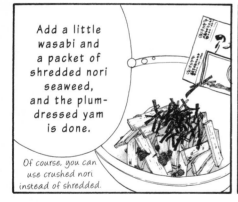

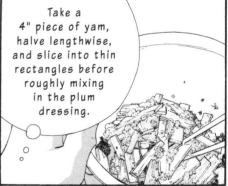

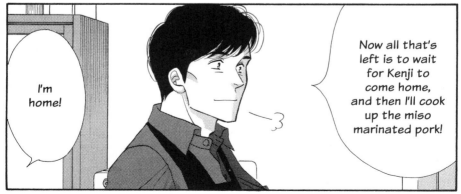

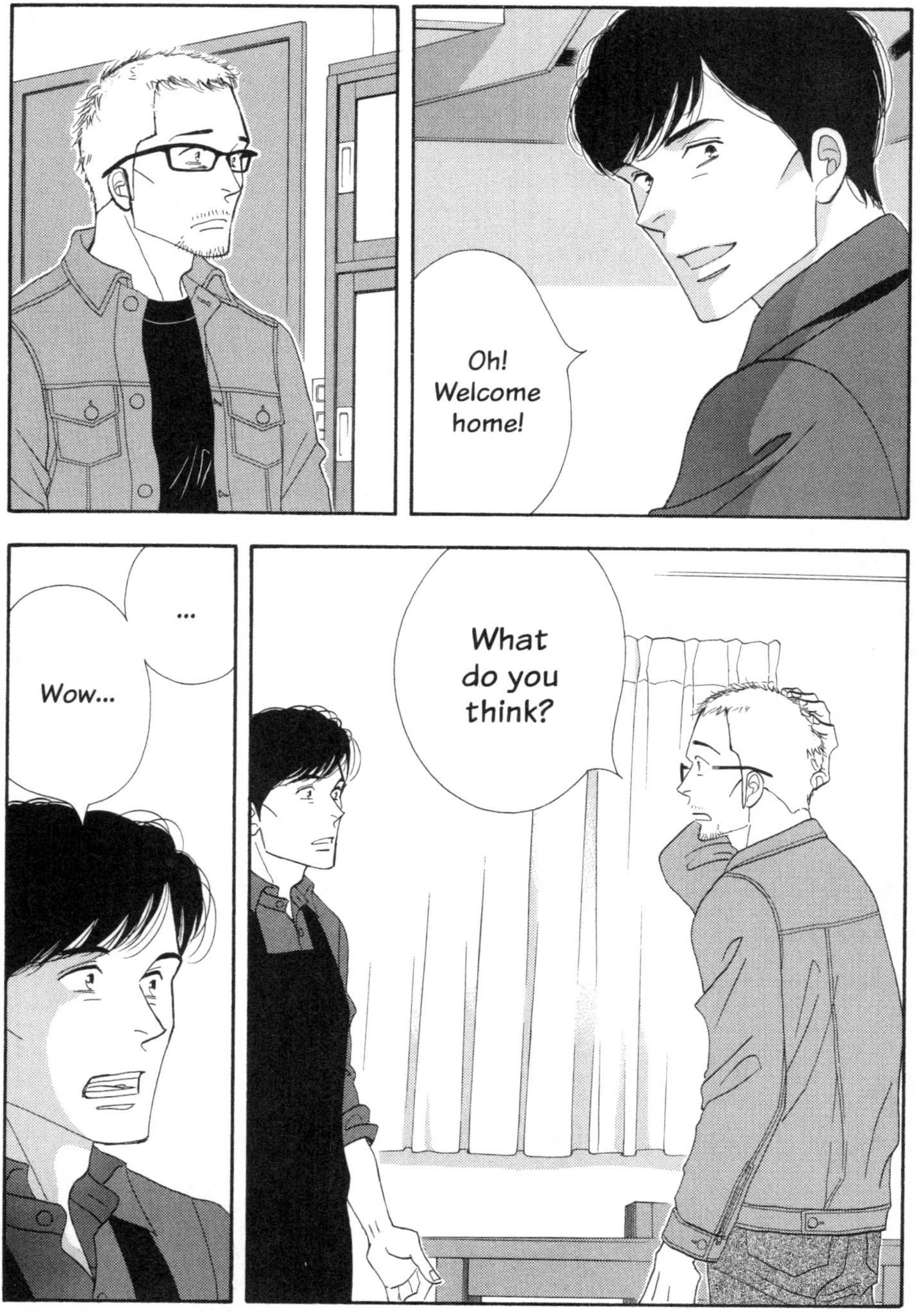
Oh! Welcome home!
What do you think?
...
Wow...

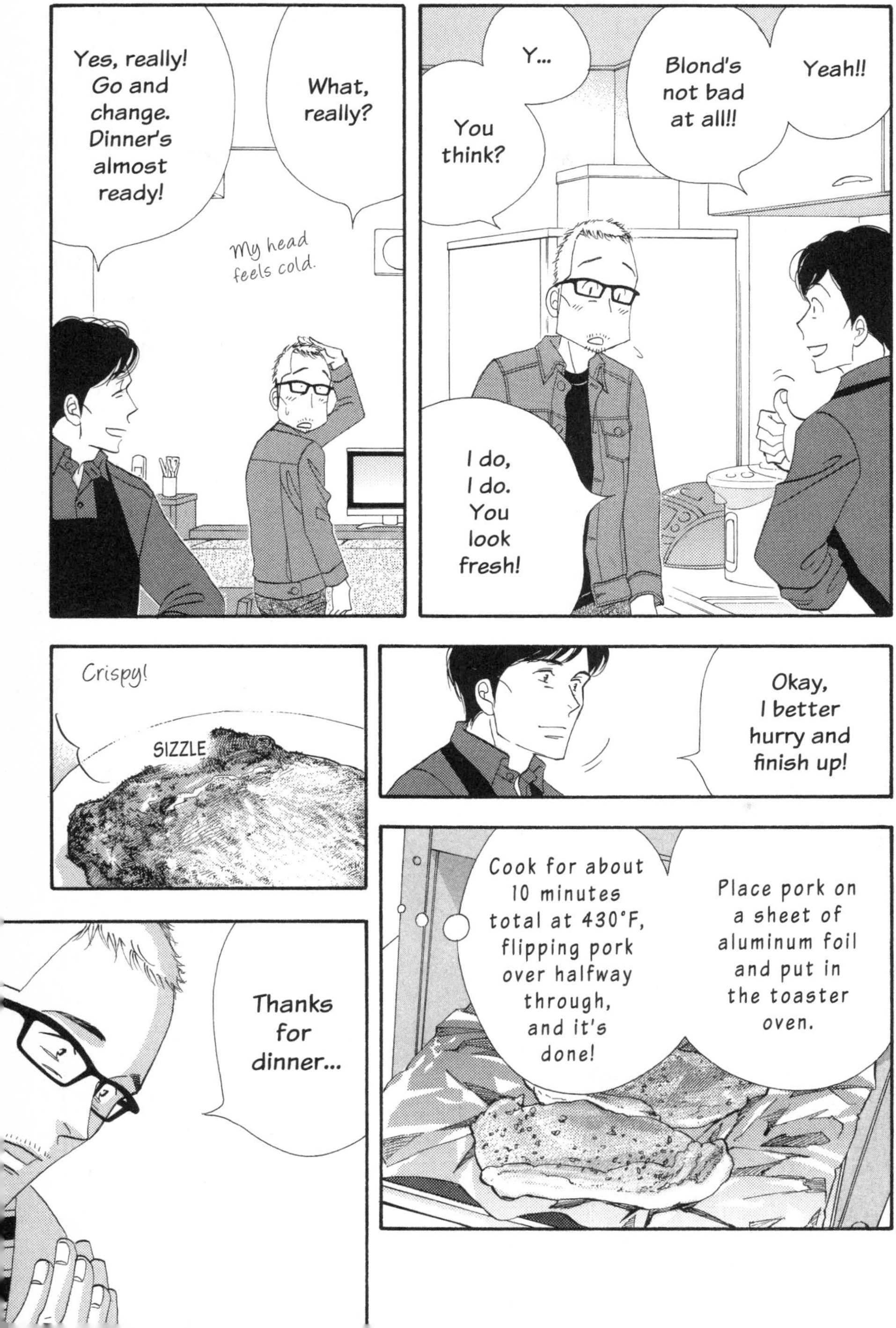
Yeah!!
Blond's not bad at all!!
Y...
You think?
I do, I do. You look fresh!
What, really?
Yes, really! Go and change. Dinner's almost ready!
My head feels cold.
Okay, I better hurry and finish up!
Crispy!
SIZZLE
Place pork on a sheet of aluminum foil and put in the toaster oven.
Cook for about 10 minutes total at 430°F, flipping pork over halfway through, and it's done!
Thanks for dinner...

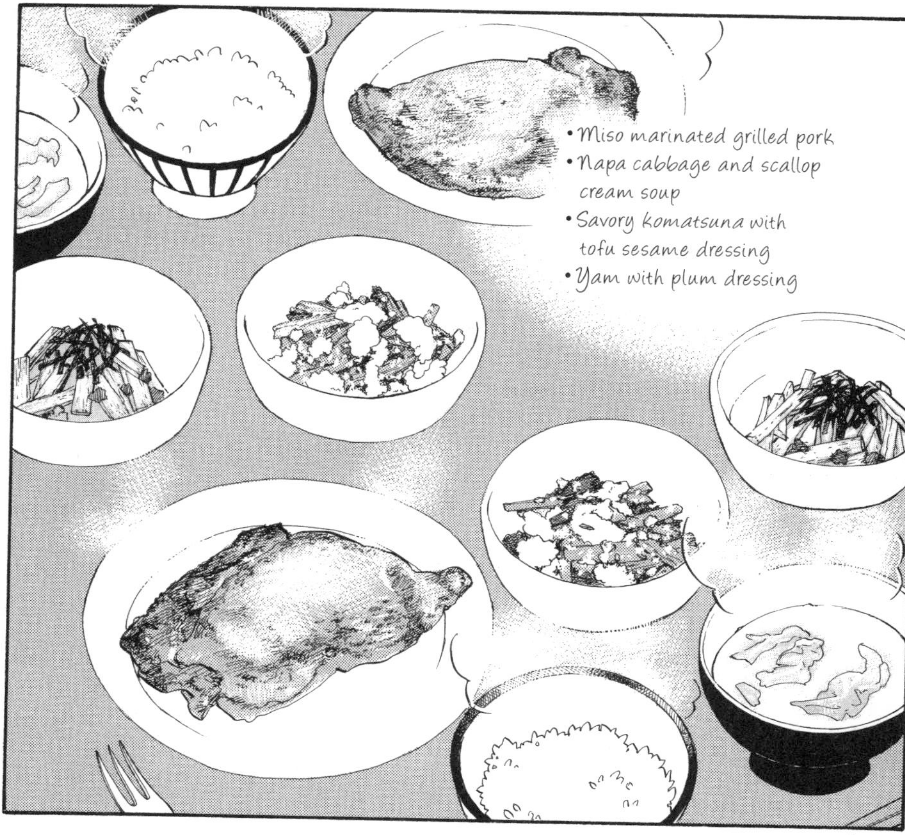
• Miso marinated grilled pork
• Napa cabbage and scallop cream soup
• Savory komatsuna with tofu sesame dressing
• Yam with plum dressing

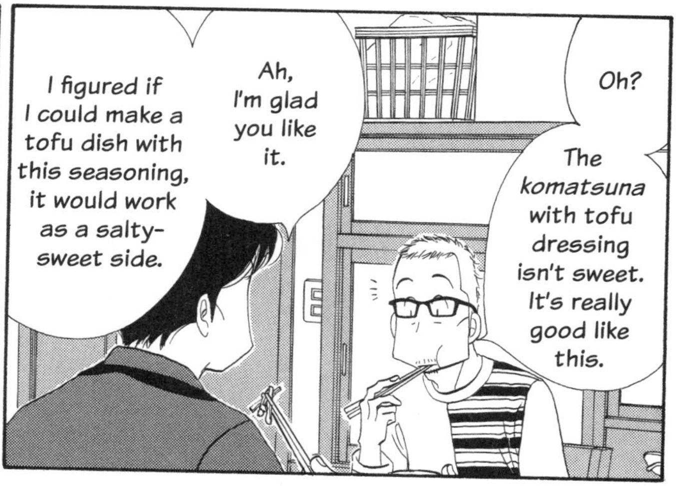
Oh?
The komatsuna with tofu dressing isn't sweet. It's really good like this.
Ah, I'm glad you like it.
I figured if I could make a tofu dish with this seasoning, it would work as a salty-sweet side.

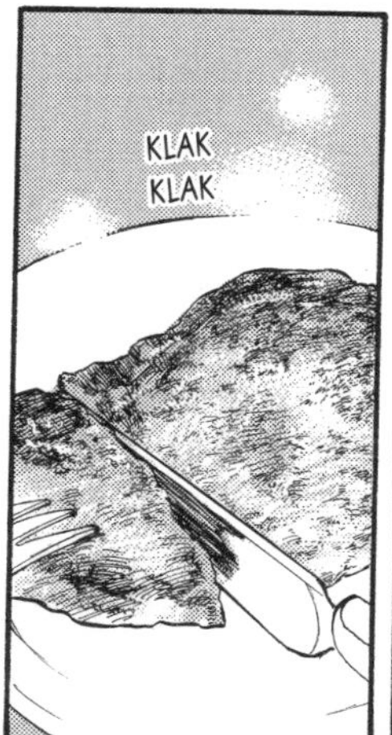
KLAK
KLAK

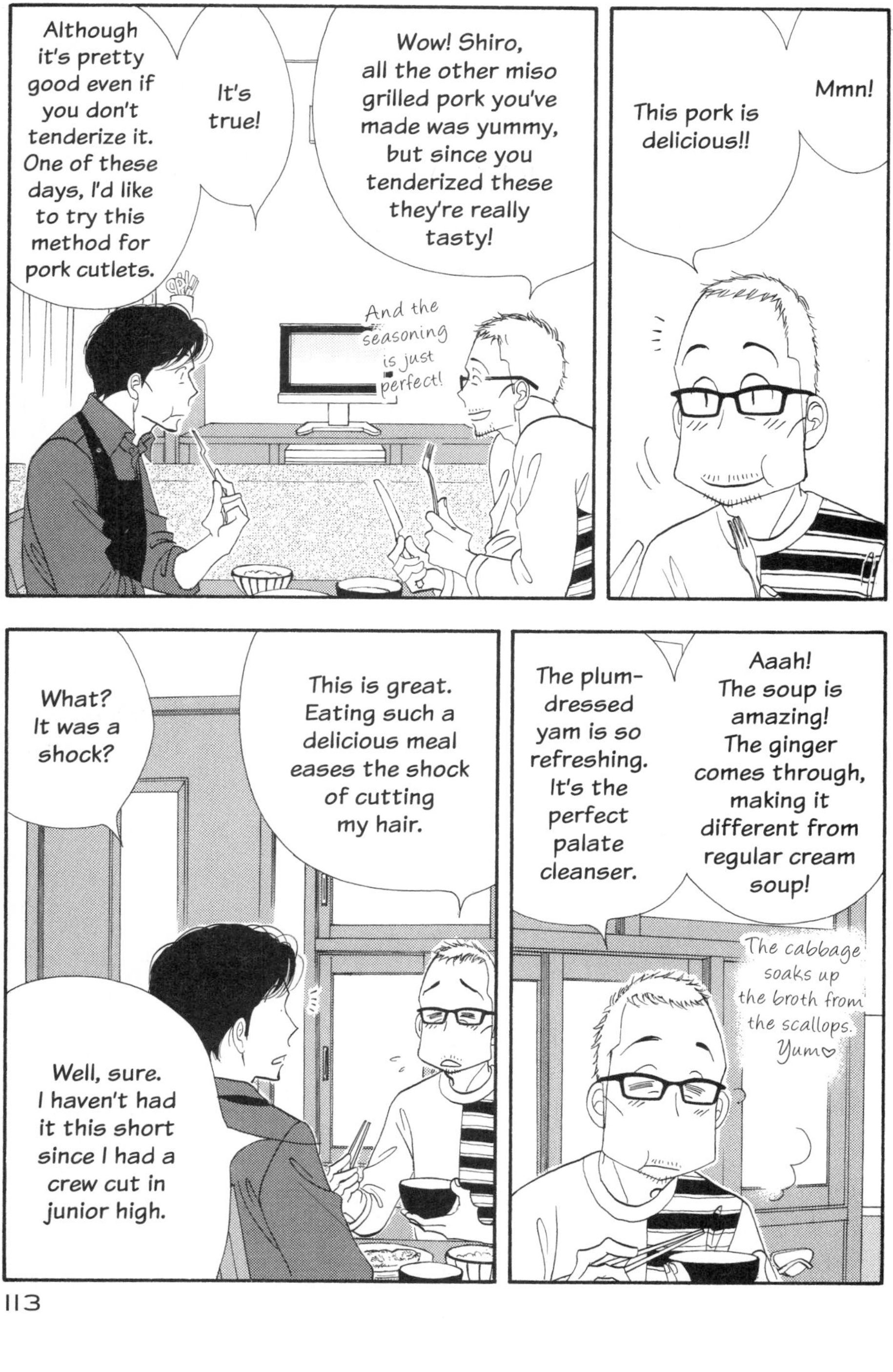
Mmn!
This pork is delicious!!
Wow! Shiro, all the other miso grilled pork you've made was yummy, but since you tenderized these they're really tasty!
And the seasoning is just perfect!
It's true!
Although it's pretty good even if you don't tenderize it. One of these days, I'd like to try this method for pork cutlets.
Aaah! The soup is amazing! The ginger comes through, making it different from regular cream soup!
The plum-dressed yam is so refreshing. It's the perfect palate cleanser.
The cabbage soaks up the broth from the scallops. Yum♡
This is great. Eating such a delicious meal eases the shock of cutting my hair.
What? It was a shock?
Well, sure. I haven't had it this short since I had a crew cut in junior high.

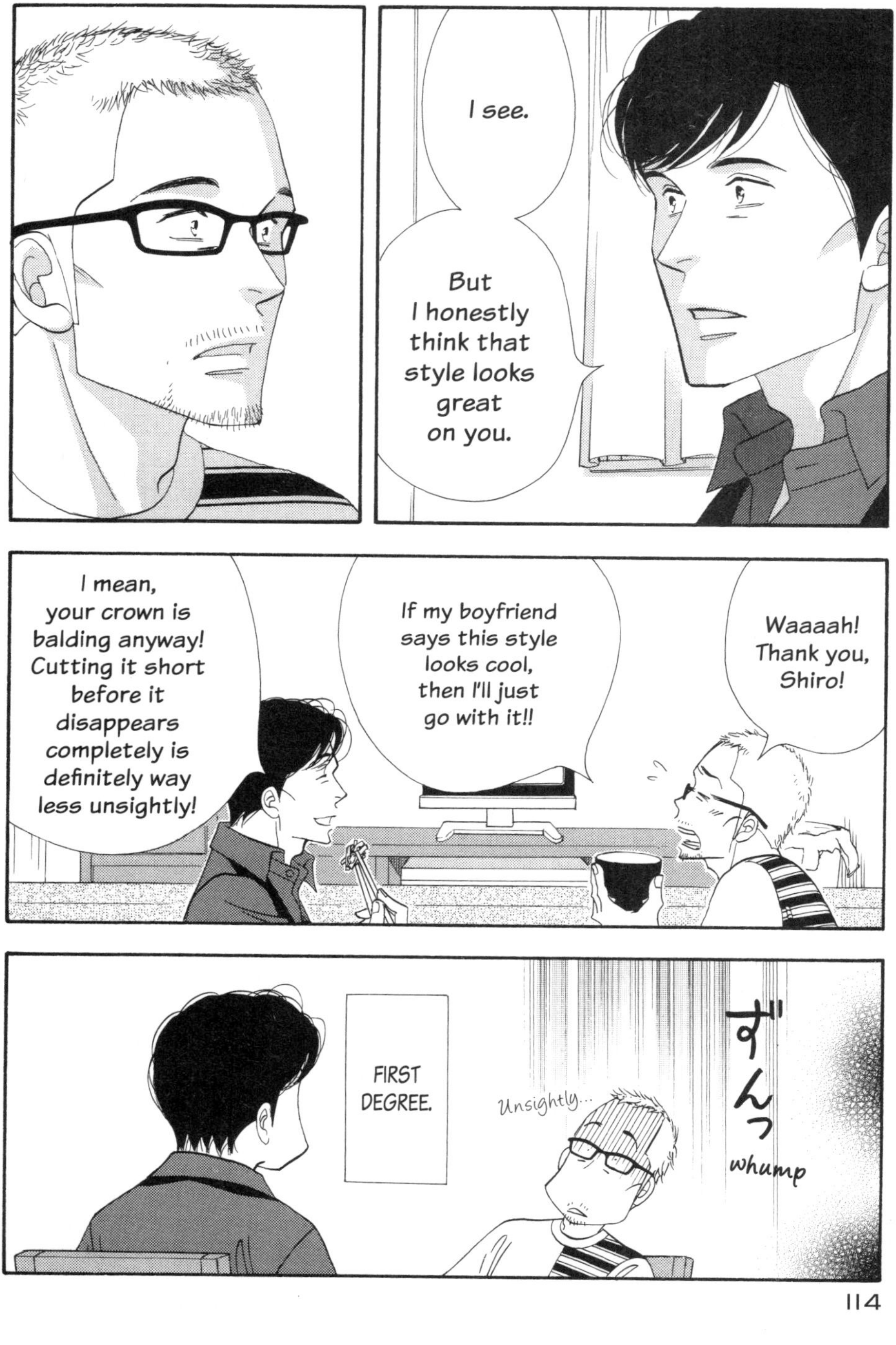
I see.
But I honestly think that style looks great on you.
Waaaah! Thank you, Shiro!
If my boyfriend says this style looks cool, then I'll just go with it!!
I mean, your crown is balding anyway! Cutting it short before it disappears completely is definitely way less unsightly!
ずんっ
whump
Unsightly...
FIRST DEGREE.

In this chapter,
the miso used for
the **marinated pork** is
Shinshu (yellow) miso.
Please season the pork to taste
in accordance with the saltiness
of the miso you have on hand.
You can also substitute soy sauce
if you don't have *yakiniku* sauce.

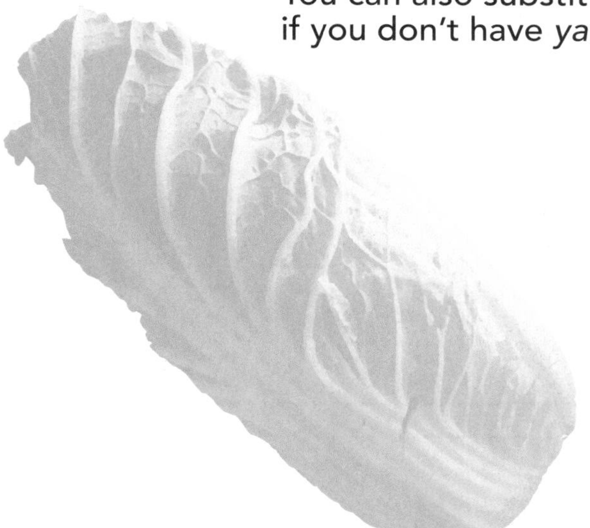

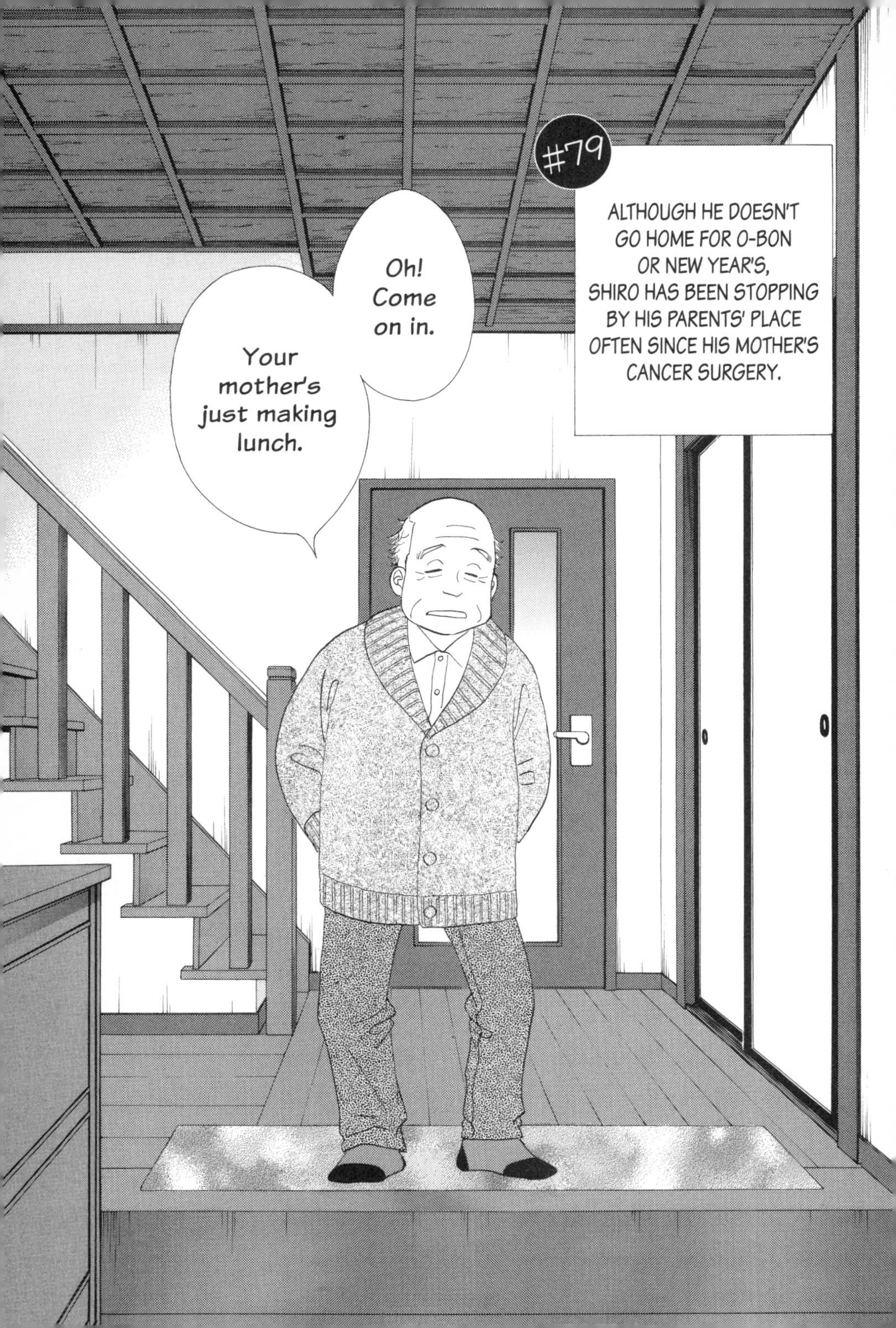
#79
ALTHOUGH HE DOESN'T GO HOME FOR O-BON OR NEW YEAR'S, SHIRO HAS BEEN STOPPING BY HIS PARENTS' PLACE OFTEN SINCE HIS MOTHER'S CANCER SURGERY.
Oh! Come on in.
Your mother's just making lunch.

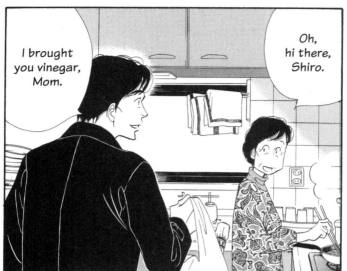

FSHHH
Oh, hi there, Shiro.
I brought you vinegar, Mom.
Oh, thanks so much. I was going to use some today, and then I looked and saw the bottle was empty.
Vinegar is like that. You only ever use a bit at a time, so you don't notice when it's nearly gone.
I also stopped in front of the station and picked up some sweets.
He brought us cake and cookies.
HE DOESN'T GO FOR ANY PARTICULAR REASON. HE STOPS BY ON HIS DAY OFF ONCE OR TWICE A MONTH JUST TO HAVE LUNCH.
Ah, I'll just run to the bathroom.

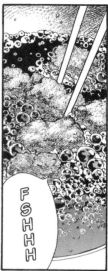

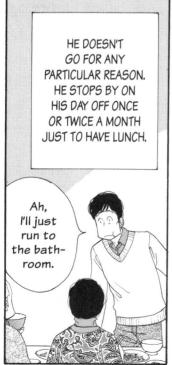

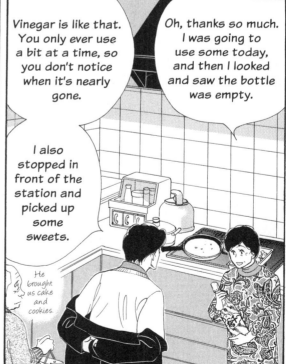

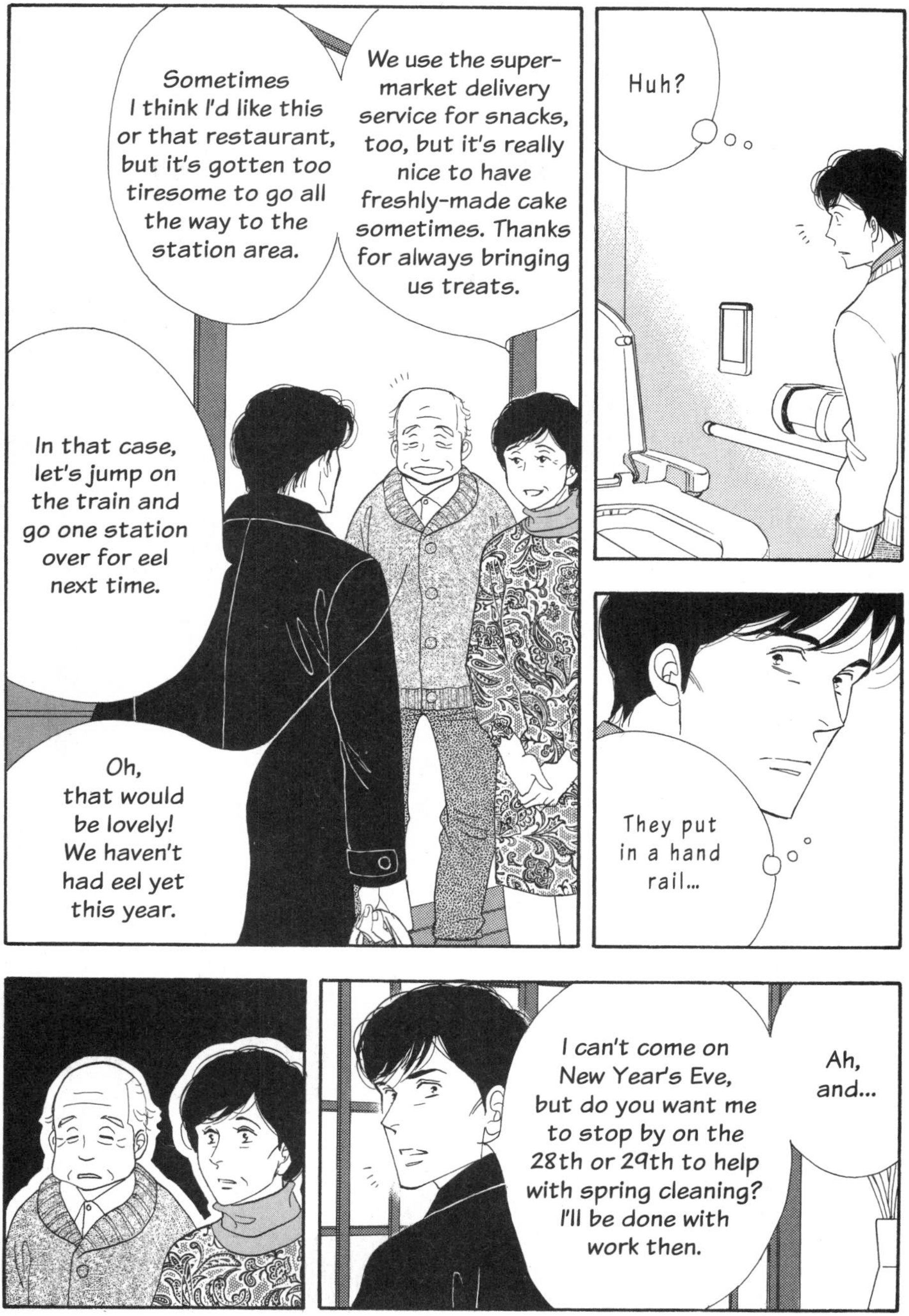
Huh?
They put in a hand rail...
We use the super-market delivery service for snacks, too, but it's really nice to have freshly-made cake sometimes. Thanks for always bringing us treats.
Sometimes I think I'd like this or that restaurant, but it's gotten too tiresome to go all the way to the station area.
In that case, let's jump on the train and go one station over for eel next time.
Oh, that would be lovely! We haven't had eel yet this year.
Ah, and...
I can't come on New Year's Eve, but do you want me to stop by on the 28th or 29th to help with spring cleaning? I'll be done with work then.

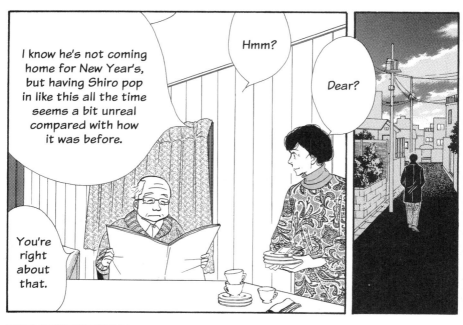

Dear?
Hmm?
I know he's not coming home for New Year's, but having Shiro pop in like this all the time seems a bit unreal compared with how it was before.
You're right about that.
Honey...
We need to make sure we stay healthy so we don't give that boy too much trouble.
True, true.
So I'll be at my folks' place all day on the 29th to help out with spring cleaning. Can you fend for yourself for dinner that night?
Sure, no problem!

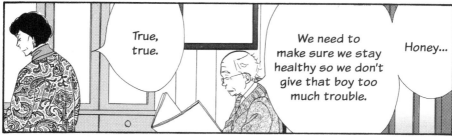

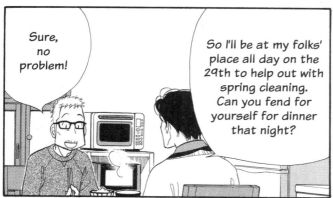

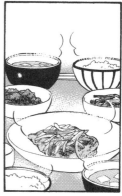

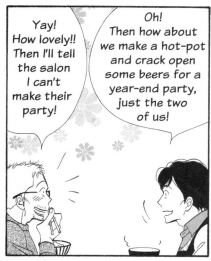

I'm done with work on the 26th this year. You?
Umm, just like last year, the salon's open until the 30th, but we're closing an hour earlier at 7 that night.
Oh! Then how about we make a hot-pot and crack open some beers for a year-end party, just the two of us!
Yay! How lovely!! Then I'll tell the salon I can't make their party!
Heh heh heh! So, Hiro, I'm doing a romantic hot-pot with my boyfriend on the 30th, which means I'll have to miss the year-end party ♡ Sorry ♡
Okay! I'm not jealous at all so go ahead ♡
AND THEN THE 29TH.
Okay, first, let's take the light covers off and clean those!

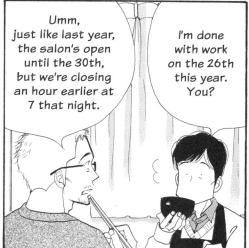

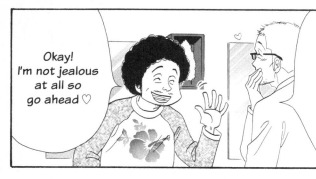

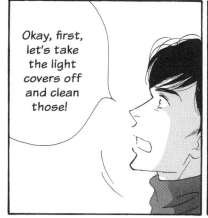

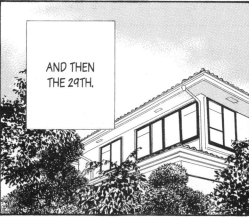

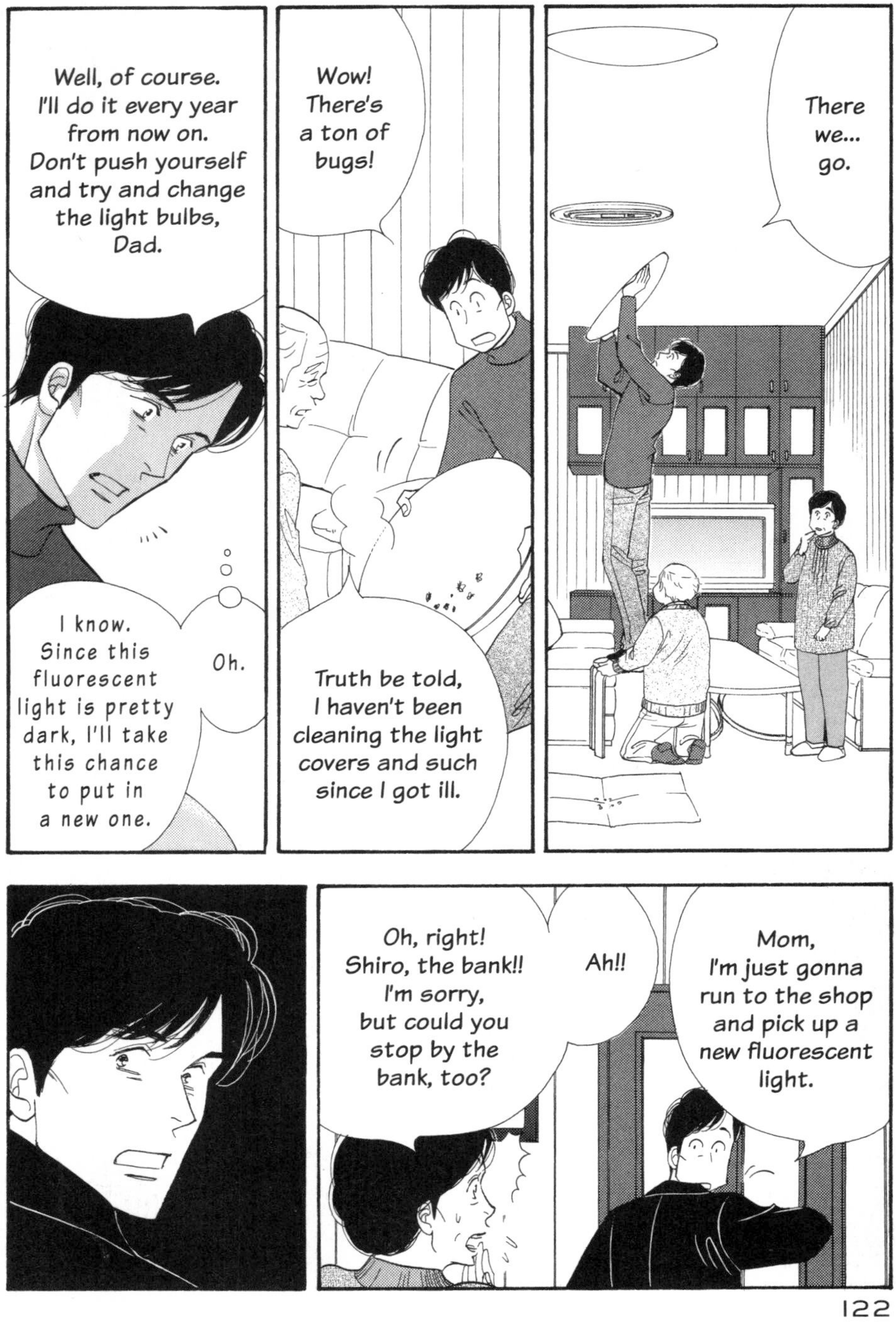
There we... go.
Wow! There's a ton of bugs!
Truth be told, I haven't been cleaning the light covers and such since I got ill.
Well, of course. I'll do it every year from now on. Don't push yourself and try and change the light bulbs, Dad.
Oh.
I know. Since this fluorescent light is pretty dark, I'll take this chance to put in a new one.
Mom, I'm just gonna run to the shop and pick up a new fluorescent light.
Ah!!
Oh, right! Shiro, the bank!! I'm sorry, but could you stop by the bank, too?

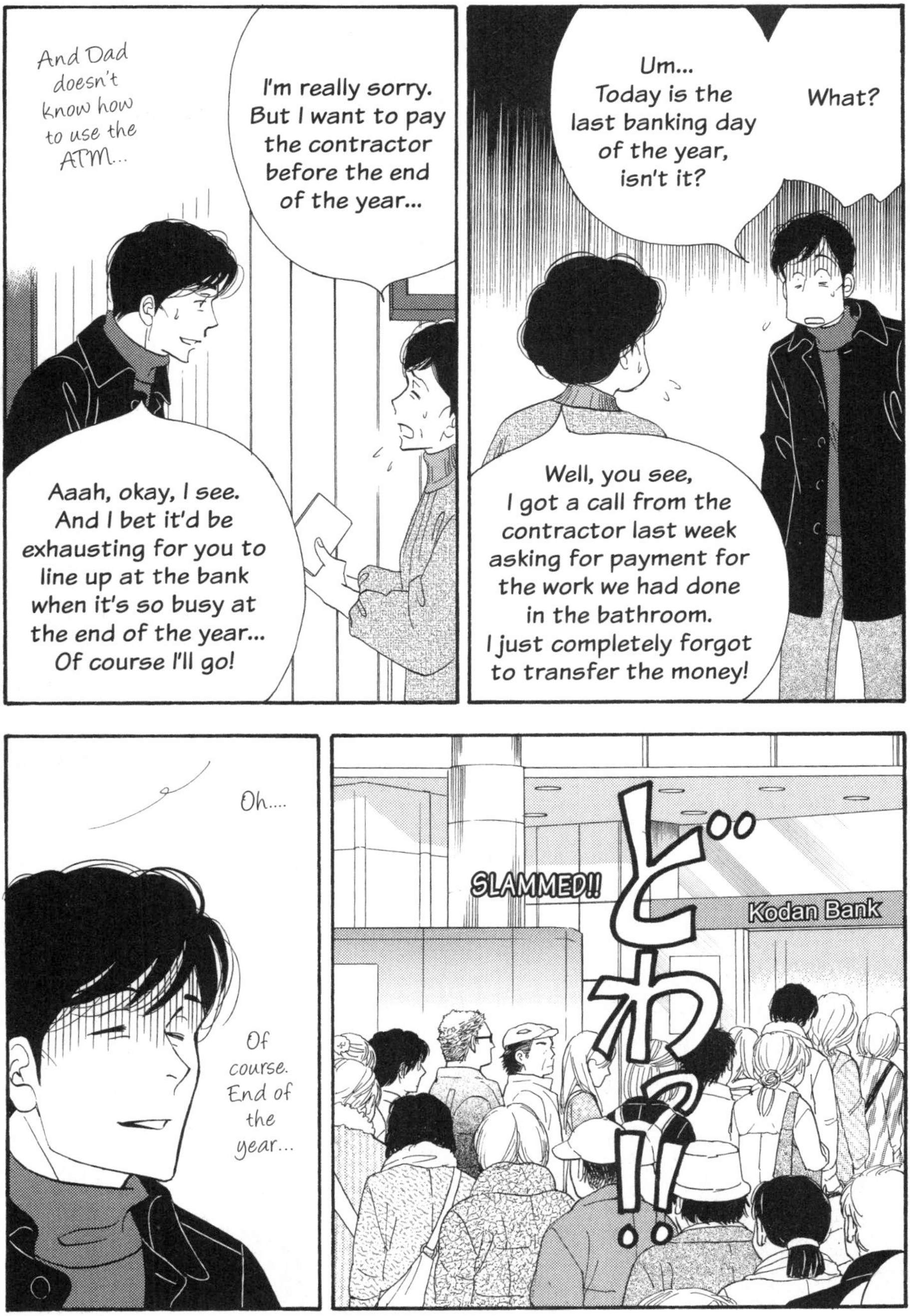
What?
Um... Today is the last banking day of the year, isn't it?
Well, you see, I got a call from the contractor last week asking for payment for the work we had done in the bathroom. I just completely forgot to transfer the money!
I'm really sorry. But I want to pay the contractor before the end of the year...
And Dad doesn't know how to use the ATM...
Aaah, okay, I see. And I bet it'd be exhausting for you to line up at the bank when it's so busy at the end of the year... Of course I'll go!
どわっ!!
SLAMMED!!
Kodan Bank
Oh....
Of course. End of the year...

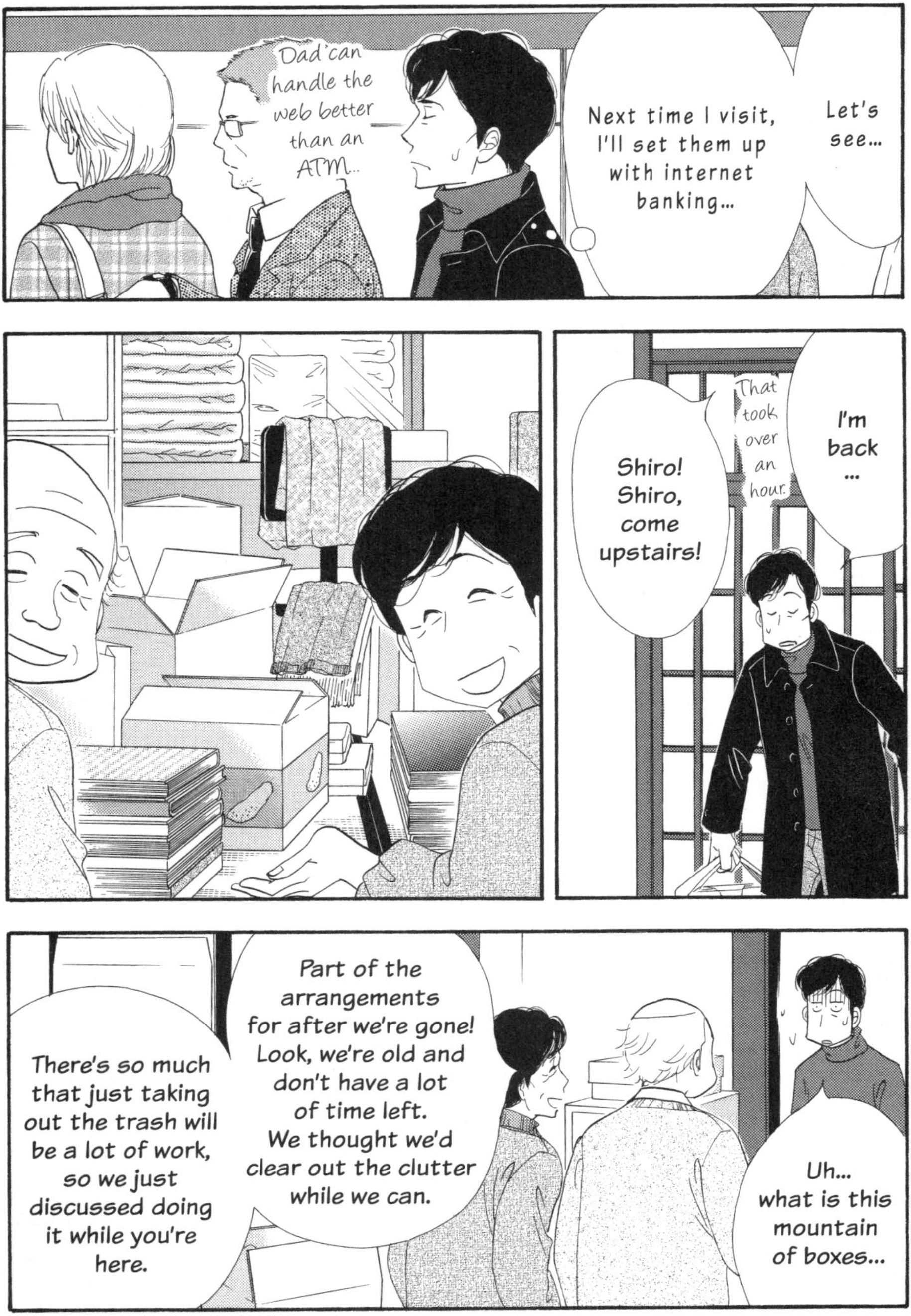
Let's see...
Next time I visit, I'll set them up with internet banking...
Dad can handle the web better than an ATM...
I'm back...
That took over an hour.
Shiro! Shiro, come upstairs!
Uh... what is this mountain of boxes...
Part of the arrangements for after we're gone! Look, we're old and don't have a lot of time left. We thought we'd clear out the clutter while we can.
There's so much that just taking out the trash will be a lot of work, so we just discussed doing it while you're here.

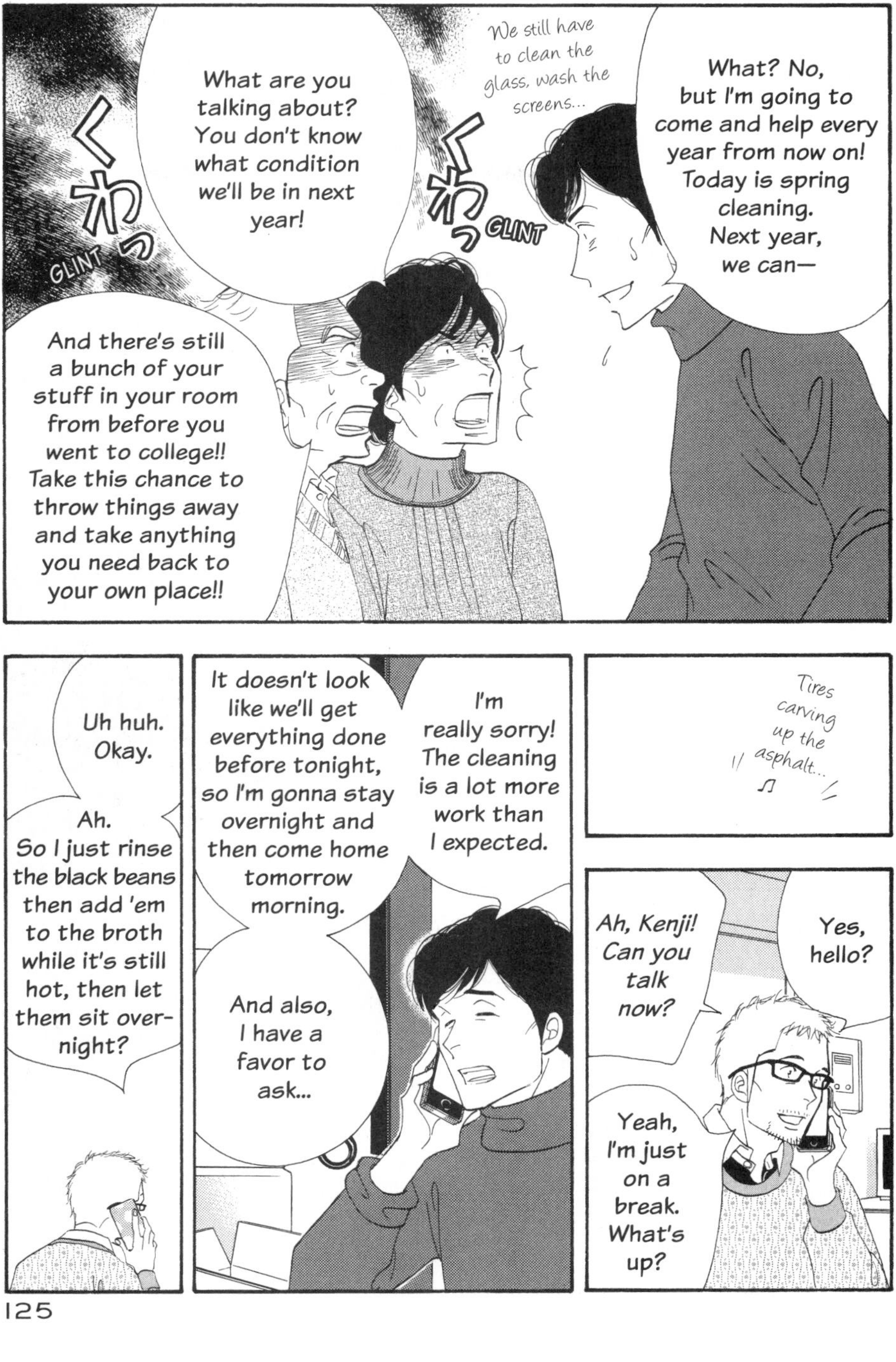

What? No, but I'm going to come and help every year from now on! Today is spring cleaning. Next year, we can—
We still have to clean the glass, wash the screens...
くわっ GLINT
What are you talking about? You don't know what condition we'll be in next year!
くわっ GLINT
And there's still a bunch of your stuff in your room from before you went to college!! Take this chance to throw things away and take anything you need back to your own place!!
Tires carving up the asphalt... ♫
Yes, hello?
Ah, Kenji! Can you talk now?
Yeah, I'm just on a break. What's up?
I'm really sorry! The cleaning is a lot more work than I expected.
It doesn't look like we'll get everything done before tonight, so I'm gonna stay overnight and then come home tomorrow morning.
And also, I have a favor to ask...
Uh huh. Okay.
Ah. So I just rinse the black beans then add 'em to the broth while it's still hot, then let them sit over-night?

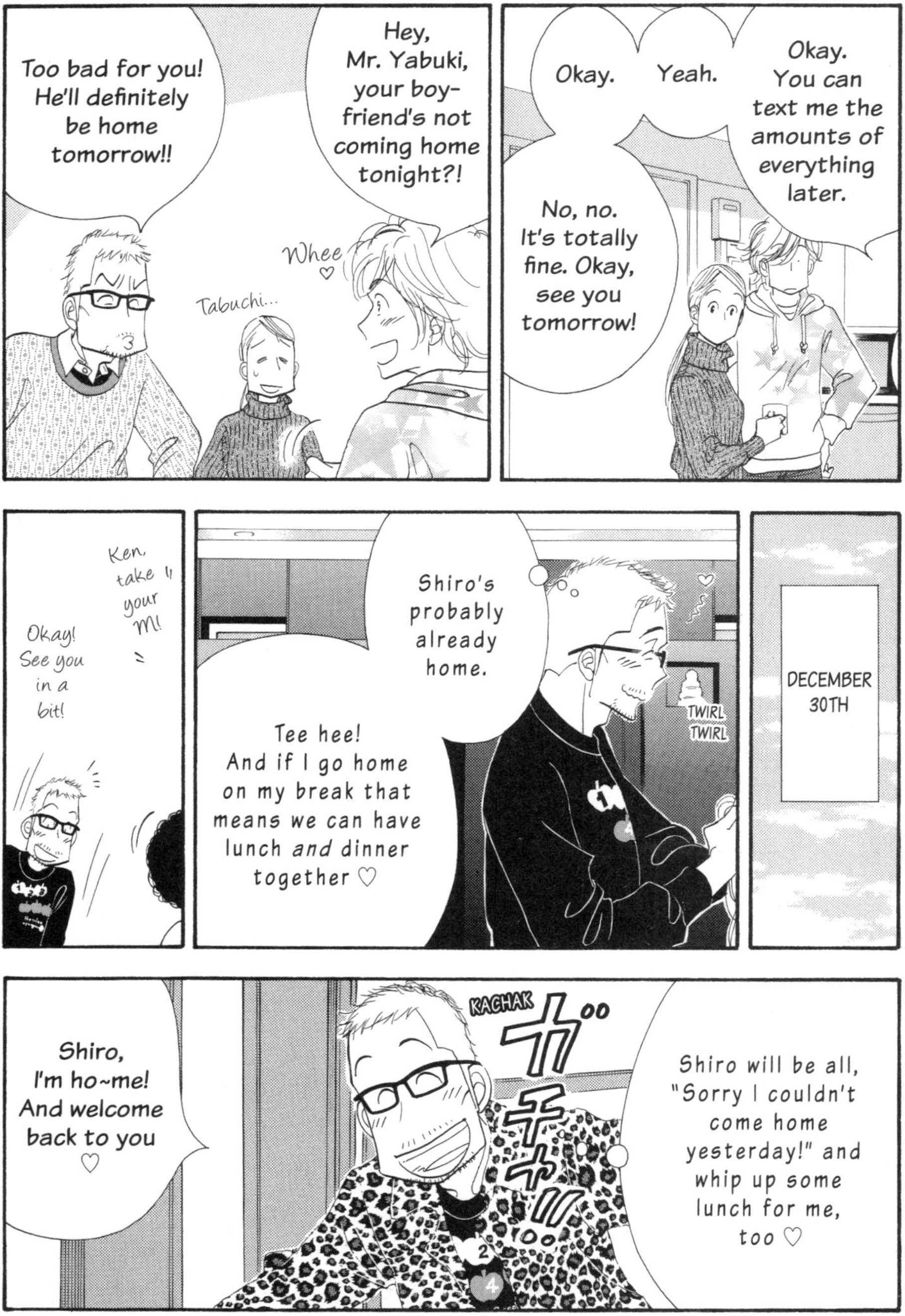
Okay. You can text me the amounts of everything later.
Yeah.
Okay.
No, no. It's totally fine. Okay, see you tomorrow!
Hey, Mr. Yabuki, your boy-friend's not coming home tonight?!
Too bad for you! He'll definitely be home tomorrow!!
Whee ♡
Tabuchi...
DECEMBER 30TH
Shiro's probably already home.
TWIRL TWIRL
Tee hee! And if I go home on my break that means we can have lunch *and* dinner together ♡
Ken, take your M!
Okay! See you in a bit!
Shiro will be all, "Sorry I couldn't come home yesterday!" and whip up some lunch for me, too ♡
KACHAK
Shiro, I'm ho~me! And welcome back to you ♡

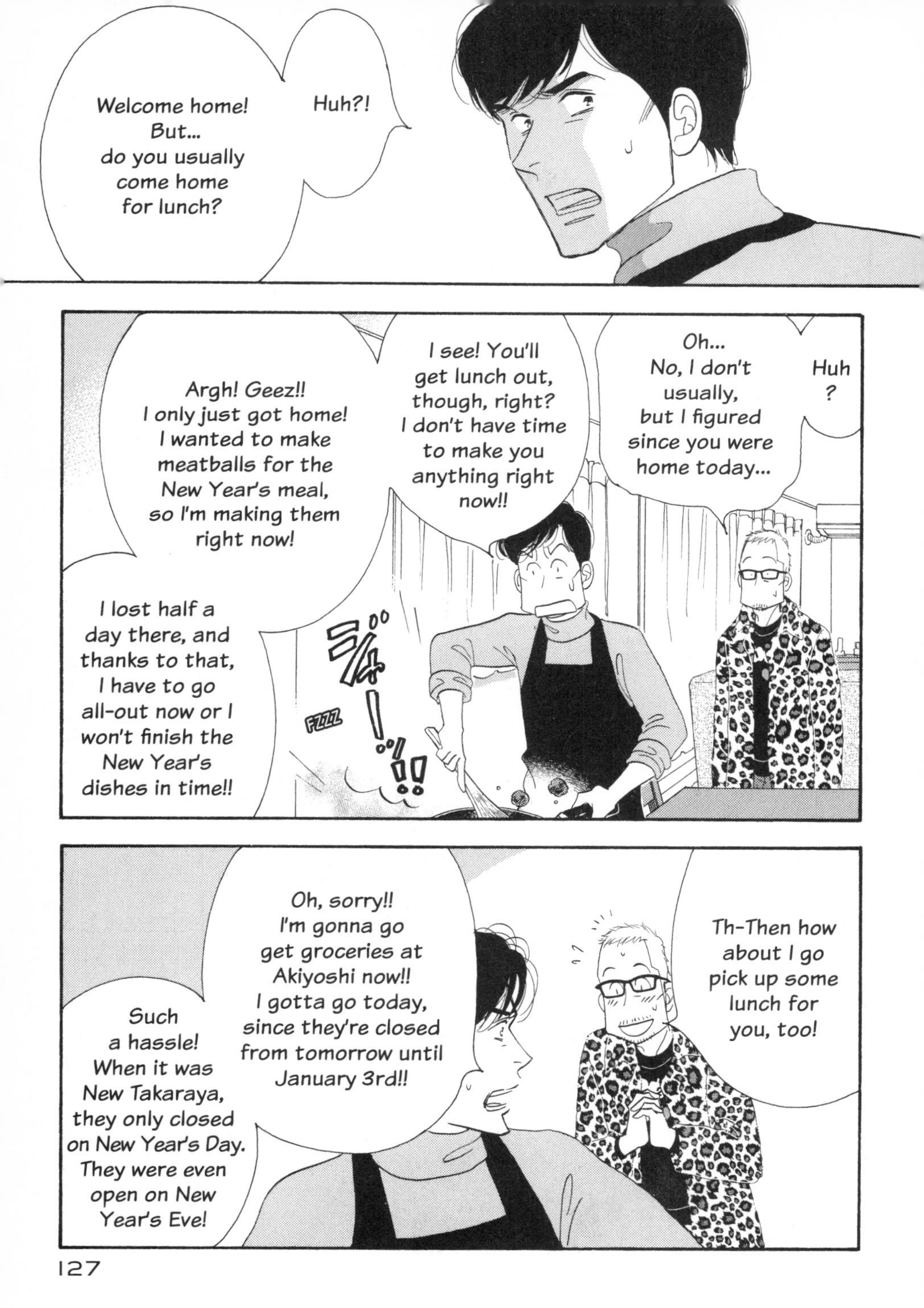
Huh?!
Welcome home! But... do you usually come home for lunch?
Huh ?
Oh... No, I don't usually, but I figured since you were home today...
I see! You'll get lunch out, though, right? I don't have time to make you anything right now!!
Argh! Geez!! I only just got home! I wanted to make meatballs for the New Year's meal, so I'm making them right now!
FZZZ
I lost half a day there, and thanks to that, I have to go all-out now or I won't finish the New Year's dishes in time!!
Th-Then how about I go pick up some lunch for you, too!
Oh, sorry!! I'm gonna go get groceries at Akiyoshi now!! I gotta go today, since they're closed from tomorrow until January 3rd!!
Such a hassle! When it was New Takaraya, they only closed on New Year's Day. They were even open on New Year's Eve!

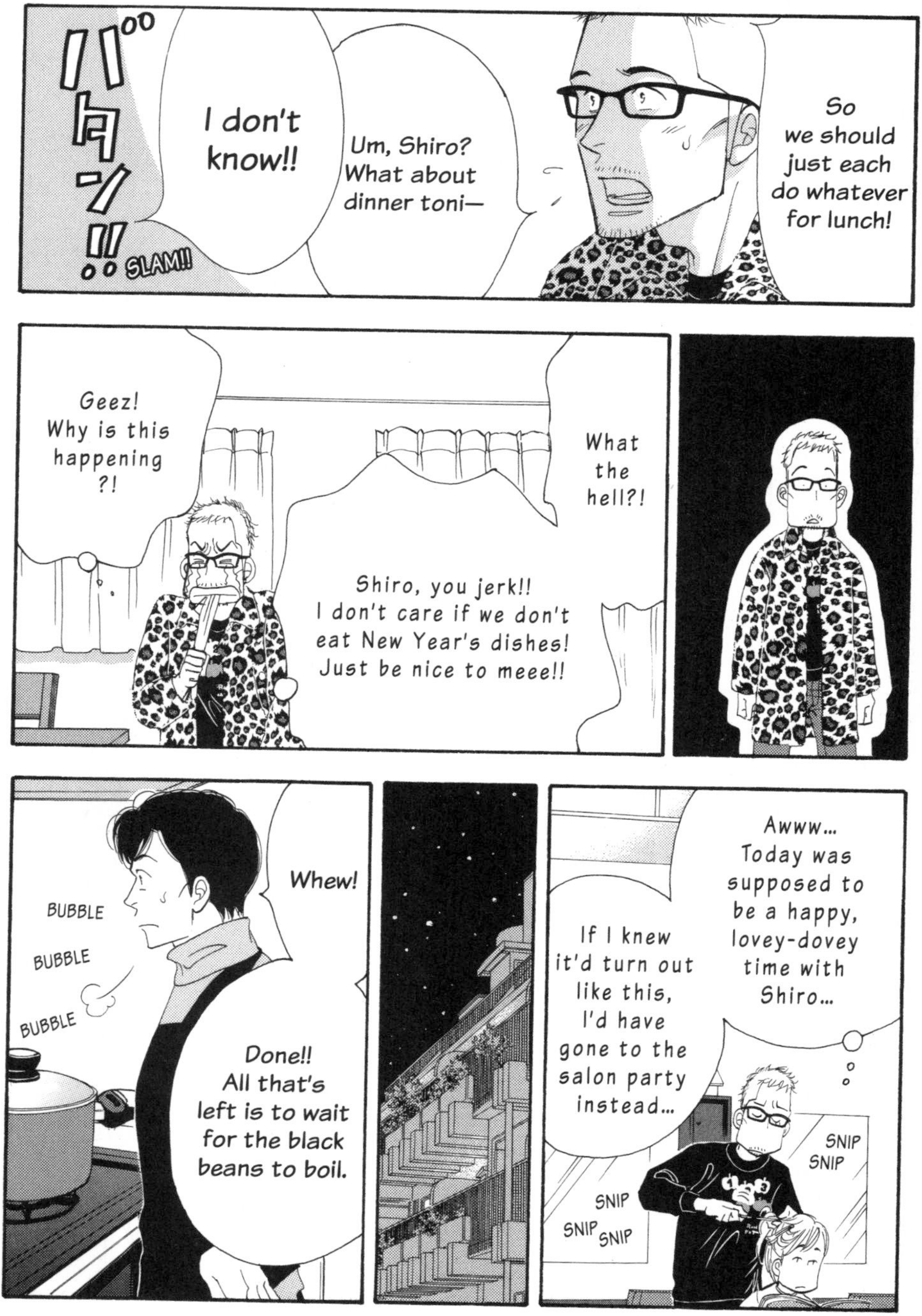
So we should just each do whatever for lunch!
Um, Shiro? What about dinner toni—
I don't know!!
バタン!!
SLAM!!
What the hell?!
Geez! Why is this happening?!
Shiro, you jerk!! I don't care if we don't eat New Year's dishes! Just be nice to meee!!
Awww... Today was supposed to be a happy, lovey-dovey time with Shiro...
If I knew it'd turn out like this, I'd have gone to the salon party instead...
SNIP SNIP
SNIP
SNIP SNIP
Whew!
BUBBLE
BUBBLE
BUBBLE
Done!! All that's left is to wait for the black beans to boil.

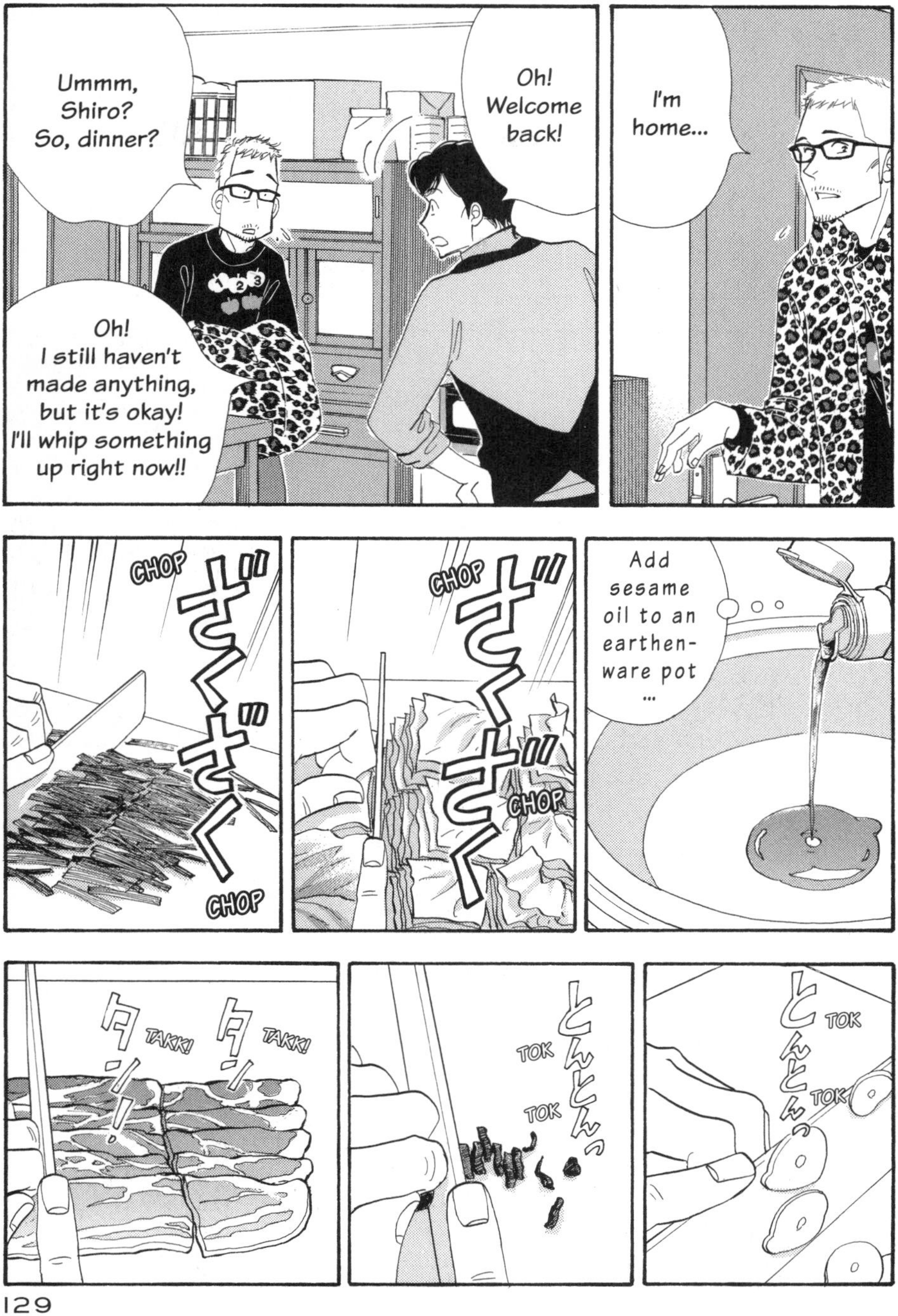
I'm home...
Oh! Welcome back!
Ummm, Shiro? So, dinner?
Oh! I still haven't made anything, but it's okay! I'll whip something up right now!!
Add sesame oil to an earthen-ware pot ...
ざくざく
CHOP
CHOP
ざくざく
CHOP
CHOP
とんとんっ
TOK
TOK
とんとんっ
TOK
TOK
タン！
TAKK!
タン！
TAKK!

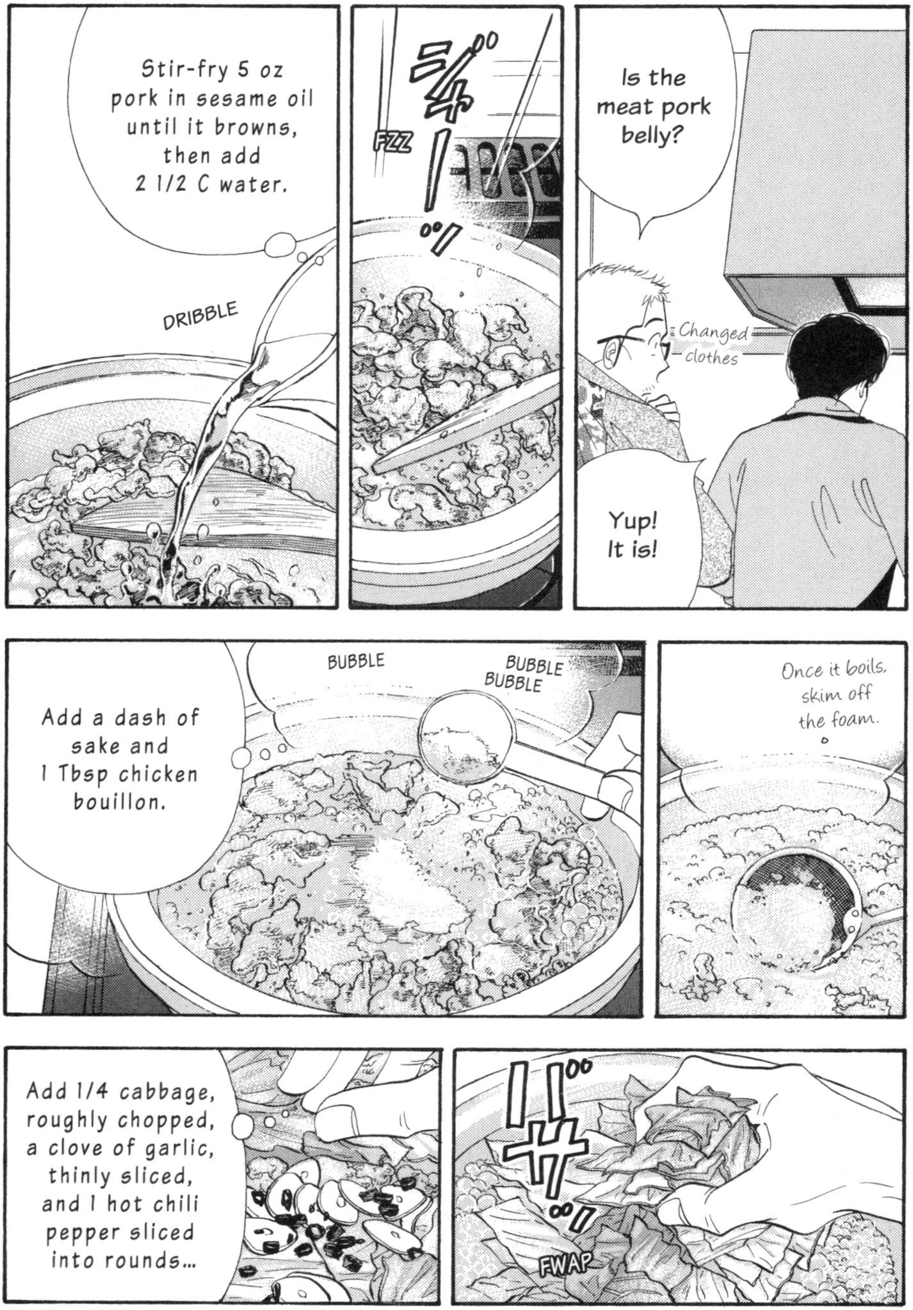
Is the meat pork belly?
Changed clothes
Yup! It is!
FZZ
Stir-fry 5 oz pork in sesame oil until it browns, then add 2 1/2 C water.
DRIBBLE
Once it boils, skim off the foam.
BUBBLE
BUBBLE
BUBBLE
Add a dash of sake and 1 Tbsp chicken bouillon.
FWAP
Add 1/4 cabbage, roughly chopped, a clove of garlic, thinly sliced, and 1 hot chili pepper sliced into rounds...

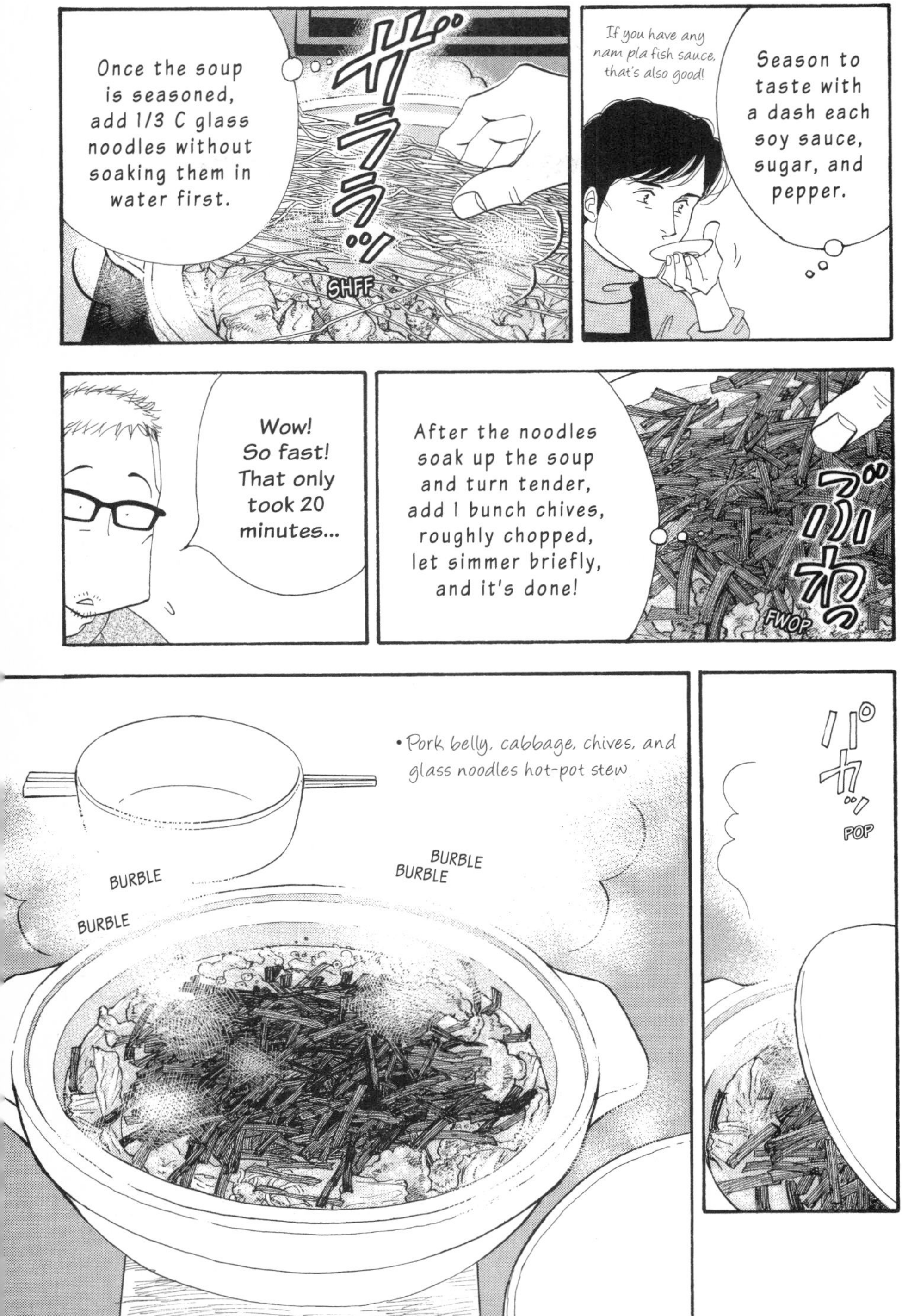

If you have any nam pla fish sauce, that's also good!
Season to taste with a dash each soy sauce, sugar, and pepper.
Once the soup is seasoned, add 1/3 C glass noodles without soaking them in water first.
SHFF
After the noodles soak up the soup and turn tender, add 1 bunch chives, roughly chopped, let simmer briefly, and it's done!
FWOP
Wow! So fast! That only took 20 minutes...
POP
• Pork belly, cabbage, chives, and glass noodles hot-pot stew
BURBLE
BURBLE
BURBLE
BURBLE

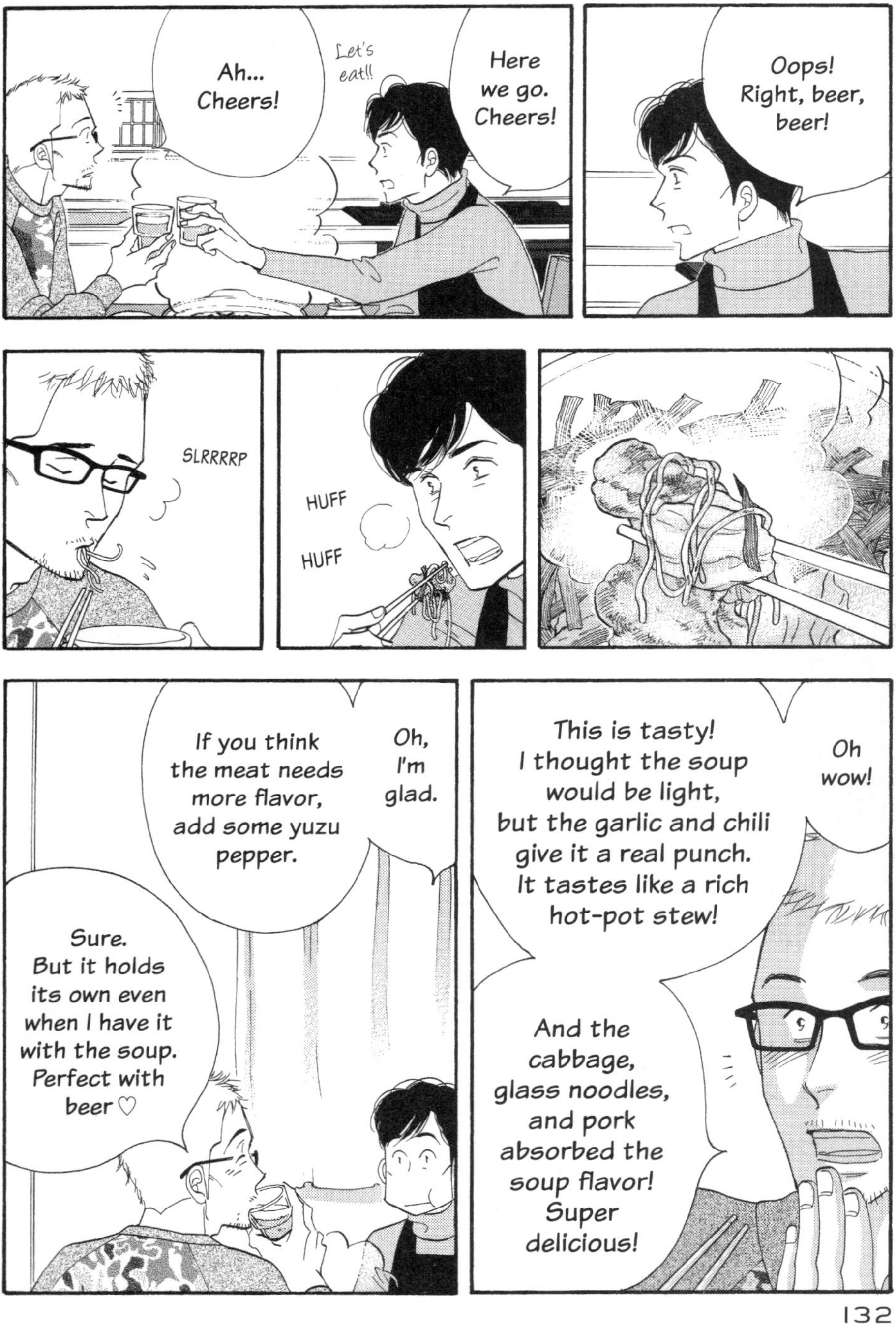
Oops! Right, beer, beer!
Here we go. Cheers!
Let's eat!!
Ah... Cheers!
HUFF
HUFF
SLRRRRP
Oh wow!
This is tasty! I thought the soup would be light, but the garlic and chili give it a real punch. It tastes like a rich hot-pot stew!
And the cabbage, glass noodles, and pork absorbed the soup flavor! Super delicious!
Oh, I'm glad.
If you think the meat needs more flavor, add some yuzu pepper.
Sure. But it holds its own even when I have it with the soup. Perfect with beer ♡

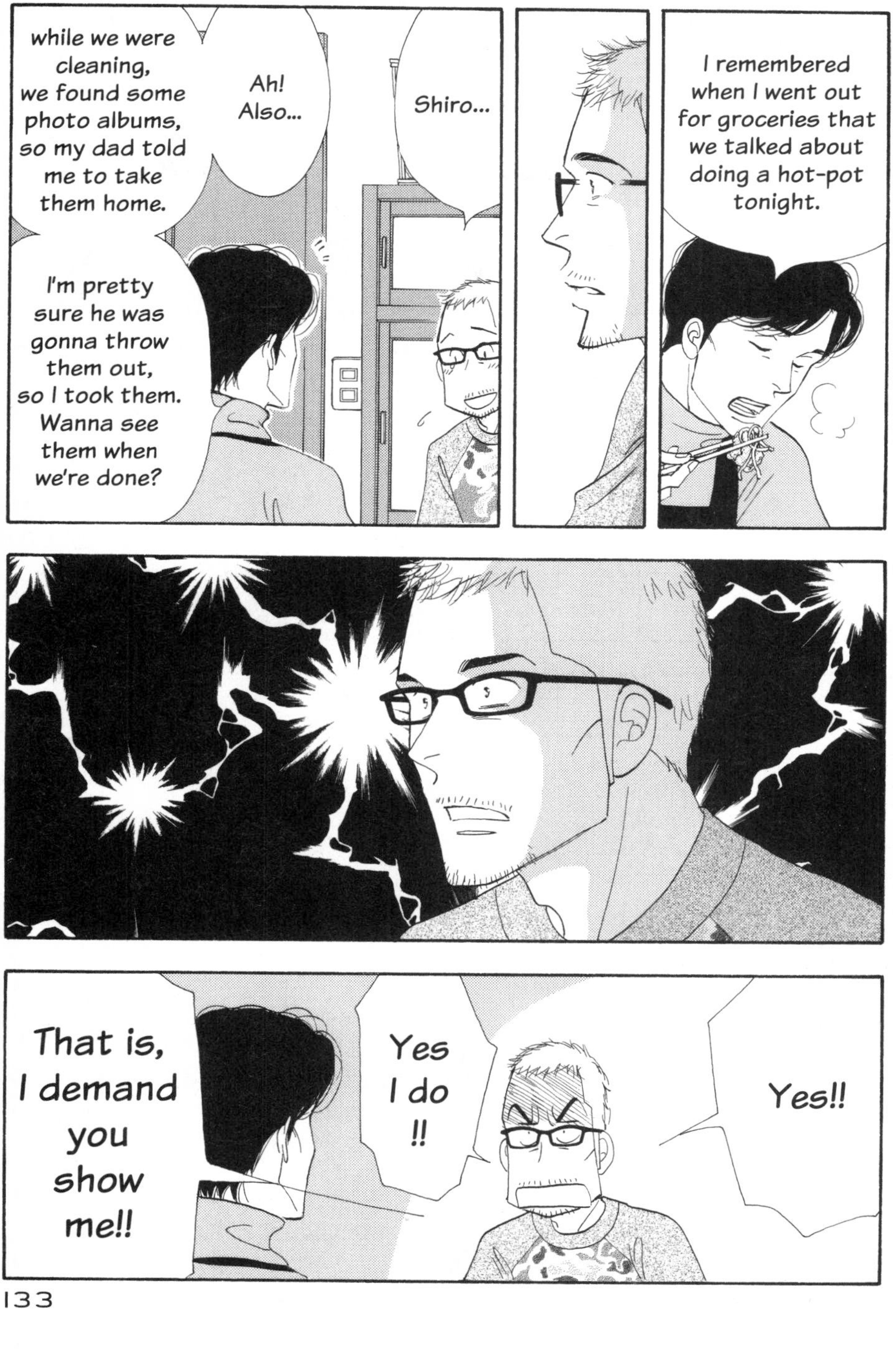
I remembered when I went out for groceries that we talked about doing a hot-pot tonight.
Shiro...
Ah! Also...
while we were cleaning, we found some photo albums, so my dad told me to take them home.
I'm pretty sure he was gonna throw them out, so I took them. Wanna see them when we're done?
Yes!!
Yes I do !!
That is, I demand you show me!!

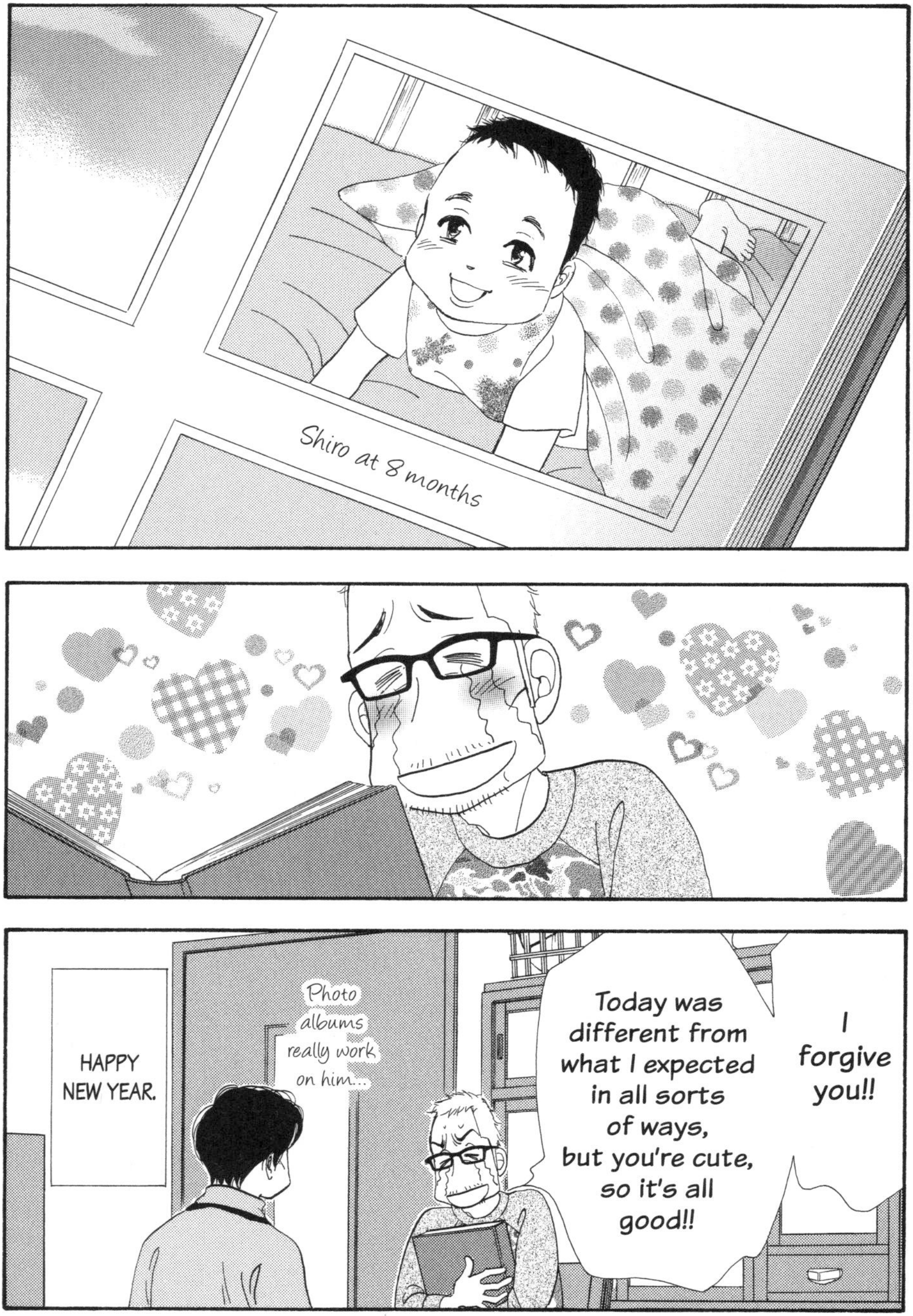
Shiro at 8 months
Today was different from what I expected in all sorts of ways, but you're cute, so it's all good!!
I forgive you!!
Photo albums really work on him...
HAPPY NEW YEAR.

Bean sprouts, burdock, tofu, and *mochi* rice cakes are some other ingredients you could add to the **hot-pot**.
Using miso instead of soy sauce to season is also delicious.

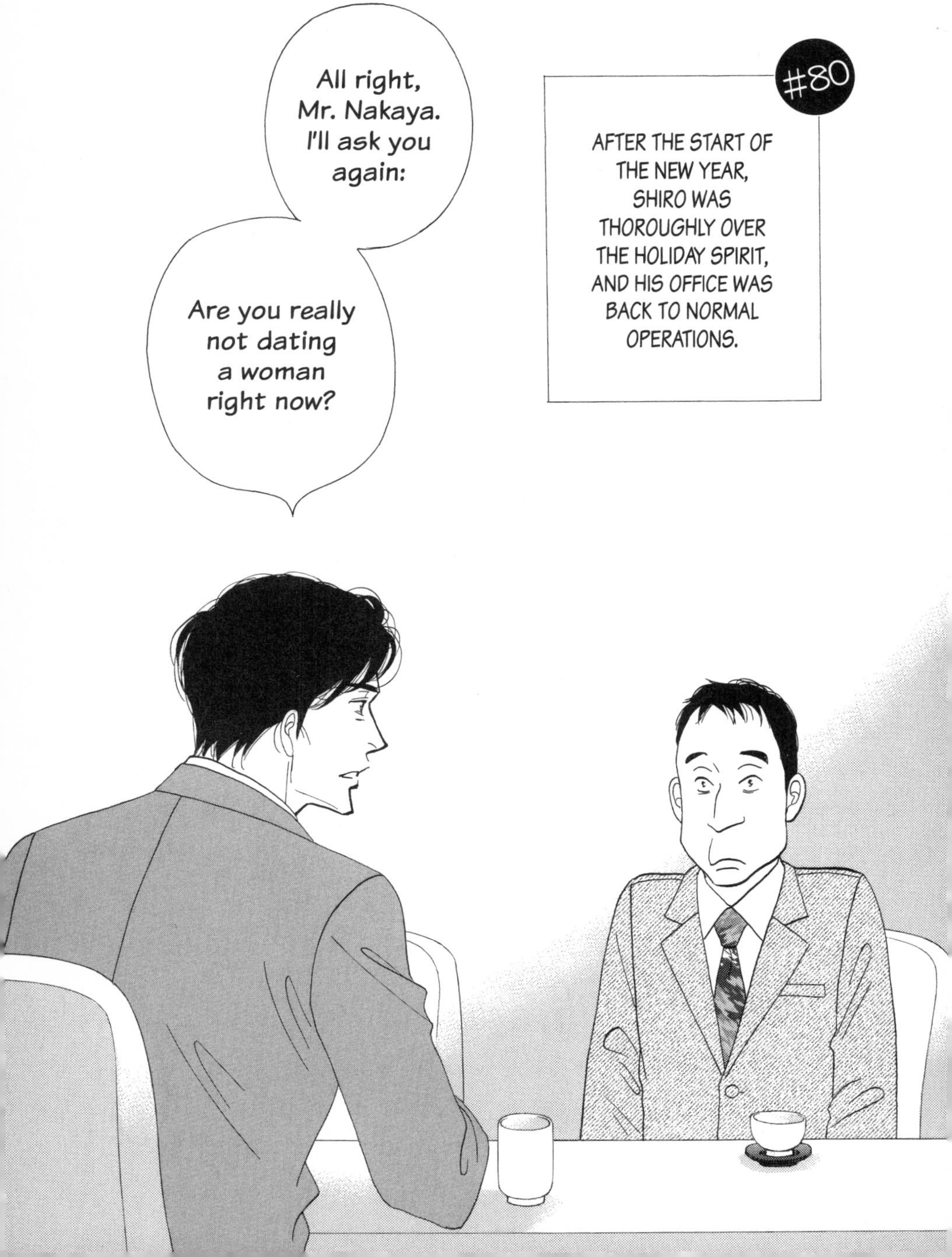
#80
AFTER THE START OF THE NEW YEAR, SHIRO WAS THOROUGHLY OVER THE HOLIDAY SPIRIT, AND HIS OFFICE WAS BACK TO NORMAL OPERATIONS.
All right, Mr. Nakaya. I'll ask you again:
Are you really not dating a woman right now?

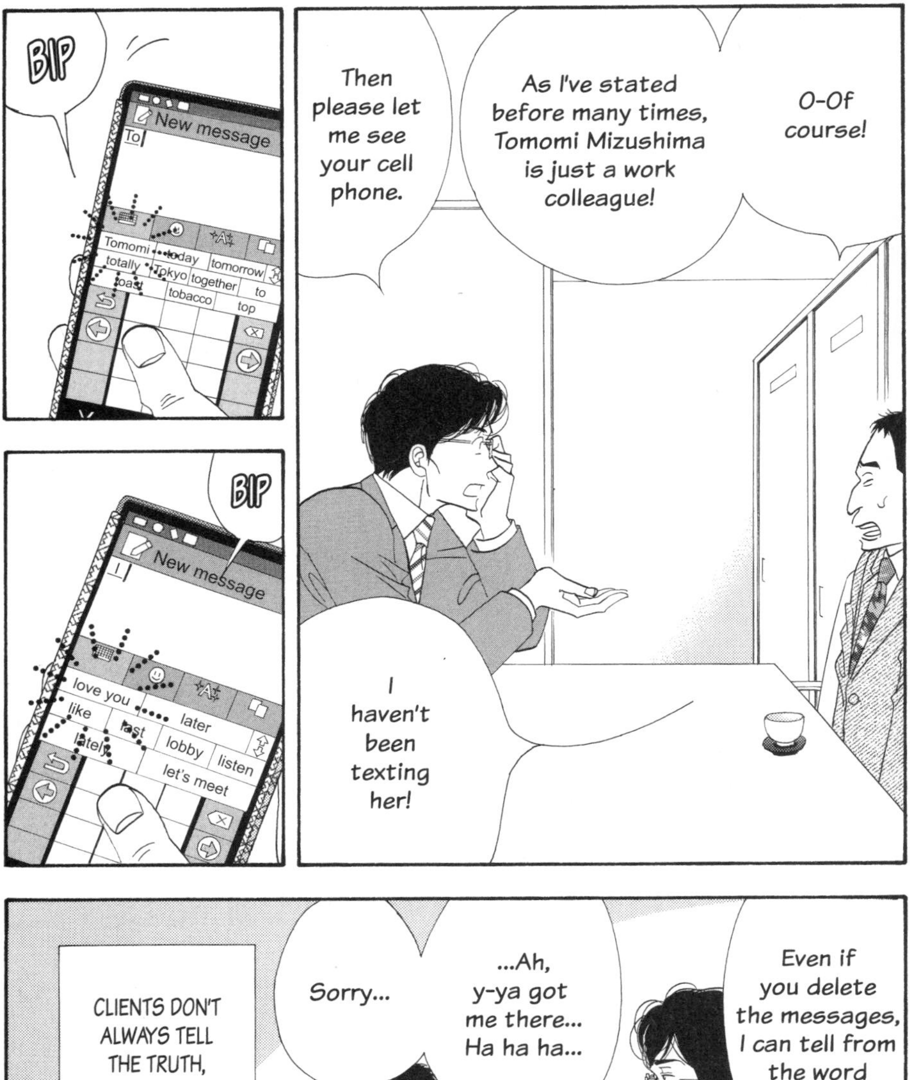
O-Of course!
As I've stated before many times, Tomomi Mizushima is just a work colleague!
Then please let me see your cell phone.
I haven't been texting her!
BIP
New message
To
Tomomi
today
tomorrow
totally
Tokyo
together
to
toast
tobacco
top
BIP
New message
I
love you
later
like
last
lobby
listen
lately
let's meet
Even if you delete the messages, I can tell from the word prediction.
...Ah, y-ya got me there... Ha ha ha...
Sorry...
CLIENTS DON'T ALWAYS TELL THE TRUTH, AND IT'S NOT LIMITED TO DIVORCE ARBITRATIONS.

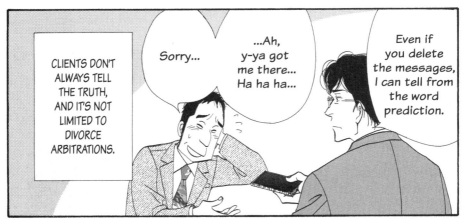

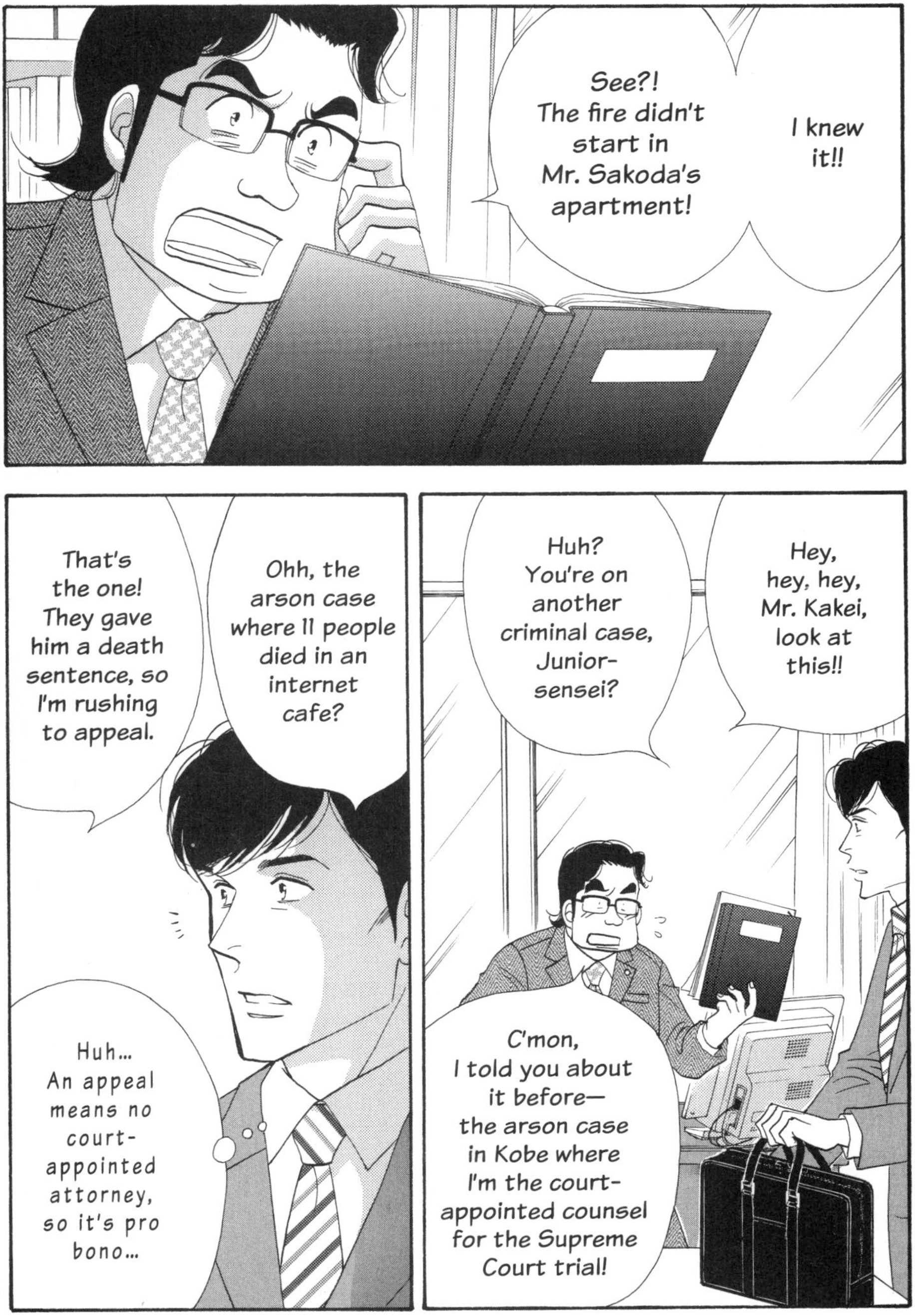
I knew it!!
See?! The fire didn't start in Mr. Sakoda's apartment!
Hey, hey, hey, Mr. Kakei, look at this!!
Huh? You're on another criminal case, Junior-sensei?
C'mon, I told you about it before— the arson case in Kobe where I'm the court-appointed counsel for the Supreme Court trial!
Ohh, the arson case where 11 people died in an internet cafe?
That's the one! They gave him a death sentence, so I'm rushing to appeal.
Huh... An appeal means no court-appointed attorney, so it's pro bono...

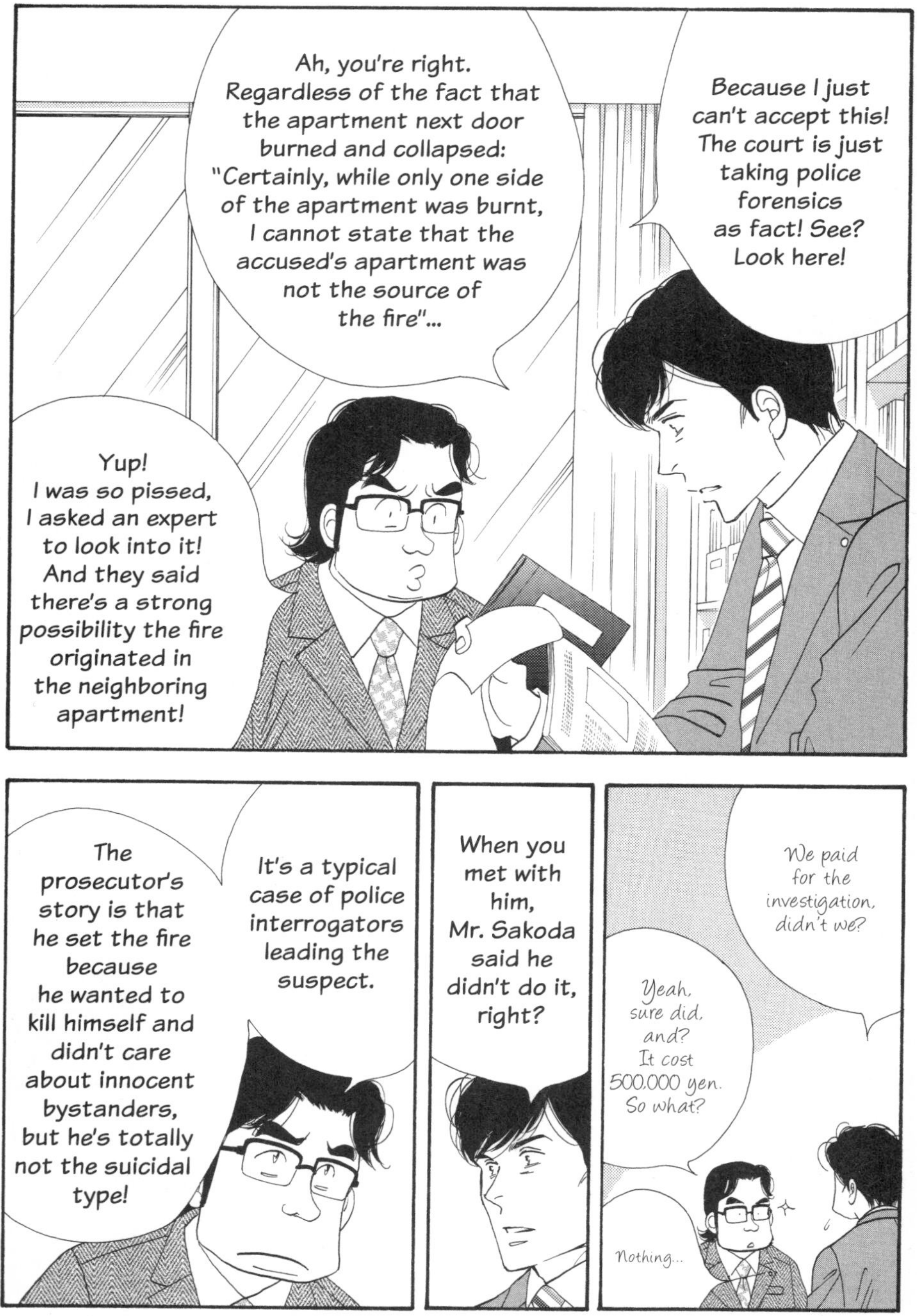

Because I just can't accept this! The court is just taking police forensics as fact! See? Look here!
Ah, you're right. Regardless of the fact that the apartment next door burned and collapsed: "Certainly, while only one side of the apartment was burnt, I cannot state that the accused's apartment was not the source of the fire"...
Yup! I was so pissed, I asked an expert to look into it! And they said there's a strong possibility the fire originated in the neighboring apartment!
We paid for the investigation, didn't we?
Yeah, sure did, and? It cost 500.000 yen. So what?
Nothing...
When you met with him, Mr. Sakoda said he didn't do it, right?
It's a typical case of police interrogators leading the suspect.
The prosecutor's story is that he set the fire because he wanted to kill himself and didn't care about innocent bystanders, but he's totally not the suicidal type!

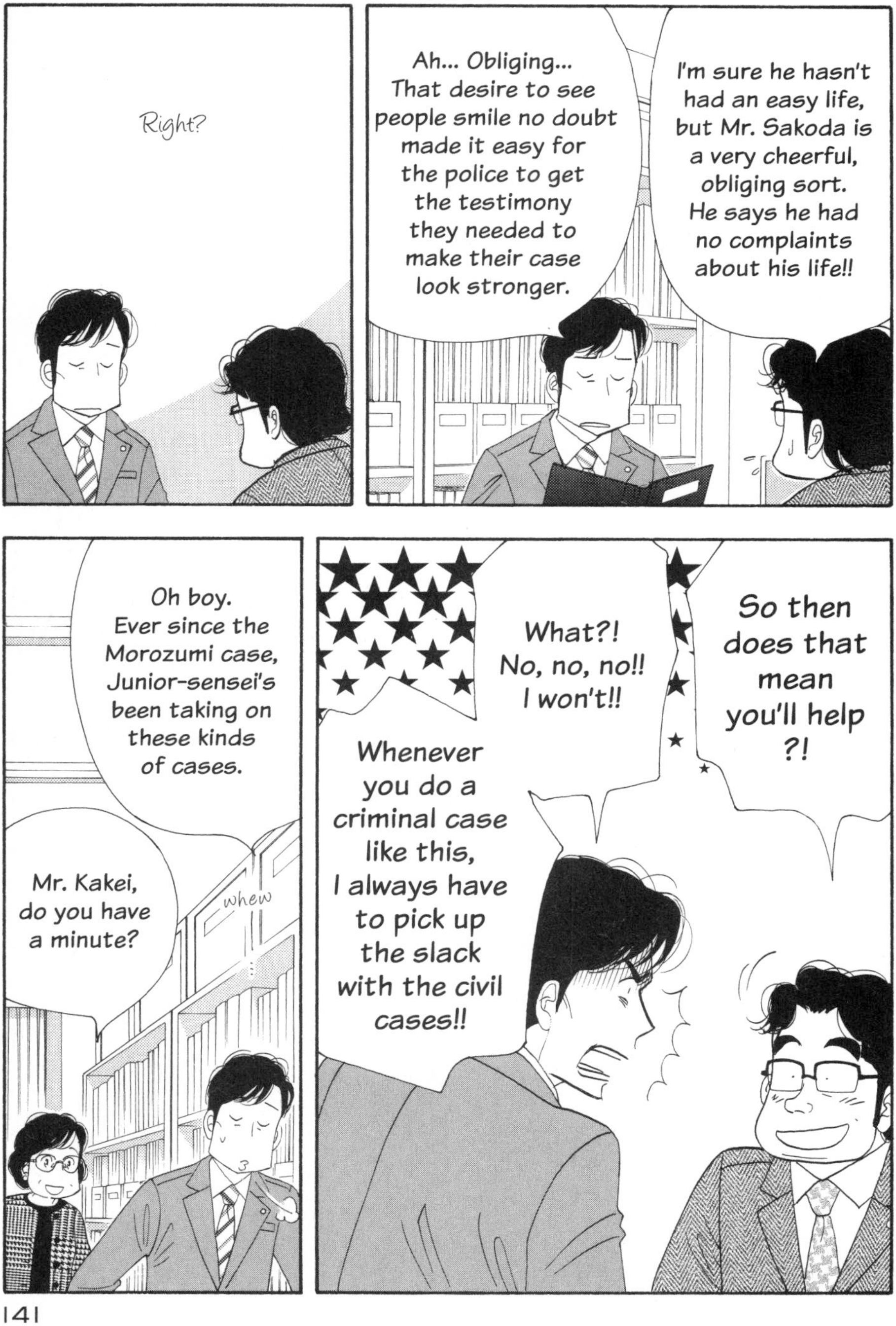
I'm sure he hasn't had an easy life, but Mr. Sakoda is a very cheerful, obliging sort. He says he had no complaints about his life!!
Ah... Obliging... That desire to see people smile no doubt made it easy for the police to get the testimony they needed to make their case look stronger.
Right?
So then does that mean you'll help?!
What?! No, no, no!! I won't!!
Whenever you do a criminal case like this, I always have to pick up the slack with the civil cases!!
Oh boy. Ever since the Morozumi case, Junior-sensei's been taking on these kinds of cases.
Mr. Kakei, do you have a minute?
whew

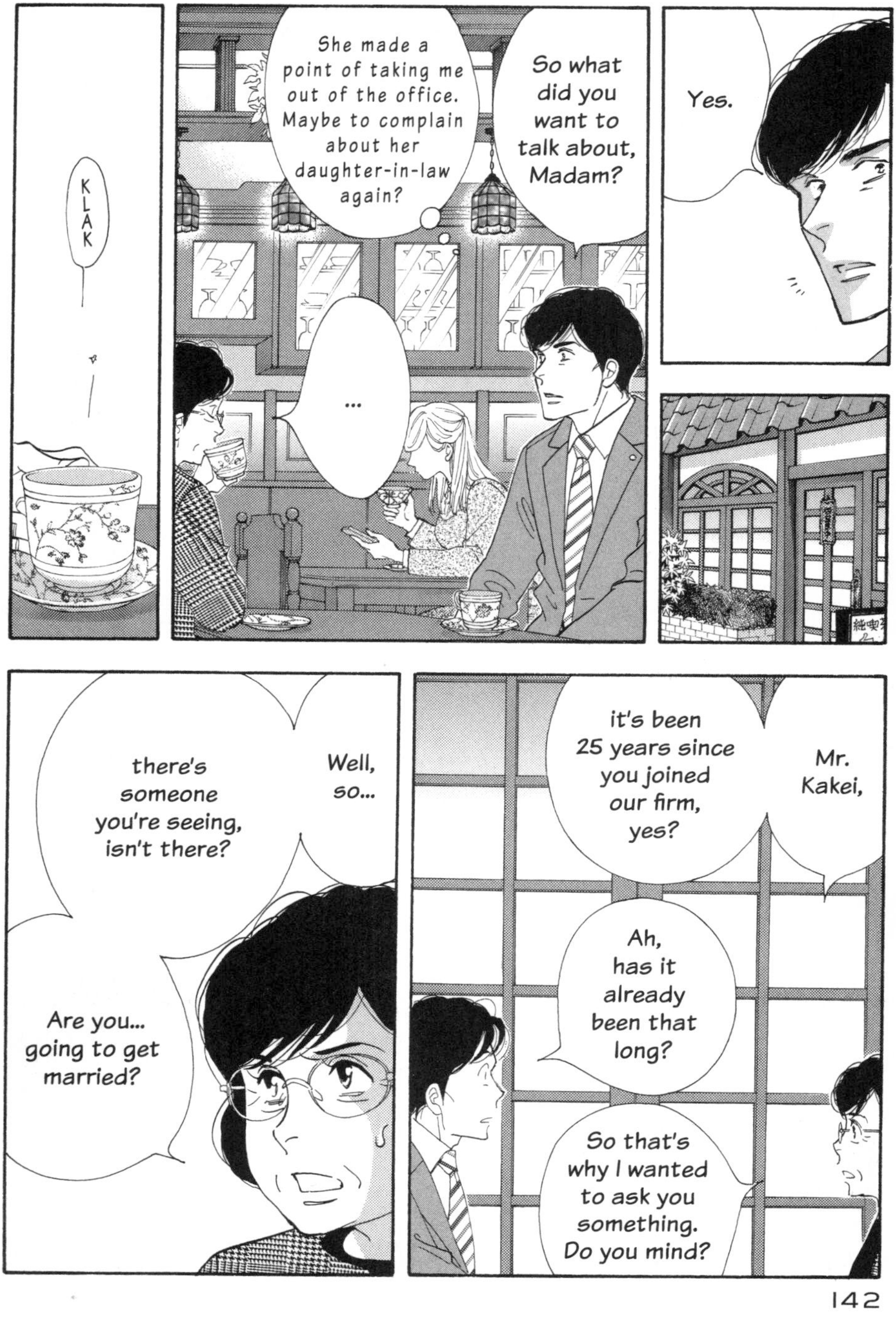
Yes.
So what did you want to talk about, Madam?
She made a point of taking me out of the office. Maybe to complain about her daughter-in-law again?
...
KLAK
Mr. Kakei,
it's been 25 years since you joined our firm, yes?
Ah, has it already been that long?
So that's why I wanted to ask you something. Do you mind?
Well, so...
there's someone you're seeing, isn't there?
Are you... going to get married?

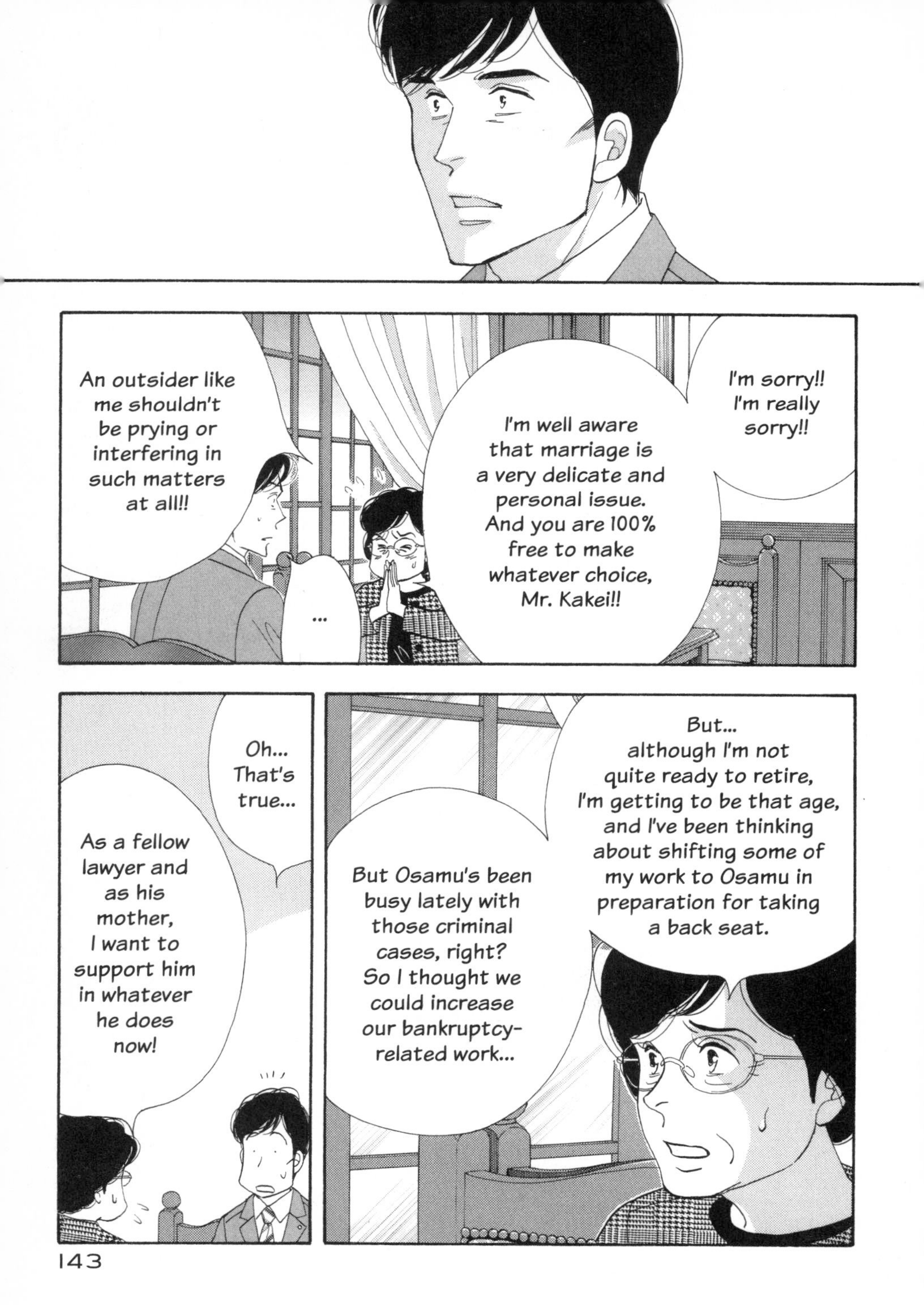
I'm sorry!! I'm really sorry!!
I'm well aware that marriage is a very delicate and personal issue. And you are 100% free to make whatever choice, Mr. Kakei!!
An outsider like me shouldn't be prying or interfering in such matters at all!!
...
But... although I'm not quite ready to retire, I'm getting to be that age, and I've been thinking about shifting some of my work to Osamu in preparation for taking a back seat.
But Osamu's been busy lately with those criminal cases, right? So I thought we could increase our bankruptcy-related work...
Oh... That's true...
As a fellow lawyer and as his mother, I want to support him in whatever he does now!

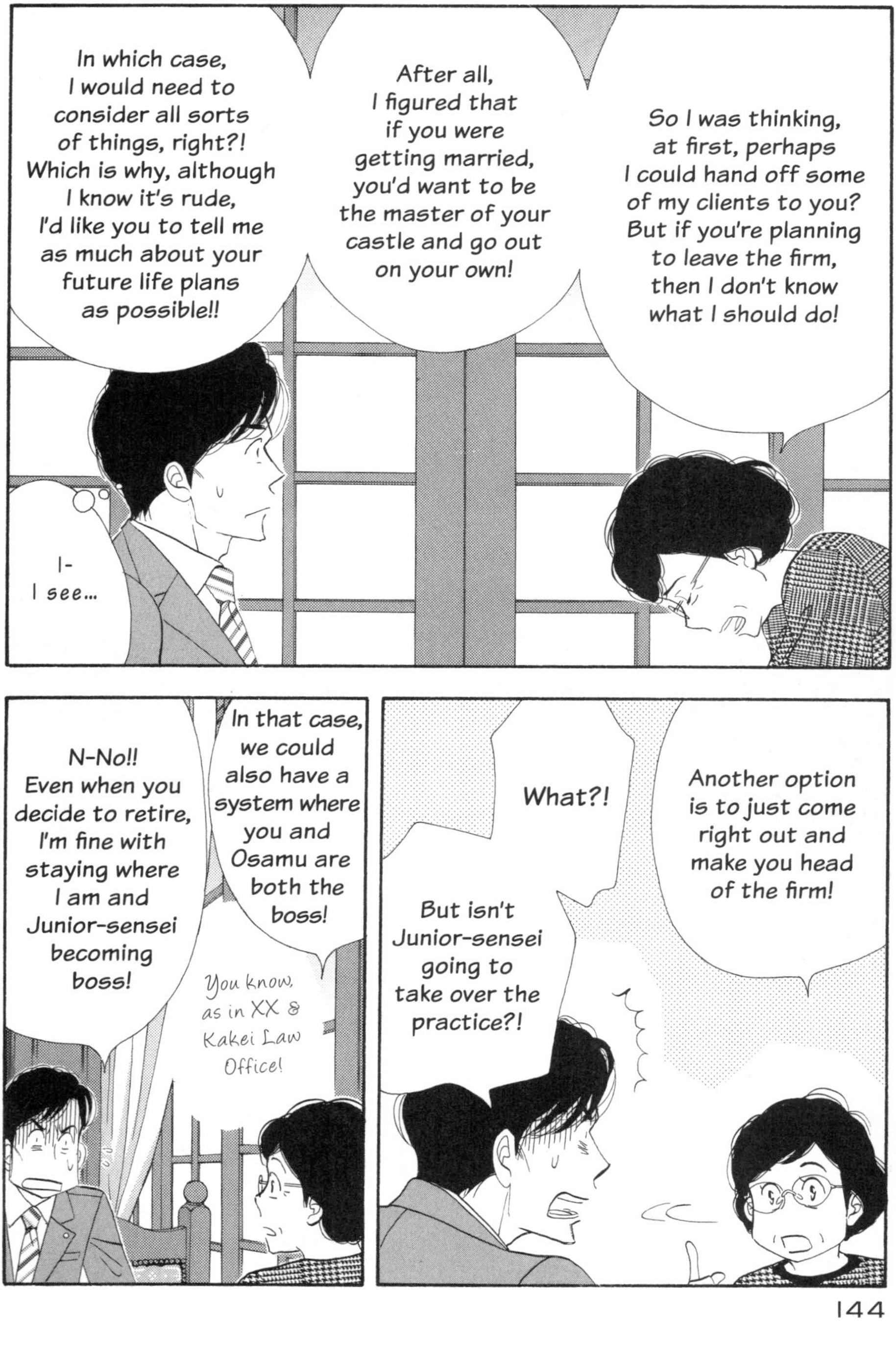
So I was thinking, at first, perhaps I could hand off some of my clients to you? But if you're planning to leave the firm, then I don't know what I should do!
After all, I figured that if you were getting married, you'd want to be the master of your castle and go out on your own!
In which case, I would need to consider all sorts of things, right?! Which is why, although I know it's rude, I'd like you to tell me as much about your future life plans as possible!!
I- I see...
Another option is to just come right out and make you head of the firm!
What?!
But isn't Junior-sensei going to take over the practice?!
In that case, we could also have a system where you and Osamu are both the boss!
N-No!! Even when you decide to retire, I'm fine with staying where I am and Junior-sensei becoming boss!
You know, as in XX & Kakei Law Office!

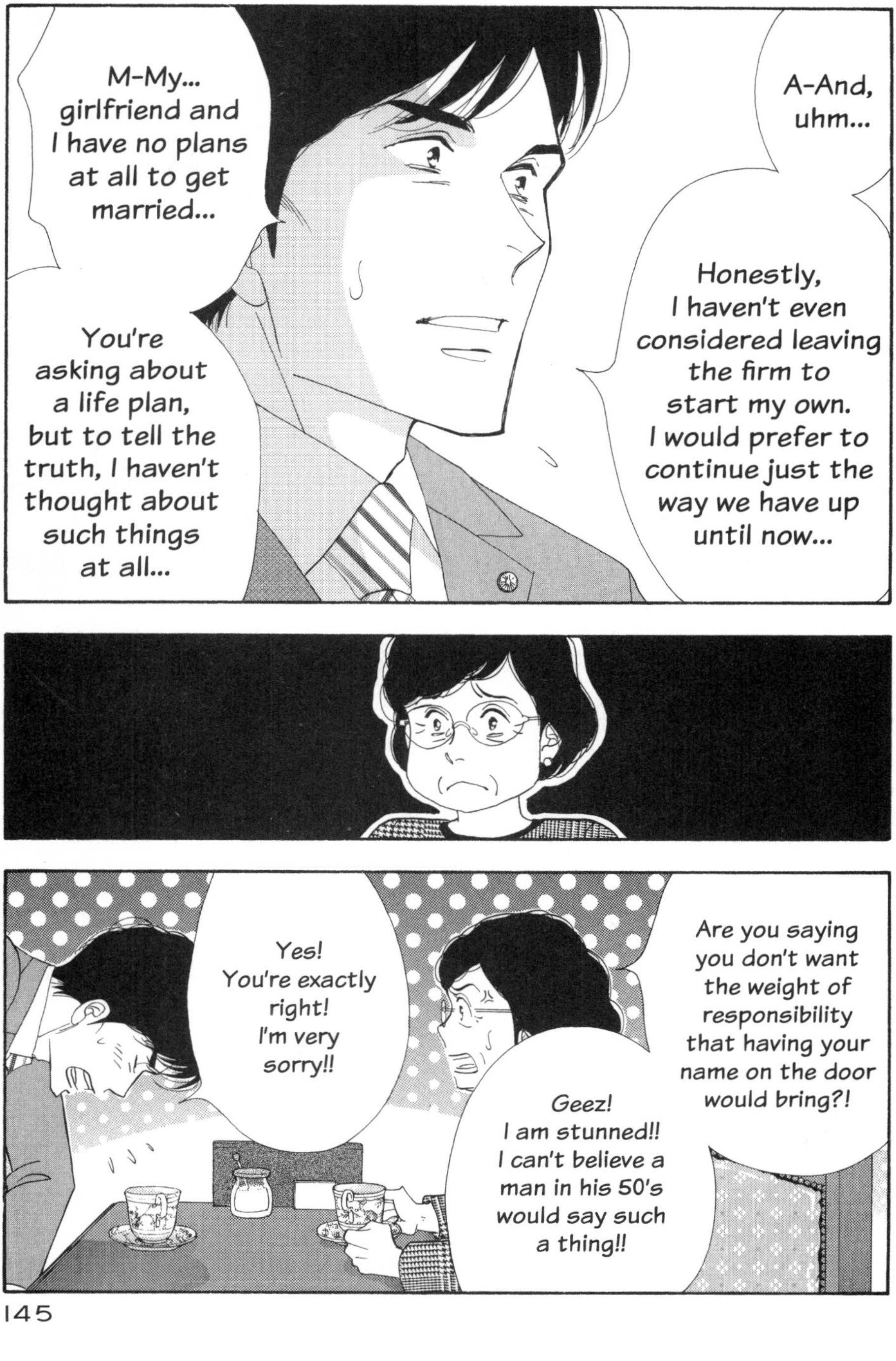
A-And, uhm...
Honestly, I haven't even considered leaving the firm to start my own. I would prefer to continue just the way we have up until now...
M-My... girlfriend and I have no plans at all to get married...
You're asking about a life plan, but to tell the truth, I haven't thought about such things at all...
Are you saying you don't want the weight of responsibility that having your name on the door would bring?!
Geez! I am stunned!! I can't believe a man in his 50's would say such a thing!!
Yes! You're exactly right! I'm very sorry!!

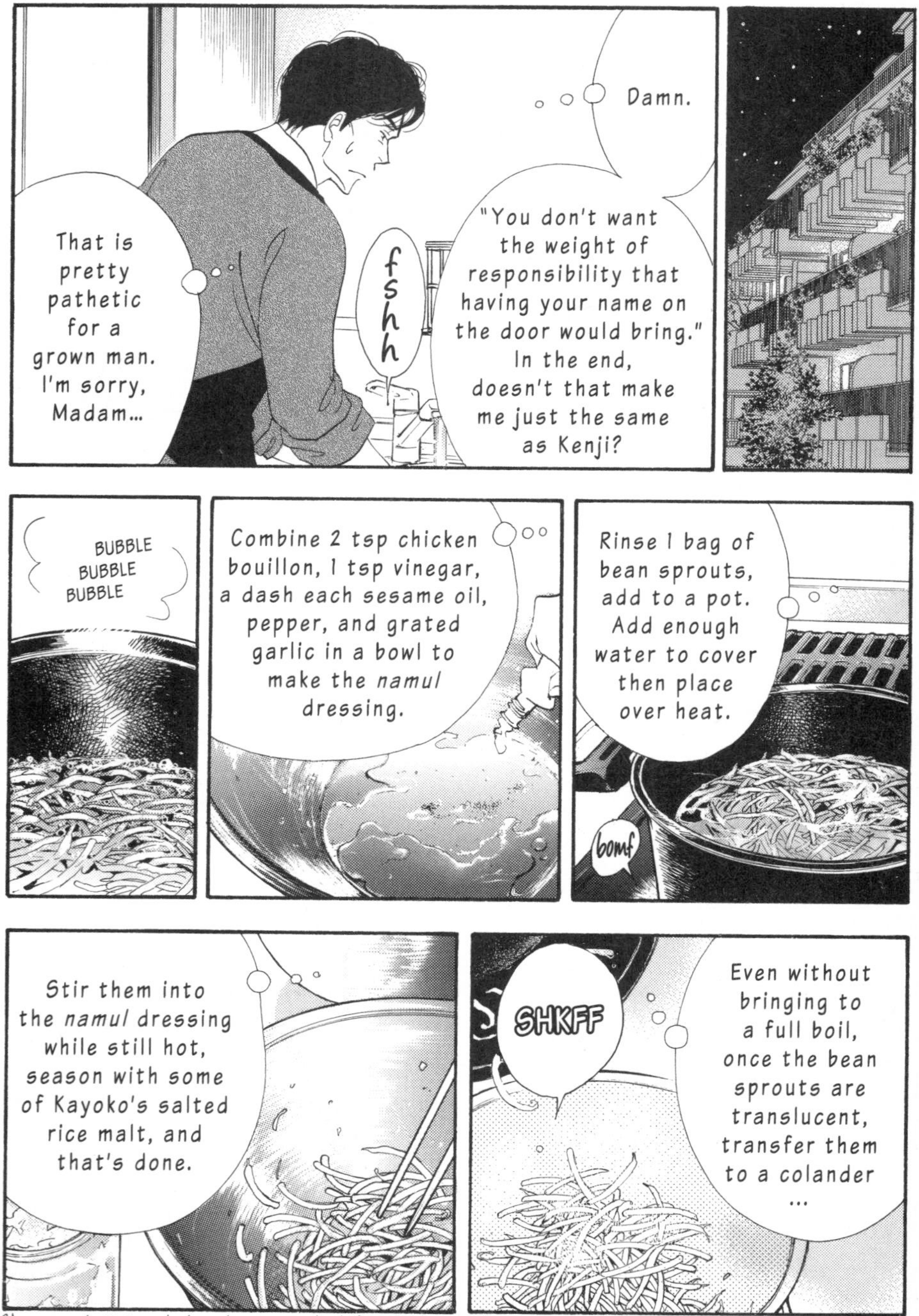
Damn.
"You don't want the weight of responsibility that having your name on the door would bring." In the end, doesn't that make me just the same as Kenji?
fshh
That is pretty pathetic for a grown man. I'm sorry, Madam...
Rinse 1 bag of bean sprouts, add to a pot. Add enough water to cover then place over heat.
bomf
Combine 2 tsp chicken bouillon, 1 tsp vinegar, a dash each sesame oil, pepper, and grated garlic in a bowl to make the *namul* dressing.
BUBBLE BUBBLE BUBBLE
Even without bringing to a full boil, once the bean sprouts are translucent, transfer them to a colander ...
SHKFF
Stir them into the *namul* dressing while still hot, season with some of Kayoko's salted rice malt, and that's done.

You can substitute a dash each sugar and salt for salted rice malt.

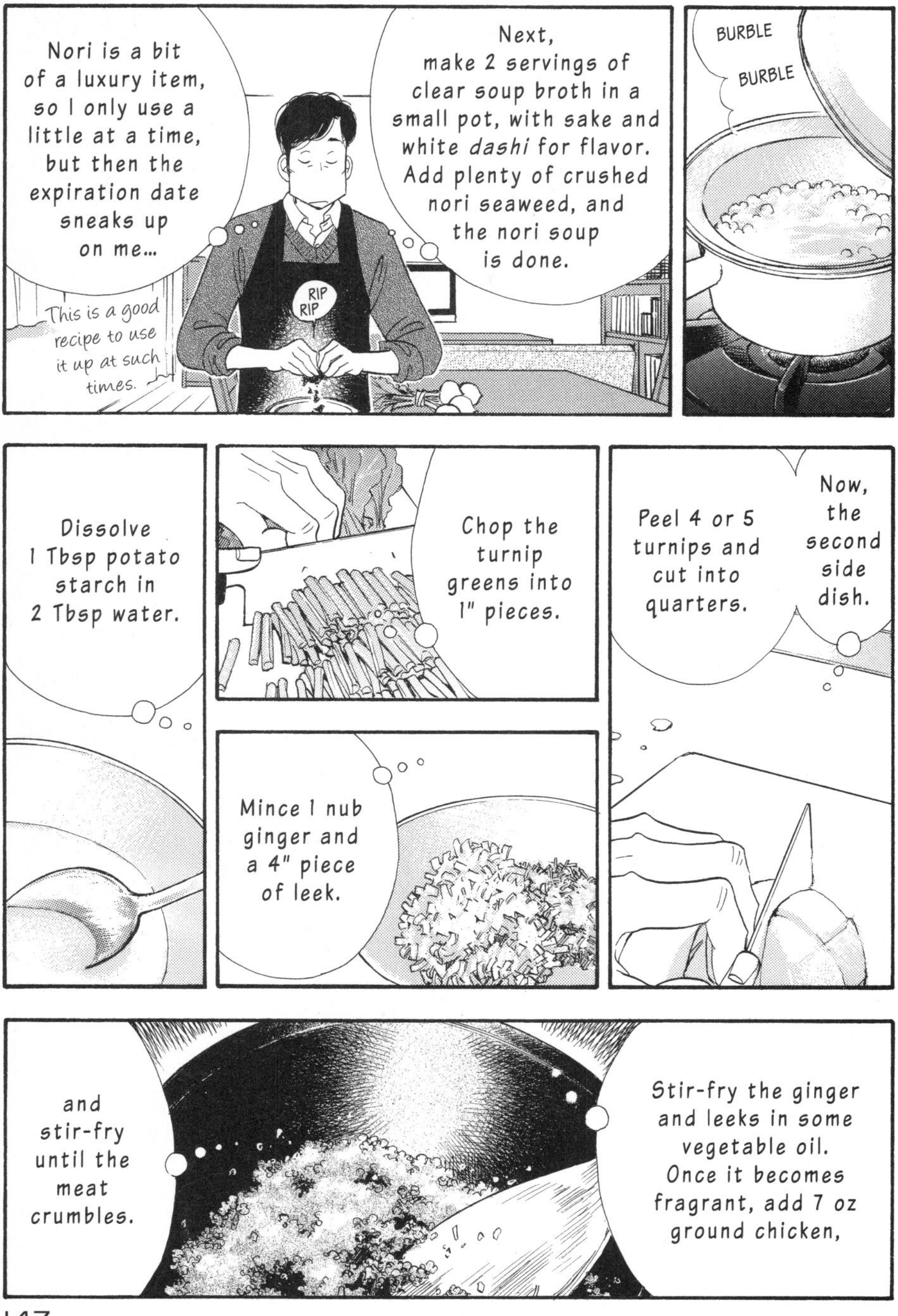
BURBLE
BURBLE
Next, make 2 servings of clear soup broth in a small pot, with sake and white *dashi* for flavor. Add plenty of crushed nori seaweed, and the nori soup is done.
Nori is a bit of a luxury item, so I only use a little at a time, but then the expiration date sneaks up on me...
RIP RIP
This is a good recipe to use it up at such times.
Now, the second side dish.
Peel 4 or 5 turnips and cut into quarters.
Chop the turnip greens into 1" pieces.
Mince 1 nub ginger and a 4" piece of leek.
Dissolve 1 Tbsp potato starch in 2 Tbsp water.
Stir-fry the ginger and leeks in some vegetable oil. Once it becomes fragrant, add 7 oz ground chicken,
and stir-fry until the meat crumbles.

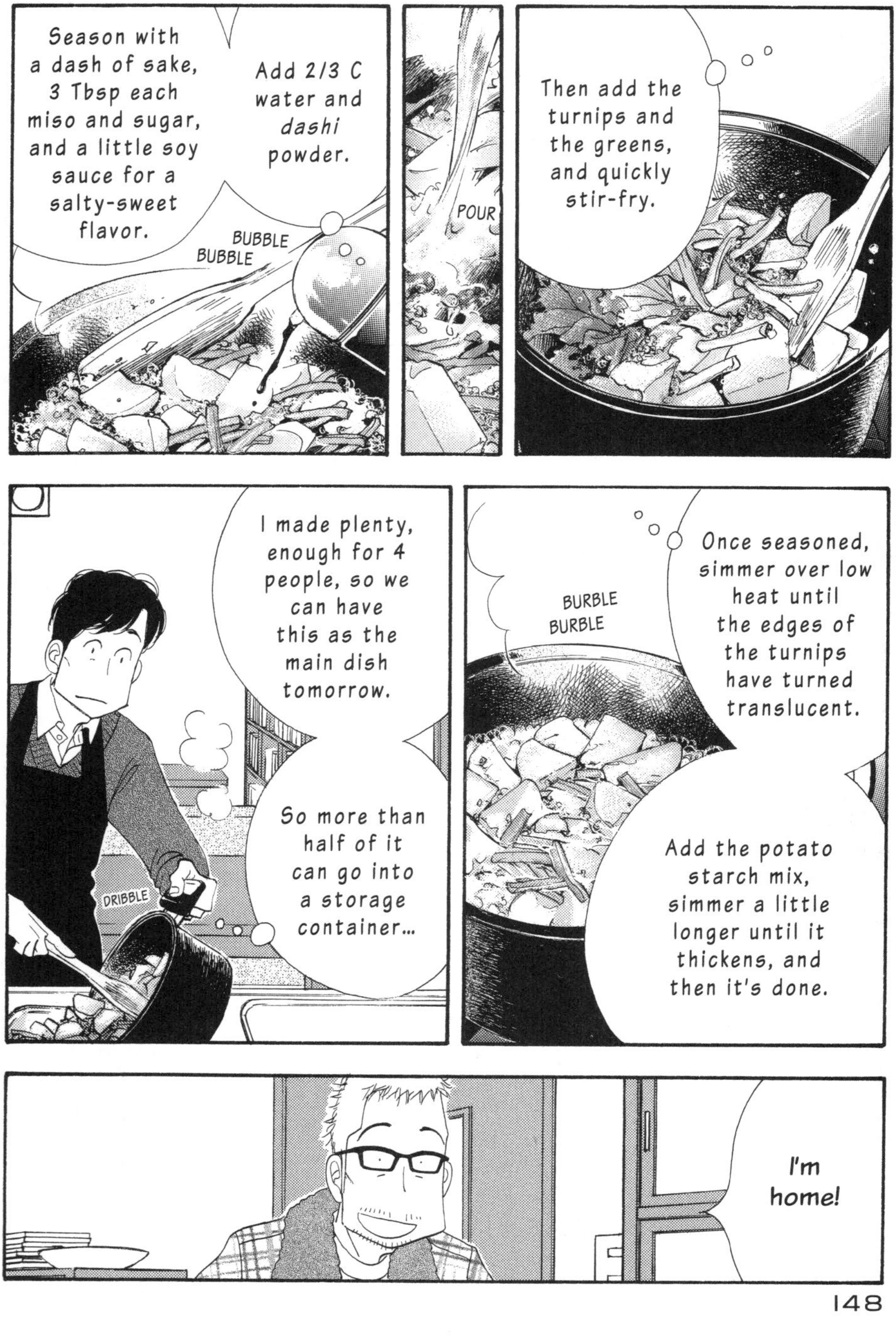
Then add the turnips and the greens, and quickly stir-fry.
POUR
Add 2/3 C water and *dashi* powder.
Season with a dash of sake, 3 Tbsp each miso and sugar, and a little soy sauce for a salty-sweet flavor.
BUBBLE BUBBLE
Once seasoned, simmer over low heat until the edges of the turnips have turned translucent.
BURBLE BURBLE
Add the potato starch mix, simmer a little longer until it thickens, and then it's done.
I made plenty, enough for 4 people, so we can have this as the main dish tomorrow.
So more than half of it can go into a storage container...
DRIBBLE
I'm home!

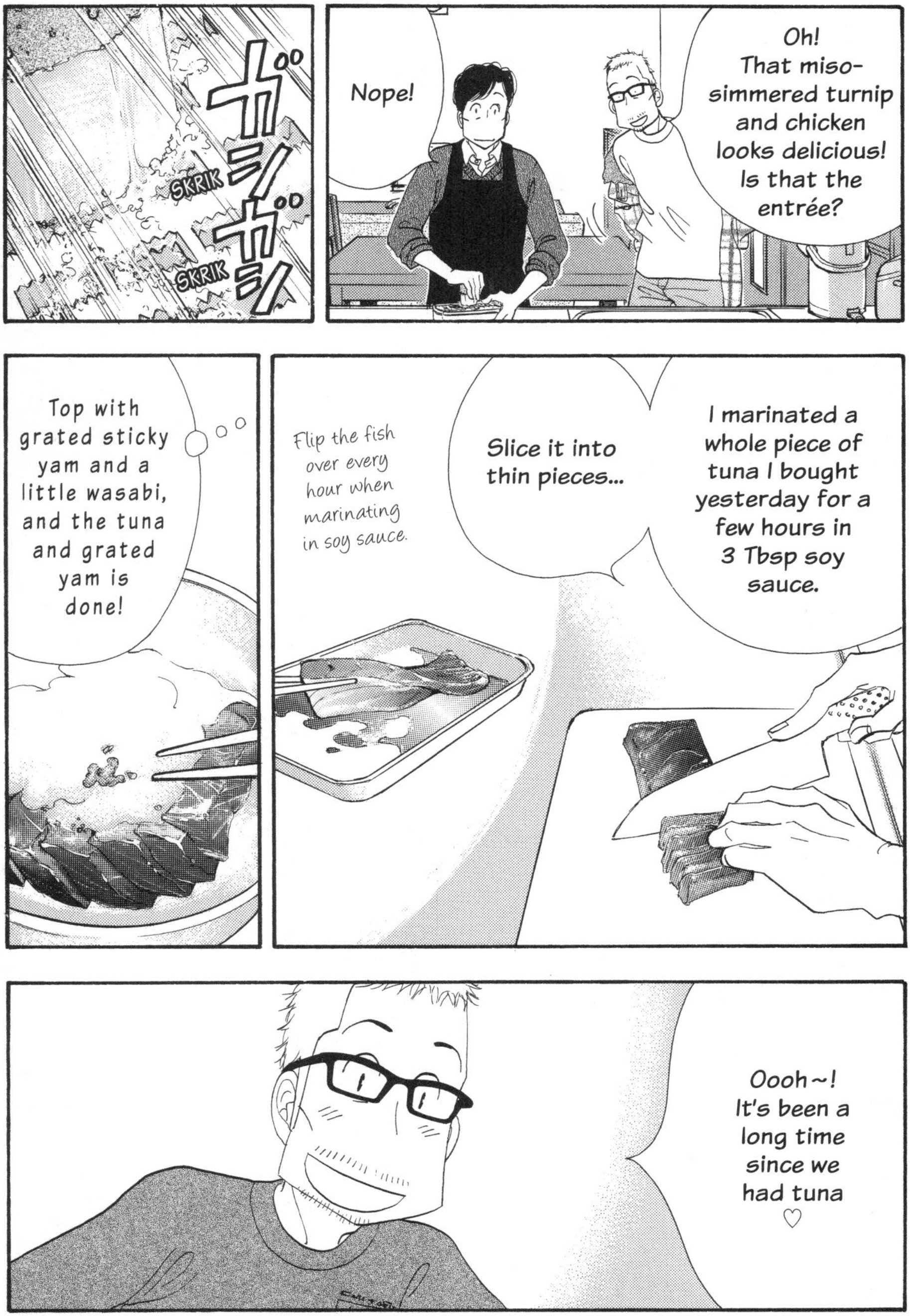
Oh!
That miso-simmered turnip and chicken looks delicious!
Is that the entrée?
Nope!
SKRIK
SKRIK
I marinated a whole piece of tuna I bought yesterday for a few hours in 3 Tbsp soy sauce.
Slice it into thin pieces...
Flip the fish over every hour when marinating in soy sauce.
Top with grated sticky yam and a little wasabi, and the tuna and grated yam is done!
Oooh~! It's been a long time since we had tuna ♡

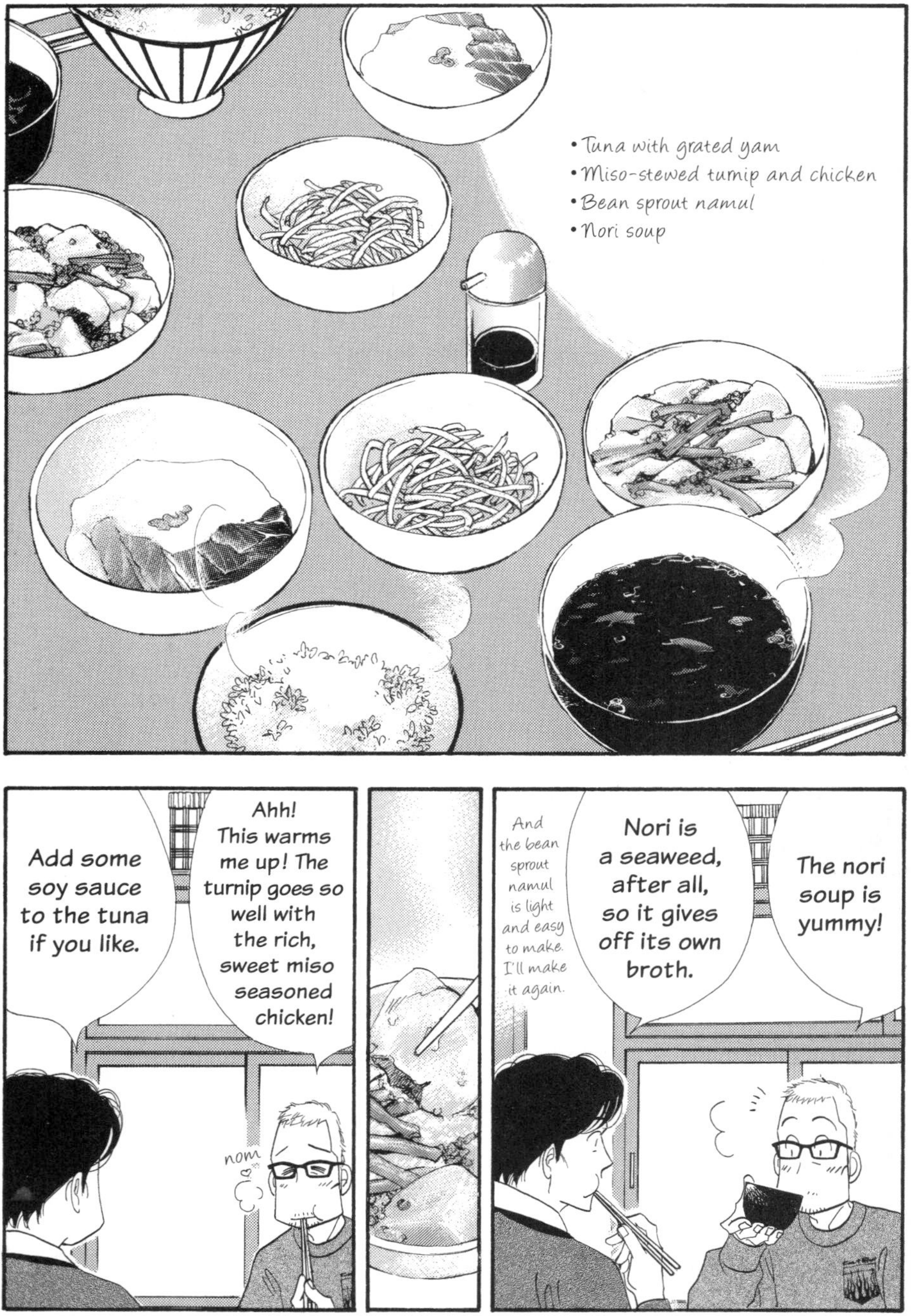

• Tuna with grated yam
• Miso-stewed turnip and chicken
• Bean sprout namul
• Nori soup
The nori soup is yummy!
Nori is a seaweed, after all, so it gives off its own broth.
And the bean sprout namul is light and easy to make. I'll make it again.
Ahh! This warms me up! The turnip goes so well with the rich, sweet miso seasoned chicken!
nom
Add some soy sauce to the tuna if you like.

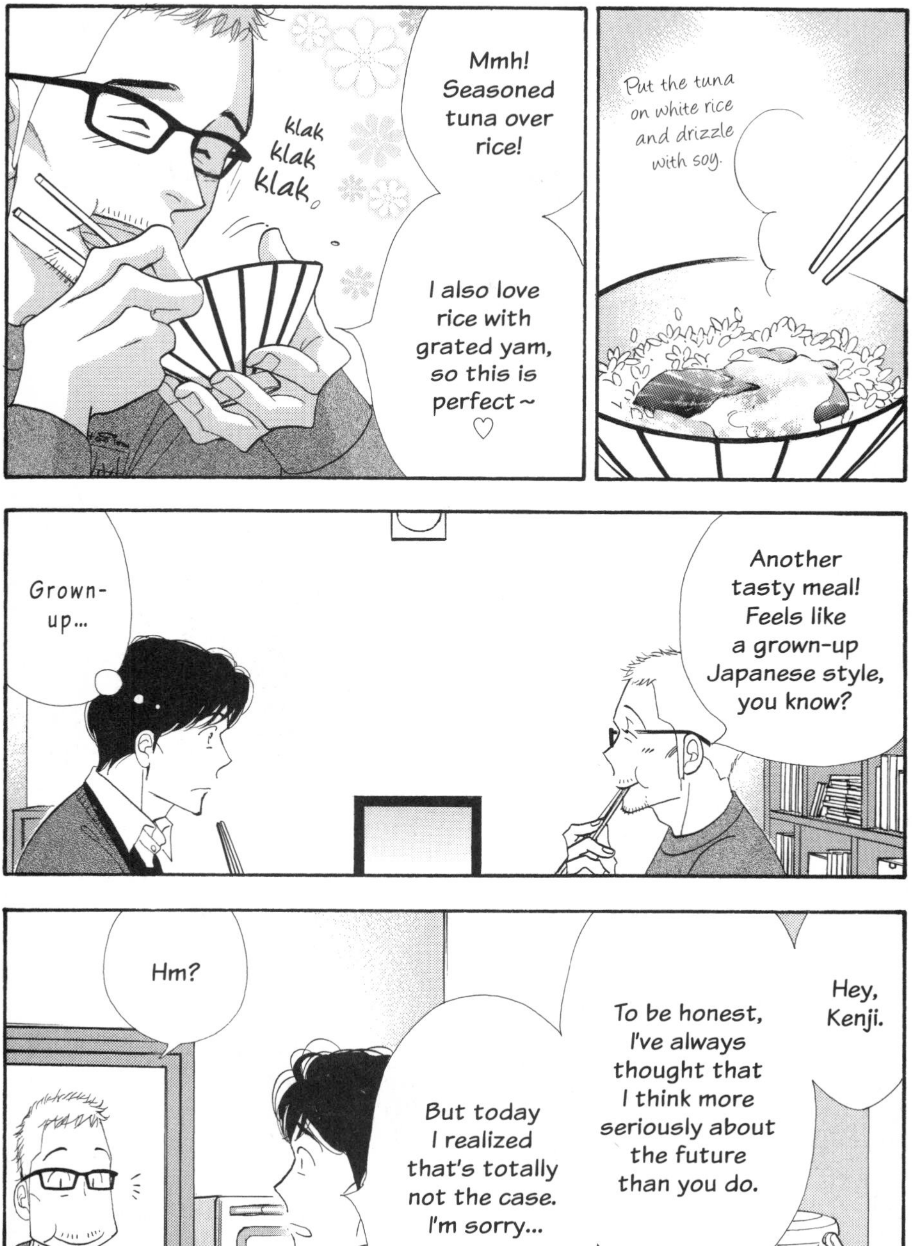
Put the tuna on white rice and drizzle with soy.
Mmh! Seasoned tuna over rice!
klak klak klak
I also love rice with grated yam, so this is perfect~ ♡
Another tasty meal! Feels like a grown-up Japanese style, you know?
Grown-up...
Hey, Kenji.
To be honest, I've always thought that I think more seriously about the future than you do.
But today I realized that's totally not the case. I'm sorry...
Hm?

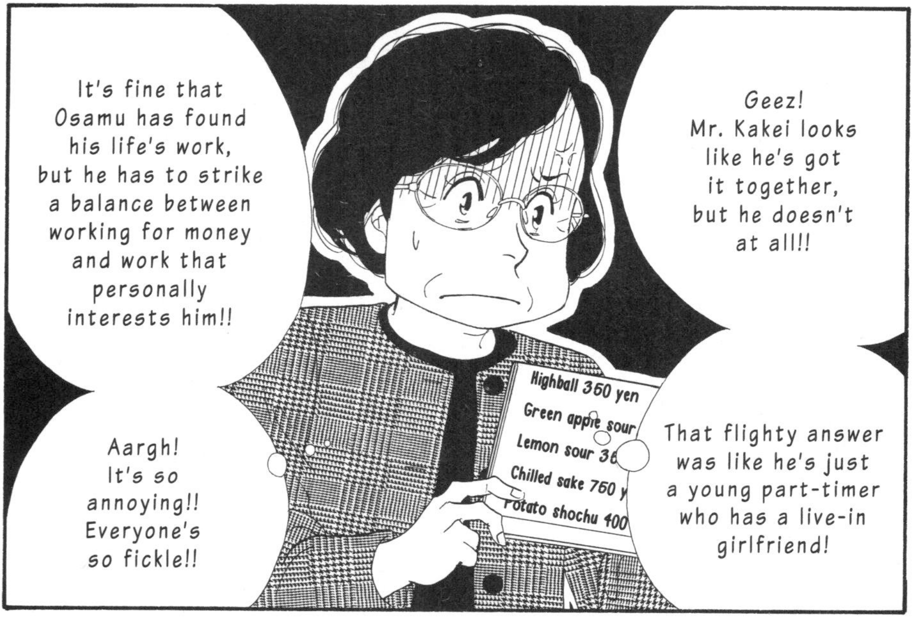
Geez! Mr. Kakei looks like he's got it together, but he doesn't at all!!
It's fine that Osamu has found his life's work, but he has to strike a balance between working for money and work that personally interests him!!
Highball 350 yen
Green apple sour
That flighty answer was like he's just a young part-timer who has a live-in girlfriend!
Aargh! It's so annoying!! Everyone's so fickle!!

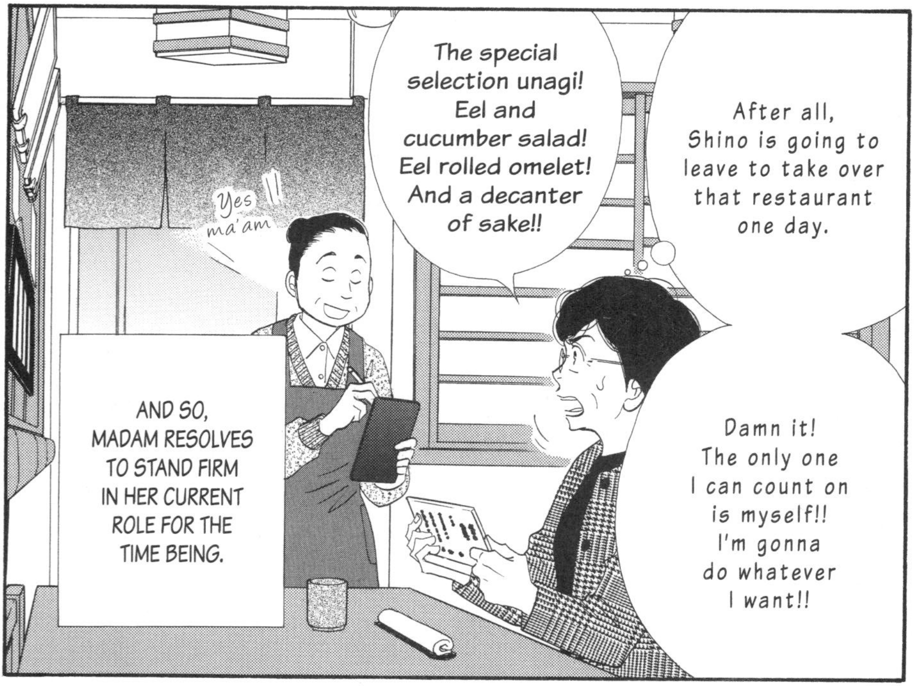
After all, Shino is going to leave to take over that restaurant one day.
The special selection unagi! Eel and cucumber salad! Eel rolled omelet! And a decanter of sake!!
Yes ma'am !!
Damn it! The only one I can count on is myself!! I'm gonna do whatever I want!!
AND SO, MADAM RESOLVES TO STAND FIRM IN HER CURRENT ROLE FOR THE TIME BEING.

If you don't have any of
the salted rice malt
used in the *namul*,
you can get roughly
the same flavor with
a little salt and sugar.
The **tuna and grated yam** is
also delicious topped with
the yolk of a quail egg.

what did you eat yesterday?, volume 10

translation: jocelyne allen
production: risa cho
tomoe tsutsumi

translation provided by vertical, inc., 2016
published by vertical, inc., new york

originally published in japanese as kinou nani tabeta? 10 by kodansha, ltd.
kinou nani tabeta? first serialized in morning, kodansha, ltd., 2007-

this is a work of fiction.

isbn: 978-1-942993-24-7

manufactured in canada

first edition

vertical, inc.
451 park avenue south
7th floor
new york, ny 10016
www.vertical-inc.com

A problem in their

steamed cod and tofu

steamed egg custard

chrysanthemum and carrot sesame miso salad

taro, scallion and fried tofu miso soup

sardine and sesame *inari* sushi

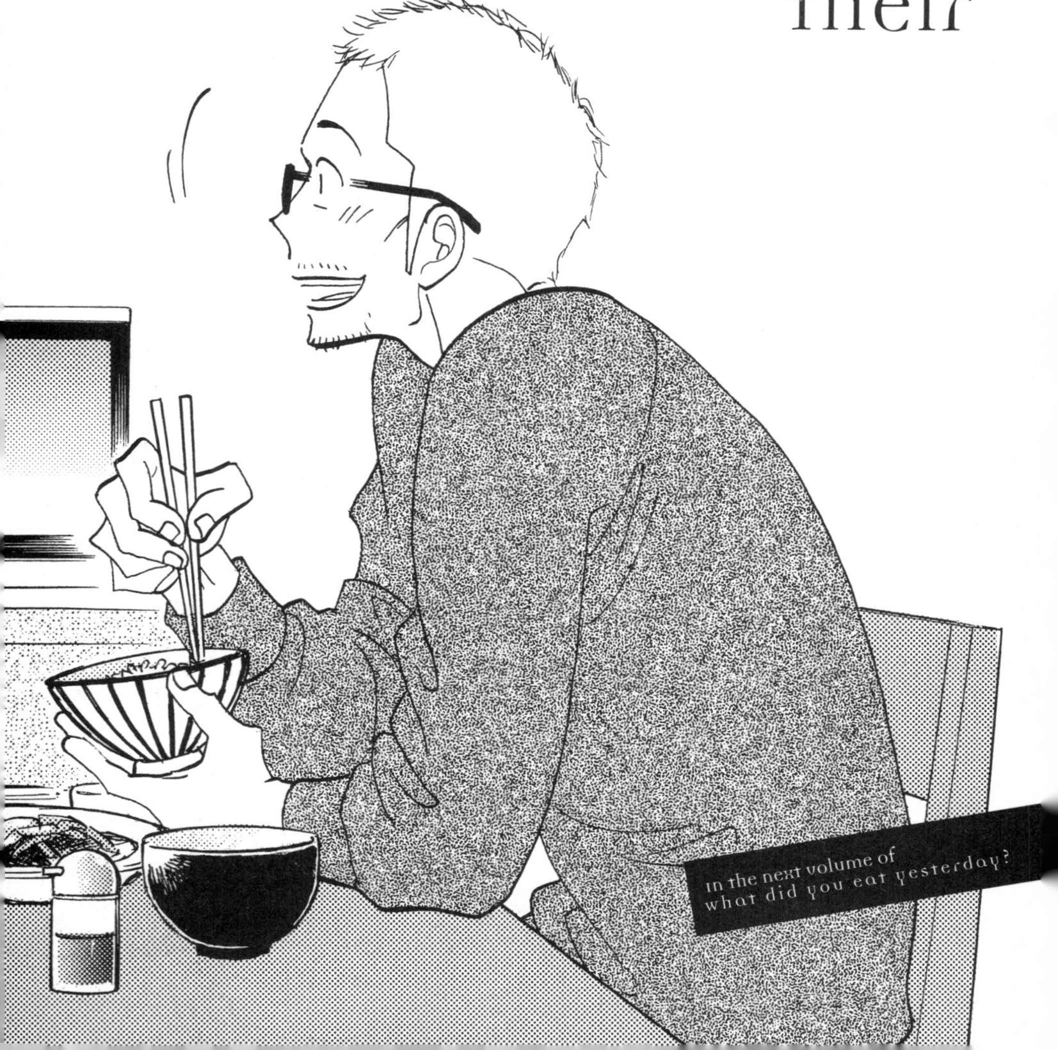
in the next volume of
what did you eat yesterday?

house-hold finances ?!

carrot and leek meat rolls
salmon escabeche
Japanese rolled omelet
Asparagus with bonito flakes

And more...

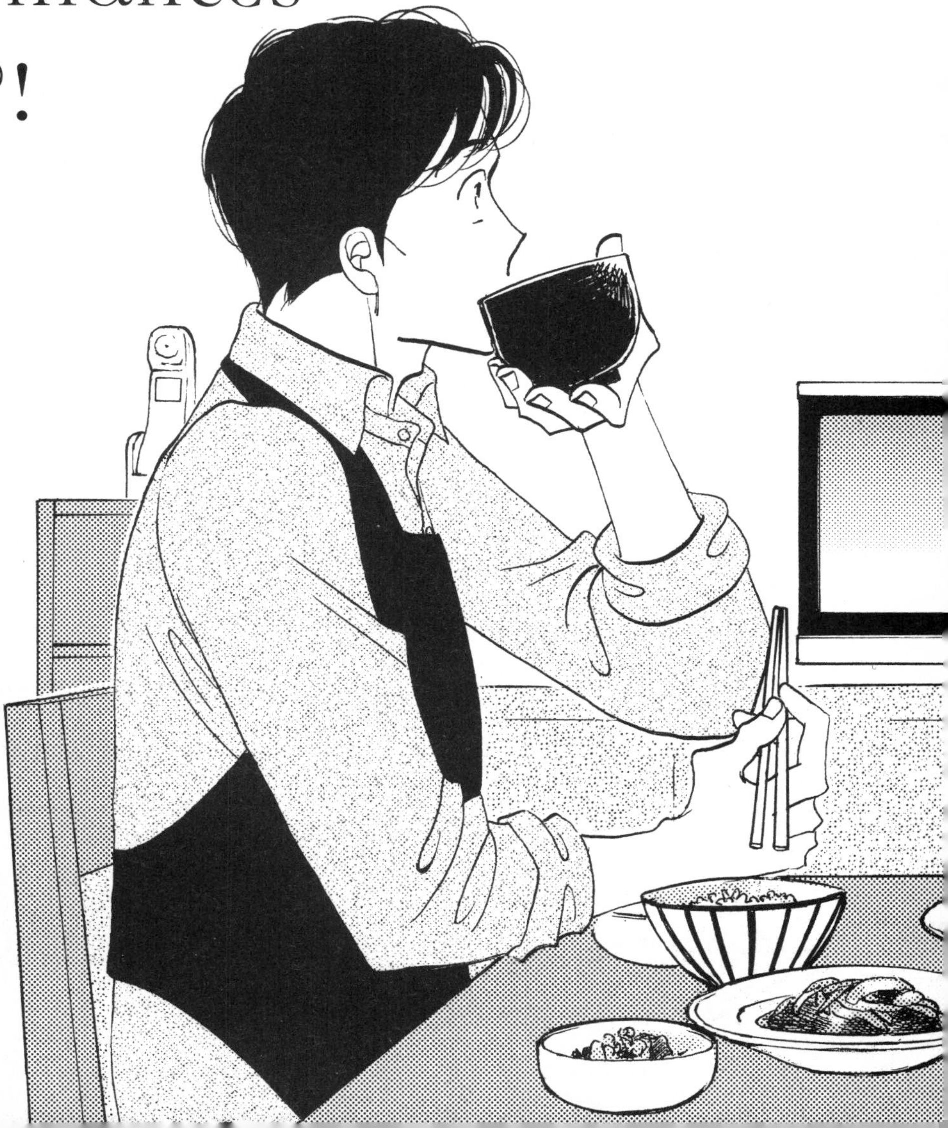

Finally available in English: the award-winning comic about wine that has been a hit not just all over Asia but also in France! Learn about legendary bottles as well as affordable secrets while enjoying a page-turner that's not about superheroes but people with jobs to keep. When world-renowned wine critic Kanzaki passes away, his will reveals that his fortune of a wine collection isn't bequeathed as a matter of course to his only son, who in a snub went to work sales at a beer company. To come into the inheritance, Shizuku must identify— in competition with a stellar young critic— twelve heaven-sent wines whose impressions the will describes in flowing terms...

"Arguably the most influential wine publication for the past 20 years."
—*Decanter Magazine*

Volumes 1-4 & New World available now in digital and print! approx. 400 pages each, $14.95 (print) | $9.99 (digital)